Diana Appleyard is a writer, broadcaster and freelance journalist for a number of national newspapers and magazines. She worked for the BBC as an Education Correspondent, before deciding to give up her full-time job to work from home, a decision which formed the basis for her first novel, *Homing Instinct*. She lives with her husband Ross and their two daughters in an Oxfordshire farmhouse. *Homing Instinct*, *A Class Apart*, *Out of Love* and *Every Good Woman Deserves a Lover*, are all published by Black Swan.

Also by Diana Appleyard

HOMING INSTINCT
A CLASS APART
OUT OF LOVE
EVERY GOOD WOMAN DESERVES A LOVER

Playing with Fire

Diana Appleyard

BLACK SWAN

PLAYING WITH FIRE
A BLACK SWAN BOOK : 0 552 77304 2

First publication in Great Britain

PRINTING HISTORY
Black Swan edition published 2005

1 3 5 7 9 10 8 6 4 2

Set in 11/13pt Melior by
Falcon Oast Graphic Art Ltd.

Black Swan Books are published by Transworld Publishers,
61–63 Uxbridge Road, London W5 5SA,
a division of The Random House Group Ltd,
in Australia by Random House Australia (Pty) Ltd,
20 Alfred Street, Milsons Point, Sydney, NSW 2061, Australia,
in New Zealand by Random House New Zealand Ltd,
18 Poland Road, Glenfield, Auckland 10, New Zealand,
and in South Africa by Random House (Pty) Ltd,
Endulini, 5a Jubilee Road, Parktown 2193, South Africa.

Printed and bound in Great Britain by
Cox & Wyman Ltd, Reading, Berkshire.

Papers used by Transworld Publishers are natural, recyclable
products made from wood grown in sustainable forests. The
manufacturing processes conform to the environmental
regulations of the country of origin.

To Beth, Charlotte and Hamish.

Prologue

If my life is a tapestry, then I am unpicking it, stitch by stitch.

Laure stands at the side of the too-small dance floor, smiling the preoccupied smile that is her first line of defence, when this thought comes to her. Before her a group of people, some she knows well, one she knows intimately, some she knows not at all, approximate the dances of their youth with varying degrees of success. One man looks as if he is sliding about on a tray while performing semaphore, and she has to stop herself laughing out loud. Only drink could make people abandon their inhibitions like this. She should join in, but she cannot. Letting go is not an option, because there is too much in her life that is fast unravelling. If she allowed alcohol to crumble her defences, then anyone might climb in.

'Drink?'

A familiar deep voice at her elbow makes her jump.

'Not for me. What are you having?' She forces a smile.

'Champagne. Started off with it, may as well carry on. Bugger the expense. It's all in a good cause, anyway.'

'And are you drunk yet?' She turns to look at him directly, her eyes gleaming to take the sting out of her words. His hair has flopped down over one eye and his black bow tie is askew. There are beads of sweat on his forehead. He is balancing a bottle of champagne and two glasses in one hand, a cigarette fixed to his lower lip. He squints through the smoke, smiling.

'What a rude question. No, not yet. A bit, but reasonably vertical. And are you bored stiff, Mrs Sober Person?' he asks, in a parody of her mockingly hectoring tone.

'Aching,' she agrees. 'And my feet are killing me.' He looks briefly down at her narrow feet, elegantly encased in high strappy evening shoes, each toenail a perfect shiny red half-moon.

'You should have brought a book.' His smile broadens. 'Then you could have gone and read in the Portaloo.'

'That', she said, 'is a tantalizing thought. Only Gerard would be furious with me.' She glances at her husband, his broad back to the bar.

'Why? I used to read books at parties all the time when I was younger.'

'For effect,' she teases him. 'To try to look intellectual. No, Gerard says that I do not make enough of an effort. I do not join in.'

Tom looks at her, surprised at such a truth in a brittle social situation. You should smile, and smile, even at things that are not funny or remotely interesting.

'Dance with me. At least I can't make you feel any worse.' He puts a hand, nonchalantly, on her bare back as he guides her to a minute gap on the dance floor amidst the gesticulating, twisting bodies, grinding out his cigarette on the parquet floor with his heel, parking the champagne and glasses on a table already overflowing with drink and ashtrays.

8

The music slows, and he holds her. His body is warm, his touch comforting. He is not as tall as Gerard, and slimmer. She lets her head rest briefly against his shoulder. It is odd to be in another man's arms. 'You're quite nice, really,' she says, into his black evening jacket.

'I aim to please. Behind this lazy exterior beats a compassionate heart.' Her grip on his hand tightens imperceptibly. She stops dancing for a moment and looks at him. Their eyes are almost level. Around them the tableau of dancers becomes a blur, and quietens. He stops too, and looks into her eyes.

At that moment, they fall in love. But neither, as yet, knows. All they think is that they have found a friend.

Chapter One

Laure

'Mum!'

'What?'

'Where's my book bag? It's disappeared *again*.'

'Sophie, *chérie*, you're so hopeless. It's where you left it.'

'You always say that. If I knew where I left it then it wouldn't be lost, would it, dur?'

'Don't use that horrible expression. And don't be so cheeky. I shall ban television completely. You watch too much of that American rubbish.'

Sophie's footsteps echo away down the York stone of the wide hallway, palely lit by winter sunlight filtering through the arched stained-glass window above the front door.

'We're going to be late, darling,' Laure calls after her retreating back.

'No, we won't be. You fuss too much. We never are.' Sophie's voice drifts out from the snug door, where she is pulling plum-coloured cushions off one of the two large squashy cream sofas. Laure sighs as she hears the cushions thump against the wooden floor. She loathes mess, cannot think if a room is untidy.

In the five years they have owned the Rectory, she

has created her own contemporary style within the gracious framework of the big old house. In rooms filled by the previous owners with country-house clutter, hulking antiques and chintz, Laure has placed large, comfortable sofas, low polished tables with just one thoughtfully placed ornament and on the walls hang striking works of modern art. The rooms, which used to be glaringly lit by ornate chandeliers, are bathed in pools of light from elegant table lamps and small, discreet spotlights regulated by a dimmer switch. Her friend Cassie says it is like living in a *Country Interiors* spread and too irritatingly perfect for words.

'Ah ha. Here you are. How did you get there?' Sophie's voice, finding her bag, precedes her through the doorway.

Laure picks up her car keys to the Renault people carrier, winding a pink and blue checked scarf around her neck, vivid against the plain black cashmere polo neck. She knots it in the fashionable way around her neck, and buttons up the tailored black velvet frock coat against the cold February wind outside. Her hair is caught up in a bun, carelessly, with a glittery bull-dog clip belonging to Sophie, and shining tendrils of her long, wavy light brown hair escape around her heart-shaped face.

She peers into the oak-framed mirror above the half-circular ormolu hall table, pulling down her mouth to tighten the unlined, lightly freckled pale skin on her cheeks and rub away a tiny smudge of mascara from under one eye. She slips the keys into the pocket of her coat, and her eyes flick back to the kitchen table, just visible through the double pale-oak doors. She hates leaving any breakfast plates on the table, but she is coming straight home. She surveys the stone hallway, looking for Bobo, the ginger tomcat who will lick Sophie's bowl, still half full of Weetabix, clean, if unattended. There is no sign of him. In fact, he is already in the kitchen, lying low under a chair until he hears the front door slam. Like all cats, he is a master of tactical planning.

'Don't care if we're late. It's double maths first thing anyway.' Sophie emerges from the snug, swinging her maroon book bag. Laure reaches out to smooth down a bump Sophie's hasty brushing has left in her blonde hair, pulled back into an untidy ponytail. Sophie twitches away from the grooming hands of her mother.

'Nick rang last night.'

'Did he? When? How is he? Why didn't you wake me?' Sophie's face lights up. She adores her older brother. In the holidays he forgets his teenage cool and they roll and tussle together like puppies, just as they did when they were younger.

'You were fast asleep, he rang after prep. Anyway, you know Nick. All he did was grunt, I hardly got anything out of him. He's in a rugby match today. I said I'd try to get up to watch.'

'Oh, I wish I could go. You never come and watch me,' she adds, wickedly and untruthfully. Sophie nurtures an unfounded belief that her mother favours Nick. It is a useful weapon when she wants something, and she is a born manipulator. The rows between Nick and Gerard fuel this opinion, as Laure has been forced to stand Nick's ground increasingly against his father.

In the last year, there have been many more rows. Laure knows that when Gerard shouts he is not genuinely angry with them, they are simply the whipping boys against the growing pressures of his work. Understanding it does not make it any easier to bear, however, and she feels she is running out of excuses for his bad moods. Not enough, is Gerard's criticism of

Nick. Not enough achievement, not enough academic work, not enough helping around the house, not enough respect, not enough thanks for all the money they were spending on his education, money they could ill afford. During the Christmas holidays father and son were like two fireworks, set to ignite each other. Laure was caught between them, trying to dowse the simmering embers. If allowed to explode, she knew that unforgivable things could be said. Sophie, ever the drama queen, picked up on the emotional tension straight away and became far more confrontational, to divert attention to herself. By the end of the holidays Laure felt worn out by constantly having to placate Gerard, and keep the children away from him when he was tired, as he seemed so often to be.

If only, she thought, she could style their lives as effortlessly and calmly as she styled their home.

'Did you hear me? Honestly, you never listen to me at the moment. I might as well not be here. I might as well go and live on the moon in a crater surrounded by aliens. Nobody cares about me.'

'Sorry, darling, I was miles away. Anyway, that is simply not true. I watched you last week, and you were on the pitch for precisely ten minutes. I stood there in the freezing cold for an hour and a half and all you did was hit the ball once and suck oranges.'

'It's not my fault Mrs Bloody Hardman has it in for me. She never lets me play a whole game. She hates me too.'

'Don't swear.'

'Daddy swears and you don't tell him off. Why is it OK for adults but not for children? Why can't I come with you? Please?' Sophie's face is pleading, but she knows the answer. Laure would never sanction an unauthorized afternoon off school, unlike Cassie who lets her three children have days off to go to pony shows.

'No. You know it's not possible.'

'Kiss.'

Sophie pauses in the doorway long enough to raise her freckled face to Laure's. Laure thinks how grown-up she is beginning to look, her round baby face developing planes and high cheekbones, her chin slightly pointed, like her own. She will be a beauty. At nine, her skin is pale, almost translucent in its purity, and already she is practising being a woman, standing with a hand on her hip when she tries on new clothes in front of the mirror, looking up from under her eye-lashes when she wants something, resting a finger on her chin in an exaggerated gesture when she is think-ing. Laure's hand smooths her soft blonde hair.

'I love you, *chérie*. Even if you lose everything you touch.'

This time Sophie leans her head into Laure's touch, like a cat being stroked. I want to keep you safe for ever, Laure thinks, fiercely. You should not be made to grow up too soon by trying to understand and unravel the tension of complicated adult relationships flying above your head. She wanted so much to give her children the guileless confidence of a well-ordered, secure home, where there are no rows and no doubt of love. A home run by two rational grown-ups, who both know when to draw the line. The confidence she had never had, because as a child she had been privy to too many adult secrets, the unwilling mediator between warring, volatile parents who felt they could behave as they liked behind the closed doors of their home. And yet here they were, despite everything she had done and tried to be.

'Yeah, yeah. I found it though, didn't I? Come on.'

Sophie runs ahead to the car, trailing book bag,

sports bag and music folder. Laure smiles. This morning she feels unaccountably happy, despite the argument she had with her father on the phone last night, and having to cope with Gerard's hangover-fuelled irritability. She and Sophie had left him alone in the snug for most of the day, with the Sunday papers and endless cups of coffee, hardly helping his headache.

The memory of Saturday night is like pulling on a warm coat. Why? She thinks hard. She was bored and rather cold in the draughty marquee at the dance, but then, what? Of course. Her smile deepens. Tom rescued her, and made her laugh. Dear, dear Tom, who sees things that others don't. She touches her sleeve, feeling the softness of the black velvet, like a caress. He made her feel safe, as if nothing bad could happen. She found herself going over the silly conversation they had while dancing. It was strange, but she could remember nearly every word. He is a kind man, she thinks.

Could she tell him? To let somebody else in, to talk openly to anyone would be such a relief, but it would also be a betrayal. She hadn't even talked to Cassie about how bad things had got. It was too humiliating, too personal. And it was all so complicated, she struggled to make sense of it even to herself. To voice her feelings would be to give her fears credence, when really it had to be just a phase, a bad patch. Everyone went through such ups and downs, and it did not necessarily mean that their problems were insoluble. No-one lived a perfect life. She must try harder to be more understanding. She took a deep breath, her hand on the door to the car, the metal cold underneath her palm.

At the heart of all this was Gerard's worry about his business. That was what was at fault, not their relationship. Their inability to talk to each other was just a symptom of that problem, and she had to be mature enough to recognize it and deal with it. She could not possibly go around talking about Gerard – especially to another man. That would be the ultimate betrayal in Gerard's eyes. If she were to take Tom aside and make him privy to information about Gerard, about their personal relationship – well, that would be like lighting the blue touchpaper and retreating. Tom might inadvertently mention something to Cassie, who might mention something to Nat, who might then offer help or advice to Gerard – it was unthinkable. Best to say nothing, to cope alone.

On the way to school they do not speak. Sophie stares out of the window, lost in thought, one foot in navy blue tights tucked under her, her black clumpy school shoes abandoned in the well of the car. Laure clicks on the radio, and the car is filled with loud pop music. Laure grimaces, and reaches to turn it off. On her own, she listens to classical music, which Sophie says is boring. Gerard's car radio is permanently tuned to a sports and news channel, with endless, chattering voices which give her a headache.

'Don't. I like that one.' Sophie is an aficionado of pop music, and claims to want to be a pop singer when she grows up, mainly to annoy her father.

A thought is floating at the back of Laure's mind. She can't quite pin it down, but knows it is a fear, unidentified, nameless. It casts a shadow over the pleasurable memory of dancing with Tom. What is it? Oh yes. From being a dark shadow, it takes shape and becomes coherent. The school fees had still not been paid, and it was a month and a half into the new term. Laure no longer accompanied Sophie to her classroom for fear of bumping into the bursar. She couldn't bring it up with Gerard either, because he had said, in his

17

don't-mention-it-again voice, that he would see to it when he could. But then he wasn't the one ducking behind the steering wheel as she drove up the main drive, creeping round the school like a criminal.

She tries to push the thought away, to bury it, or else her mind will start the interminable round of 'if only's'. The world is full of 'if only's'. There is no life plan, she thinks, changing gear. You can never think, phew, I'm safe now, everything is sorted, and pull up the drawbridge. Life is a series of unpredictable, chance happenings. Always expect the unexpected had been her motto. But she had not seen this coming, nor the way it would twist Gerard into a man she felt she barely knew, who thought he could behave as he liked and she would absorb it without consequence because she was his wife.

She tightens her grip on the steering wheel. Stop it. Do not think of it. Things will change. It can't stay like this for ever. She had to be optimistic. The fear wraps a steel cord around her heart, tightening. To ease the pressure, she had tried to tell him they could move to a much smaller house, or rent, take the children out of their schools, she should go back to work full-time. He was outraged by the suggestion, the implication of his failure. Then, after the shouting, he apologized for his bad temper and hugged her. And that, she thought, was supposed to make it all right.

And, if she was totally honest with herself, she could not bear the idea of giving up the house. It was a fixed point, a sanctuary in what had become too much of an uncertain universe. When she walked in through the tall front door, it was as if the house folded its secure arms around her. Gerard teased her about being spiritual and airy-fairy, but she genuinely believed that houses have a soul, and all the conversations, the memories, the births, the family events

18

and the deaths of the inhabitants were somehow absorbed into the stone walls, the beams, the quiet places. Houses knew things, and either loved you, or didn't. The Rectory was not populated by ghosts, exactly, but to Laure it had a personality all of its own and it was on her side.

When she had first walked in with the estate agent, she had felt immediately at home, there was a connection. The house welcomed her, and it was a happy house. She had never been more content than when she was supervising the renovations, choosing materials, deciding on the colour schemes for the big square rooms with their high sash windows and window seats. But then they weren't living under a constant shadow. She thought it would be theirs for ever, the house in adulthood her children would look back on as their home, unchanging, secure. Sophie had been just four when they moved, Nick ten, and she intended never to move again until it became too big for the two of them, once the children had left home.

In the winter, log fires blazed in the stone fireplaces in the hallway, the snug and the large, impressive drawing room they hardly ever used, and in the summer sunlight streamed through the high old windows, and doors were left open to let in the scents of the garden she had enthusiastically brought back under control, uncovering weed-filled flower beds, stone steps and moss-covered planters. At the back of the house was an ancient greenhouse, covered in mould, and she had loved rolling up her sleeves to scrub the glass, mend the benches and restore it to its full Georgian glory. Laure liked to work hard to create the perfect backdrop to her family's life. She planned ahead, to make their lives as pleasant as possible. All their friends agreed that Gerard was a lucky man, a spoilt man. Cassie teased her about being a 'proper' wife while Laure shrugged and said that she genuinely enjoyed making a home. Sarah, Tom's wife, remarked sourly that it was all very well if you actually had the time to whisk about making scones and laying fires – other women had to live in the real world and work full-time. Life, she implied, had moved on from this kind of cosy domesticity which was no longer valued by the outside world. What she failed to see was that it was Laure's career in just the same way as journalism was Sarah's.

No expense had been spared on the renovations, but then Gerard had encouraged her to spend. He was so proud of the Rectory. It was the tangible symbol of his achievement, symbolically a million miles from the pebble-dashed two up, two down terraced home of his childhood, row upon row of grey slate roofs in a grey slate town.

Coping with the practicalities and logistics of the move from a smaller house had shifted Laure's feet onto firmer ground at a time of personal insecurity, and she drew much comfort from the fact that her mother would have adored the Rectory. Her father, downsizing to a flat from their former family home in the year after her mother's death, had given her and her sister most of her mother's furniture and paintings, gathered over a lifetime as a dealer importing antiques and modern art from France to Britain. When she had come to place them around the house, she felt her mother's hand and eye as surely as if she was beside her, hearing her rapid, didactic Parisian accent. Her mother refused to speak to them in English when they were on their own, even when they were at primary school and desperately trying to lose their 'foreignness', which made them the object of teasing. When Laure had first met Gerard, he had thought her parents so exotic, with their opulent country house – paid for by her mother – colourful parties and endless free-flowing alcohol at all times of the day. That was the life he wanted – stylish, extravagant, glamorous. She, meanwhile, admired his mousy, loving parents in their tiny, orderly house with tea on the table at the same time every night, the unthreatening rhythm of the lives that Gerard thought so small.

Laure and her sister had dropped everything to care for their father in the immediate months after their mother's death from a stroke. They listened to him telling them again and again how much he had loved her, how she was irreplaceable, with their lips buttoned against the obvious retort. They had lost the driving force when she died, but they still felt they had at least the tattered and bruised remains of what passed for a family in their father. Was it really worth laying bare the truth that their parents' shouting matches and their father's infidelity had created a childhood full of fear and lies? That it was hypocritical in the extreme to mourn a woman he had so constantly betrayed? Not that their mother was without blame; she could not be seen as the victim. Laure had adored her, but could see she had made their father's life hell by constantly picking holes in his ambition and his achievements.

Laure's sister Françoise had once remarked that it was like being brought up in a Tennessee Williams play, never knowing what the next act would bring. Night-times were the worst, because that was when the drinking started and the shouting began. The result was that both sisters craved peace and routine. Laure's deepest ambition in life was not to replicate the chaos of her childhood. When Nick was born, she held him tight in her arms and breathed that she would keep him safe for ever, and build walls of love

21

around him so the monsters of her childhood never came.

Whatever her father did was never good enough for her mother, and Laure did not know if the infidelities came before his acceptance that he would never be the man she wanted, or afterwards. What was clear was that they should have divorced, many years before, but hadn't not only for the sake of their children but because her mother was a staunch Catholic. She wore her religion, like the pain of her husband's infidelity, like a hair shirt. As a child, Laure had been told, again and again, 'Never marry a man like your father!' At times she had felt sorry for him, as her mother was so obviously the stronger character, but she knew he was a coward who preferred to live a life of half-truths and escape.

He plunged into the role of grieving widower with the enthusiasm with which he had plunged into his numerous affairs, but after six months he shook himself, decided enough was enough, and found a new girlfriend. Then another, and another. All this was par for the course, although they were getting embarrassingly young. Then, three months ago, to their astonishment, he announced he wanted to marry. But then, as Françoise pointed out, he could afford to. They'd got the furniture and antiques, but he'd got the money from the sale of the house, and it occurred to them that their father, no fool, was keen to find someone to look after him in his later years. He was now sixty-four, and a little more mindful of mortality.

Although she wasn't surprised by her father's decision, she was surprised by how hurt it made her feel, how little she wanted a stepmother younger than herself. And, God! He might start another family. All the ground she had recovered, all the emotional stability, had been pulled away from under her once more. She was furious with him for being so thoughtless, so utterly self-absorbed. Although her childhood had been filled with the uncertainties and pain of his affairs, he had, at least, only one wife. Now even that precarious honour was to be usurped. Gerard, who had been patient and understanding about her grief over her mother's death, now felt his patience tried by what he saw as her overemotional reaction to this new relationship. Her father had been having affairs for years – why did getting married again make any difference? She detected, as she often did, a sneaking admiration in Gerard for the charming old roué. He did not understand the chaos and insecurity of infidelity and the long shadows it cast.

Then, just before Christmas, Gerard had dropped his own bombshell and for the first time in their marriage Laure began to wake filled with the same kind of fear she had experienced as a child – the fear of insecurity, of not knowing what each day would bring. The business was in dire trouble. It was, in a tiny way, a relief as it explained why he had been so bad-tempered, but then the realities crashed in; they were now living a life they simply could not afford. Laure was determined to shield the children from the truth, but it was getting harder and harder.

Sophie's foot swung in time to the music, and Laure noted that a toenail was beginning to shine through the thin blue cotton of her tights. She must get her a new pair.

'Yellow car.' Sophie reached over and lightly punched Laure's arm. 'No returns.'

'I wish you wouldn't do that.'

'Did you know that the sky is never totally black at night? It's only ever a deep, deep blue. Mr Harwood in Science told us that.'

'Really?'

'Can we see *The Lion King* at half-term? Emily's been and she said it was so cool.'

'We'll see.'

'I hate it when you say that. It means no.'

'No it doesn't. It means we'll see.'

No, she thought. It would cost way too much. Everything had to be accounted for. From spending hundreds of pounds in the supermarket on luxury foods, fresh flowers and expensive shampoo and bath oils, she now wheeled her trolley with a calculator in her head, buying own-brand makes and two for the price of one. She could see how unthinkingly spoilt she had been, and had jumped at the chance to do something to help, to be practical. She had stopped using her credit card immediately and only used cash, although Gerard seemed intent on trying to carry on as normal until their credit card had been stopped. That had been a killer blow, unarguable evidence of how deeply they were in debt.

Laure could see it was all about saving face for Gerard, keeping up appearances, whereas her inclination was to pull up the drawbridge, and there was a growing resentment between them because he was reluctant to rein in their lifestyle. He told Laure she didn't understand how business worked, that this was simply a temporary problem which would be rectified when he found new investment. Every week this new investment was just around the corner, but never arrived. And all the little things, every day. Stupid things. Bobo had to go to the vet because he had stopped eating. He needed to have his teeth out, as he had a severe gum infection. It cost a fortune, and Gerard said it wasn't a priority. 'Buy a new cat,' he said. 'Sophie will cry for half an hour and then we'll give her a kitten.'

'You don't mean that.' Laure was appalled by his insensitivity.

'Oh, but, Laure, so much? You could buy ten cats for that amount of money.'

'But not this cat.' She held him up to her face. His soft ginger body, too thin, vibrated against her cheek. He had become much more affectionate now he was ill. The other night, when Gerard was away on business, he had slept on their bed for the first time and Laure had woken to feel a small, warm pressure against her leg. In the darkness she had made out the outline of the cat, and she smiled and slept, reassured. Love that was worth anything was made up of shared experiences. Only their love did not seem to be strengthened by this. It was rubbish to say that adversity brought you closer together. It tore you apart. The problems had apparently begun almost a year ago, but he had not told her. Now, looking back, she could see how he had gradually begun to change. He had been unusually snappy with Sophie and Nick, distracted, reluctant to make love or touch her.

The business, which manufactured hard-wearing textiles for industrial use, was strictly his affair, and he did not want her to be involved at any level. He had built it up from scratch, from a small derelict mill he'd bought near his parents' house when he was in his twenties, four years after leaving a local grammar school. He could have gone to university, but he preferred to get out into the world of work. He had asked his father for a loan to buy second-hand machinery, money his father had saved painstakingly over his years working for the local trades union as a supervisor. His father had refused. Gerard had never forgiven him for that, and it made him all the more determined. He borrowed the money from the bank, and had then taken on a partner, an older man who later proved incompetent and Gerard had had to buy him out. He had so much to prove, to find the escape route he had been charting since childhood.

Laure, who found the English class system baffling and absurd, did not fully understand what drove her husband. She could not understand why he became so angry at things she did not consider important. She could not understand why he didn't bother to keep in touch with his parents, why she had to ring to arrange visits, remember birthdays and to take the children up to see them. To Gerard, his parents were a constant reminder of the life he desperately wanted to leave behind. When he bought the mill everyone in the area had said that he was mad, that textile production was dead. Most of the old mills were abandoned to become architectural relics, but he was determined to prove that he could make them work, and drag the industry into the twentieth century with the latest, very expensive, machinery and a small, specialized workforce.

After the first ten years of their marriage, when they had lived in a rented house, then a small cottage, then two cottages knocked together, he had made the first mill a success, then bought a purpose-built unit on an industrial zone in the north, and finally the big new site in the south, which had precipitated the move to the Windrush Valley and the purchase of the Rectory. When they had looked around the house, they had both fallen instantly in love, but Laure had said, 'Are you sure we can afford this?' and Gerard answered, impatiently, that of course they could.

Then the bottom had begun to fall out of the market. The strong pound made it harder to sell into Europe, the anticipated sales in America and Australia had not arrived in the way he had planned. He had borrowed heavily on the strength of sales which did not materialize. Interest rates soared, and the first mill had been closed down earlier in the year. He'd tried to sell it, but there were no takers. He told his parents he no longer needed the extra capacity. They knew the people he had put out of work, and were not impressed. Gerard said they didn't understand the business, but his father understood more than he liked to think. Now the bank was being very difficult and he wished that he had not named the Rectory, worth close to a million, as collateral. Admitting this to Laure had not been easy. She thought the house was safe.

In the early days of their marriage she had teased him about being old-fashioned and wanting to be the breadwinner and the head of the family. He liked the fact that she only worked occasionally, that her career was on hold to bring up a family, and he wanted her to be there for him and the children. She fitted perfectly into the mould of the wife he wanted. When the children were younger she was quite happy to be the person he wanted her to be, because she was so caught up in their lives and she loved being a home-maker. But now they were older she did want more of a life of her own. One of the things that most attracted her to him when they first met was his decisiveness, his ambition, and his determination to take control. She had never before met a man who took her over in such a way and gave her no time to think. He was so driven, so sure of himself. After the chaos of her childhood, she thought, here was a man who would keep her safe, who would make all the right decisions.

When she talked to him about the business, about what she could do to ease their financial pressure, she was trying to help. But Gerard saw it as interference in issues which did not concern her. His mother had never questioned his father. He had absorbed far more of the traditional roles of his parents than he would care to acknowledge. The roles in his and Laure's marriage were beginning to shift, and as the balance of power tipped Gerard became more aggressive, more determined to have his way whatever. And now Laure could see that he was not always right.

Sometimes I look at him and I cannot understand who he is, or if he loves me at all, she thought. I wonder if he loves simply the thought of who I am, the way I look and the home I make for him?

'Six thirty. It's swim squad tonight.'

'I won't forget. And bring the rest of your games kit home. I haven't washed it all.'

'Will do.' Sophie's hand paused on the door.

'I love you.'

'I love you more.' Sophie got out, and disappeared into a sea of blazers.

Chapter Two

Laure

'I hate my children.' She loved the way he said her name, sounding the 'e' at the end. Sometimes she saved and replayed his messages about the children's social arrangements, just to listen to his beautiful voice. It made her smile.

'No you don't. You're just saying that.'

'School was invented to stop parents murdering their children. Do you know what Mickey did this morning? He wrapped up a bloody hen in his school jumper. The only clean one.'

'Why?'

'The others had ostracized it, vicious buggers that they are. Now I know why it's called a pecking order. They peck the top of its head until it bleeds to drum it out of the herd or whatever hens have. Mickey found it barely alive behind the henhouse.'

'How horrible.'

'I love the way you say that. Say it again.'

'Stop teasing me.'

'I'm not. Would I do that? Anyway, so now we have a hen in the kitchen, dropping hen crap all over the floor and no doubt answering the phone saying, "There's no-one here but us chickens." And by this time it's quarter past eight and . . .'

'Tom, calm down.'

'I've had it with being a housewife. Why didn't anyone tell me what a nightmare it is? My nerves are in tatters.'

'You could be putting on a pinstriped suit and catching the seven thirty into the City, you know.'

'Christ, that's true. Be thankful for small mercies. As it is I have a house that looks as if it's been vigorously burgled, as usual, a pile of work I cannot bring myself to do and a hen to rehouse. Are you hands-free?'

'No. Why?' She held the phone with one hand, and was driving with the other.

'You can get arrested for that, you know. Didn't you see me at school? I was waving at you like mad.'

'Like mad? I like that. I was in a bit of a dream. Oops. Oh God. Sorry. Nearly hit a tractor.'

'Do you want me to ring you back when you get home?'

'No, it's fine. What do you want? I'm still exhausted from Saturday. It was fun, wasn't it?'

'You know it wasn't, stop lying. I'm too old for late nights.'

She smiled. 'Ten is late for me, these days. I'm usually fast asleep on the sofa by nine.'

'Look, tonight . . .'

'Yes?'

'Lucy's hatched this plan.'

'Oh yes?'

'She wants them to have a sleepover.'

'On a school night?'

'She said something about a play rehearsal. *Diogenes the King*, or some such pretentious bollocks. Whatever happened to *Oliver*? Do you know anything about it?'

'I know they'll be late.'

'Well, do you want me to pick them up and then Sophie can stay here? I promise not to let them watch *Scary Movie II*. I'll chase them into bed.'

'What about Sarah?'

'Who?'

'Your wife.'

'Oh, that Sarah. She's got some awards ceremony she has to go to, she's going to stay in town.'

'Oh. OK.'

'What about Sophie's things?'

'I'll drop them off. I've got to come past you on the way back from shopping today anyway. Will you be in? About two? Then I promised to go and see Nick in a match.' She paused, a thought striking her. 'You could come with me, if you like.' The words were out of her mouth before she thought about them. Why on earth had she said that? She was in danger of using Tom like a security blanket.

'Excellent idea. More work avoidance. Thanks, I probably will. It will be good to see the old school again.'

'Are you sure you're not banned? I'm not sure I want to be seen with you. I have a reputation to maintain, you know.'

'I very much doubt there's anyone still there who remembers a pot-smoking incident in 1978, vivid as it remains in my memory.'

'I don't know, some of the teachers there go back a long way. I will be seen, consorting with a known criminal.'

'They didn't charge me, just made me go home for a bit. Suspension, it was called. I quite liked it, like a mini holiday only with very cross parents. The beginning of my glorious descent. Just think what I might have been. I might have scaled the corporate

31

ladder and been a captain of industry like Nat or your successful husband. Thank God for Sarah, eh?'

'You can't really be that lazy.'

He laughed. 'Try me. At least if I go with you to the school I won't be tempted into the pub.'

'On a Monday?' Laure was scandalized.

'You've no idea what a jumping place the Slug and Lettuce is on a Monday lunchtime. It's the AGM of the women's darts team.'

'Don't tell me you are an honorary member?'

'I'm waiting to be asked.'

'Sarah would never let you.'

'God, no. Darts. I mean, there's country life, and there's country life.'

'I can't see Sarah being very pleased by you not working. Hasn't she left you a long list of things to be done?' Laure's voice was teasing.

'Yup. I chucked it in the bin. I refuse to be dictated to by my illustrious wife. I am not a rich woman's plaything. I have standards. I am on the cusp of writing a very successful novel.'

'Tom, you've been on the cusp of writing a very successful novel all the time I have known you, which is nearly five years. It is no longer a valid excuse to do absolutely nothing. Now shut up. I'm nearly home. I'll see you at two-ish. Try not to set the world alight before then.'

'By the way.'

'What?'

'You made Saturday bearable. Without you, I would have eaten my bow tie through sheer boredom.'

'Go away.' She pressed the 'end call' key decisively, and swung the people carrier into the wide drive. Then she stopped, and sat in the car for a moment, staring at nothing, smiling.

* * *

32

The sound of hooves on the drive interrupted her morning-tidy routine. Not, as Cassie would say, that there was much tidying to be done. Laure kept the house immaculate, with the help of a cleaning lady who used to be daily but who had now been reduced, as an economy measure, to once a week. In comparison Cassie's house, the old manor on the other side of the church, was a tip. She told Laure it was quite unreasonable to be so bloody perfect and that it reflected badly on her normal friends. Laure replied that she loved the manor, she just couldn't function if there was not complete order.

What she ought to do was work. There was a commission she had been offered on a big house in a neighbouring village. It was a full-scale renovation, working with an interior architect, and Laure had initially leapt at the idea, because the money would be so useful. Gerard didn't want her to take it. In the past months she had been tentatively putting out feelers, telling friends she wanted to get back to work, and the commission had come through a friend of a friend. She had been delighted, but Gerard was furious, because she did not consult him first.

Having accepted the commission, despite Gerard's objections that she didn't have time, met the clients and looked round the house, she now felt daunted by the sheer scale of everything that needed doing. And she found it so hard to concentrate. Whenever she sat down at her desk and tried to get on, to phone stockists, to draw plans, thoughts crowded into her mind in squadrons, each one more frightening than the last. By performing endless, mindless tasks like tidying up, washing and gardening, she could keep these thoughts at bay. She knew she was procrastinating too much, but each day every little thing became more of an effort. It was like wading through deep water. I wish. She stopped, her arms full of cushions she was plumping. If wishes were horses then beggars might ride.

Cassie's Jack Russell, Hector, jumped down off the front of the saddle and landed at Laure's feet.

'Do be careful,' Laure said in alarm, as Cassie's large bay horse suddenly skittered sideways, spooked by the sheets Laure had hung out on the line to flap in the early March wind. Cassie laughed and expertly straightened the horse, tapping it on the side of its neck with her whip. Laure stepped out of the way of its enormous hooves. She did not like horses. They moved too suddenly and unpredictably, and she could not understand the English obsession with being cold and muddy. She loved the English countryside, but as one would adore a painting, to look at. She did not want to tramp about in it.

'How can you keep an eye on both of them?'

'You get used to it. Ouch. Get off.' Cassie had slid off the horse, and was now standing by its head holding the reins. The horse abruptly rubbed his face up and down her coat, forcefully. 'You big ejit. Stop it.'

'Coffee?'

'You're an angel. I didn't get time, what with chasing the kids out of bed.'

Hector pattered behind Laure into the kitchen, through the big double doors which led from the terrace, and cursorily touched noses with Laure's old Labrador, Victor, who was lying, as usual, as if stuffed, in his basket. Just a quick social call, Hector seemed to be saying. No need to get up. Victor made do with thumping his tail against the side of the basket as a response, and then closed his eyes once more. As Laure boiled the Aga kettle, she watched Cassie from the window. The horse was now resting its head against her shoulder, as she stroked his face. Nat was right. She probably did love that horse more than him.

'And was the dance as excruciatingly boring as you predicted?'

Laure handed a mug of steaming coffee to Cassie, who had looped the reins over one arm. 'Was it that obvious?'

'You didn't exactly set the dance floor alight, unlike *moi*. I only saw you dance with Tom towards the end. I had to keep your bloody husband entertained – I've still got the bruises. I'm too old to rock and roll and he does throw you about, doesn't he? Was I visibly drunk? I felt like an alien on Sunday morning. I had to keep checking I was wearing clothes.'

'Yes.'

'At least I didn't fall over.'

'I caught you. Going up those rickety steps to the loo. Don't you remember?'

'Nope. Everything after nine is a blur. I didn't snog anyone, did I?'

Laure smiled. 'Not that I actually saw. Anyway, there wasn't anyone there you would want to', she hesitated over the word, 'snog.'

'Your husband was on good form. It's the first time I've seen him so cheerful for ages.' Cassie looked sideways at Laure over her coffee cup. God, she was beautiful, even on a Monday morning with no make-up. It was quite unreasonable to have a best friend with cheekbones like that. Laure had the kind of face which would never age, because her bone structure was so good. Cassie, feeling her face first thing in the morning, knew there must be bones under there, otherwise her face would fall down, but she couldn't actually find them. This morning it had been even more of a struggle to get her jodhpurs on. She'd had to lie on the floor to do up the zip. She must lose weight.

It was so hard to be elegant when you had short legs and a serious addiction to delicious food like cake. Laure must starve herself, she thought.

'Stop staring at me.'

'Sorry. Look, tell me if I'm putting my foot in it but is everything OK? Whenever I looked at you on Saturday you were standing on your own like patience on a monument. Smiling at grief.'

'Oh, *merci*. What an attractive picture that paints. I must have been a real asset to the party.'

'I don't give a toss about that. Is it your father? You will tell me, won't you, if I can do anything to help? I'm not fishing, really I'm not, but Gerard said something weird . . .'

'What?'

'It was probably nothing. I just asked him if you fancied coming skiing with us at Easter because we've got space in the chalet and he said he didn't even know if you would be here by then. I think a holiday would do you good after everything you've been through, and my kids would love it if you all came.'

'He didn't know if we would be here?'

'Odd, isn't it? You're not planning to move, are you? I won't let you. I'll lie in the drive in front of the removal van. Who would catch me when I fall?'

Laure glanced over her shoulder, at the old square stone house behind her.

'You'd have Tom. Anyway, we're not moving, of course we're not. I would have told you something like that, don't be silly.'

'Is everything fine? With the business, I mean? It's just Nat said that, well, he may have been speaking out of turn but things aren't great, for anyone, at the moment and he knows someone who said that— Oh.' She saw the expression on Laure's face. 'I am putting my foot in it. I'm sorry.'

'It isn't the end of the world,' Laure said, reaching out, tentatively, to stroke the horse's soft chocolate-brown nose. It breathed deeply at her. She could not meet Cassie's eyes. 'Gerard says — well, to be honest you probably know as much as I do because he's stopped talking to me about it.' How much can I say, she wondered. It was a relief that Cassie had picked up signs of disquiet, giving her some justification to let Cassie know at least something of what was happening. 'It's a bit of a taboo subject between us because whenever I bring it up he just gets cross and it ends in an argument. He says I don't understand and that I am panicking, which is not what he needs right now.'

'Can we help? I mean, Nat . . .'

'Nat is the last person Gerard would take help from. You can see that, can't you? You are our friends.'

'I didn't just mean financially. I meant in terms of advice, support . . .'

Laure looked at Cassie incredulously. 'You know Gerard, and you can say that?'

'I am a very stupid person. Nat's right. I should think before I open my big gob. I should stick to horses and leave business to him.'

Laure had a swift and uncharitable thought. If it weren't for Cassie's family money, there might not have been Nat's flourishing media consultancy, big-name clients and no need for Cassie to work.

She heard Cassie's voice. 'Sorry, what? I'm a bit vague this morning.'

'I said, come for dinner on Saturday. Well, supper really, you know I can't do a whole proper dinner, not like you. It'll just be a casserole full of brown stuff, barely edible, but at least you won't have to cook yourself. Bring Sophie. Nick's not home, is he?'

'Not this weekend. It's his exeat the following one. But we owe you.'

'Who cares?'

'I don't . . .'

'What?'

'We're not desperate, you know. We can afford to eat.' The words came out much more sharply than she intended. Cassie looked surprised and hurt. Laure was never prickly, she had the sunniest temperament of anyone Cassie had ever met, and often left her feeling like a complete witch for being the slightest bit mean about people.

'I never said you were, you daft thing. But you've got to work and I know Gerard is so busy. Nat, meanwhile, my adorable husband, ought to be more of a man of leisure as he's allegedly sold off half the company, only of course he isn't. And I – as my husband would say – do bugger all apart from shovel horse muck and shout at the children. I keep telling him to take things a bit easier but he never stops. He's away so much I'm convinced he's having an affair.' Cassie laughed.

'You don't really think that?'

'Oh, who cares? Who knows what goes on in men's mysterious little minds?'

'He adores you. He'd never do anything like that.'

'Well, he should stop going on about my fat arse, then.'

Laure laughed. 'He doesn't mean it. You should see the way he looks at you.'

'He's just trying to tot up how many glasses of wine I've had and whether I'm likely to fall over. I wish I had your control. How do you not drink? Isn't it hideously boring? I better go.' The horse was starting to get restless, moving about, pulling at the reins in Cassie's hand. 'Thanks for the coffee.' She handed the empty mug back to Laure. 'What will you do with the rest of the day?'

'I've got to look at the plans for the house in Guiting

Power. Going back to work is so scary – I'm not sure they will take me seriously.'

'Don't be silly, you're fantastic at interior design. It could be fabulous, couldn't it? I used to know the people who lived there. Bonkers. He kept coming up with mad inventions and she used to wear a hat indoors. Friends of my mother's, needless to say. It was wonderful, but decaying around them. Don't let them take out all the old features, will you?'

'Of course not. Would I?'

'It will all be done in the best possible taste.' Cassie flashed a wicked smile and led the horse over to a low wall, which she climbed on to mount. 'Don't panic. If you do it like you've done the Rectory it will knock their socks off.'

'I spoke to Tom,' Laure said, once she was safely back in the saddle.

'Did you? When?'

'This morning. He rang about a sleepover plan the girls had hatched. He was trying to get it fixed up.'

'You two were thick as thieves at the party.'

'Were we? We were taking the mickey out of everyone else's dancing. He is so funny.'

'Lovely, lovely Tom. Where would we be without him? Our little window into the strange workings of the male psyche.'

'I'm not quite sure if Tom qualifies as male. He's too much in touch with his feminine side. Too gossipy.'

'Oh, he's male all right. Don't go underestimating our Tom, I've known him a lot longer than you have. He used to be a real ladies' man. All the girls round here used to fall for that little-boy-lost routine and diffident charm. The only one who's come anywhere close to taming him is Sarah. Do you think she had a good time on Saturday?'

'Well, it's not really her scene, is it? Not very

glamorous or full of famous faces. *Un peu* provincial.'

'Lady Hetherington was there,' Cassie said, defensively. 'Although she may come more under the heading of "crustaceous old bag" than "famous person". We were a bit short on pop stars, admittedly. But what do I know? I'm just a housewife who wouldn't recognize a Jimmy Choo shoe if it bit her on the leg.'

'Don't be unkind. Sarah has a lot of good qualities.'

'I know. I'm a vicious bitch who is jealous of her success. Actually, I'm not. Imagine being in an office today.' She looked up at the clear blue sky, the barely budding hedgerows full of birdsong and the deep pink flowers dusting the hawthorn tree by the gate.

Laure smiled. 'We are lucky.'

'Go and work, you lazy cow.'

'And go and tidy up your messy house. Some house-wife you are.'

'Ouch. See you, darling. Pick up the phone – it's the getting started that's hard. Says she who hasn't worked properly in ten years. Ta-ra. Call me about Saturday, and give my love to your husband. Tell him I hurt in places I haven't hurt for years.'

'I'm not sure I dare!' laughed Laure. 'Ride carefully.'

Cassie took up the reins and called Hector, who appeared from a flower bed, and positioned himself obediently at the horse's heels, just out of kicking distance. She jogged away down the drive, the horse snatching at the bit, moving sideways, eager to have the gallop he would be denied because of the depth of the mud on the bridleway. Laure turned back to the house, mentally girding herself to pick up the phone and speak to the architect, to find out if the buyers had actually made a decision about what they wanted yet. She could hardly start planning the decor if they didn't know if they wanted walls knocking down. She would feel much better once she had started, Cassie was right. It was just making that initial move. But then the thought came to her. What on earth had Gerard meant? They might not be here? Cassie must have misinterpreted what he had said. He couldn't possibly take a decision like that without consulting her.

Chapter Three

Laure

'God, this takes me back. The scene of my misspent youth.'

They were winding their way up the long drive towards Nick's boarding school, where Tom had been educated, as, he said, in the loosest sense of the word. The school had been through a rather lean time until ten years ago, when it had decided to open its doors to girls. Now numbers were buoyant, and there was a waiting list. Sophie was desperate to go, but Laure knew there was no way they could make that kind of financial commitment at the moment. She didn't even know if Nick would be able to stay, and leaving would break his heart. He'd taken to boarding like a duck to water, and she thought he had grown up a lot in the two years he'd been there. Gerard disagreed. He said that Nick was more surly than ever and that he took his privilege for granted. Laure had to bite her lip, because she rarely saw that side of her son.

The spires of the chapel rose above the treetops and, as they rounded the bend, the front of the wide, gracious Edwardian building came into view.

'Were you happy here?' Laure turned to look at Tom,

who had slouched down in the passenger seat, as if he feared being spotted.

'No. I hated it. I was terribly bullied. That's why I rebelled. It wasn't touchy-feely like it is now, it was all cold showers, stiff upper lips and having your head flushed down the loo.'

'Were you really bullied?'

'God yes, I was a dreadful wimp, under all the bravado and bad behaviour. Not the intensely masculine presence I am today.'

'You could have dressed a bit better.'

'What's wrong with me?'

'Tom, you are a dear friend, but you are a mess. Those trousers are filthy, and that coat looks like the dog slept on it.'

'Probably did. Are you ashamed to be seen with me, then?'

'Yes. Walk ten paces behind me. I only said you could come because I felt sorry for you. And please don't smoke those disgusting cigarettes in my car.' Tom sheepishly put away his tobacco tin. 'I don't know how Sarah stands you.'

'Sarah says that too,' he said, happily. 'It hasn't changed at all,' he added, looking out of the car window. Wound around his neck was a thick pink scarf belonging to his elder daughter Lucy, incongruous against the muddy khaki shooting coat. It should have looked ridiculous, but instead it made him look glamorous, in a faintly dissolute way.

'Well, it wouldn't, would it? It's a listed building. Are you going to send Mickey here?'

'Can't afford it. He'd probably burn it down, anyway. Sarah wants to, but I think it's a waste of money. It works against you, you know, getting into university and that kind of thing. They favour comprehensive students, and quite right too. The day of the toff is over. The old class system should be dead and buried. It's a load of crap.'

'Did you go to university?' Laure realized that she didn't know.

'For a bit, an unimportant one, a jumped-up polytechnic in all but name. I was, without putting too fine a point on it, a severe disappointment to my family. I got bored, went off travelling, and then when I came back I managed to lie my way into a job on the local newspaper and that was that.'

'The beginning of your meteoric career.' Laure smiled.

'Miaow. Did you go to university?'

'College, in Paris, to study art and design. Not a real degree, as my father would say.'

'I like your father.'

'You would. You like everybody.'

'Are you implying I have no taste?' A loud bang on the driver's window made them both jump. Outside stood Nick in his rugby kit, the collar of his shirt turned up. Laure opened the electric window, and, leaning out, kissed him on both cheeks. Her beloved son, his dark, spiky short hair brushed forward at the front into a fashionable quiff, his skin only slightly marked by acne. His eyes, Gerard's ocean grey-blue. She said something rapidly to him in French, and he smiled.

'Hi, Tom. What are you doing here?' His attractive voice had the effortless, confident public school inflection, sentences ending on a rising note.

'Visiting the old alma mater. And to see you triumph in the first eleven, of course. Not to mention the free tea.'

'It was cool of you both to come. Look, I have to go now, the match is about to start. See you afterwards. Can you take me out before prep? I have like no money and I have to buy some books. And other stuff.'

'Possibly. As long as you don't spend all my money on CDs.'

'Would I?' Grinning, he wandered off, the studs of his boots shedding mud on the gravel drive. Laure found a parking space, in between a Mercedes estate and a Discovery. The Discovery had a wicker basket in the boot. What, Laure wondered, was it about upper-middle-class women and wicker baskets?

'Do we have to get out of the car? It's nice and warm in here.'

'There's not much point coming to a match if you don't actually get out and watch it, is there?'

'Can't you just keep coming back to tell me what the score is, and bring me buns? Or better still, stay and talk to me?'

'No, Tom, I cannot. I drove you all the way here to keep me company.'

'I could be with you in spirit.'

'You are not sitting in my car smoking. You're just scared you might meet someone you know.'

'There is that.' Reluctantly, he opened the passenger door, as Laure pulled on her black velvet coat. Tom thought how proud he was to be seen with her. A group of boys in sports jackets, clutching files to their chests, paused to gawp at her on their way through the imposing front door. Nick was lucky to have such a gorgeous mother. Tom would have been thrilled if his mother had looked remotely like Laure, because if there was one thing that made you popular at school, it was a beautiful mother. His own had looked like a trout in a headscarf. He thought, not for the first time, that Laure resembled a painting by Raphael. Flowing, unworldly, intensely feminine. There were no hard edges to her.

'Does he like it here?'

'Nick?'

'Of course, Nick.'

'He didn't at first, but now he's passionate about it. I couldn't drag him away. I said he could leave next year, after his exams, and go to the sixth-form college in Claydon, but he won't hear of it. Worse luck.'

'Why worse luck?'

'Because it costs an arm and a leg. Not that you'd remember.'

'You're rich. Aren't you?'

She forced a smile. 'Of course we are, silly. Fabulously.'

It was very strange, but she did not feel able to meet his eyes. She was aware of the fact that their easy, casual relationship had shifted, minutely, since Saturday. When they had moved to the Rectory, they had formed an inter-couple friendship with Nat and Cassie, Tom and Sarah. Tom and Cassie had been friends since childhood, and she and Cassie had clicked immediately. Then their daughters Lucy and Sophie had formed a friendship at school, and Tom and Sarah naturally weaved into their lives, ferrying the children backwards and forwards between the two homes, arranging trips to the swimming pool and sharing dinner parties and barbecues in the summer. It was a pleasant, recreational friendship, suiting the whole family. She'd always thought Tom was fun, without counting him an intimate friend in the way that Cassie had become.

On Saturday a boundary had been crossed into uncharted territory, a connection made, and she did not know how to step back. The connection, she realized, with an intake of breath, was that, somehow, her subconscious had registered him as sexually attractive. She had never seen it previously, but now she could not understand why it had not hit her before. When she talked to him, she found herself

46

looking into the distance, or at his ridiculous scarf, feeling flustered. She was unusually conscious of how she looked, and one hand reached up to run through her hair, lifting it away from her face. She shook herself. How could you know someone for five years and suddenly see them in a quite different light? She was being so silly. Nothing had changed, and it was purely a by-product of her hypersensitivity at the moment. She was clutching at straws for comfort and reassurance, and Tom was kind and seemed genuinely to like her and find her interesting and funny. As a friend, she said firmly to herself. And she had never, in all the time she had known Gerard, ever contemplated infidelity because it led into the long shadows.

Tom, walking round the back of the car, tucked his arm companionably in hers. Despite herself, she felt a flash of warmth, of illicit pleasure. She looked down at his arm. 'You'll cause a scandal,' she said.

'Why?'

'Because all those women over there by the pitch, the ones with sunglasses on their heads even though it's March and we are hardly bathed in sunlight, are currently looking at you and me, and have no idea that you are simply my very good friend who is here to skive off doing any work.'

'Interfering old bats. How about if I snogged you?'

'Don't be an idiot,' she said, sharply. 'Put me down.'

'All right.' Grumpily, he disengaged his arm. One of the schoolboys by the front door turned to stare at them, and nudged a friend. Unaware, Laure steered Tom towards the distant group of fellow parents on the far side of the pitch beyond the drive, standing in a well-dressed huddle. She had better introduce him, or word would be round the parents' mafia like wildfire.

'He's pretty good, isn't he?' Nick, tall and athletic, had scored a try. 'Has he got a girlfriend yet?'

'I don't know. He won't tell me. But he won't let me see his phone. Keeps it under his pillow when he's at home, and it's the only thing he never loses.'

'He has, then. Doesn't Gerard come to these things?'

'He's always at work. Anyway, they bore him. He's always loathed anything to do with the children's schools. They make him uncomfortable, I don't know why.'

Laure's eyes were on the match, watching her son, and Tom studied her profile, the curve of her unmade-up eyelashes, the faint blue shadowing under her eyes and the smooth hollow of her cheek. He felt a wave of protectiveness towards her. It was unexpected. He had never felt sorry for Laure before, she seemed so self-possessed. Untouchable. Today there was a fragility about her that was disturbingly appealing. He was aware of a warmth between them, a kind of force field. Suddenly he felt the same bat-squeak of sexuality he had experienced holding her on the dance floor, which he had, at the time, hurriedly dismissed as too much champagne. He jammed his hands in his pockets and looked down at the ground, scuffing the muddy grass with the toe of his boot. Just standing next to her was seductive. Where had this come from? He had always found her attractive, any man would, but he had a mental firewall protection against sexual attraction, he just did not go there. Ever. This feeling was quite new, and different. He felt as if all the time they were together they were making connections, little tiny sparks. But there was no way – with Laure, ridiculous. She and Gerard, besides Nat and Cassie, were one of the happiest couples he knew. In their close circle, it was only he and Sarah who seemed unable to . . . no. He closed the thought down. He was sick and tired of trying to analyse what was wrong.

'Did you have a girlfriend when you were here?'

Laure's voice was deliberately light. He was aware that she had moved a little away from him.

He stared at the boys running up and down the field. That had been him, twenty-odd years ago. In his mind's eye he saw his childhood self, small for his age, talented at English but hopeless at science, irritatingly cocky and an irresistible target for bigger, powerful boys freed from parental restraint. God, he had hated rugby matches. An excuse for legitimate violence. The early years at the school had been hell on earth, until he learnt how to sidestep physical attacks with humour, and had begun to win admiration by being both amusing and rebellious. He cultivated a dilettante image, and developed a reputation for taking more drugs than he actually did. In his first year he had once made the mistake of trying to tell his mother he was being bullied, and she looked at him in horror. 'Of course you are,' she said. 'It's part of your education.' He could not remember a time when she had physically touched him when they said goodbye.

'There were girls in the sixth form. First year of intake, thank God for that. Otherwise we'd all have died of exhaustion from wanking and buggery,' he said.

Laure pointedly ignored his profanity. When she had first met Tom she'd been shocked by his language. Now she was used to it.

'So?' she said, teasingly.

'Well, what do you think? Of course I did.'

'Did you break hearts?'

'One or two.'

'Did you get hurt?'

'Never.' He was regarding her with a curious intensity, and she looked away, uneasy. She was acutely aware of a subtext. He *was* treating her differently. She hadn't imagined it.

49

'Did you, you know . . . smuggle girls into your room?' Her voice was studiedly light.

'Yes, I did, you dirty beast. Do you want details?'

'*Dieu*, no. It makes me think of Nick doing the same thing, not that he is in the sixth form yet.'

'He's a good-looking boy. It's bound to happen sometime.'

'I guess so. I just feel so protective about him. He's mine. Is that strange?'

'I suppose I feel the same about Lucy. It's a boy–girl thing. I don't worry about Mickey at all, apart from his tendency to set fire to things. I just expect him to cope, to be like me. Well, not exactly like me, obviously. I hope he will be rather more of a success.'

'I'm glad you came,' she said. She bit her lip, and looked away. 'At the moment I feel like everything's so . . . I'm not very . . .'

'So, what? Are you OK? You do seem a little . . . Look, tell me.' His voice was urgent, full of concern. She swallowed, and to her horror, her eyes filled with tears. She turned her head from him and coughed, hurriedly wiping her eyes with the back of her hand. What on earth was wrong with her? She realized that if she had been with Gerard, they would probably not have exchanged a word for the entire match. It was such a relief to be with someone who chatted, who listened. She felt overcome with waves of emotion and exhaustion, and the one thing she longed to do more than any other was throw herself into his arms and sob, 'We're broke, we might even lose the house and I think Gerard hates me.' That's it, she thought. I am officially insane.

She turned back towards him, hoping her eyes did not betray the fact they had filled with tears. She was taken aback by the intensity of his gaze. She frowned at him slightly, unnerved, and he looked quickly away, a shadow of embarrassment crossing his face, as if he had been caught out. We're acting like teenagers, she thought, and took a deep breath. 'I'm fine, of course I am. No, I just meant that if you hadn't come I would have had to get into the one-upmanship of these women.' She gestured at them, forcing a laugh, and he knew that she was lying, something was wrong. Surely she could trust him with it, whatever was worrying her? The feeling of protectiveness was unusual, and he thought, suddenly, I want to know every tiny thing about you.

'You know,' she carried on, 'cars, houses, clothes, where were we going skiing at Easter? They intimidate me. Even the most innocent question is actually a highly subtle exercise in establishing a social pecking order. It's a game, you see – they look like they're having a conversation, but in fact they're all madly topping each other. I detest it. There are some nice ones, but for most of them having a son here is simply another social badge.'

'They do look a bit like hens, now you come to mention it. Hens with identical blonde bobs.' Laure laughed, grateful that they were moving on to less dangerous, less personal ground.

'Oh rahly?' A self-consciously loud voice floated over to them, the kind of voice that is meant for people to overhear and think, gosh, you must be smart. 'We're going to Lech this year. Are you? Oh. Last Easter the lifts in Courchevel were *so* crowded and there were simply hordes of Russians. Hugo said never again, and I quite agree.'

Laure and Tom snorted.

'See?' said Laure. 'That's put her in her place. Courchevel is just *so* last year.'

'I'll have to cancel the chalet. Damn,' he said, in an exaggerated version of his own accent.

Laure nudged him. 'You don't even have to pretend. You're one of them. I'm the outsider, the foreigner. You understand all this. You're part of it.'

'Bollocks,' Tom said. 'I left all that behind long ago. Don't you dare say I'm part of that brigade. What have I got to show off about, anyway? I can't remember the last time I went skiing, and we're paupers compared to your family and your great big humungous house.'

'Shut up. Can you ski?'

'Like a racing demon.'

'Seriously?'

'Seriously? I used to, but I'd be crap now, I haven't been for years. Anyway, it's just sliding pretending to be a sport. We used to go every Christmas.' He grinned at her, his voice full of self-mockery. 'The only good thing I remember was the après ski. I used to get as drunk as a monkey in Dick's Tea Bar in Val d'Isère from the age of about twelve. Don't actually remember much skiing at all.'

'You drink too much.'

'I know. It's to stave off boredom. Anyone's interesting when you've had a drink. Sarah says . . .'

'What?'

'She says I drink to escape from my lack of ambition.'

'Is it true?'

'Probably. I don't really care any more. I just like the way it makes me feel.'

'Or not feel.'

'There may be a grain of truth in that. You're being quite judgemental today, aren't you, Mrs Sigmund Freud? Anyway, psychoanalysing me is pointless. There's nothing underneath. What you see is what you get, I'm afraid.'

'The man with hidden shallows.'

Tom laughed. 'That's it. Come on. They must

have set up the tea. I'm freezing my knob off out here.'

'You are such a child. There are times when I pity Sarah. She must have the patience of Job.'

'She doesn't, believe me. I drive her nuts.'

Tom had eaten an embarrassing amount of cake and the other mothers had avoided them as if they were surrounded by traffic cones, and they had had an enjoyable wander round town where Nick managed to extract money Laure could ill afford for a new pair of jeans which barely covered his underpants. They were now on their way home. Tom's phone rang in the pocket of his muddy coat.

'In the car. Why? No, I haven't. I've been busy. Just stuff. Work.' He caught Laure's eye, and she had to stop herself laughing. She felt light-headed, irresponsible, as if today was a day off, a holiday. Being with Tom was like entering a sunny parallel universe. It made her realize that with Gerard, she always had to weigh her words. When she was with him she was constantly on alert, antennae quivering to pick up his mood, conscious as to whether the children were annoying him, or if he was bored. With Tom, she felt much more herself. Or, at least, the Laure she used to be. She could relax and not have to feel that if he was in a bad mood, she was somehow to blame.

'Now? With Laure. On the way back from Uplingham. To see Nick. I was bored at home. Hang on.' He held the phone out near Laure's ear, so she could hear Sarah's strident voice.

'Why have you got my idiot husband?'

'He volunteered himself,' Laure shouted at the phone.

'Christ.' Sarah's voice was full of irritation. 'You'd think he had nothing to do. He didn't embarrass you, did he? What is he wearing? Not those combat trousers?'

' 'Fraid so,' Laure shouted.

'Jesus. Put him back on, will you?'

Tom obediently put the phone back to his ear. 'No, I haven't forgotten. Yes, of course, of course I will. Have a good night. No I won't go to the pub, I know I've got the kids. Drink the minibar dry. Have you? Well, tell me later. You too. Bye.' He slipped the phone back in his pocket, a shadow of irritation passing over his face. Sarah always succeeded in making him feel that he ought to be doing something much more worthwhile. Most of their conversations these days seemed to revolve around her giving him orders and instructions.

A paperback book lay in the well of the car. Tom reached forward and picked it up. He studied the back cover. 'Have you read this?' he said.

'No, I just put it in here for effect,' Laure laughed. 'Don't be silly. I brought it just in case you changed your mind about coming, so I'd have something to do if I had to wait for Nick. Have you read many of his?'

'All of them,' Tom said. 'I love Edward Farrell. Been reading him since I was thirteen. He's saved my sanity several times. I tried to pretend I actually was him when I was younger and infinitely more dashing. It gave me hope that my future didn't have to be deathly dull and predictable. That you don't have to settle for the life that is expected of you.'

'Hence the travelling the world,' Laure said, understanding.

'In a battered panama.' Tom nodded. 'And not giving a toss. Treating each day as if it might be my last,' he added, with mock bravado.

'I never had the courage just to take off,' Laure said. 'Maybe someday. He's my favourite English writer. Not as good as French writers like Camus, of course.'

'Of course,' Tom replied, smiling. 'It's really amazing you love him. Most people have never even heard of him. Sarah says he's pretentious. I think that actually he just uses too many words of more than one syllable.'

'That isn't very kind,' Laure said, disapprovingly. 'She's my friend, remember.'

'I rather hoped you were *my* friend,' he said. Laure glanced at him.

'Can't I be both?'

'No,' he said, decisively. 'I claim you for my own, which means I'm allowed to bitch about my wife and you have to be on my side.'

'Sometimes you are very childish. He killed himself, you know. He was only in his forties. Living your life on the edge and all that drinking . . . there's such a thing as too much passion.'

'At least he lived. He travelled. He didn't bury himself in fucking suburbia like most of us and lead lives of quiet desperation.' He gazed out of the window at the grey sky.

'You don't have such a bad life!' Laure laughed. 'You have the children, Sarah, a nice home . . . you can't constantly look for adventure.'

'I know, you're right. I am a whingeing sod,' he said, moodily hunching his shoulders and burying his chin in the pink scarf. 'It's just that sometimes I think, what's the point? I had so many big dreams and now look at me . . .'

'You've grown up,' Laure said, looking sternly at him. 'Being a parent means you can't just take off, doesn't it? Or you shouldn't, anyway. You can't just choose what you want to do and do it, because you have other people to consider. That's not a bad thing.'

'It's no bloody fun, though is it?' he said. 'I'm bored,

bored, bored, bored, bored, bored.' He looked at her. 'Bored.'

Laure regarded him sardonically. But that's partly your fault, she thought. For not pushing ahead with your career. You chose to be at home. 'It's a different kind of fun,' she said. 'Less selfish.'

I have been happy, she thought. I have been quite happy with my life until this last year, I don't feel I have given anything up – the children have enhanced my life, made it much, much better and given me a purpose I never had before. If only Gerard could see how incredibly fortunate we are. Tom is wrong. There can be joy in a safe, routine life.

'His books are about escape, aren't they?' she said. 'But that isn't always courageous. It can mean that you are running away from your responsibilities – it makes you more of a coward than an adventurer. He never married, did he?'

'No,' Tom said. 'He didn't. Although he had a child, I think.'

'Whom he never saw.' She nodded. 'A daughter. I think that's why he killed himself in the end. He didn't know what it felt like to be loved unconditionally. He ran away from responsibility because he was scared. Maybe his books are more about insecurity than escape.' She looked thoughtful.

'I'd like to see the adaptation of *The Blood Red Sky* that's on at the theatre at the moment. At the Almeida, I think. It's got great reviews. I read about it in the paper on Sunday,' he said.

'I would love to . . .'

'Why, would you . . .'

'What?'

'Like to see it? Maybe next week?'

'I'll have to see if Gerard is free. He's so tied up with work at the moment.'

'Oh.'

'It's so hard to get him to go anywhere. And, to be honest, he hates the theatre. We used to go when we were first together, but he only went to please me. After we got married he admitted he loathed it. When I think of all the plays I made him sit through, and I thought he was enjoying it as much as I was, whereas in fact he was just counting the minutes until the interval. He hates sitting still for so long, and you can't smoke. There's something about theatre audiences that drives him insane, too.'

'Sarah doesn't like it much either. She goes, but mostly it's just to say she's seen the latest play with rave reviews.'

'Stop being mean.'

'Sorry.' They caught each other's eye and smiled. Tom smacked himself hard on the hand. 'Bad Tom.'

'How's her job?' Laure said.

'Oh, you know. Frantic. Desperately important. She hardly ever gets home before nine at night. Look, I really would like to see that play. Would Gerard mind if you came with me?'

'Why on earth should he?'

'I'm very irritating, though,' Tom warned. 'I hate it if people cough. I have been known to lean forward and tell them off. I can be quite scary.'

'I'm sure I can bear you.'

'Shall I book it?'

Laure hesitated. It would be expensive. She couldn't just go around wasting money on what was effectively a luxury. 'I'll call you about it,' she said.

His heart sank. It wouldn't happen, and he felt unreasonably deflated. He shrugged. 'Whatever,' he said, studiedly careless. 'You owe me one treat, then. I need cheering up.'

*   *   *

At home, he looked around his messy kitchen, plates from breakfast still in the sink, the morning paper spread out on the table. He sat down slowly at the table, and let his head fall onto his folded arms. He felt overwhelmed by utter despair. Nothing had changed. He looked at the clock. Christ, he had to pick up the girls in a minute.

Gerard was standing at the Aga frying steaks when she walked into the kitchen, shedding her coat, shaking out her hair. Victor thumped from his basket, and she bent to stroke his nose. 'Have you had your tea?' His martyred eyes, beseeching, said no, he had been quite forgotten.

'He's lying,' Gerard said without looking round, his pale pink work shirt stretched tightly across his back, his pinstriped suit jacket hung on the back of one of the kitchen chairs. 'I fed him half an hour ago. No Sophie?'

'She's staying at Lucy's. Tom's gone to pick them up. She's got a late play rehearsal. How was your day? You're early. I went to see Nick in a match. Tom—' She stopped, realizing she suddenly felt uncomfortable about saying it. 'Tom came with me.'

'Useless tosser. Hasn't he got anything better to do?'

'Apparently not. You know Tom. How was your day?'

'Fine. I had a meeting in Chalfont so I thought I may as well come home. I picked up steaks on the way. Could you make a dressing for the salad?'

'Mmm.' There was a pile of post on the hall table, neatly stacked by the cleaner. She thumbed through it. Two bills and a bank statement. She opened it and had to look at the amount twice. How much? How? Maybe somebody was sneaking into their bank account and spending their money. Well, not their money. The bank's money. It was horrific. She felt physically sick, and put the statement face down with a shaking hand.

'Anything nice?'

'Hardly.' She handed it to him. He turned it over, glanced at it, then, opening the top of the swing bin, chucked it in.

'Don't you think we ought to keep them?'

'Why? What's the point?'

'Just to check it's correct, to see what's going out . . .' Her voice trailed off. Her light-hearted mood, the feeling of holiday, had evaporated the moment she saw his car in the drive. It was like stepping out of the sun.

Gerard had turned away from her, and his words were clipped, angry. 'Could we just not talk about it for one night? I'm tired.' Laure saw that he had bought a bottle of red wine, which was warming by the oven. They had decreed that they would not drink during the week, only at weekends. Drink must be a treat, not a habit. It must have been a bad day. The words were out of her mouth before she could stop herself.

'But we never talk about it. What happened? At the meeting?'

His back went rigid. 'I said, I do not want to talk about it. Nothing's final.'

'What's not final?' She had a growing sense of alarm. Something new. Something bad. She saw him draw his shoulders in, then suddenly drop them. He would tell her. He turned.

'It was about the equity in the house. I went to see the building society. It wasn't a business meeting, and they're allowing us to release another chunk. I told them it was to build a garage, do some landscaping. It means I can pay off more interest on the loan, give us a bit of clear water. Nothing too alarming.'

Laure stepped away from him, colliding with a chair. 'No! You promised! That was only as a last resort for the school fees, and we haven't paid them yet. You know that, Gerard. Why? There's practically no equity left. And it means the mortgage payment goes up, yet again. We can't survive on nothing. I'm trying – I have the manor to do – but that won't be paid for months. What will we do in the meantime? Live on fresh air? Can you imagine what it is like, being here when the bills arrive, knowing that we have no way of paying them?' She knew her voice was rising with hysteria, and she breathed deeply, trying to keep calm. He hated her losing her temper.

He banged his glass down on the table, his face furious. 'Christ, yes, it must be awful for you, mustn't it? Being in this house day after day, while I'm out there working my ass off. You cannot compare your stress level, Laure, you really can't. Look,' he smiled, a ghost of a smile. 'Let's not do this, shall we? It really isn't your problem. Let's not spoil what can be a nice evening. Things will be fine. I promise. You just have to trust me, and leave me to sort it out. There's nothing you can do.'

Laure couldn't stop herself. 'But it's the not doing anything that's killing me! You're shutting me out. Cassie said . . .'

'What?' His voice was dangerously quiet.

'Cassie said you said something about not even being here at Easter. What did you mean?'

'It's one of the reasons I had to see the building society.' His voice was studiedly casual, as if it was unimportant. 'The stupid bank didn't pay the mortgage last month. We really have got to change banks, they are such arseholes. They had this idiotic notion that we might have to put it on the market. Of course it's rubbish, it's never going to get that bad. I was only joking to Cassie, she caught me at a bad moment.' His voice was very firm, daring her to challenge him. He ran a hand through his thick dark hair, shot through with grey. His face still handsome, but lined around his eyes and with a deep groove running down each cheek. A tic was beating under one eye.

'What! Why didn't they ring us?' Her heart was beating wildly. They could lose the house. They really could.

'They did. They rang me. I didn't want to worry you. As I said, it's just a blip. Forget it.'

'We can't go on like this.' The words were out of her mouth before she could stop them.

Gerard's expression was cold, threatening, his grey-blue eyes narrowed. 'What do you mean?'

'I mean that we need to sit down, and work out what is possible and what is not. We cannot keep borrowing and borrowing until there are no escape routes left. I can sell some of Mama's furniture, a painting or two. They are quite valuable, they would bring in thousands, something to live on. It seems so crazy to live here and not even be able to pay the phone bill. We have to be practical. We can't just carry on living a life we can't afford.'

'That is my decision. Not yours.'

'Why? Why is it just your decision? Couldn't you try and sell at least a part of the business? Nat says he knows someone who . . .'

'Please tell me you haven't been talking to our friends about this.'

'Of course I haven't. Cassie mentioned it when we were talking about something else. She said that Nat knows someone who . . .' He cut her short.

'Please do not interfere in things you don't understand. I am really not going to give up now. Survival is just round the corner, Laure, honestly it is. Trust me.' The nervous tic beat more strongly under his eye. She wanted to reach out and smooth it away, but she knew he would brush off her hand. He could not bear to be seen in a position of weakness. Laure clenched her hand into a fist, her fingernails digging into her palm so hard it hurt. Why was everything she said wrong, making him more angry? She *did* understand. Why couldn't they try and work this out together? He refused to treat her like an adult. Couldn't he see he was pushing her away? She looked at him, at his exhausted face, and was overcome with pity.

She shrugged. She felt numb, exhausted. Arguing was not going to make the slightest bit of difference. She took a step towards him and put her arms, from behind, around his solid shoulders in the smart pink shirt she had bought for him at Christmas, before she knew they had no money for luxuries, breathing in his smell of cigarettes and aftershave, the smell that always used to make her feel safe. She leant her head against his back, but his body was rigid, and he did not respond by turning and putting his arms around her. It was like trying to hug an inanimate object, and his body language was defensive, unyielding. She dropped her arms, and stepped back from him, hurt.

Before Christmas, Sophie being away would have been seen as an ideal opportunity for them to make love. Now, they had not made love for what – three months? Certainly several weeks before he had told her what was going on. She hadn't cared too much at the time, too absorbed in her own worries about her father, but now she realized how long it had been, what an effect it was having on their relationship. She'd made excuses for him, he was tired, she was tired, he needed to work after she went to bed, he'd had too much to drink or the children were still awake – but she was running out of excuses.

He had always been so tactile, desperate to make

love to her whenever he could. But now he no longer seemed to desire her. If she rolled over to touch him in the night, he turned away from her. He had either ceased to find her sexy, or, perhaps, he did not want to try to make love because he might not have been able to. And that, to Gerard, would have been the worst thing in the world. Many times she had tried to get him to talk about it, but he always said the same thing. 'Not now. I've just got too much on my mind. Don't make a big issue out of it.' Making love had always been their haven, their way of making everything better. Now he either did not need her, or they had created too much of a barrier between them to have that kind of intimacy.

She turned away, defeated. The image of Tom, with his floppy wayward hair, childish grin, weather-tanned face with bags beneath his dark brown spaniel eyes, flashed into her mind. He wouldn't talk to her like this, as if she was a child who could be dismissed. She longed to call him, just to hear his voice. Maybe she could ring him later about the hairbrush Lucy had left in her car. Stop it, she said to herself. You're just leaning on him because you know there will be pleasure in his voice when he hears you. None of this was his problem, his affair.

Chapter Four

Sarah

'Sex has never been so good for the over-fifties.'

'Gross.' Liberty, twenty-three, clad from head to toe in Prada, screwed up her pretty elfin face in a grimace. 'Fifty-year-olds don't have sex, do they? Ew.'

Sarah glanced at Charles's offended face, and smothered a laugh. 'Of course they do, Lib. Fifty isn't old any more. I propose a double-page colour spread on very attractive fifty-year-olds who say they have multiple orgasms.'

'I may have to leave the room.'

'Well, obviously, they don't have to actually be fifty, we can just say they are. And for "orgasm" read "fulfilling love life". We don't want to give the collective middle class a heart attack over their Sunday morning cappuccino. Cosima, can you fix that? Ring Annabelle. She can find anyone.'

Under the banter, the Monday morning planning meeting was even more tense with undercurrents than usual. Something was up with Charles, the executive editor of the weekly and Sunday title, who liked to sit in occasionally on their meetings and create an atmosphere of subdued panic, which he much enjoyed and made him feel powerful. Normally he joined in, but this morning he was sitting quietly, steepling his fingers, frowning. She felt, not for the first time, that he was the organ grinder and they were his performing monkeys. Sometimes they made him laugh. Sometimes they irritated or disappointed him. But they all danced for him.

'And now,' Sarah looked at her list again, 'the woman who has persuaded her grandmother to carry her baby.'

'Surely that's not possible.'

'I kid you not. They're a bit pond life, but we can posh them up at the shoot. Say the prospective nineteen-year-old father's a business manager, not a factory worker. They want fifty thousand. Is that OK, Charles?'

'What?'

'Fifty? For an exclusive?'

'I'll see,' he said, coolly. That meant no.

'We need to get back to them soon or they'll go elsewhere. Now, fashion shoots. Tiny bolero jackets are the in thing for spring, and then Marcia has a great underwear shoot. Big pants are apparently the new thong.'

'Great,' said Michael, the newly married health editor, morosely. 'How sexy. Not.'

'They're more like shorts than big pants, really,' Sarah said. She made a mental note to buy some one lunchtime this week. That was one of the great things about working in the capital – you had access to all the shops.

'Little sexy shorts?' He cheered up and flashed her a flirtatious smile, which she ignored. He was all over her like a rash in front of other people and nothing was too much trouble, while she knew he had been secretly lobbying for her job and spreading rumours behind her back that she was planning another baby, which was complete rubbish. She was so paranoid about being portrayed as a 'mummy' she didn't even have any pictures of the children in her office.

'You are pathetic,' she said, witheringly. 'We've persuaded that girl from the soaps, you know, the lesbian-kiss one, to model them. Very upmarket shoot. On the staircase at the Café de Paris.'

'What's that?'

'Lesbian, Michael. There, now I've got your attention, can you tell me what's on your list for health and well-being?'

'Fifty is the new forty,' he said, triumphantly. Everyone around the table hooted. He held up his hands in front of him in mock horror. 'It's true,' he said. 'And I've got the medical evidence to prove it.'

Christ, I'm tired, Sarah thought, as Michael ran down his list, feature ideas she had heard a million times before. She looked out of the window at the cars sixteen floors below, crawling up the high street like so many ants. This morning she had got up at six to be at the office by half past nine, and tonight, after finishing work at eight, she had to go to an awards ceremony which meant staying over in town in a hotel. She hated that, although it did mean she'd get a better night's sleep without Daisy crawling in with her. At three, she still loved to sleep with her and Tom. Some nights it was sweet. Other nights it was a pain in the neck, as she wriggled and kicked. Last night had been a wriggly night.

She meant to prepare for the ideas meeting on the train but had fallen asleep instead, probably with her mouth open. She had woken abruptly, her head jerked back by a sudden movement of the train, and there was a little dribble on her designer-jacket collar, which she quickly wiped away. Once awake, for the last ten or so miles, she resolved to go through the newspapers and make notes, but instead stared out of the window, not fully conscious, at the scrubby waste at the side of the track, dyed a pale mauve by the pollution from the trains.

The intense green of the fields had given way to a seamless morass of old blackberry bushes, bent low, with sparse buddleia and trees raising skeletal grey arms to the sky, behind which stood faceless dark buildings. Trees you could never imagine in leaf, embalmed by the mortality of the urban air, trapped under leaden clouds. Then the sudden plunge into a tunnel, when people's mobiles abruptly stopped working, a roaring sound, cutting out the rhythmical clunk of the wheels. The steady creak of the brakes as the train pulled into the station, winched to its destination by the graffiti-strewn walls. Then it stopped.

Welcome to my world, Sarah thought, as she gathered up her unread newspapers, stained empty polystyrene coffee cup and pen. About now Cassie and Laure would be sitting down to a cup of coffee in their kitchens with the newspaper, looking out over the garden, surrounded by the blissful silence of a child-free house. They really had no idea how the rest of the world functioned. Sometimes, chatting to them when she had a spare moment, which was rare, she felt as if she was captured in a 1950s time warp. They seemed to have all the time in the world, whereas she felt she hardly ever paused for breath.

None of the children had been awake when she left the house, for which she was profoundly grateful. She loved them all deeply, but with a fourteen-hour day ahead, coping with farewells and hugs and requests for presents even though she was only going to be away one night would have been too much. Tom could cope. Anyway, he didn't appear to have anything better to do at the moment. Which reminded her. She must ring him about that phone call she'd had from

Martin. He could push some work Tom's way, he'd said. He'd worked with them both, years ago, on the regional paper where they had met, and now ran a successful news agency. That was before Sarah started to climb the career ladder, and Tom effectively retired to write his novel and look after the children. They had never formally decided he would become a house husband, it had just evolved as she failed to find a nanny she liked and Tom failed to do anything about either his freelance career or his writing. He had drifted into the role, and it was now accepted as a fait accompli.

'Can I see you later?' Charles said in his acquired upper-class drawl, as he gathered up his notes at the end of the meeting.

'Sure. When?'

'Lunch. I have a little proposition for you.'

Sarah's heart skipped a beat. Not more budget cuts then, thank God. She knew that her department haemorrhaged money, but then they had to over-commission because Peter the Sunday editor was so bloody fussy they had to get at least three spreads ready per page every week, two of which got chucked away and were never used, despite the expense of the journalist's fees and the cost of the shoot. The paper made squillions, but was always proposing budget cuts. This was part of the regime of fear, which kept everyone on their toes, eyes swivelling for the sudden plunge of the dagger.

A proposition. That could only mean one thing. Promotion. Sarah had been angling for more of an executive role for years – she wanted to oversee all of the features output, rather than just the women's pages on the mid-market Sunday tabloid magazine. Venetia, the senior features executive, was useless – she only kept the job because she was a friend of Charles's wife and married to a politician, thereby the source of some useful information. Sarah burned with all the little indignities Venetia heaped upon her, when she knew that she was so much more able and had, since her women's-page editorship, increased the paper's circulation by over half a million.

This year, the magazine might just win an award. It was read by most of the wealthy women in the country, and Sarah knew just what they wanted. A heady mix of fashion, sex, scandal and confessional journalism of the 'I'm a working mother, I feel so guilty, but look at how much I earn and how nice my shoes are' variety. But then she was well placed to edit such pieces. I've been there and got the T-shirt, she thought, ruefully, regarding her expensive designer shoes. And the footwear. An old university friend of hers had recently returned to work after having five years off with young children, and said the thing she liked most about it was being able to wear high-heeled shoes every day and going to the toilet on her own.

The job could well be Venetia's. Eureka. Charles had seen the light. It must mean at least a bigger salary, not to mention a car. You may as well get all the toys for the boys, she thought. What should she have? She allowed her mind to dawdle along tantalizing lines of a smart new car, which they had never been able to afford, while idly flicking through shots of a mother and daughter talking about dating in the new millennium. God, they were ugly. What must they have looked like before the shoot, without that amount of make-up? You could almost smell the chips, and no amount of designer clothes or hairstyling would waft it away. And she should know. She'd got the T-shirt there too. No chance of getting it past Peter, then. He had placed an embargo on anyone he considered 'rough or common'. She made a mental note to pay the journalist a kill fee. She'd protest, but tough.

She was sure Venetia had only got the job in the first place because she was part of the same dinner-party social circle as Charles. Tom resolutely refused to get drawn into any work-based socializing or 'crawling up the editor's arse', as he termed it, and anyway they lived too far out of town for it to be feasible. Of course what was so infuriating was the fact that he had the class credentials she didn't, which would have opened many doors in the rarefied world in which Charles moved – Tom was the one who had been born with the silver spoon. Now he appeared to be at his happiest in the pub. Talking about nothing, to anyone.

She put down her pencil, realizing she had been tapping it furiously. That was the effect Tom had on her at the moment – he made her furious, literally boiling with anger. She knew that she got on at him all the time, but it was such a waste of his talent, sitting in that bloody pub, or mooching about, having coffee with Cassie and Laure. She felt short-changed by him, as if she had been sold a pup. Daisy could easily have gone to a full-time childminder so Tom could actually do some work, as he claimed he wanted to do, but he kept finding excuses and said she was far better at home with him – and yet he took her to nursery three mornings a week, so he did have time to work.

And here she was, day after day, chained to her computer, chairing meetings, sucking up to men like Peter and Charles, juggling office politics with an expertise born of long practice, while he did practically nothing. Yes, of course he got the children to school and Daisy off to nursery but it was hardly brain surgery, and she'd happily pay for childcare if only he would do some bloody work to justify the extra expense. He kept talking about writing his novel, but did he ever do anything about it? What he should be doing was some freelance journalism, rather than sitting about waiting for the muse to strike. Meanwhile she had to work so hard to pay the mortgage and bills on the four-bedroomed modern house at the opposite end of the village to Cassie and Laure.

But, at heart, despite the moaning, she would not have wanted to give up her career. She loved the frisson of power, of being where the action was, the recognition for doing well, the being in control. Staying at home with the children all day would have bored her rigid, and she didn't understand how Tom could be so patient. When she wasn't at nursery he spent hours drawing with Daisy, making a tree house for Mickey and creating that awful menagerie which made a mess of the back lawn.

Her mother had been thrilled to bits when the rather scruffy young man Sarah was dating turned out to be the Honourable Tom Cotterill, second son of Sir Rupert Cotterill. Until she met Tom and his family, Sarah didn't think that people like that existed any more. But, as she'd discovered, the country was still full of pockets of these dinosaurs, hoary old families clinging onto their dwindling acres of land in decaying old country houses full of tack and muddy boots, devoted to their horses and dogs, doing a bit of charity work, hunting, glimpsed infrequently like rare species with their red faces and loud voices, pushing trolleys inexpertly around Tesco and trying to engage the checkout girl in conversation as if they were still in the village store, while she looked at them as if they were Martians. Relics, trying to cling onto a forgotten time, when people still knew their place and they were top of the heap and could patronize the lower orders.

Sarah's mother, misguidedly, thought the way

would be paved to a life of material wealth and ease for her tough, determined daughter, who had made it clear from an early age that she wasn't going to get dumped on by a man as her mother had been. Only, as Sarah carefully explained, being posh didn't mean you actually had any money. Tom's parents certainly didn't. Since his father's heart attack they were living in just two rooms of their filthy huge old house, which was falling down. Buckets littered the upstairs rooms as the roof gradually caved in. Even Tom said they ought to move, but his mother wouldn't hear of it. She talked perpetually about the need to keep 'the inheritance' for his older brother Henry, whereas renovating the house from its current parlous state would probably cost more than it was worth, and death duties would eat away at whatever tiny investments they had left. Henry, who lived in Hong Kong and worked in equity, made it clear he didn't want it. Sarah would have felt sorry for his parents if they hadn't been such appalling snobs, desperately trying to preserve a life that nobody wanted.

Sarah had decided from an early age she was always going to have a lucrative career so she wouldn't be left high and dry without a proper income and have to take low-paid jobs cleaning and working shifts in a petrol station, as her mother had. Well, she'd certainly achieved her own success – only she hadn't quite planned to be the sole breadwinner. It was only a matter of time, Tom said, before he sold the rights to his novel. She knew he thought she didn't appreciate him or the way he ran the house and looked after the children – but she found it very hard to respect a man who didn't bring in any money. Having been brought up without it, she had an inbuilt terror of not having enough, whereas Tom didn't give a damn. He claimed she was obsessed with material possessions. But then he'd grown up absorbing his parents' disregard for the practicality of money, talking about which was simply not done. Their current situation was one they resolutely ignored. Both of them had grown up in large houses with servants, and the money had only started to run out after they had finished paying school fees. Their childhood too had been a quite alien world to Sarah – a world of governesses, nannies, the top-floor nursery and shaking hands with your parents before sitting down to dinner.

Now Tom's parents lived off next to nothing, and the first time Sarah met them they ate Heinz tomato soup barely heated up in a kitchen encrusted with years of grime, and she had to move a mouldy old dog's lead from one hairy chair before she could sit down. A cat weaved its way around the plates and a Labrador rested its head heavily on her lap, long drools of spit hanging from its jaws. Sarah was too embarrassed to push it away, although she found it revolting. Her mother would have died at the thought of the bacteria. Tom's mother Jumbo (Sarah had never found out what her real name was, she couldn't have been christened Jumbo, could she?) seemed to spend her life in a grubby green sleeveless husky and a headscarf, indoors and out. At that first meeting his father, in a wheelchair, was covered in a tartan rug smothered in dog hair. A Jack Russell growled faintly on his knee. Both man and dog had rheumy, watery eyes and seemed scared stiff of the formidable Jumbo.

The children thought their house was brilliant, because you didn't have to take your muddy wellies off at the door and Grandma let you cook gooey cakes and meringues on the ancient Aga. They weren't remotely intimidated by her and she seemed to adore them. Sarah was fanatical about cleanliness and never let them make cakes at home because it made too much mess. She was similarly discouraging about painting.

When she first met Tom, on the regional newspaper, she had rejected his overtures of friendship, viewing him with suspicion because he represented a life she had despised in a certain social set at her university. Soon, however, she realized he was far from a snooty Hooray, despite his cut-glass accent, and he in fact despised that kind of person too. As the years passed she realized that his initially charming disregard for society's rules characterized a chronic disability to engage with anything that remotely resembled real life. Having been brought up with nothing, she yearned to acquire the badges of wealth and privilege, and it was she who insisted on sending the children to private school, although Tom said quite rightly they couldn't afford it, and they'd be much better off at the village school, where Cassie's children went. She was determined to fight tooth and nail to give them what she hadn't had, and she loved expensive designer clothes and shoes, which Tom thought were a pointless waste of money. He'd happily wander about in ripped old jeans and it drove her mad that he didn't bother to dress the children up – Lucy and Mickey were too old to be told what to wear, but did he have to put Daisy in a tatty pair of trousers and paint-splashed T-shirt for nursery? What really irritated her was the fact that everyone else thought he was such a saint to stay at home and look after the children. Sarah could understand what people saw in Tom, but then they didn't have to live with him and his chronic lack of ambition.

Tom's mother told all her friends, prior to their marriage, that she thought Sarah was 'tremendous' and was so relieved that someone was prepared to take hopeless Tom in hand. She credited Sarah with jerking him back onto the straight and narrow after his infatuation with drugs and his endless, pointless globe-trotting. When Sarah met him he was on the brink of chucking in his job at the newspaper – he'd been there for a year when she joined as a junior reporter – to go off travelling in a war-torn region of Africa. Sarah said he couldn't run away all his life, and that if he left she would not be waiting for him. He had acquiesced, surprising not only his family but himself. He admired her guts, and he subversively enjoyed introducing someone of Sarah's background into his family's long line of well-bred country 'gels'.

Sarah, Tom thought, would be the key to a quite different life. She was the first person to tell him that he was a talented writer, and seemed to believe in him. Up to that moment, he was determined to thwart anyone who thought he might have potential – at school, the English master had nurtured him to the point where Tom, secretly terrified of failure, deliberately wrote practically nothing in his English exam. His friends thought it was deeply cool, but Tom had unsettling memories of the man's puzzled, hurt eyes when he read out the results. Better not to try and fail, than try and fail.

Once they were a couple, Sarah made most of the decisions. Tom, inherently lazy, found that he liked the novelty of having someone to organize his life. He loathed snobbery and elitism, and it didn't occur to him until much later that Sarah was, in fact, as much of a snob as his mother. All this became apparent in the first six years of their marriage, but by then Tom had fallen passionately in love with his children. Besides, most of the time, he liked looking after the children, running the house in a haphazard way and wandering about the village. It was really only in these last few years, when he felt that what he and Sarah wanted from life seemed to be diametrically opposed, that he was beginning to experience the niggling desire to take off, to change his life.

In the first few years together he and Sarah had a fantastic sex life, but perhaps inevitably it had taken something of a back seat as the children arrived. Sarah seemed to now diligently regard their sex life as part of her 'must do' list. Tom made Cassie laugh by saying, quite untruthfully, she had a list pinned up in the kitchen, which read 'Pick up clothes from dry cleaner, book car in for service, shag Tom'. Cassie replied that most married couples substituted a chilled bottle of Sauvignon or a cheeky Rioja for a great sex life, so what was new?

He'd learnt to switch off when she nagged about his lack of ambition. He knew, underneath it all, that he was perfectly capable of being a writer. Inside him was a nugget of talent, just waiting to be cracked open. The desire was there, only the confidence and application were lacking. He would start tomorrow. Or the next day. The time had to be just right, or the magic would be lost. Snatches of dialogue came to him all the time, phrases in his head perfect in structure and meaning. But then when he sat down in front of the computer, facing the blank white screen, they vanished. It was like trying to grasp smoke.

Sarah's phone rang. Jesus Christ, it was nearly eleven and nothing was laid out. Cosima, Sarah's PA, put her head round the door, She pointed furiously at the phone.

'It's Charles,' she mouthed. Sarah picked it up.

'Sarah, darling.'

'Yes?'

'Lunch at one. I have a very interesting suggestion to put to you. I'll send the car, it'll be at the front.'

The car. This was good. Normally she had to get a

taxi and charge it to expenses. She was going up in the world. After the lunch, she made a mental note, if it was good news she would ring her mother and tell her first, which would please her. She drove Sarah mad by being so timid, but her anger was tinged with guilt because she knew how much her mother had scrimped, saved and sacrificed her life for her. It was one hell of a debt to repay. Whenever she rang, she'd say, 'Is this a good time? Are you sure I'm not disturbing you?' Sarah knew she shouldn't, but she despised her mother's accent, her clothes and her chain-smoking. She knew she was lonely, and would have loved to move nearer to them, but Sarah couldn't face that. She had left that life behind her, and having her mother living nearby would be bringing a piece of it far too close for comfort. She had created a new life through hard work, a life her mother neither reflected, nor enhanced.

She arrived at the restaurant five minutes late – long enough to show Charles she wasn't too keen, but not long enough to make him angry. Once there, she shot into the loo for a respray. Her relationship with Charles was an unsettling mix of the fatherly and the sexual. He treated her as an indulgent father would, proud of her achievements, lauding her to his colleagues and demanding she sit next to him at press award ceremonies and the annual ball, where he would rest his hand, as if by accident, on her thigh. Then, abruptly, he would cast her out into the cold. Angry memos about overspending would arrive, and little cutting comments would be made about the suitability of the case studies in the magazine, while Venetia smiled like the cat with the cream. Charles liked to foster bad feeling among his senior staff, as he worked on the 'divide and rule' principle.

Carefully, Sarah drew lipliner around her mouth

and filled it in with red lipstick, redrew the black eyeliner under her eyes and brushed her chestnut hair, expensively highlighted at a smart salon by a celebrity hairdresser, who gave her a discount because she had featured him in the magazine. She looked critically at herself. The black Armani jacket was always reliable, so well cut it gave her a tiny waist, and today she'd teamed it with a red wool skirt by Marc Jacobs, slightly flared and just above the knee. It had cost an arm and a leg but was, as Marcia, the fashion editor, told her, an investment. The whole outfit was finished off by her black Manolo Blahnik high-heeled shoes. She looked, she hoped, sexy and intimidating. Years of working in newspapers and bossing journalists and subordinates around had taught her that a little intimidation went a long way towards getting what you wanted.

'Darling.' They clashed cheeks, as Charles half stood up from the table. Social kissing was a skill she'd had to acquire, because her mother shied away from personal contact and regarded social kissing almost as a form of perversion.

As they kissed, Sarah knew he was looking down the front of her jacket. She had noted, as she walked through the packed restaurant, that he had a bottle of champagne chilling at the side of the table. Good sign. You weren't very likely to give champagne to someone you were about to sack. He signalled to the waiter to open it and pour them a glass.

She leant back and took a sip, as he stared at her.

'What do you think of Venetia?'

She was well used to his technique of trying to wrong-foot people by asking them blunt questions which were practically impossible to answer. She had to say what he wanted to hear, but he would also spot immediately if she was lying.

'I think she relies too much on the position of her

husband, spends too much time having lunch and delegates important tasks.'

He gave a short, barking laugh.

'Well, that's a shame,' he said, taking a sip of his champagne. 'Because he's not going to be reselected.'

'How do you know?'

Charles tapped the side of his nose. 'A little insider knowledge. Now, to business.' He leant forward towards her, and put his hand over hers. It was warm, and slightly sweaty. 'You and I both know that she is not up to the job. But she has been very useful, with all the people she knows, and keeps up the – how can I put it? – the *tone* on the magazine. On the other hand, you . . .' He looked at her slyly out of his dangerous, hooded eyes. Sarah smiled charmingly at him. The utter, utter bastard. What he was saying was that she was a social nobody with zero kudos but she worked hard, and she delivered. He needed a grafter, and he needed someone who could produce the kind of features which played on the darkest fears of their readers, while pandering to their aspirations.

'I, what?' Sarah said, looking sexily at him from under her lashes. She was far too clever to let him provoke her or be offended. Who cared, as long as she got the job?

'You don't have the same contacts, but you've proved yourself.'

'Thank you.' She raised her glass to him. 'I know I have.'

'How would Tom feel if you had to travel more, spend longer hours at the office?'

'He'd be fine.'

'And the children?'

'Tom looks after them, as you know. Anyway, if you're going to pay me the fortune I am about to demand, I can afford a full-time nanny.'

He smiled, and tightened his grip on her hand. She tried not to wince. 'You're like me, Sarah. A lot like me. Nothing will stand in your way. I'll demand blood, you know.'

'I wouldn't expect anything less,' she replied, smiling flirtatiously at him.

'I aim to make this the best-selling Sunday tabloid in the country. The others won't stand a chance; we're already snapping at their heels and as for that supposedly upmarket broadsheet – they can't touch us, even though they're trying to reduce the age profile and get rid of the old-fashioned image. I want you in my inner sanctum, Sarah. I need you right by me.' His leg pressed insistently against hers. She did not move away, not yet. She would do it discreetly, later, so he would not take offence.

Sarah took a long drink of champagne. Until I displease you, she thought, or fresh meat comes along. It would mean several years of living on her nerves, her antennae permanently on red alert. But the rewards would be great. More money, so they wouldn't have to worry as much as they did at the moment – or rather, as she did – about the prospect of three sets of school fees. A new car, not the ancient estate they had now. Power. It was everything she had ever dreamed about, but he was dead right when he said he would demand blood. It would mean late nights every night, phone calls at all hours at the weekend, the need to drop everything and rush in when he demanded it, with no time off for good behaviour. I can bear it for a couple of years, three at most, she thought. Then I can think again. It will put us on a much sounder financial footing, and we might even be able to send Mickey to Uplingham. We could pay off some of the mortgage, have proper holidays. It will take back-breaking hard work, endless ego-stroking and a lot of fancy footwork to stay one step ahead of the game. But most of all, it would be one in the eye for snooty women like Venetia, who thought you had to have been to the right school and have the right accent to climb to the top of the ladder.

'Have you told Venetia yet?'

'Of course not, darling. I wanted to sound you out first, see if you wanted the job.'

'Of course I do.'

'Marvellous,' he said, sitting back in his chair. 'Let's order then, shall we? I fancy the sea bass. Now, tell me about your children. Where are you thinking of sending them? If you need a word in the right ear, I can help, you know. And how is Tom? Still writing his novel?'

That was the business over. He would not allude to it again, and the meal passed in inconsequential chat about their children's lives, Tom, Clarissa, his wife, holidays, politics. He had the ear of the Prime Minister, and was hilariously, bitchily indiscreet about the great and the good. On top of the champagne he ordered a bottle of vintage claret, and although Sarah meant not to drink too much, it was too delicious to resist. They returned to the office together in his chauffeur-driven car, and Sarah had the satisfaction of bumping into Venetia in reception. 'I won't let you down,' she said, kissing Charles's drink-flushed cheek. 'It was lovely. Hello, Venetia. Been shopping?'

Furiously trying to banish her post-lunch hangover, she worked like a demon all afternoon, and got three spreads ready. At six, an email arrived in her inbox direct from Charles. There were too many moles in personnel. It said that if she accepted, she would be offered a satisfactorily increased salary and a choice of car. She didn't reply at once, but picked up the phone to call her mother. She should call Tom, too. Maybe he'd actually be working. Her mother cried on hearing the news and said she'd always known Sarah would be such a success, but then added – what about the children? Wouldn't it mean much longer hours? Which was exceedingly irritating. I'm doing this *for* the children, she said to herself.

Next she dialled Tom's mobile. Of course he wasn't working. He was in the car on some fool's errand with Laure. She'd tell him all the details later, and he would pretend to be impressed, for her sake, even though he hated Charles, the newspaper, and everything it stood for. But then it was all very well for him to sneer at its materialistic middle-class values. She didn't have the luxury of the moral high ground. Tom argued that if she found the job so stressful she should quit, they could live on far less if she wanted to freelance, the children didn't have to be privately educated. But he knew, as she did, that she loved the high-octane world, the politics, the adrenalin, the sense of achievement. This is one of my best-ever days, she thought, on a high. The children would see even less of her, but she would be able to give them everything she had never had. The sacrifice would be well worth it.

Chapter Five

Cassie

Hector had disappeared. One minute he was in front of her on the narrow lane, his little piglet legs going like pistons, on the scent of a rabbit, and the next there was no sign of him. Cassie stood in the lane, and called, and called. Blast. It was nearly four, the light was fading and she ought to go and get the children from school. They were late because they had matches that afternoon. She could leave him, and he would make his own way home, but there had been ructions in the village about people allowing their dogs to wander and mysterious signs had appeared warning of fines if dogs were allowed to foul the pavements.

The local farmer had a lot to say on the subject, as he had on most things. They went along the lines of 'Bloody townies, they move out here and moan when my dogs wander the village which they've always done. Then they complain about mud on the road from my tractor – why don't they just move back to the city if they object to it so much?' The fact that the land on which the modern homes were built had been sold by him, in the first place, to a builder for a huge profit didn't seem to figure in this argument, and Cassie always thought it best to leave that little detail unsaid.

The building of the new houses had effectively divided the village, into the people who lived in the old houses and cottages around the green by the church, and those who lived on the outskirts in a series of ribbon-like 'executive housing' estates, each house, no matter how substantial, built just feet from its neighbour, identical but for the odd detail of an outside porch or a gable end. They had been given deliberately countrified names to make would-be purchasers feel they were buying into the rural dream – The Paddocks, Yew Farm Close, Meadow View, The Grange. The rural dream, that is, minus the inconvenient mud. Even though many of these houses sold for twice the price of the farmhands' old terraced cottages by the green, the unspoken social divide remained.

It was a point of which Sarah was touchily aware. At the time she and Tom bought the four-bedroomed 5, Yew Farm Close, which stood on the corner of one of the developments and so had marginally more garden than the rest, one of the old cottages had been for sale, and Tom had wanted to buy it instead, pointing out that it was much cheaper. But Sarah said it was poky, far too small (only three tiny bedrooms), and much harder to keep clean. It was also too close for comfort to Cassie and Laure, and their big old detached houses. She liked the convenience of the modern house, the uniform square rooms and the fact that it was newly wired and centrally heated and the kitchen came with all the latest appliances included. Tom, his soul shuddering, acquiesced, for the sake of peace.

Cassie got on well with George Hetherington, the farmer. They hunted together and her family had lived at the manor for as many generations as his family had farmed the land. George wasn't so sure about

Cassie's husband Nat. Nat wasn't an easy man to get to know and he belonged to an alien world, a world of suits, commuter trains and business meetings. The idea of working in London was anathema to George, who spent all day in the high, open fields. He'd had ideas about Cassie himself but hadn't been quick enough off the mark.

She'd surprised everyone by marrying Nat, whom she met on a sailing holiday in Cornwall, when she was in her early twenties. They had moved away when they first married, but came back to the manor when Cassie's father died and her mother, Martha, decided the house was too big to live in alone. She now lived in one of the cottages at the far side of the green, and was away travelling most of the year, to a series of challenging and unsuitable destinations for a woman in her early seventies with a dodgy knee.

As Cassie rounded the bend, she saw George heading towards her in a big new tractor, pipe in mouth, black Labrador sitting sentinel at his side. He slowed down, and shouted above the noise of the engine. 'I just saw your little dog. Running like hell he was, towards the lower barns. After rats, I'd think. If you see Tom,' he leant forward and bellowed louder, 'tell him to bring his gun down to those barns and shoot the bloody things.'

'I'll tell him,' Cassie shouted back. 'If I see him. Bye.'

Oh, sod Hector, she really didn't have time. He'd ignore her anyway if he was ratting. She took a quick look at her watch. Five past four. She would be late, but they'd probably start walking home on their own. Only Beth, at six, needed watching on the road, and Arthur and Tilly would look out for her. It was a silly new rule that children had to be met at the gate, and meant that far more people would drive to school rather than walk, clogging the narrow village lanes even more. She and her brother William had negotiated their way to St John's Church of England Primary every morning and back every afternoon on their own without being flattened, but then there had been far fewer cars.

The new villagers were now talking about getting up a petition for speed bumps and traffic-calming measures, which made her snort with laughter at the thought of what George would say. The bumps would bounce his Labrador out of the cab, not to mention dollop even more mud onto the road. Nor would he wait his turn, if they got their way and put in the priority arrows that had been talked about at the last parish council meeting. Not many motorists would argue with a twenty-foot-high tractor surmounted by a farmer breathing out furious pipe smoke even if they had right of way.

A group of the newcomers had decided that joining the parish council was a duty not to be shirked, and had transformed what had been sleepy meetings in the Slug and Lettuce over a pint into proper meetings with minutes and a chairman in the village community hall without a pint in sight. George had resigned in disgust. Cassie had stayed, out of a sense of duty. George's wife, Mary, also remained a member but was too mousy to voice her opposition to the speed bumps. But then living with George and his trenchant views would make anyone incline towards timidity, Cassie thought. She did a sterling job with the Women's Institute though, you couldn't fault her for that.

Cassie religiously went along to all of the WI meetings, as her mother had before her, and got roped in to run the cake stall at the summer fete, which she hated because she couldn't cook to save her life and her cake was always the one left at the end. Laure generally saved the day by bringing along her delicious offerings from French recipes, which Cassie then pretended were hers. Sarah thought it was hilarious that anyone would have the time or the inclination to sit on monthly committees with an agenda of road signs and dog-fouling, or raise a few hundred pounds to extend the playground at the village hall by selling cakes and throwing sponges at the vicar. 'Why doesn't Nat just give them the money?' she said, and Cassie replied that wasn't the point. She had been about to say that it brought the village together, and then stopped herself because it made her sound about ninety-three. Even her mother, since her father's death, had opted out of village life, saying she was sick to the back teeth of standing behind white elephant stalls recycling old tat and had more than done her bit for the church roof fund and the new community hall that no-one ever used apart from the bossy parish council.

Cassie had long ago accepted she was a disappointment to her mother. She'd expected her to go to university, as she had done, and reap the harvest of women's emancipation, and all Cassie had ever done was be a particularly inefficient secretary and then marry Nat and have children. Her mother had studied classics at university and had then wanted to become a lawyer, but it wasn't the done thing for upper-middle-class women and, after having the children, she'd given up any idea of a career and burned with thwarted ambition – mainly as she was much cleverer than her husband Robin and would have made a much better lawyer. With her husband dead, she now had the time and money to do exactly as she pleased, which consisted of throwing caution to the winds scrambling up Everest and, most recently, trekking the Inca Trail in the company of young Australians who thought she was terrific.

Now the children were school age Cassie didn't

really have an excuse not to work, but she did have the horses, and they took up all the time not swallowed by the children or Nat. The thing was, even though she knew she ought to aspire to greater things, she was quite happy with her little life. Measured against Sarah, with her glittering career, and Laure, with her beauty, style and gorgeously decorated home, she knew she was a bit of a B+, must try harder. But she didn't really care.

It was only before parties, when she threw open her wardrobe door and groaned aloud that everything she owned – most of which she'd had for years – neither matched nor fitted properly, that she regretted the fact she didn't dedicate more time to her appearance. But whatever she did to herself didn't seem to make much difference – her hair was thick, shoulder-length, dark brown and wavy, and never looked neat or stylish no matter how expensive the haircut. She had once tried to straighten it using Tilly's electric straighteners and ended up looking as if she was wearing a medieval helmet. A lot of the time it was squashed under a riding hat and went flat at the front, prompting Tilly to remark, 'Bad hair day again, Mother.'

Because she spent so much time outside, her skin was weather-beaten to a freckled brown like a free-range egg, and whatever make-up she put on seemed to disappear in the face of such high colour. Mascara smudged as soon as it was applied, and lipstick only ever lasted a minute. She spent her life in jodhpurs because then there was no hassle about what to put on in the morning and it didn't matter if they got covered in mud. It was just a shame it made her bottom look like two ferrets fighting in a sack. She was more stocky than fat, and, although she had tried diets, she loved food too much to starve herself. Occasionally she would read magazine articles about models or actresses who said, 'Often, I forget to eat. I have to remind myself,' and Cassie would think, 'How? Silly tarts.' Of course it would have been much more of an issue if Nat had minded the way she looked. But she had looked like this at twenty-one, and he had never once suggested she slim or dress more elegantly. It was one of the things she loved most about him.

When she was first introduced to Nat's smart clients – something she tried to avoid like the plague – she couldn't miss their double take. Tall, impossibly glamorous Nat with his film star looks should have been married to a willowy blonde with pencil-slim legs, not a short outdoorsy woman with unruly hair. She had no desire to plunge into Nat's corporate world, with lunches and corporate trips to Henley and Glyndebourne, which called for designer clothes and inconsequential small talk. She hated being away from home, anyway, and Nat liked her to be there. He often called, during the day, just for a chat. He would say, 'What are you up to?' and she would tell him about Hector, or the activities of the grumpy cat, or a funny incident Tom had relayed about the dodgy members of the pub crowd. She relaxed him with her village tales, a little oasis of calm in his high-stress working life. No matter how awful his day, the moment he walked into the manor and its attendant chaos, noise, milling animals and children, none of it mattered any more. He was home.

When she first saw Nat on the boat she was crewing for a family friend, she literally had to hang onto the sail to stop herself falling overboard. He was ludicrously good-looking, with white-blond hair swept back from a tanned forehead, deep green eyes framed by thick black lashes and a square jawline. He was tall, broad-shouldered and wearing de rigueur sailing clothes – a loose-fitting navy blue fleece over a white T-shirt, baggy khaki trousers and leather deck shoes with no socks. He appeared to have the assurance of the boys she'd grown up with, golden boys, who treated her like good old Cassie, one of the lads, who was always ready to have a drink and didn't spend hours putting on make-up. Popular, yes, but not in the way she wanted. She'd had numerous crushes on her brother William's friends, but they'd never taken her seriously as a girlfriend. They'd tell her how terrific she was, while gazing over her shoulder at her slim, feminine friends who flicked their hair and giggled.

She thought someone like Nat would never consider asking her out because she wasn't beautiful or thin enough. When she was introduced to him, she was surprised to hear a trace of an accent. He was actually quite shy. He told her he was taking an MBA at a business college, with her best friend Sophie's brother, Max. Accepting the fact she stood no chance with such a god, she chatted to him quite unselfconsciously. Meanwhile Sophie was practically tying herself in knots trying to get Nat to look at her, swinging her mane of dark brown hair and sitting, in a tiny pair of shorts, with her pipe-cleaner tanned legs up on the rail around the boat.

They spent lazy summer days together, and as they shared chores and swam in the freezing sea, Cassie learnt he was an only child and that his parents were divorced. He didn't talk about his father, and Cassie quickly deduced it was a taboo subject. He told her he had to work his way through college, behind a bar. He said, without a trace of irony, that he was going to make a million before he was thirty. Cassie, brought up among people who took having money for granted, found him rather noble. He didn't try to hide anything, or seem embarrassed about not having the same upbringing. There was an air of authority about him, not just from the way he looked, but from a quiet and powerful determination. He was much more focused than her pleasure-seeking friends.

The first time he kissed her, after a disco in the back room of a heaving pub on the quayside, she thought she had died and gone to heaven. She had never felt such an overpowering attraction to anyone, and was terrified she had fallen in love with a man who must, surely, reject her. The next morning she was tortured by self-doubt – after all, he could have had anyone. Months later, when they were accepted as boyfriend and girlfriend, she asked him why he had chosen her rather than Sophie. He said that girls like Sophie bored him rigid because they had nothing to say. She was real and she made him laugh. But she had never quite shaken off the feeling that she didn't deserve him. He, on the other hand, could not have achieved any of his success without the security of knowing that Cassie was at home at the end of the day.

Nearing the house, Cassie remembered she'd locked the back door because Laure had rung her earlier about some sneak thieves reported in the local evening paper who were taking advantage of their country laziness in not locking doors, and stealing from cars and houses. Cassie, who regularly left her house wide open and unattended, determined to be vigilant and lock things up but it was a massive pain because she now couldn't remember where she'd put her keys. They were in a safe place, but where? Once they had gone away for the weekend and Laure had rung her on the mobile, laughing, to tell her she'd left the front door wide open.

By the time she reached the village green, the sky was beginning to darken, and there was still no sign of the children. The manor was set back on the far left, on the other side of the church to the Rectory. This was by far the prettiest part of the village. The Norman church, with its square tower, stood beside a graveyard filled with the green shoots of daffodils, as yet unopened, and cherry blossom trees, just beginning to bud. As she watched, the old clock on the church tower struck half past four and the bell chimed over the darkening roofs. The Rectory was taller but not as long as the manor, with its odd wings and additions. Being Georgian, it was neat and precisely symmetrical in a way that the Tudor manor was not, rambling along dark corridors which ended surprisingly in store rooms or doors to the courtyard. New guests at the manor often found themselves lost when looking for the loo, stepping confidently into broom cupboards or abruptly ending up outside in the courtyard.

They only used half the house – if they entertained more they would have opened up the old drawing room, the size of a small ballroom, which in her parents' day had been used for dances and village events. Now the children used it to play football and it housed a rickety table-tennis table at the far end. When they had friends for dinner Cassie preferred to eat in the kitchen, around the scrubbed pine table, because it was heated by the old cream Aga. The rest of the house was incredibly cold, inefficiently warmed by storage heaters. Nat kept telling her to get a quote for central heating but it involved so much upheaval that Cassie thought it easier to wear more clothes, and the children never seemed to feel the cold.

After the gate clanged shut behind her, she reached out to turn the old metal door handle on the back door. Blast. Of course, it was locked. The key was not under the bucket, or the clay pot containing lavender. Where? She pressed her hands against the pockets of her battered Barbour, feeling a wave of relief as she encountered the solid shape of the big old key. Anyway, she would have left a window open somewhere, for the cat to get in and out.

As she put the key in the lock, she heard the children. They were on the far side of the green, and even from this distance she could tell, from the high-pitched shrieks, that the older two were tormenting Beth. A fierce little girl, she was very easy to wind up as she loathed not being taken seriously. If she cried, they were generally tears of rage. Looking across the green, she saw Arthur was carrying Beth on his back, and he was holding a book in his hand, his arm stretched out away from her. Tilly followed on behind, dreamily, her school bag swinging and, as Cassie watched, she stopped to touch the nodding heads of the snowdrops, clustered on the grassy bank by the red telephone box.

Beth saw her and yelled, 'I came top in spelling! Arthur won't give me my book back! He's so horrid!'

'Well done,' Cassie shouted. 'Arthur, hand it back. Come on, it's going dark.'

'Have we time to ride?' Tilly called, knowing the answer. Cassie never said no to riding unless it was pitch black. She knew she ought to be as strict about homework coming first as Laure, but couldn't be bothered.

Cassie looked up at the fading light. 'Just. If you're quick. But first can you ... oh, never mind.' Minutes later they charged past her into the house, dumping their school bags in the dim light of the stone-flagged hallway. On the chandelier, only two bulbs out of seven were working, and part of the wiring was exposed at the fitting. That was probably caused by the great jumping sessions Arthur and Beth had on Beth's bed, which shook the old house to its foundations.

All the horses were stabled in a big barn at the moment, because the fields were too wet and muddy to turn them out. They were lucky to have kept four large paddocks out of the original estate, most of which had been sold a generation before to pay off the death duties from her grandparents. Over a hundred acres were let to Mr Hetherington for cattle and sheep.

Cassie had been surprised when her mother suggested she and Nat move back into the old house when her father died – she'd thought her mother would want to stay. But her mother, with character-istic bluntness, said she was sick of being freezing cold and had no desire to rattle around in a house far too big for her, when it should be filled with children. She'd moved happily to the little stone cottage at the far side of the green, with a tiny garden and two bed-rooms, which meant not all the children could stay over at once, which suited her perfectly. She had had enough responsibility for a lifetime, she said. Now it was her turn to be entirely selfish and do exactly as she pleased. Besides, she said, it was good for the children to have individual attention.

Cassie piled the bags into a marginally more tidy heap, and rooted through them for any letters from teachers which the children would forget to give her. The grey cat weaved around her legs, mewing furiously. 'Do shut up and give me a minute,' she said, looking down at her. She seemed to spend most of her life feeding things. Even the fish in their green algae-ridden bowl in the kitchen swam to the surface and opened their mouths as soon as she walked in. At that moment there was a bashing sound on the door, out of all proportion to the size of dog, and Hector trotted in. He was completely black, from head to toe, and stank of cow slurry. He grinned ingratiatingly at her, showing little pointed teeth, and his whole body shivered as he wagged his docked tail furiously from side to side.

'You', she said, 'are a disgusting creature. It's the hosepipe.' He paused, turned tail, and shot back out of the door. If there was one thing Hector hated, it was the hose. She ought to start making tea, but Beth would need help mounting. The other two said she ought to be able to get on her pony on her own by now, despite the fact that her head only came as high as the stirrup. They always said that at six they hadn't needed a leg-up, which was rubbish. Beth was much braver and stronger than her compatriots at school, because her brother and sister expected her to be able to do everything they could, and Cassie was often taken aback at quite how wimpy some children could be. Beth had friends who came for tea and shrieked when Hector so much as put his paws up on them.

Arthur, who was the oldest, had inherited her old hunter, Mulberry, who was getting on in years now at fifteen but still had a lot of life in him. Arthur was agitating to ride Fred, her new young horse, but he was still a bit unpredictable on the roads and frightened of lorries and tractors, so Cassie said, not yet. Tilly had a showy fourteen-hand grey which was the envy of the pony club and had cost them an arm and a leg last year, and Beth, bless her, had inherited the family armchair, a chestnut part-Welsh mountain with a white muzzle called Dougal, who looked like a mobile carpet. His eyes, if you could find them beneath the mass of hair, displayed a weary cynicism at the world and everything it had to throw at him. In his youth he had been quite active but, at twenty-five, he now thought it was about time he was allowed to take things rather more easily. He would consent to hack out, but mostly he slept. Leave him alone for any length of time during a lesson at pony club, and he nodded off.

Cassie stood looking over the half-door at the back of the house, watching them lead the horses into the yard, tying them to rings before they tacked them up. Oh dear. None of them were very clean. Fred trumpeted his despair at being left alone from the barn and kicked the door, and Mulberry raised his head and whinnied in response.

Turning, Cassie delved about in the big chest freezer they kept in the back kitchen, the former scullery, and pulled out a pack of frozen fish fingers and oven chips for tea. That would do, with some French bread she'd bought that morning from the Spar shop at the end of the village. The shop was experimenting with some new lines, which everyone in the village, bar Sarah, was very excited about. When Sarah caught Tom and Cassie with genuine enthusiasm talking about the fact you could now buy fresh baguettes at the Spar, she rolled her eyes and said, 'Get a life.'

'It may not be very exciting to you,' Tom said in a camp voice, folding his arms over a mock bosom. 'But it's quite made my week.'

'Mum,' Beth called to her from the yard. Cassie pulled on the Barbour she'd slung on the hooks by the back door and walked down to them. She shivered. It was getting chilly. They'd have to be quick, or the light would be gone.

'Hurry up, Mum! They'll go without me.'

'Would we?' Arthur said, grinning, already mounted.

'Yes, you would,' Cassie said. 'Just hang on. One, two, three.' She expertly hoisted Beth's sturdy bulk onto Dougal, who groaned. She tightened his girth, making him flick his ears back, and, reaching up, made sure Beth's chinstrap was fastened securely, while Beth wriggled away.

'Do not be long,' she said sternly to Arthur, who was pulling on a pair of her riding gloves. 'And do not canter on the green. You know what the vicar says.'

'Stupid rule,' Arthur said. He kicked Mulberry forward and the three of them trotted out of the yard. Plunging her hands into the pocket of the old coat, she watched them go, Beth's little legs flapping on Dougal to make him catch up with the other two.

'Have you got your mobile?' she shouted at Arthur, but he was already too far away to hear.

They won't be long, she thought, as she turned back towards the house. God, if only she could give Nat frozen fish fingers.

Chapter Six

Nat

Nat stared out of the window of the train, into the inky darkness. In the distance, he could just see the lights of the village approaching. If his mobile rang again, he was severely tempted to hurl the bloody thing out through one of those irritating little sliding train windows which stuck open and gave you a stiff neck. There was no point during the day when it was not ringing – he now had three mobiles, one for incoming, one for outgoing, and one to take messages he didn't check often enough from his long-suffering PA. He could not complain about how busy they were – well, he shouldn't, but there was a part of him which longed to shout, 'Just go away!' whenever one of the phones rang. They were all connected by email via his laptop and work PC and diverted via God knows what, probably a satellite on Mars, to find him wherever he was. It was like being electronically tagged.

He was beginning to wonder just how long he should, and could, carry on. He'd made enough money. The promotional DVD wing of the company had been sold off last year, for a very satisfactory sum. The thought of financial security should have made him happy. He should have felt that he'd achieved everything he wanted to achieve, and he ought to feel, for once, at peace with himself. But he didn't feel peaceful at all. He woke with just the same raging drive, just the same raging ambition to get out there – and, what? Conquer the world? Make millions? That had always been his goal, as a student, to make enough money so no-one could touch him. No-one could make him go back. It would give him freedom, 'fuck off' money which meant he was beholden to no-one. What he hadn't thought about, all those years ago, was that the more success you had, the more responsibility you took on. A workforce of over sixty depended on him, another twelve in the recently opened New York office. Even if he did sell the whole lot, and there was no doubt several of his competitors would love to get their hands on the consultancy, he'd have to stay on for at least a nominal three years as chairman before he could get all the money out. Three years. At that moment, tired and stressed, it felt like a lifetime.

It's a very odd thing, he reflected, to achieve your life's ambition while you were still in your late thirties. Where do you go from here? Some of his business friends who had made a mint when they 'hit the exit' had gone off sailing around the world. He used to enjoy sailing, but he didn't want to follow the herd. It was such a cliché, to sell a business and buy a boat. He often lay awake at night, next to the sleeping form of Cassie, thinking, What do I want? He had everything, on the surface, that anyone could ever want. Maybe they should buy a house abroad. He thought hard. France? Cassie would never leave the horses. It was just taking on more stuff, and he was bored of stuff.

There was one thing he wanted. He would love to own an estate in Scotland. When he was a child his mother had taken him on a truly dreadful camping holiday to the Highlands with her parents, crammed into a Morris Minor with a tent and a smelly dog. He'd gone fishing every day to escape their smothering adoration and had wandered the fells, looking for remote little lochs full of trout. He'd even caught a salmon on the spinner on a fast-flowing river, and then had to run like hell when a gillie spotted him from the opposite bank. Something about the landscape, the wildness, the sheer nothingness of it all had caught his soul, and he had never felt as peaceful as he did standing at the side of a loch stretching away from him like glass, the only sound the call of a buzzard overhead. He loved the feeling of being completely alone. It was so odd – the more you had, the more you realized you did not need, and instead of making your life more comfortable and luxurious, possessions and responsibilities became just heavier weights around your neck, dragging you down. He now worried just as much about the company stock and interest rates as he once had about his tiny overdraft as a student. God. Was it the human condition, never to be satisfied with what you had? Too much, or too little? Cassie was the only truly optimistic, happy person he had ever met.

Downsizing. That was the answer. Lead a life that was far more meaningful, instead of getting on a bloody train every day and ducking and diving in the City. He laughed to himself. He was beginning to sound a bit New Age. Maybe he should go to a retreat and thrash himself with birch twigs and sit under a pyramid. But how would he ever persuade Cassie to leave the manor? Her family had lived there for six generations, and she had a strong sense of tradition. Maybe he could persuade her to buy a second home, and then slowly introduce the idea of moving lock, stock and barrel. Mobile phones wouldn't work up there, either. Nirvana.

The train jerked to a stop. Fulbrook station. The village nestled in a hollow of the Windrush Valley, flanked either side by gently undulating hills, and the station was tucked away down a cul-de-sac, not far from the school. The village would have been chocolate-box picture-perfect without the small new estates at the far end, but Nat quite liked that. He was irritated by the 'us and them' attitude of some of the villagers, and if he had had his way would have supported any new low-cost housing.

He was regularly approached to join the parish council, but there was no way he could. He was having to spend more and more time in New York, where the consultancy had just opened a new PR office, and had gained several five-star-hotel clients in the last two weeks. He must fly out in a couple of weeks and check out what was happening. The thought did not excite him. People thought that travelling on business was glamorous. It wasn't. It was twelve exhausting hours in a metal tube breathing in recycled air, even if you could stretch your long legs in business class and eat marginally less gruesome food.

The truth was, he missed home. He missed the chaos and the noise and Cassie. He missed being able to reach out to her in the night, and wrap himself around her comfortable form. He found it hard to sleep in anonymous hotel bedrooms, no matter how luxurious. Other men, like him, at his age, took lovers, younger women. He had lots of offers. He knew the effect he had on women, and it bored him. He had a finely developed radar for people who wanted something from him – business, money, glory by association. Several clients had even laid on hookers for him. One night last year he had arrived, late and tired, at the Central Plaza in New York to find a gorgeous eighteen-year-old sitting on the radiator outside his hotel room. She was wearing a very short skirt and a bright smile. 'Boo,' she said. 'Thank you,' he said, 'but no.' Her face had fallen. She wouldn't get paid, then.

Nat didn't despise his clients, his friends, who took advantage of this frequently offered form of 'hospitality', nor did he turn down the invites to lap-dancing clubs which proliferate in the male-dominated corporate world. They were no longer seen as sleazy, as strip clubs would have been, and many of the invites came from big clients. He went along, and smiled, and drank champagne, and did not even see the girls gyrating around poles right in front of him. He was probably the only one who told his wife exactly what he had been doing. 'Not lap-dancing again?' Cassie would say when he phoned her to say he would be late. 'Have fun.'

She was not remotely jealous, and he loved her for it, just as he loved her complete disregard for the trappings of wealth. Someone like Laure, he was sure, would have run through his money like a knife through butter. When he met Laure, he had, for the first time in many years, felt a frisson of attraction. But he knew when to retreat. There were some places you just did not go to maintain a happy marriage. Anyway, Gerard had become a friend. Or as much of a friend as anyone was to Nat. Only Cassie ever got close to the man his staff regarded as an enigma.

He gathered the papers up from the grey Formica table, and snapped shut his laptop. He was working on a presentation for a big new corporate client, who wanted him to oversee the media training of their top executives. He had collected together a number of big-name reporters to head up the presentations who had formerly worked on the main terrestrial news channels, as his clients loved to listen to war stories and feel they were in the presence of a genuine hero. Even better if they'd been shot at. He paid them well, and charged the companies a fortune. He dropped the phone that was lying on the table into his brown leather briefcase, and clicked it shut.

Opposite, a girl with sleek brunette hair watched him over the top of her evening paper. She had travelled on the same commuter train as him for a year, but he had not noticed her. Every morning she looked forward to seeing him, her heart lifting as he strode down the platform, like a comic-book hero with the sun glinting off his hair, the collar of his overcoat turned up against the wind. She fantasized about being his wife, and having two little blonde-haired children, replicas of him. When he was on the phone she'd lean forward, trying to overhear, to glean clues about his life. What was indisputable was the solid gold band around his wedding finger. She dressed in the morning for him. One day. One day he would look up, their eyes would meet and he would suddenly realize that she was the woman for him. It was a good job he was on the phone such a lot or he would have heard her biological clock ticking like a time bomb.

He stepped out of the train, and the automatic doors slid shut behind him. The cold air made him draw in his breath, and he pulled his navy cashmere overcoat more tightly around him. With his briefcase and lap-top bag under one arm, he walked up the concrete ramp towards the car park. Around him were other commuters, people who had become nodding acquaintances over the years. Next to him a man in a long tweed coat flipped open his phone as it bleeped with a message. The security spotlights created surreal orange pools of light among the dark shadows of the lines of parked cars. Behind him the train began to draw away, the lights fading into the darkness through the wire netting separating the car park from the platform. The locking systems on cars clicked, and headlights flicked on. A woman yards from him murmured, 'Goodnight,' as she laid her briefcase on the back seat of her car. Another day done.

'Good evening, Nat.'

'Evening, Dave.' He smiled at the car-park attendant in his little Portakabin, who liked to think he knew all his regulars by name. Nat had a season pass to the car park as well as an annual rail ticket. He hated buying the pass each January. Another year. Another year very similar to the last and probably very similar to the year after it. Once the cut and thrust of business had excited him. It was a game to be won, and every day was a challenge. Now, it was all just the same. The buzz had gone. He pressed the fob to open the doors of the Range Rover, and the lights flashed. It was brand new, top of the range, and had a satellite navigation system which Arthur thought was deeply cool. Beth and Tilly loved the fact you could watch TV in the car when it was parked. They were lobbying for an in-car DVD, but Cassie said that was a silly waste of money. He would have given way, but Cassie held firm. She saw no point in expensive cars, and drove an ancient Toyota full of muddy tack and wellingtons.

Nat, flicking the indicator to turn left out of the car park, smiled to himself at the thought of her, and home. The girl on the train leant forward to catch the last possible glimpse of him. Of course he had a gorgeous car. Life really was not fair. She pictured his wife. Probably a former model, still beautiful with high cheekbones and liposuctioned thighs, who would greet him with a gin and tonic and usher him into a perfect firelit drawing room while she put the finishing touches to a gourmet meal.

* * *

'Not the butter! Not the sodding butter!' The cat, spotting the fact that the lid was off the butter dish, had leapt gratefully up and was hastily polishing off the end of the Lurpak that Cassie had intended to shove into the baked potatoes which were by now turning a deep black in the hot oven of the Aga. 'Ow, ow, bugger,' she said, juggling them as she tried to lift them out with a tea towel which was frankly too thin for the purpose. The oven gloves were nowhere to be seen. They were, in fact, making a snuggly bed for a small rabbit and Tilly's guinea pig, which had been smuggled into the house.

All three children, their cheeks glowing from their ride – they had almost had to feel their way back in the dark – were lying prone under a duvet in the TV room on a very smelly sofa, which had been used as an impromptu drying aid by Hector, still pungent from the farm. They were watching *Friends*, which wasn't allowed, but they knew Cassie would be busy in the kitchen for at least the next half-hour. No homework had, as yet, been done. Arthur, who was naturally bright and the most hard-working of the three, would do his in the first break tomorrow. Beth only had a bit of reading to do, and Tilly had left her homework at school anyway.

Artists, Tilly said, shouldn't have to do maths. It was bad for the soul. She wrote extraordinary poetry full of wild imagery and misspellings, and Nat thought she was a genius. She had achieved, in the exams before Christmas, the amazing feat of getting eighty-seven per cent in English and nought in maths. 'Didn't you even write your name at the top of the paper?' Nat had asked, trying not to laugh. 'Can't remember,' Tilly said. Arthur thought it was hysterical, and Granny said, well, she was obviously going to be a world-famous artist and writer so why bother about a few exams?

Cassie said that was hardly the point and no-one was taking this seriously apart from her.

She knew for a fact that Laure sat down and did at least an hour's homework with Sophie every night, even though she had prep at school. Nick had won a part scholarship to Uplingham and she was sure that was because Laure was so diligent and even bought them *Maths Booster* videos. God damn and blast Laure for being such a good mother on top of being thin. Sophie even did her piano practice every night. Tilly's music teacher had given up writing practice notes in the little blue exercise book because Cassie never filled them in. When Cassie thought of it, she went hot with shame. She didn't even have Sarah's excuse of being at work all the time. Even Tom made a rudimentary effort to keep on top of the children's homework and music practice.

I must try harder, she thought. I must be more organized. Far too much time was spent with the horses, and that wasn't going to get the children into good schools. Her aim was to make sure they all passed their exams and went to the nearby grammar school – they could have afforded school fees but Cassie had been deeply miserable at her boarding school and didn't want to impose that on any of her children, nor did she want not to see them for weeks on end. Nat had been through the comprehensive system without a scratch and also believed that school fees were a complete waste of money. Most of the time, all you were paying for was a smart accent and an inflated sense of your own importance, he said.

The back door slammed. Oh hell, there was Nat, and the chicken casserole thing had only been in for half an hour. The recipe said at least an hour and a half, and she'd forgotten to put the flour in until after she poured on the chicken stock, which meant that it had rather off-putting balls of hard white flour bobbing about. She'd have to give them all a good bash later. Either her casseroles ended up too thick, like glue, or they were like thin soup. The cat sat on the stained beechwood work surface, regarding her with barely suppressed ridicule. She opened the kitchen window, and pushed it out. 'Go and be a cat, cat,' she said, and then felt guilty because it was so cold outside. As she did so, she felt Nat's arms enfold her from behind.

'Talking to the cat again?' he said, into her neck. 'You need to get out more.'

'That cat hates me. It looks at me as if it could run the house ten times better than me.'

'Probably could,' Nat said, leaning on the dresser, flicking through the post.

'Wine?'

'God, yes.'

Cassie turned and reached up to slide a bottle out of the custom-built wine rack at the side of the chimney by the log-burning fire. 'We're running a bit low.'

'Um. I'll get some ordered. What is that interesting smell of burning?'

'Jacket potatoes. Oh.' Having been at least the same size as when they went in the oven, if a bit black, they now had an unappetizing look, like deflating balloons.

'And what culinary delight is in here?' Nat asked, grinning, as he opened the door to the baking oven.

'It's a casserole. At least it was when it went in. It could be anything by now.'

'That's what I love about your cooking,' Nat said. 'The constant surprise. Ouch.'

Tilly, having heard his voice, belted into the kitchen and flung her arms around his waist as he stood up, standing on his feet. 'Daddy! You're home!'

'No need to be quite so dramatic. I do it most days.' He walked clumsily over to the end chair by the table, with Tilly still standing on his feet, and levered himself down into it. Tilly reached forward and took a sip of his wine.

'Mm, nice,' she said. 'French.'

'This child is going to be an alcoholic.'

'Like mother, like daughter,' Cassie muttered, lifting up the lid to the simmering plate to steam some beans.

Beth appeared in the doorway, trailing her disgusting blanket with the well-sucked end. 'Me too,' she said, and clambered up onto Nat. He sat one on each knee and regarded them mock sternly. 'And have you done your homework?'

'Noo . . .' Tilly said. 'Not exactly.'

'Don't tell me you left it at school,' Cassie said. 'Not again.'

'Tilly, you're going to have to get more of a grip,' Nat said, trying to be cross.

'I got a star for art,' she said, brightly. 'Yow. Beth's pinching me.'

'Could you be a love and take them up and listen to Beth read?' Cassie's voice was muffled as she peered into the murky depths of the oven. 'Dinner will be about half an hour. If it hasn't spontaneously combusted.'

'Off to bed.' He put Tilly down onto the floor and stood up, with Beth still in his arms.

'I don't have to go to bed now,' Tilly said, aggrieved. 'It's only eight o'clock.'

'Yes you do,' Cassie and Nat said, together.

'But she's younger than me. I don't get any privileges. It's not fair. If I have to go to bed, Arthur has to go to bed.'

'Just take them away, will you?'

'Off, now.' They passed the entrance to the snug, where Arthur had completely submerged himself under the duvet. 'I know you're in there,' Nat said. 'Half an hour.'

'Fine, Dad,' said the duvet.

Tilly's room was a tip. No matter how often her mother tidied it, it took her precisely five minutes to upend her drawers, strew felt tips all over the floor and cover the place, mysteriously, in screwed-up balls of toilet paper. Usually she was making dens for her various pets, and a bemused guinea pig was often found sitting in a shoe at the bottom of her wardrobe. 'Argh! Forgot!' she said, as Nat tried to usher her through her bedroom door with his arms full of Beth. She shot out from under his arm and disappeared down the stairs.

Beth leant against his shoulder, and put in her thumb. Her eyes were already closing. After the ride she had pulled on an odd assortment of clothing, from pyjama bottoms to her pony-club sweatshirt and big furry horse's head slippers which neighed when you pressed an ear. Nat debated taking her into the bathroom to brush her teeth but decided to leave it until the morning, as she was so sleepy. She didn't stand a chance of doing her reading.

He carried her down the narrow passageway to her bedroom, ducking his head to avoid the beam. It had a low, sloping ceiling, with a furry llama rug on the polished floorboards, a present from Granny on her last trip to Peru. She'd also bought her a woolly hat with ear flaps, which Beth insisted on wearing in bed. She had inherited her grandmother's eccentric dress sense. Nat laid her down on the bed, and gently pulled off the sweatshirt. He found a clean pyjama top in the drawer, and put it over her head. Beth did not open her eyes. He pulled back the duvet to reveal a sheet lightly coated in grey cat hairs. Beth liked to sleep with the cat tucked under the duvet with her.

The cat was nowhere to be seen – in fact, it was lurking at the top of the stairs waiting for Nat to go, because occasionally he put his foot down and said it ought to go out at night because that's what cats did. When Cassie pushed it out of the kitchen window it had done its usual circuit of the house, jumped onto the boot-room roof and then up onto the main roof and in through the top bathroom window. Nat pulled the duvet over the prone little body, and bent to kiss her warm cheek. 'Story,' she said, without opening her eyes.

Nat groaned. '*Cuddly Duddly*,' she said. Nat fished the book out from down the side of the bed, and sat down.

'There once was a penguin,' he began. God, he could recite this book in his sleep. Looking at Beth, she seemed to be fast asleep and had turned over, away from him, her arm around the hideous toy wolf she also took to bed. He gingerly turned over three pages. 'And then they all shouted Hurrah!'

'You've missed some out,' said Beth, into the wall. He sighed, and backtracked. Tilly stood at the door. She'd loved this story too, and had passed the book on to Beth. Cassie didn't believe in throwing books away, ever, and the loft was full of boxes to be passed down from child to child. Nat patted the bed beside him. Tilly ran over, and Nat was glad to see she'd put on her pyjamas. She had been known to go to bed fully dressed.

'This doesn't count as my story,' she whispered.

'You're too old for stories,' he said.

'No, I'm not. I like it when you make up the voices.'

At the end of the book he bent to kiss Beth. He tucked her in firmly, and as the two of them headed towards Tilly's room, a streak of grey shot past them.

'Why', he said, sadly surveying the chaos on the floor, 'are the oven gloves in here?'

'Ah,' Tilly said. 'Well.'

He picked the gloves up and shook them. A small selection of guinea pig and rabbit poo fell out. 'This is not pleasant,' he said, picking them up, and, opening the window, he hurled the offending pellets out. 'Where are the creatures of whom this poo was once an integral part?'

'Back in their cage. Honest.'

'Really? Not watching television? Not drinking my drink? Not making long-distance phone calls to Peru?'

Tilly laughed. 'You're so silly.' In fact, they were nestling in her bottom drawer amongst her warmest jumpers and she'd put a bit of food in there for good measure. What parents didn't know didn't hurt them.

She handed *The Worst Witch* to him. 'You must have read this millions of times,' he said, but resignedly found the turned-down page.

Once he'd finished, she said, as she said every night, 'Put my tape on.'

He clicked off the light. 'Not too loud.'

He started to go back down the stairs but then decided to check on Beth. She was curled around Howler, her toy wolf, the fluffy grey head of the cat just poking out of the top of the duvet. His heart turned over. The yellow gingham curtains weren't quite closed, and he stepped quietly across the room to draw them. From Beth's window he could see the church, the tower and clock illuminated by a spotlight on the ground among the graves. As he watched, one of the heavy gilt hands on the clock clicked onto twelve, and a deep chime rang out over the shadows of the green. A light was switched off in the Rectory, and he could just make out the shadow of Laure passing by the landing window.

You are a lucky man, he thought. Then he remembered. New York. Another week away.

Chapter Seven

Cassie

'What's up?'

Nat swirled the red wine around in his glass. 'I've got to go away in a few weeks.'

'Not again,' Cassie groaned, making a sad face. Actually, she was secretly pleased, because it meant she didn't have to cook for him and could watch whatever she wanted on TV. She hated it when he was away for more than a week, missing him intensely, but if he was away for just a few days it felt for her like a holiday from her wifely duties, however badly she carried them out. She could slob around in jodhpurs or tracksuit bottoms and not worry about looking as if she was being pursued by wriggling vermin. She could lie in the bath until midnight, or go to bed at nine. Men, no matter how lovely, always seemed to need attention of some sort. They were very bad at being left alone, and if she did ever go and watch a television programme she really wanted to see when he was in the house – such as a costume drama – she felt absurdly guilty, and he had an irritating habit of repeatedly popping in saying, 'Hasn't it finished yet? I want to go to bed.' Or standing in front of the television saying, 'This is so dull. You can't want to stay up watching this.'

' 'Fraid so. Unavoidable. I'd send someone else if I could, but I think it has to be me,' Nat said.

'But you promised to come to the show. I have faithfully promised Beth she can go for the first time without a lead rein.'

'On Dougal?' Nat raised his eyebrows and smiled.

'He wakes when he's in company,' Cassie said. 'Honestly. He takes even himself by surprise. You should see him, his little legs go like mad. He's a different horse.'

'Will Beth be able to handle him? I've got visions of her disappearing over the horizon, kidnapped by a flying ginger carpet.'

'She'll be fine, I'll look after her.'

They were both sitting at the kitchen table, Nat flicking idly through a country life magazine, his feet, out of his suede brogues, entwined with Cassie's. A fire flickered in the log-burning stove, and Hamish, their fifteen-year-old golden retriever, slept heavily by their feet, snoring, his fat butter-coloured paws twitching. Hector lay in one of the dog baskets, curled into a cross little ball with one eye open, wondering if he could get away with a leap onto Cassie's knee. A branch of the Virginia creeper, covering the kitchen roof, tapped against the window, and the wind made a distant howling noise as it swirled up the pipe from the Aga.

An advert in the magazine caught his eye. It was a full-page photograph of heather-covered mountains, and, in the centre, a white shooting lodge nestled in the valley. The Glengarry estate, he read. 2.2 million, with two thousand acres of grazing land, moorland, two lochs and a well-stocked pheasant and grouse shoot. There was also stalking, with twenty hinds accounted for last year. As well as the main house, which had twelve bedrooms, there was a tenanted farmhouse and four estate cottages in need of repair.

Derelict, then, he thought. Apart from the house and the small cottages, there was literally nothing for miles. The land included a mountain. Quite a small one, but still a mountain.

'Look at this.' He handed the magazine over to Cassie, who was gazing into the fire, trying to summon up the energy to clear their plates and wondering if she could be bothered to have a bath before bed.

'What? What am I looking at?'

'This one.' He leant over and tapped the page. 'This estate.'

'Why?' She raised her eyes from the magazine, dubiously. 'What has an estate got to do with the price of fish?'

He thought hard for a minute. 'It just seems the right time. The market in general is pretty flat at the moment and this could be the time to buy, with interest rates going through the roof. The money's just sitting there in the account and I'd rather put it into property than take a punt on what's a pretty unstable investment market. It makes sense to put it into property and Scotland's the place to be. More and more people are buying estates, it's a growing market.'

'But not to live there?' Cassie said, slowly. 'Not to up sticks and leave here and actually live on the—' she peered more closely at the photograph – 'moon?'

'It's not the moon,' he said, a trifle testily. 'It's actually thirty miles north of Inverness.'

'The moon,' Cassie said, conclusively. She had a sinking feeling in the pit of her stomach. Nat didn't have whims. If he wanted to do something, he did it. Which was why he was so successful in business. He didn't just talk about things, he quietly got on with them. If he was planning to buy an estate in Scotland, then he would do it, or her name wasn't Morag McKinnon. Not that it was. Obviously.

'Don't dismiss it out of hand. It's just that', he leant forward towards her, his voice suddenly passionate, 'I sat on that bloody train tonight and thought, how long can I do this for? How long can I spend commuting backwards and forwards and saying the same things on the phone to the same people and having all the same worries, day after day? We don't have to do this, I don't have to do this. We're lucky people, Cass, we sold at just the right time. We can afford it. I want to make a big move. A life-changing move.'

Cassie reached forward and put her hand over his. 'This big a change?' she said, gesturing at the magazine. 'In Scotland?' She looked more carefully at the advert. 'North of Inverness? I didn't know there was a north. I thought you just fell off into the sea and hit the North Pole.'

'I worry about your geography. It would be fantastic,' Nat said, his voice warming with enthusiasm. 'The children would be totally free to develop without all the pressures of growing up too fast around them – they could sail, and ride for miles – you'd love that – and we wouldn't have to worry about what school they went to and all that rubbish because they'd just go to the local school, well, localish, and we could spend a lot more time together.'

'I can see why you want it,' Cassie said, slowly. 'It's just, well, does it have to be so far away? Couldn't we retreat a bit nearer home?' I don't want to leave here, she was thinking. This is my home. And Scotland is cold. Not just cold occasionally, but cold all the time. Like a big heathery fridge.

'Couldn't we just buy a second house? The children –' Nat looked at her – 'the children have a life here. Their friends. The horses. The pony club. Pret A Manger. You know. Civilization.'

'I am not going to arrange my life around your

115

bloody horses,' he said. 'I want to do this for the children. I think it would be fantastic. We could get rid of everything. No television. No mobile phones . . .'

'No people,' Cassie pointed out. 'The reason most normal people don't want to move to Scotland is because there is nobody there. I went to Scotland once and everybody was out.'

'But that's the point! I'm sick of people. We'll both be forty next year. I don't want to spend the next decade doing exactly the same thing and the brilliant thing is that this is the perfect time to sell. I can ease myself out of the company and you could go on ahead and set things up.'

Cassie looked at him beadily. 'On my own?'

'You'll be fine.' He laughed.

'I am not going to live in a derelict house in the middle of nowhere that is virtually the North Pole with only seals to talk to. I would grow a beard out of boredom.' She read the details more closely. 'One of the estate cottages is called Pointless Cottage because there is no road to it,' she said.

'Brilliant.'

'You are barking mad,' she said, getting up to throw another log on the fire. 'And don't you dare tell the children about this. You'll upset them. They love living here.'

'They'd love it.'

Cassie admitted this to be true, but refused to agree out loud. Why did she feel so strongly opposed to the idea? Mostly it was fear of the unknown, but it was also fear of leaving the manor. She'd grown up here, she knew every inch of the house and she felt a responsibility towards it. It was Their Home. It Was Where They Lived. Continuity was so important. People upped sticks all the time now and moved around and no-one seemed to belong anywhere any more. Nat didn't understand, because he'd moved house frequently when he was a child, what it felt like to have such a long historical association with a house. She knew that he needed a change, but did it have to be quite so dramatic?

'Oh, I forgot to tell you, everyone's coming to dinner this Saturday.'

Nat groaned.

'Don't be like that.'

'Who?'

'Just Gerard and Laure, Tom and Sarah. No-one you have to be nice to.'

'Thank God for that. I've got the week from hell. I'll have to stay over a couple of days.'

Cassie idly traced a finger in a spilt bit of chicken casserole on the table. 'Do you think I should go back to work?'

'What? Where did that come from?' He regarded her face, creased with thought, with amusement.

'Laure's doing something. A commission on a big house in Guiting Power. I feel that everyone seems to be going in new directions but me. Does it irritate you that I don't do anything?'

'You do lots of things. You look after the children. You cook like a dream, and you make this house shine like a new pin.'

'Get lost. You see, I don't do anything. I don't even do what I'm supposed to do very well. I'm not a very good wife, am I?'

He reached over and stroked her cheek. 'You'll do.'

She smiled, and rested her cheek against his hand. 'But I'm beginning to feel like a dinosaur. Mother keeps insinuating that I ought to do something with my life, something a bit more challenging. She's talking about climbing Kilimanjaro this year.'

'Like what?' Nat leant back in his chair.

'I dunno. Maybe take a course.'

'You could take a course in estate management,' Nat said, grinning.

'Oh, right, as if. You'd have me out in all weathers, mending tractors and building fences.'

'Excellent. That's what I want. A good, sturdy wife who can turn her hand to anything. I knew you'd come in useful.'

'I sometimes think that you don't view me as a sublime sex goddess.'

He smiled at her. 'You're lovely. Just as you are.'

'Not too fat?' This was a frequent preamble to their love-making.

'Perfect. I like a woman who doesn't blow over in a strong wind.'

'Handy for Scotland.' They both laughed. The phone rang.

'Oh, piss off. Don't answer it,' said Nat. The phone rang six times and then the answerphone clicked in. After the recorded message, in Cassie's best telephone voice, Laure's voice echoed into the hallway. 'I know you are both there,' she said, in her soft, accented voice. 'And don't tell me to go away. So rude. I'm just ringing to check Saturday is still on. Let me know if you want me to cook anything. I'd welcome the change from this ghastly work. They seem to expect me to do it every day.' Nat and Cassie smiled at each other. 'Ring me when you feel like communicating with the outside world. Don't drink too much, Cassie, it's a weekday night. Remember, you said no more than two glasses. Love you, darlings.' The phone went dead.

Cassie looked down at her third glass of red wine, and grimaced.

'She was a bit subdued on Saturday,' Nat said. Cassie glanced at him, surprised he'd noticed. 'She's usually more fun than that.'

'She does seem a bit worried about something,' Cassie admitted. 'I think – well, is Gerard's business OK? He always seems very bullish but he said a weird thing to me about not knowing if they were still going to be living at the Rectory by Easter. At first I thought it was a joke, but then he backtracked and tried to pretend he didn't mean it. He was quite drunk, admittedly, as was I, so maybe I just misheard.'

Nat had privately thought for a while that Gerard was taking on a lot by expanding so fast in the current climate, but it was none of his business. They rarely talked shop together, preferring to discuss fishing or shooting, relaxing boys' conversation.

'I have heard a few rumours,' he said. He did know that Gerard had taken on a hefty mortgage with the Rectory, much bigger than he would ever have done, but it wasn't his place to pass judgement. With interest rates as high as they were, the repayments on that alone must have been a fortune, then with the children's school fees on top, it was quite a financial commitment.

'Do you think Laure is beautiful?' Cassie said, suddenly.

'Why?'

'I was just wondering. She is. And she's exactly the same age as me. I ought to be thinner. And her clothes . . . I'm going to start, I really am. I'm going to join that aerobics class at the leisure centre and get back to a size twelve.'

'You won't stick at it,' Nat said, pouring her another glass of wine.

'I shall detox.'

'Oh, God. Please don't. You'll be miserable.'

'Don't you want a slim gorgeous wife?'

'No,' he said, reaching for her. 'I want you. Come on, bed.' He leant forward, and took her hand. She let him pull her upright.

'I ought to clear the plates.'

'Sod it, just leave them.'

'But it's a fag in the morning. Can you put the dogs out for a pee?'

'Come on, you great fat thing,' he said, nudging Hamish with his foot. The old dog groaned, and heaved himself to his feet. Hector pointedly turned the other way in his basket. He hated going out in the cold and the wind. Nat walked to the back door, and slid back the bolt. He whistled to the dogs, while Cassie began to clear the plates from the table, running them under the tap before stacking them in the dishwasher. Hamish creaked past him, and he followed him out onto the terrace at the back of the house. In the light from the stables, he saw him crouch down on the lawn. Hector shot past him, and lifted his leg on the old oak tree, before bolting back into the warmth of the house. It was cold, there'd be a late frost in the morning. Nat's breath hung in tiny ice crystals in the air before him. The moon was bright, a perfect pale globe in the indigo sky. He waited as Hamish arthritically kicked non-existent earth over the soiled patch with his back legs. He held the door open as the dog walked slowly past him, and it occurred to him he had probably spent hours and hours waiting for Hamish. But then there were worse things to have spent your life doing.

Cassie was bending over the sink and he put his arms around her, resting his face in her hair, which smelled of shampoo, fresh air and the leather tack she had been cleaning earlier on. His hands slid up to her breasts. 'Bed,' he said. 'Now.'

He clicked off the lights behind them and as they climbed the stairs, Cassie reached backwards, her palm flat, to link her fingers with his.

Chapter Eight

Tom

A Conflict of Interest

By Tom Cotterill. By the Hon Tom Cotterill? Nope. Too ridiculous.

There. That was the title done. He looked at it admiringly. It was a good title. It summed up the book that was to come, about the conflict in Sierra Leone from which he had only just escaped alive when he was wandering the world in his early twenties, before hitching a ride home on an air force plane to Nigeria and from there to Rome. He knew he had been rather idealistic travelling to such a potentially dangerous country, but he had had a mad idea about becoming a diamond trader. Only he hadn't found any diamonds, just a lot of very dangerous teenagers high on drugs and toting AK47 guns. He knew it was time to leave when a bullet just missed him and hit a wall. The food hadn't been up to much, either. It was all very well try- ing to live an Edward Farrell novel in theory, but in practice it was a trifle hair-raising. However, it was a life experience just waiting to be turned into a fast- paced thriller, in the style of Farrell. Only younger. And not dead, obviously.

Now. He had the title, a pun, very clever. Only below it was a screen with no words on it. It was awfully white. And awfully empty. And it went on being awfully white and awfully empty for page after page. How long did a book have to be? He consulted the *Writers' and Artists' Yearbook*. At least eighty thousand words. Blimey. Did the title count? He counted it. Four words. Just seventy-nine thousand nine hundred and ninety-six to go. Piece of cake. Hmm. That window was very smeared. There were also lots of little marks on his computer keyboard. He scratched at one with his fingernail. Little grey bits came off. Oh. He had typed six 'e's. That didn't count. Unless he was going to start the novel by falling out of a plane. He looked up, drawing his lower lip over his top one. That must make him look a bit like a gorilla. Maybe he ought to check it out in the mirror. No. God, his fingernails were dirty. Maybe he should just type anything, just to get started.

'The helicopter blades scythed the fetid air.'

Scythed? Scythed the air? What a cliché. And how did you spell scythed, anyway? Spellcheck. It was correct. It didn't look right. 'C' and 'y' together. The phone rang. Please let it be Laure, he thought. I don't care if she's calling about Lucy promising Sophie one of our baby guinea pigs, or telling me the whole family has nits, just let me hear her voice.

'How far have you got?'

He let out his breath with a rush, and forced himself not to sound ecstatic. Or even grateful.

'Seven words. Not counting the title.'

'Oh.'

'They're very good words,' he added, defensively.

'Try me.'

'The helicopter blades scythed the fetid air.' Read out loud, they sounded ridiculous.

'Is scything a real word?'

'How would you know? You're French.'

'Pardon me. I have a qualification in interior design. I am not uneducated, you know.'

'Of course. How silly of me.'

'How long have you been at it?'

Tom looked at his watch. 'Twenty-five minutes.'

'Seven words per twenty-five minutes. This book could take a long time.'

'At least I've started.'

'So you have. The helicopter blades scythed the fetid air.' Laure started laughing.

'I don't think you're being awfully kind,' Tom said. 'Remind me to ridicule you when you try to create great art. We writers are very sensitive people. You've probably set me back years. I may have to go and lie down.'

'I'm sorry. It is unkind of me. Are you coming to Cassie's on Saturday?'

'Sure am. What do you think she'll cook? Soup that tastes like wet dog? Rissoles with bits of gravel?'

'I don't care, as long as it isn't that pudding again. Chocolate pithivier, do you remember? From one of my recipes?'

'The one that tasted like a sliver of Marmite in flaky concrete?'

'That's the one.'

There was a long pause, and then they both spoke at once.

'I think I might take a secret supply of chocolate biscuits.'

'Did Lucy tell you . . .'

'Sorry, you first,' Tom said, gazing into the phone, a vivid mental image of her in his mind, long hair hitched behind one ear, Roverphone cradled under her chin, sitting in her immaculate kitchen.

'I was just ringing to ask if Lucy had told you they've fixed up to see each other on Saturday – have you got anything planned?'

'No, that's fine.'

'Great, I'll . . .'

Don't go, he thought. Just talk to me.

'At least we'll have lovely wine to drink.'

'When?'

'On Saturday,' he said. She must think I'm an idiot, Tom thought. Why can't I talk normally? I must have spoken to her on the phone hundreds of times. The receiver felt sweaty in his hand, and he realized he was squeezing it.

'Yes, Nat has a great cellar,' Laure said. To Tom, her voice sounded slightly puzzled, as if he was talking gibberish. He coughed.

'You hardly ever drink anything. Lightweight,' he teased. He must act as if nothing in their relationship had changed. But nothing would ever be as it was for him, and, he thought, I have no idea where to go, what to think and what to do. From the moment I get up, through driving the children to school, taking out the bins, clearing out the bloody guinea-pig hutch, loading the dishwasher, my mind is full of you. You are the movie in my head and everything else in my life is a distraction, even the children. I am moving inexorably towards you, and I cannot make myself turn back.

'So? I can watch you all enjoying it. Just think. When "The helicopter blades scythed the fetid air" –' more suppressed laughter – 'make you a multimillionaire novelist, you'll be able to create a wine cellar too.'

'Where will I keep it? In the airing cupboard? There's no room in this horrible box.'

'It's lovely, you exaggerate. Anyway. You'll be able to move.'

'That's all right for you to say, Mrs Lord of the Manor.'

'You aren't poor. Sarah keeps you in style, you lazy man.'

'Oh yes,' he said. 'Did I tell you? She's been given a big promotion at work. Senior features editor or some such meaningless rubbish. It means she gets to use the executive toilet and all her underlings have to prostrate themselves in front of her and she walks over their backs in stilettos.'

'I can quite see why Sarah loses her temper with you. Be supportive. She's done fantastically well, and all you can do is make fun. I think you should take her out for dinner in celebration. There's a new restaurant in Claydon. Italian. It isn't too expensive.'

'She's never home in time. I don't much fancy eating at midnight.'

I want to go there with you, he thought. Everything in my life would be bearable, even putting out the bins, if I was with you. He was beginning to understand how stalkers feel, how obsessions develop. When he saw a big silver car approaching him on the road, he longed for it to be her people carrier so he could wave at her and watch her face light up with pleasure at the sight of him. If he saw her at school, even from a distance, it was a good day. He had to stop himself driving past her house, just to see her car in the drive and know she was there. Last week he had parked on the other side of the road from the Rectory and sat, with his chin on the top of the steering wheel, willing her to walk past a window just so he could see her. She hadn't.

He told himself this was very sad, but he was powerless to resist. And – this was hard to admit – he had begun to imagine what it would be like to touch her, to feel the softness of her hair, her skin. He only had to close his eyes to visualize running his hand down her face, tracing the outline of her lips, to feel her skin against him – just thinking about it made him feel faint with desire. He tried to tell himself it was a crush, a kind of midlife crisis that many men went through, that she was simply the receptacle for emotions which might have hit him anyway. But he knew this was rubbish. It wasn't a teenage crush, because he was an adult and his feelings were adult. It was love for her and her alone, with all the attendant complications and pain. Which was both far, far worse, and far, far more wonderful. It was now, and it was Laure.

But if she ever found out – which of course she wouldn't – she would think he had gone quite mad. She could never, would never, reciprocate that love in a million years, and he had to keep telling himself that it could never be anything but an enormous secret, locked up inside him. It could ruin their friendship if she ever realized, and he would lose the gossamer contact that sustained him.

'You don't sound very pleased for her.'

'Who?'

'Sarah. Her new job, you lunatic,' she said, patiently.

'I am, I suppose, but she's going to be away even more. The kids . . .'

'What's the matter?'

'They're not that thrilled. Sometimes I think she doesn't understand, or won't see, how much they miss her. She's never at home. Not that I . . .' I want to tell you, he thought, savagely. I want to tell you that I do not love her and I do not care if she leaves me for ever. I hate the fact that you do not understand how I feel, that my hands are tied.

'Tom, you can't have everything. You know how hard she has to work.'

'Because I have not, as yet, achieved success in my professional life?' He tried to laugh. You think I am useless, he thought. I have to make this book work, to make you see what I can achieve. Besides, we'd need money to live on if ever . . . Shut up. Shut up. Shut up.

'Sometimes you make me really angry by being so pathetic. You are not a failure. You're just fishing for compliments because you know that bringing up children is just as important as working and you do that very well. You can't both be doing high-profile, demanding jobs, can you? Who'd look after the children?'

'Other couples manage.'

'Yes, by paying a nanny an absolute fortune and never seeing their children at all. If I worked like Gerard goodness knows what would happen to the children. You've taken a very brave decision to be at home.'

'Don't patronize me. And you called me lazy. I shall sulk.'

'I'm not. Look, at least you've made a start. Writing a novel is a job.'

'Is it?' Tom picked at his bitten nails and looked moodily out of the window at the back garden, with its jumble of cages and hen house. Two fat brown hens were pecking around the flower bed he'd meant to weed last weekend but hadn't had time.

'Oh bugger. I haven't fed the guinea pigs.'

'I thought the children were meant to do that before school.'

'We overslept. I drove them to school in my pyjamas.'

Laure laughed. 'I hope you didn't get out of the car.'

'I put a jumper on top. And wellingtons. I couldn't very well send Daisy into nursery on her own, could I? God, they'll be calling in social services soon. That's all I need.'

'Cheer up. You're supposed to be riding with Cassie

this afternoon, aren't you? I bet Daisy's excited about coming with you. Will she be safe? She's so little.'

'She can hardly come to any danger on Dougal. I might tie her legs to the saddle.'

'You can't do that!'

'My mother did. I used to go hunting with my legs lashed to the stirrup leathers with bits of twine. Once I went right round and ended up upside down for two fields before anyone noticed.'

'Tom, I think that sometimes you make things up.'

'No, really. Eventually my mother spotted the fact that there was a gap where I was supposed to be, reached down and pulled me the right way up. She told me off for not holding on tight enough. My parents were bonkers, weren't they?' he said, as if realizing this for the first time.

'It's official. English people are insane.'

'Did I tell you my mother once dropped me in a river at the age of four and told me to swim?'

'No! You poor little thing. No wonder you're so strange.'

'Strange? Strange and lazy? Thanks.'

'Maybe not strange, but . . . it is not normal to drop a child into a river and expect it to float. Look, don't you have to get on with your book? Aren't I stopping you? You haven't got long before you have to get Daisy.'

'No. Don't go. Chatting helps the creative process, honestly. My mother worked on the theory that puppies learn to swim by being chucked into water by their parents, so why should we be any different? It has left me with a lifelong fear of water in my ears.'

'So what happened? Did you swim?'

'Nope. I was going under for the third time before my father took pity on me and fished me out.'

'Your parents don't seem awfully kind.'

'They never told me they loved me,' he said, mock tragically. 'It has blighted my life. I was parcelled off to school at the age of seven with a trunk that was bigger than I was. It has left me emotionally retarded for life. But then I look at Mickey, the big thug, and think he'd be better off at boarding school.'

'Where are you going to send him?'

'Well, he won't pass the grammar-school exam, that's for sure. Sarah wants Uplingham but I can't see how we can afford it.'

'Can't your parents help?'

'Are you mad? It's all gone, whatever there was. Nothing for my dear brother Henry but a mouldering old house and inheritance tax. Not that he needs it, he's making a fortune.'

'You two must be very different.'

'How can I tell that's not a compliment?'

'You wouldn't want his life, though, would you?'

'God, no. And his wife is the bitch from hell. They have two Filipino nannies and I don't think Caroline could pick out her children in an identity parade. She spends all her time at the beauty salon being waxed and not eating lunch.'

Laure laughed. 'Does he look like you?'

'Hardly. Henry's handsome. At least Sarah thinks so, as she tells me repeatedly. And of course he's making millions so that must mean he's perfect, because that's how we judge success, isn't it?'

'I don't think Sarah only judges people on the amount of money they make,' Laure said, carefully.

'You don't know her. Anyway, at the moment she's so . . .'

'That isn't fair, Tom. I don't want to know.'

There was a long pause.

'Well,' she said. 'I ought to go now. This is stopping you from working and I have to get on. Have a good ride. Send my love to Sarah and say well done, I'm thrilled for her.' Her voice was brisk, impersonal. 'I'll see you both soon, and don't forget about the girls and Saturday.'

Tom thought he might be imagining it, but she seemed to emphasize the 'both'. It's a warning, he thought, his heart sinking. Back off. She knows, and she thinks I am an idiot.

'I better go too,' he said, carelessly. 'I've got to get Daisy in ten minutes. You never know, I might be able to write another seven words by then.'

'OK. Bye.'

You hang up, Tom thought, and then I will. But she didn't.

'Are you still there?'

'Yes,' she said. Her voice was much quieter, there was something in it which told him she had something to say.

'What is it?' he said, gently. 'Please tell me. I'm all yours. Honestly. I don't feel in the mood for writing anyway.'

Laure thought hard. This, she could tell him – and confiding in him would be such a relief. It was fairly harmless information, would not lead anywhere. She took a deep breath. 'It's just that Gerard won't listen to me about my father any more but I feel so – well, I feel so angry with him. He's going to get married at a register office and he wants us all to go. I don't know if I can face it. Gerard says I'm being unfair and that of course we should go, but then I think he's taking my father's side. It's OK for him to talk – he hasn't seen his parents for nearly a year.'

'Why do you feel so angry?' Laure was quiet for a moment, and Tom realized she was trying not to cry. 'I'm here,' he said. 'Go on.'

'It's as if he's throwing our life away, our childhood.

I know he was never faithful to Mama but at least he did love her a little, or I thought he did. You have to feel that your parents love each other, don't you? Or you think, why did they make me? I know their marriage was a charade but at least Mama tried to keep things relatively together but now it's as if he doesn't need us at all any more. I have this fear – and I know you're going to think this is completely *fou* – but I am so scared he'll have another family and then he won't need me at all any more. I'm losing my place. Does that sound crazy? I know I should change, and adapt, but I don't want him to have another life. I want him to grieve for her, not replace her.'

'It shouldn't change how you feel about him or your mother. People should be allowed to do what they want. You have to move on, and nothing's ever perfect. I'd say let him get on with it. You can't stand in judgement on anyone's life. You're not inside it. I used to think . . .'

'What?'

'I used to think that people who split up a marriage when they have children are totally selfish and stupid. But I'm coming to realize that unless you are inside that marriage, you have absolutely no right to judge. Some things . . . some things just can't be borne, I suppose, and anyone can be taken over by love no matter how careful they are.'

There was a moment's silence, and then Laure said, slowly, 'I can see that's fine in theory, but surely it is about exercising control. You can't just indulge yourself . . .'

'Sometimes you can't stop yourself,' Tom said. Oh, bugger it. Why not let go? He didn't have to be specific. 'It sounds such a cliché, but maybe anyone can be overtaken by love when they least expect it. I'm not sure it is about choosing, any more. You have no idea how you will react until you meet someone who fits what you want so entirely . . .'

'What do you mean?'

'We change all the time, don't we? When I met Sarah she was completely different from anyone I had met before and she seemed to represent a life that . . . a life that I thought I wanted too. But, gradually, you alter and the same things no longer feel so important. Maybe it's an intellectual thing but I'm not sure we connect any more. I want to talk about things that don't interest her, do things, like go to the theatre and read books which have no significance to her whatsoever, and I find that I'm getting so impatient with her determination to spend money on stuff which is just . . . irrelevant. Am I going on?'

'Yes. And it isn't fair to Sarah to talk about her behind her back.'

'OK. Point taken. But do you see what I mean? That no matter whether you set off from the same place, you don't always end up heading in the same direction. I wonder if her goals are mine, any more, and I look into the future and . . .'

'I had no idea you two were unhappy,' Laure said, quietly. 'You're not . . .'

'What?'

'Nothing. Look, I have to go. Cheer up. It can't be that bad.'

You don't know, he thought. You really don't know. There was a long pause, and Tom closed his eyes, pressing the top of the phone, painfully, against his forehead.

'What are you doing?' she said, into the silence.

'Nothing. I'm just . . . ow. Sorry. Just ignore me, I'm having a midlife crisis brought on by overwork.'

She laughed. 'So you think I should go to my father's wedding?'

'For the sake of your children, yes. Otherwise you're saying to them that their grandfather is doing a bad thing, and he's not.'

'I don't want them to think that marriage is temporary.'

'Your mother died,' Tom said. 'He's free to move on.'

'But so quickly? It makes me wonder if anything is permanent, even grief. Maybe we can get over anything. Now I really am going. Have I cheered you up?'

'Oh, absolutely. I may go and do a handstand in the garden.'

'So silly.' And then the phone clicked. He sat listening to the continuous whining tone for several minutes, before replacing the receiver.

Chapter Nine

Tom

'You know I'm not one to gossip . . .'

They were ambling down a country lane at the back of the village. Cassie was riding her horse Fred on the inside, to protect him from any scary vehicles, wheelie bins, grates in the road or flapping plastic bags just waiting to leap out and savage the unwary horse. He skittered along on the tips of his hooves, ears pricked forward, quivering, every sinew alert to the possibility of danger and the need to take flight. He wasn't an awfully relaxing ride, Cassie thought – thank goodness he was so brilliant across country. Already this season she'd jumped hedges she couldn't see over. Tom was on steady Mulberry, towing Dougal along beside him, who kept stopping to eat grass on the verge, whereupon Daisy yelped and tried to haul his head up. Several times already he had taken her by surprise and she'd slid down his neck to land with a thump in front of his munching face. She was quite a phlegmatic child, and sat on her plump little bottom picking at leaves until Tom jumped off and lifted her back onto Dougal's broad back.

'I think Gerard's in trouble.'

'Ooh. Where does that come from?'

'He said something inadvertently to me on the night of the ball. The night you', she twisted in the saddle to look sternly at him, 'got so drunk you told the master of the hunt you could see the point of being a saboteur.'

'He's so pompous,' Tom said, grinning. 'I wanted to wind him up. They think they can carry on like this for ever in their little bit of England but they don't realize that the country is changing. You can't just bury your head in the sand and think that modern views and twenty-first-century life won't catch up with you. Most of the population don't approve of ripping little foxes to bits in the name of sport. You have to accept that. No wonder it's been banned.'

'But you supported hunting. You go shooting. You would have hunted if you could have afforded it.'

'I know, Mrs Smartarse. That's not the point. I supported it from the point of view of sensible land management and pest control, not some outmoded belief that I could put on a red coat and roar about looking down on people.'

'The ban hasn't made much difference, and anyway we don't look down on people,' Cassie pointed out.

'You don't, but some of them do. They believe there is an "us" and "them", that the landed gentry still rule. It even exists in government, you know it does. The kind of gentleman who has to buy his own furniture, all that patronizing rubbish. It's the little snipes at people. It's a class thing, you can't get away from it. Class isn't dead, it's rampant in this stupid petty country and anyone who gets any money starts running around in a tweed jacket trying to ape the gentry. I'd move away if I could. Ouch.' Dougal, taking advantage of his inattention, stopped dead and plunged his head downwards. With a practised arm, Tom grabbed Daisy's anorak to arrest her rapid descent.

Cassie said nothing, gazing over the damp hedges at the ploughed fields, stretching away as far as the eye could see. The fields which had been seeded were already turning green with the first shoots of grass, ready for the spring grazing. The cows would be turned out soon, to gambol about on stiff legs after their long winter cooped up in shippons. The winter-born lambs were growing quite big now, and it was only weeks before the daffodils would be fully out. Of all the seasons, she liked spring the most. Each year it seemed to take her by surprise, as if she was seeing it for the first time. The hawthorn tree by the gate, a riot of white flowers as if covered in frothing lace, the host of daffodils on the top lawn and the clematis pregnant with little pink buds about to burst. After the damp, heavy winter with its squally rain and incessant mud underfoot, it was so cheering to think of new life, the ground drying out and the days lengthening.

'Gerard is a strange chap, isn't he?' Cassie said. 'Sometimes I look at him and Laure, and think, you wouldn't put those two together. She's so beautiful and gentle and elegant, and he's like a pugnacious street fighter. A bit chippy sometimes, too.'

'Oooh,' Tom said. 'Get you. Snobb-ee. And that's tautology.'

'What is?'

'Saying the same thing twice with different words.'

'Whatever, clever clogs. He is chippy.' She flashed a grin at him. Having known Tom since the early days of her childhood gave them a shorthand so she could say things to him she wouldn't dream of admitting to anyone else, even Nat. 'One moment I think I really know him, and then he backs off into a shell. It was as if he was going to confide in me when he said they might be moving, but then he thought he'd said too much and clammed up. I tried to talk to Laure about it but it was weird, she wouldn't discuss it either. It was almost as if she was frightened. I just wish to God she'd let us help if there is anything wrong. You know, there's a side to him I don't quite trust. I bet he can be hell at home, but Laure would never say. I think she puts up with a lot.'

'Surely if they were in trouble she'd tell us?'

'You'd think so. But he can be weird. Sometimes he's as nice as pie but the next he's in a foul mood. I wouldn't like to get on the wrong side of him. He's got quite a temper, I bet.'

'No-one is talking to me,' Daisy said, crossly, from the level of their feet.

'Sorry, darling,' Cassie said. 'It is very rude of us. How was nursery?'

'Boring. We did finger painting. That's for babies. Why is Dougal so dirty?'

Stop looking a gift horse in the mouth, Cassie thought, peeved. 'I didn't have time to clean him. Maybe you could give him a brush when we get back.'

'Please. Can we do this every day? I like riding.'

'Sarah's going to kill you. You'll end up having to buy her a pony.'

'Where would I keep it? In the hen house?'

'You could keep it with me. Look, Beth's going to outgrow Dougal very soon, Daisy could have him. I'm hardly going to be able to sell him, am I? Who would want him?' They both looked down at Dougal, who promptly stopped and closed his eyes. Daisy's little legs windmilled and he reluctantly shambled on, without opening them.

'Laure's not herself at the moment,' Cassie said.

'Do you think so?'

'Yes, she keeps half confiding in me and then stops. I get the feeling Gerard's told her not to say anything.'

'I wish she'd tell me. I'd hate to think she's secretly worrying about something. I know she's dreading her dad's wedding but I bet there is something else, you're right.' Cassie looked at him sharply. Why had he said 'me'? They were both her friends.

'My guess is that she feels it's too disloyal to spill the beans. I know whose side I'd be on, though. Still, she'll tell us when she wants to. I don't want to push her, not when she's got this new work to do. Have you spoken to her today?'

'She rang me at lunchtime. When I was writing.' He dropped the last sentence in, casually. Cassie reined her horse to a stop and looked at him in amazement.

'Christ, have you started? That's brilliant.'

'I haven't got very far,' he admitted. 'At all.'

'But it's the starting that's the hard part. You'll be like a runaway train now.'

'More like a stalling Skoda.'

'Look, let's just ask her outright. I can't bear the thought that she's worrying on her own.'

'We shouldn't force her.'

'Oh, sod that. I need to know. What if they did sell up and move?'

'That cannot be allowed to happen,' he agreed.

'I can't bear the thought of change,' Cassie said, firmly. 'I like everything the way it is. Even bloody Nat's on about moving us up to Scotland.'

'No!'

'Oh, it won't happen. I'll find a way of thwarting him. He's got to go to New York in two weeks. That will take his mind off it for a while. I think . . .' She leant forward confidingly, and Fred took advantage of the sudden shift of balance in the saddle to spook at a plastic bag in the hedge. All four feet left the ground as he leapt sideways, barging into Mulberry, who sighed and moved over. 'You useless tool. Stop it. I think he's having a male midlife crisis and he's going to start brushing his hair forward.'

'He hardly needs to. He's got a lot more hair than me. I'm sure I'm starting to go bald. Then no-one will fancy me.'

'No-one fancies you anyway,' Cassie pointed out.

'How do you know? I may be the object of panting lust for the entire female population of the village. I wouldn't mind going to New York. I wouldn't mind going anywhere, really. I need a change.'

'God, you too? Are all the men around me hitting a midlife crisis? You could start a little self-help group in the community hall. Make a change from toddler groups and whist drives.'

'You're not a very supportive person, are you? Don't come to me when you start waking up with night sweats and standing at the top of the stairs with a kettle in your hand, thinking, "How did I get here?" I just feel,' he scratched his face with the reins in one hand, 'I just feel that I need something else in my life. Something a bit more exciting. I look ahead and the years stretch away and the kids grow up, and then what?'

'You are a maudlin sod today. Then you and Sarah have more time together. It's a good thing, a new phase. I can't wait to be free of my lot.'

'You don't mean that,' Tom said. He knew, in the blinding flash of that moment, that he would not grow old with Sarah. He shuddered.

'What's the matter with you?' Cassie looked at him curiously. 'You look a bit peaky.'

'Someone must have walked over my grave,' he laughed.

'Excuse me for saying, but even by your standards you are quite bananas today. Anyway, Nat's going to New York on business. He isn't exactly going to be ice-skating in front of the Rockefeller Centre. But he does get to travel first class which means having one of those cabins where you can stretch out full length and nibble canapés while watching twenty-five different films. Imagine. I'd just love it.'

'You'd miss the horses too much,' Tom pointed out. 'When I'm rich and famous I will travel the world. What do you think, Daisy? Am I going to be a rich and famous daddy?'

She looked him up and down in his faded jeans, tucked into wellingtons, and battered old coat. 'No,' she said, after a few seconds' thought. 'You wouldn't be my daddy then. And you have to stay my daddy.'

Chapter Ten

Gerard

He turned over and looked at the clock. Damn. Three o'clock again. He'd got into a cycle of waking in the middle of the night, as if an alarm went off inside his head. How did your body clock know? He moved his legs restlessly under the too-heavy duvet. He was sweating again, the interminable sweats that had been plaguing him for around six months. He woke in a pool of moisture, the bedclothes creased into tight folds underneath him, his heart racing. Through the gap in the heavy lined curtains the sky was pitch black. He liked to sleep with fresh air in the bedroom, and the half-opened window made the curtain billow and flap. The wind was howling, roaring through the big oak tree on the back lawn. There'd be more branches down this morning, it sounded close to gale force. He should get up and close the window, but if he did that he stood no chance of getting back to sleep, his brain would be activated and all the thoughts that pursued him during the day would start to run through his mind, darting here and there, trying to work out solutions, find ways to circumnavigate the slow slide towards disaster.

Everything had come at once. The failure to sell the

northern factory, the sharp rise in interest rates and therefore borrowing, the lack of cash to fund the Australian and American launch. He'd had such big dreams, but one by one the house of cards was beginning to tumble. No sooner did he prop up one side with a new loan, than the other fell down. And then yesterday he'd received a letter from an American firm of solicitors. One of his clients was suing for the money he owed them, money for material he'd had imported. He'd found a cheaper supplier and had ditched his old one, very unfairly they thought after ten years of good service, but that was business. Maybe they'd had to lay off men too. The responsibility made him groan.

When things were going well, it was like sailing a yacht – you zipped along on top of the waves, flushed with the euphoria of success. The firm's name had been impeccable, they'd collected a reputation for speedy, quality service and the fortune he'd spent on advertising was reaping rich rewards with great contracts. News spread by word of mouth, and he'd received order after order. But then, two years ago, the downturn had started. He'd suspected it might, nothing could be this good for ever, but he'd made the mistake of borrowing more than he could really afford to fund the expansion of the factories and set up show-rooms in Australia and America. He was flying, and he thought he was invincible. The bank seemed to love him, wining and dining him, and his big suppliers took him to all the main society events, lunching him in top restaurants.

Then there was a drip-drip of bad news. He should have employed a PR firm to brief the trade press in his favour, but he thought he could do the firefighting himself. How wrong he had been. At that stage the situation was not too serious, he was only half a million down, but a snide little article in the main trade paper had started to breathe the word throughout the industry that he was in trouble. Late payment for goods – normal in the business world – was questioned more harshly, and coupled with the downturn in orders, cash flow began to be a problem. The bank, normally so expansive, were now looking into his accounts with a forensic eye.

His financial director said they had to cut back. They had to give up the idea now of expanding, and concentrate on the core business. But Gerard said they were committed. He agreed to put Australia on ice, initially, but spent a month in New York trying to drum up secure contracts before he put the team in place. No-one knew him there. He didn't have a history, and no matter how personable and persuasive he was face to face, without a track record he was nobody, just another Brit with a bright idea. After a month he'd come home with his tail between his legs and admitted they had to stall.

The workforce of sixty began to get scared. They knew that things were bad because the work wasn't coming in, and he'd had to lay half of them off for six months. Aside from the sales team and office staff, he had ten highly skilled technicians who were brilliant at their job, real craftsmen. They couldn't afford to be sitting around at home, but what could he do? Day after day they pored over the books. He looked at the cost of more advertising, bringing in a PR firm. He'd even thought about talking to Nat, the ace communicator and PR whiz-kid, but then he'd have to reveal just how deeply in the shit he was. And he could never do that. Nat was someone he admired more than anyone in the world. He seemed to have the Midas touch. He rode the market while Gerard sank. But then he was in the gold-dust business, the communications industry. That was what everyone wanted, marketing, promotion. Without it, it was almost impossible to survive.

How much had Nat sold the film wing for? Two point five? Not a fortune, especially over three years, but better than a kick in the head. Gerard would struggle to offload the whole lot for under a million at the moment. Less than the Rectory was worth. They'd been on the point of floating on the stock market five years ago, and then the value of the company had been close to ten million. Ten million! But with the loss of business, the failure to expand, the soaring price of materials and production costs, it was dwindling away. To a handful of dust.

He had to get up to go to the loo, it was no good. He glanced over at Laure. She was sleeping, as she always did, without any movement or even the sound of breathing. He knew that he snored, and it was getting worse. She was so lovely and didn't really complain about it, although it must be a pain. She would gently touch him on his shoulder, and try to shift him onto his other side. In the dim light he looked at her sleeping face. Quite perfect. Her long hair fanned out on the pillow, one tendril caught in her mouth, and he reached over, to gently lift it away. She didn't stir. She slept naked, as he did, and for a moment he thought about reaching his hand under the duvet to stroke her smooth skin, maybe even to wake her. He felt a stirring within him, but he put the thought away. He was too hot, he'd be sticky to the touch, and the thought revolted him.

He didn't feel confident about himself, angry at the flabbiness around the waist where once he had had a taut stomach. He was medium height and stockily built, with strong, broad shoulders and short, muscular legs. He wasn't too bad for his age, apart from the fat around the midriff, but he didn't like to catch sight of himself naked in the mirror. The flabbiness was too much wine, too many business lunches and no time to jog or go to the gym. He was eating all the wrong foods at the moment – the only decent meals he had were at home. In the office he'd given up going out for lunch, didn't have time, and snacked on chocolate, crisps and sandwiches. He drank coffee after coffee, which he knew was bad for him and he woke every morning with sour breath. Only alcohol lifted his mood, and he knew he was drinking too much. But it was such a relief to be able, briefly, to lift some of the pressure – the depression – that weighed so heavily upon him.

He must stop drinking, and try to make time to do some exercise. Laure couldn't find him attractive in this condition, and he longed for her. It had been months since they'd made love, and that was his fault. He couldn't. He simply couldn't. He didn't even dare try because he was terrified he wouldn't be able to manage it. The pleasure side of his brain seemed to have shut down, and he was conscious from the moment he woke of a great dark cloud hanging over him. What had Churchill called it? His black dog. Not to be able to get an erection was terrifying. They used to have a great sex life. Laure kept trying to talk to him about it, but he couldn't discuss it. Maybe it would be OK. Once everything had ... what? Exploded?

It was so frustrating to long to make love to someone, but know that you might fail. Better not to try, and make excuses. But love-making was his way of showing Laure how much he did love her. Without it, he was lost and inarticulate. He knew he was losing his temper too much with both her and the children, but they were the only escape valve he had. And if he

145

shouted at Laure and she stayed, then she must love him.

The first time he had seen her, seventeen years ago, standing with her back to him in an antiques shop, something about her had struck him, and it wasn't just her beauty. She looked so elegant, so effortlessly stylish. She represented a life he wanted. She was wearing a long skirt, high-heeled boots and a soft green cashmere jumper. Around her neck was a wide, darker green scarf, knotted with a style which told him, somehow, she wasn't English. Then she turned, and he saw her profile – the tiny, heart-shaped face with an upturned nose, wide hazel eyes framed by long, curling eyelashes. When she stepped behind the desk he realized she wasn't a customer, but worked there. He later discovered it was her mother's showroom, and she was helping out during the summer holidays, while she studied in France. He was seeing someone else at the time but the moment he saw Laure he knew she was the one he had to aim for. He'd always been fussy about girlfriends, and had a reputation at home for being aloof, even arrogant. But he'd known from his early teenage years that he wasn't staying, that the girls in his home town would never be enough.

In the bathroom he ran the cold tap, and splashed water on his face, before drinking some out of his cupped hands. He was fully awake now; there was no way he was going to go back to sleep, he'd only wake Laure by tossing and turning.

He headed down the stairs, the coir carpet scratchy under his bare feet. In the hall, he flicked on the lights and heard Victor yawn. A ginger body pressed against his legs, mewing furiously. That damn cat. He didn't like it much – it sat on the work surface in the kitchen waiting to be fed, and he thought it unhygienic. He was surprised Laure tolerated it, because she was so fanatical about cleanliness. He shooed the cat away, and it gave him a furious look before shooting up the stairs to find a bed to sleep on.

In the kitchen, Victor thumped his tail against the side of the basket. Gerard went over to him, and bent down. 'Hello, old man,' he said. The dog's grey muzzle pressed against his hand, and with the other he stroked the smooth black hair on his head. He was getting a bit plump, but then that was hardly surprising because he hardly left his basket any more. Laure had put down a section of carpet in front of it, because he couldn't get a purchase on the smooth stone of the kitchen floor to haul up his creaky back end. His poor front legs skated about and a desperate look came into his eyes.

It's only a matter of time, Gerard thought. God, Laure would be devastated. He'd bought Victor for her in the second year of their marriage, just before she'd become pregnant with Nick. She'd had a Labrador when she was a child and her parents were still living in France, and she had told him she'd loved that dog more than anything else in the world. He'd bought the puppy from a breeder, and driven home with it throwing up on his best overcoat. He'd never had any pets as a child – the house was too small, and his mother didn't like the mess and the hairs. He had no idea dogs threw up. He drove with one hand on the steering wheel and the other on the squirming fat body of the dog, which repeatedly licked his hand and tried to chew his shirt sleeve. Unsentimental by nature, he was surprised how much the puppy, with its big brown eyes, appealed to him. He'd shut him in the garage overnight, hoping its anguished squeals wouldn't wake Laure, and in the morning he placed it in her lap while she was sitting up in bed, opening her cards. She cried. The ecstatic puppy writhed about and tried to lick her face. She looked up at him, and said, 'Thank you. I love you so much.' Then the dog had been sick on the duvet.

He'd become part of the geography of their lives, the grinning, wagging presence that bumped into his legs when he came home from work, the one delighted 'woof' he uttered when he heard his key in the door. He took up residence in their kitchen, and although Gerard had meant to have a run built for him outside, Laure wouldn't hear of it. She quickly and efficiently housetrained him, and since then he had led the life of Riley. Two good walks a day, regular meals and endless amounts of love. Nick had grown up hanging onto his ears and riding him round the garden, and Sophie, as a toddler, used to watch television lying on the floor with her head propped up on his slumbering back as he curled himself protectively around her.

His hands around the comforting warmth of his coffee cup, Gerard looked into the old dog's eyes, and saw his life reflected. 'I'll miss you, old mate, when you go,' he said, as the tail went thump, thump, thump. A tear, unbidden, swelled in his eye and then trickled down his cheek. That's it, he thought. I'm losing it.

He ought to get out his laptop and work on some figures, but that was too depressing a thought. He reached for yesterday's paper, but the newsprint swam before his eyes. Laure. He could not fail her. If he lost his business, what did he have left to offer her? It was all he was. He'd go back to being Gerry Nobody, not worth a bean. The thought turned his heart to stone. I will go mad, he thought, pressing the heel of his hand hard against his forehead.

Chapter Eleven

Tom

'Can I steal you?' Tom was leaning casually against the side of her car. He looked, as usual, as if he had only just learnt how to dress himself, with one side of his shirt hanging out of his trousers and his collar sticking up by his ear. She had to stop herself reaching forward to tuck it inside his navy jumper. She transferred the games bag she was holding into her other hand, and pressed the key fob to open the doors.

'Why?' She tucked a loose strand of hair behind one ear.

'I just thought you needed cheering up,' he said. 'You sounded so down when I spoke to you on the phone, and what with me suddenly having a free morning . . .'

'Tom, you always have free mornings when Daisy is at nursery.'

He looked affronted. 'Remember I am a novelist. We are never free. The muse can strike at any time.'

'Really?' She sounded as if she was trying not to laugh.

'Indulge me. As you will not let me take you to the theatre, I am whisking you away on the trip of a lifetime. Well, maybe not exactly the trip of a lifetime, but the trip of a . . . week? To the new art gallery opening today in Claydon. And I', he said, flourishing two tickets, 'have exclusive invites to the launch.'

'Can't be so exclusive,' Laure said, laughing. 'Not in Claydon.'

'We may not be trampled to death by critics from the national newspapers, but in its own small way I am sure it will have something to contribute to the artistic oeuvre.'

'Artistic oeuvre, eh?' she said. 'Is Cassie coming?'

'She couldn't make it,' Tom said, quickly. 'Horsy stuff, you know.'

Laure paused for a moment. Then she smiled. 'I'm all yours,' she said.

They stood in the middle of the gallery. 'It's almost Matisse,' Tom said pompously, his head on one side. 'In his baroque period,' he added, loudly.

'That's architecture,' Laure hissed at him. 'It's terrible.' They were the youngest people there by about thirty years. Around them wandered grey-haired women with half-moon spectacles, balancing cups of tea on their programmes.

Tom looked around him. He leant towards her, and whispered conspiratorially in her ear, 'Shall we do a runner? What say I turn your head with chocolate cake at the Singing Kettle? This is shite, isn't it?'

'I'm easily bought,' Laure whispered back. 'You're on.'

'I'm not entirely sure about baroque,' he said, stirring his tea. 'Maybe it was more chocolate box. You know all about art, don't you?' he added, pointing the teaspoon accusingly at her.

'A little,' she said. 'My mother was the expert. She had the most fantastic eye. Most of my paintings came from her, you know.'

'Are you like her?'

'I'm not sure.' Laure leant back in her chair. 'I'm like her in some ways – I look like her, certainly, but I think I am less sure of myself. She had so much confidence and style. Maybe I am half like her.' She laughed.

'Would she have liked me?'

'Why is that important?'

He shrugged. 'I don't know. Your father likes me, doesn't he?'

'Yes. What did he say? He said you were fun. I think he finds Gerard a little hard work sometimes. Papa likes to play, and I don't think he can understand someone who is much more interested in work than playing.'

Tom looked at her thoughtfully. 'Gerard does seem a bit . . . well, especially just recently . . .' he said, carefully.

Laure picked up one of the packets of sugar from a small wicker basket in the middle of the table, and appeared to be reading the contents on the label. She felt her face becoming warm, and reached out with her left hand to push up the sleeve of her light blue cardigan to her elbow. The thin silver bracelets she often wore jangled together, and Tom could not take his eyes off the pale brown hairs on her arm, glinting against her pale skin. She had such slim wrists, like a child. Then she looked up at him, and he thought how beautiful her lips were, curved into a sad smile.

'He has a lot of worries,' she said, quietly.

'Really?'

'Yes.' She put the sugar down, and rubbed a finger up and down the tablecloth. 'It isn't easy, but things are not . . .'

'What?' He realized he was holding his breath.

'Much fun at the moment.' She shrugged. 'But it will blow over. It always does. It will be fine. He's just . . .'

She frowned, hunching her shoulders, 'he has a lot of worries and I think, I don't know, but I think he is depressed. Not just worried, no, more than that, depressed.'

'And you?' Tom leant forward.

'And I, what?'

'Do you love him?' he said. 'Do you want to stay with him?'

Laure looked at him aghast. 'How can you ask that?'

'Because I want to know,' he said. 'I need to know.'

'This isn't your . . .'

'I know. But I can't help it.'

She closed her eyes and sighed. After a moment she said, slowly, 'The honest answer is that I do not feel I know him at the moment. I see him, the man I married, and he has not changed so very much. He has always been driven, obsessed with his business, and that is how he is. But lately, I don't know, there is such a cloud, such a cloud over him and it is as if everything I do is not right. Do you know what I mean? However I try to reach out to him I do it in the wrong way and I feel as if I am making things worse, not better.' Her eyes filled with tears. Tom had to stop himself leaning forward to try to smooth them away.

'I am sorry. This is so silly of me.' She ran the fingertips of her right hand under her eye, pausing in the corner. 'I don't mean to impose on you.'

'No,' he said. 'It isn't and you aren't, at all. Because . . .'

'Because what?'

'Because I am in love with you.'

On the next table, a woman cleared her throat and turned the page of her newspaper. Laure's eyes widened, and for a moment she thought she might faint. The room swam, and she pressed her fingers tight against the edge of the table.

'That's not possible.'

'Why? Why the hell is it not possible?'

'Because it is too dangerous.'

'Don't see the negatives. Please.' He reached forward, and his hand sleepwalked across the table. His fingers closed over hers, and warmth flooded through her. She pressed her lips together, her eyes never leaving their entwined hands, fascinated, as if they were a quite separate entity over which she had no control.

'Nice to see a couple so happy,' said the waitress, clearing their plates. 'Some couples come in here and say nothing to each other the whole time. I hate that,' she added, wiping a cloth over the table. 'You have to talk.'

'This is madness,' Laure said, once she had gone. She could not help laughing. 'I feel as if I am in a play.'

'I feel rather crazy,' he said. The relief of having finally told her made him light-headed. He felt languorous with pleasure, intoxicated by the extraordinary sensation of being able, permitted, to touch her. And she hadn't pulled away from him. He turned her palm over, and with his other hand gently caressed the base of her thumb with his finger. 'I can't tell you how long I have wanted to do this.'

Laure felt as if she was in a dream, as if she was moving slowly under water. She allowed her eyes to meet his for a long, sensual moment, caught in time. He held his breath. She feels it too. She has to. He felt wildly exhilarated, reckless. Gently, he began to make circular movements on the palm of her hand with his fingertips, and she closed her eyes, her body coursing with waves of intense desire. I did not think I could ever feel like this again, she thought. This could not be happening. Every fibre of her being concentrated on the sensual touch of his hand. To love, and be loved. Then her eyes flew open and she saw how flushed his cheeks were, the tip of his tongue running along his top lip. With her other hand, she reached forward and ran her finger down his cheek. He leant against her hand and stared at her, so blatantly sexually aroused that she wanted to cry out.

'That'll be two pounds fifty,' the waitress said, banging the saucer with the bill on it down on the table. Laure snatched away her hand. They were back in the tea room in Claydon on a sunny March morning and the world had not stopped, after all.

They stared at each other, astonished by what they had allowed to happen. Something, they both knew, that could not be undone.

'We must go,' Laure said. Every word she uttered felt completely irrelevant, every movement an effort. The spell, whatever madness had possessed them, had been broken and she felt both exposed and vulnerable. What were they thinking? How could she, for even a split second, have thought they had the right to do this? Her mind was full of rational thought, while her body screamed, make love to me.

'I'll get this,' Tom said, reaching in his back pocket. Laure stood up, feeling behind her for her jacket, and stumbled over the chair leg. He caught her under the elbow to steady her, and for one breathtaking moment she felt the length of his body against hers, slim, hard, strong. Each touch was like an electric shock.

'Don't,' she said. 'No.'

They walked back to the car in silence. Laure put her hands in the pockets of her jacket, and kept her head down, refusing to look at him. Her mind raced with competing, confusing thoughts. We are not teenagers. We cannot play this game, it is far too dangerous. But it is irresistible, came the siren call. You both want to so much. Can you really prevent this happening? This is out of your control.

154

A woman pushing a toddler in a buggy paused to stare into the newsagent's windows as they walked past, her eyes running down classified adverts written up on postcards and pinned to the back of the door. Tom reached out to steady an old man leaning on his walking stick, who had stumbled over a raised pavement slab. He was wearing a dark brown trilby hat and ancient tweed overcoat, breathing heavily, his old hand gnarled like a claw over the bone handle of the stick, the veins on the back of the hand raised, pumping dark blue blood through the waxy parchment skin. 'There you go,' Tom said.

'Thank you, young man,' the old man wheezed.

The sun shone, quite strong for the beginning of March, and Laure lifted her face briefly to feel its warmth. It was an ordinary day in the busy market town, an ordinary Monday with people taking library books back, shopping for milk and bread, buying newspapers, chatting to acquaintances unexpectedly encountered, while holding onto bored young children zigzagging around them, whining. A banner had been unfurled across the main street, advertising the latest production by the Claydon Players, flapping in the breeze. An ordinary day, she thought. An ordinary day to be told that I am loved.

In the car she stared out of the window at the hedges, fields and trees. A group of lambs had gathered on a grassy knoll and were practising jumping off, with wild leaps and excited flicks of their tiny curly tails. So full of the joy of just being alive, being there in the warm sunshine, with the security of their mothers close by.

She knew that if she caught his eye, he would stop the car, pull her urgently to him and kiss her. And that would be the beginning of an awesome, terrifying, ecstatic journey. It was like watching a whirlwind coming towards you, knowing it would sweep you up and take you out of your life for ever. And yet you could step out of its path, and be safe. I can stop this, she thought. I will stop this because I do not have the right to choose. And so she did not catch his eye. The most she permitted herself was a glance at his arm as he changed gear, the navy blue jumper revealing an inch of light blue denim shirt, the dark hairs against the tanned skin of his wrist. The gold of his wedding ring.

He dropped her off outside the Rectory, and did not get out of the car to say goodbye. She lifted her hand to wave, but he had disappeared, the speed of his car throwing up gravel.

Chapter Twelve

Cassie

Carole lounged against the dresser, and carefully removed an overhanging dog lead that was sticking into her back, before reaching forward to take a red grape from the big plate Cassie was hurriedly filling with cheese. Cassie put the cling-film wrapper between her teeth and ripped. 'Yuk,' she said, as a bit of it stuck between her teeth. 'Oh, bugger and damnation,' she said, looking at the clock. 'They'll be here in ten minutes. Ow, ow,' she said as she lifted a steaming casserole from the warming plate of the Aga, to put into the simmering oven. 'These things have got holes in.' She held up the oven mittens, where Hector had chewed neat little holes in the top. They were also suspiciously furry inside, as if some kind of small creature had been secreted within. But that was impossible.

'Anything I can do to help?'

'No, you just stand there and eat the grapes which cost five pounds a pound,' Cassie said, aware her face was bright red from the heat of the oven. 'How are you, anyway?'

Carole moved the grape from one cheek to the other, and looked thoughtful. 'Crap, obviously,' she said.

Cassie's heart sank. She'd invited her to the dinner party because it was her first weekend back from holiday, her first holiday as a single woman following the divorce, and Cassie thought it might cheer her up. But, so far, it was a bit like having the Grim Reaper for dinner. Laure said inviting her was a great idea and a very kind thing to do, but Cassie knew that Sarah would be furious because she loathed Carole and thought she was a moaning minnie and hadn't been surprised at all that her husband had buggered off with the au pair of one of their friends.

Carole did seem determined to remain glued to her hair shirt, and the holiday, with her mother, clearly hadn't made her any more jolly. For the dinner party she was wearing no make-up whatsoever, a heathery purple jumper and ill-fitting and slightly too short jeans of the type normally favoured by elderly mothers. But then, as she had explained to Cassie with weariness, every married woman she knew now seemed to think she was after their husband, so that was why she deliberately dressed down. 'Except you,' she added, loyally. Privately Cassie thought that getting a job would be the best thing for her to do, but then she was hardly in a position to extol the benefits of full-time employment. Carole lived in one of the new houses on the estate near Tom, with her teenage son, Milo. The atmosphere of the house was palpable with grief and loss, and Cassie wished there was more she could do to help and thought it must be hell for Milo.

Tilly strolled in and reached over to take one of the chocolates, for after the meal, that Cassie had put out on a plate. 'Yum, minty,' she said. She unwrapped one and popped it in her mouth.

Arthur slunk into the kitchen, also looking for the treats which often came with a dinner party. He regularly complained that Cassie did not buy chocolate and biscuits, but, as she pointed out, if she did, she would just eat them. 'There's no arguing with that,' Arthur said, making circular motions by his ear with one finger and whistling.

'Tilly, those are for the guests,' Cassie said, crossly.

'I'm starving. Why do we get sandwiches and the grown-ups get proper food?'

'Casserole,' Cassie said, licking the rim of the wine glasses and polishing them with a tea towel.

'Ew,' Tilly said. 'Maybe we're better off. At least you know what's in a ham sandwich. With Mum, a casserole could contain anything. Who's coming?'

'The usual,' Cassie said, bending down to take some potatoes out of the bottom of the vegetable rack. 'And don't be so rude. Tom and Sarah, Laure and Gerard . . .'

'And me,' Carole said.

'You don't count,' Tilly said. 'You're always here.'

'Do tell me if I'm getting in the way,' Carole said, making a face at her.

'You're getting in the way,' Tilly said, standing up and wandering out of the kitchen. She was wearing a grubby mucking-out anorak and pyjama bottoms, with Beth's too small horse-head slippers, the backs bent over.

'I do apologize for my children,' Cassie said. 'They don't get any better. How's Milo?'

'He won't talk to me,' Carole said, dramatically. Cassie and Arthur exchanged a secret look, as Arthur helped himself to another chocolate. 'He's just shut himself off from me and he won't let me in. I keep trying to talk to him, but he's internalizing. It's not good for him. I'm trying to talk him into attending family therapy sessions, but he doesn't seem to want to come along. He spends all his time in his bedroom playing computer games and listening to music.'

'Sounds normal to me,' Arthur muttered.

'Did he stay with Mike while you were away?' As soon as she said it, Cassie regretted uttering the Forbidden Name, the 'M' word, as soon as it had left her lips.

'And the slut, yes,' Carole nodded. 'Christ knows how confusing it is for your teenage son to stay with his father, knowing that he is sleeping with a girl only seven years older than him.' Cassie shot a glance at Arthur, who had his head down and was apparently absorbed by the newspaper. She knew perfectly well that he was drinking in every word. She did wish that Carole might bear her grief and anger a little, well, a little more stoically. But even now, a year on, she was still determined to twist the knife as often as she could. Only she wasn't twisting the knife in Mike, who was blissfully unaware, but in herself.

'I mean, can you believe it? You'd think he'd have the decency to run off with a grown woman, but no, he has to run after a child. He slept with her in our bed, you know. He took great delight in telling me. And how many times.'

'Yes, well,' Cassie said, hurriedly. 'She's not exactly a child.'

'She's hardly a grown-up. It won't last, of course. He's incapable of staying faithful to anyone. I know I'm better off without him, I just wish I hadn't wasted fifteen years finding that out. The utter, utter bastard.'

Cassie mentally hunted about for a way of getting her off the subject. 'Have you thought about taking any of those courses at the college?'

Carole examined her unpainted nails dismally.

'I might. At least it would get me out of the house.' I'd quite like you out of my house, Cassie thought, and then felt tremendously guilty. Why did I invite you? At the moment it was better to be with Carole on her own, then you could give her your full, undivided attention because she was hypersensitive to the tiniest perceived slight. Cassie knew that Carole's skin was less than a millimetre thin, and even turning her back on her to get on with the cooking was viewed as a signal that Carole was boring and had nothing to say and should stay at home. On her own, with a few glasses of wine inside her, she came close to resembling the old confident Carole, and could even see the darkly funny side of the situation, but in a group of people she clammed up and took every opportunity to rush into the kitchen to start washing up and being 'helpful'. Cassie didn't want her to be helpful. She wanted her to let her hair down and be loud and happy and look forward instead of constantly looking back.

Would she be like this if Nat left her? Hopeless, half a person? She hoped very much not. The only pleasure she and Laure could extract from Carole's situation was the fact that it gave them an excuse to pour over the property pages of the local newspaper, which they very much enjoyed, looking for lovely cottages with pretty gardens which might cheer her up. But, as Carole frequently said, divorce was like a bereavement and you needed time to grieve. Or wallow, Cassie thought, and then felt guilty again. She had been really looking forward to a relaxing evening where she could get happily drunk among close friends, but then Carole had rung and she'd found the words, 'Do come to dinner on Saturday,' falling out of her mouth, as Nat made slitting gestures across his throat.

'Right, that's it,' she said, moving the steaming pans onto the warming plate. 'I'm just going to get changed. You'll be OK, won't you? Read the paper, or something.'

'I'll start washing up some of the pans,' Carole said.

'No,' said Cassie quickly. 'Please don't. Relax.'

The doorbell rang just as she was drying her hair

upside down. She glanced at the alarm clock by her bed. Only five minutes late. How dare people who knew her so well be just five minutes late for a dinner party? They knew she wouldn't be ready. Nat wandered in, sliding cufflinks into his blue shirt. His hair was wet from the shower and he looked impossibly glamorous. 'Nice arse,' he said, as Cassie hurriedly righted herself. She twisted round to look at her bottom in black trousers. 'It does look OK in these, doesn't it? Not too much like a rhino?'

He slid his hands around it. 'Nope. Like a peach. Or maybe a melon. Or maybe,' he gave it an exploratory tweak, 'a pumpkin. Do we have time?'

'No we definitely do not,' Cassie said firmly. 'And pumpkin is bad.' She straightened up. 'Oh Christ,' she said. 'Mad hair.'

By blow-drying it upside down she usually managed to give it a nice lift at the front, but obviously she had gone on too long because now she looked as if she had had a particularly nasty fright. Nat peered at her reflection in the mirror. 'Vertical hair is very in,' he said. 'I like it. It gives your face a certain questioning quality.'

'Sod off and let the people in,' she said. She was still in her bra, and started hunting about for a top that would make her look slim. Black cashmere would be good, but it was in the hand-washing pile behind the laundry basket, from which items of clothing rarely returned. Black stretchy top from Gap? A possible option, only she couldn't tuck it in because then she would have a visible roll of fat at the top of her trousers. Not a good look, as Tilly would say. On cue, Tilly wandered in, having replaced the anorak with a sparkly halter neck. 'Gross,' she said.

'Thanks,' Cassie said. 'What do you think? Pink jumper or black stretchy top?'

'Neither,' Tilly said, and wandered out. Cassie could hear the murmur of voices downstairs. Tom and Sarah. She could hear Nat offering them drinks, and their footsteps heading to the kitchen. Sarah would be wearing something wonderful by an expensive designer, she thought, darkly. And Laure would be in one of her beautiful flowing outfits while she looked like a heffalump beside them. She pulled the stretchy top over her head, and decided to try it outside her trousers. Her head on one side, she looked at herself critically in the mirror. She sucked her tummy in and put one foot in front of the other. That wasn't too bad. She put her hands on either side of her thighs, pressing them in. If only she didn't have that bump there, her legs wouldn't be too bad. She looked at herself more closely. She put her hands between her thighs and pressed them in again. There. Thin legs.

'Cassie . . .' Nat's voice floated up the stairs. 'Stop trying to make yourself look thinner and come down and get a big drink, will you?' She grinned into the mirror.

Downstairs, Sarah was standing with her back to her, as Nat gave her a large glass of red wine. Tom put his arm around Cassie.

'Darling. Have you lost weight?'

'Shut up, you toad,' she said, kissing him loudly on the cheek. 'You look smart.'

'Thank you. I thought it was about time I updated my wardrobe. I bought a new shirt. I think it rather suits me.'

Cassie stood back to look at him admiringly. He did look smart, for once. He was wearing a pale blue linen shirt, and his newly washed hair looked as if he had actually run a brush through it. A pair of clean cream chinos, neatly pressed, and dark brown deck shoes completed the outfit. Nat handed him a glass, and he drank a third of it in one gulp.

'Don't *do* that,' Sarah said, turning round. She was wearing a patterned gypsy skirt, and an absolutely exquisite distressed tweed jacket.

Cassie reached out and felt one of the fronds. 'That's lovely,' she said.

'Marc Jacobs,' Sarah said. 'It bloody should be for the price.' She took out a cigarette from her bag. 'Carole. I didn't know you were coming.' Her voice suggested it was not an entirely pleasant surprise. Carole had materialized from the gloom of the boot room, where she had been getting another bottle of chilled white wine out of the fridge. Hector pattered about their feet, trying to attract attention to himself by dancing around on three legs, waving one front leg in the air and shimmying his wriggly piglet body. He made several abortive attempts to jump into Sarah's arms, landing against her thighs.

'Get off, you horrid creature,' she said, pushing him down. His black boot-button eyes registered affront. He would not forget. She would be made to pay.

'Bad move,' Tilly said. 'The last person who pushed him away like that was found at the bottom of the pond.'

'Don't be silly. Ignore her,' Cassie said, making a face at Tilly. None of her children seemed to like Sarah.

'Cassie took pity on me,' Carole said, leaning forward to air-kiss Sarah's cheek. 'I hope I haven't spoiled the numbers.'

'Of course you haven't,' Cassie said, quickly.

'Yes, stop being such a bloody martyr,' Tom said, kissing her. 'Still in victim mode, then, I see?'

'Lovely Tom,' she said. 'Always so rude.'

Sarah blew out smoke through cherry red lips. Her hair was wavier and more auburn than usual, Cassie thought. It suited her. Leaning against the dresser, she looked out of place in the messy room, as if she had stepped out of the pages of a fashion magazine. Cassie couldn't remember ever seeing her without make-up, even first thing in the morning or at the weekends. Sarah was the only woman she knew well who actually wore foundation. Everything about her was impeccable, from her glossy hennaed hair to her long red nails. Cassie looked enviously at her boots. They were calf length, in soft navy suede with a very pointy toe. Cassie thought she would love a pair of boots like that, but on her she'd look like one of Robin Hood's merry men.

She smoothed her hands down her thighs, noticing with amusement how Sarah smiled flirtatiously up into Nat's eyes when he topped up her glass. When she had first met Sarah she had marked her down as one of those women you had to watch around husbands, but it didn't worry her. As she frequently said to Nat, if he wanted to be with someone far more beautiful, then she would understand. Only of course she would first have to rip his toenails out with pliers and then dance upon his grave. His response was to say that he would keep her posted. He knew that she did not worry, she had never clung. That was one of the many things he loved about her – she didn't treat him like a possession. She caught his eye as Sarah smiled up at him from under her lashes. Cassie raised a sardonic eyebrow at him and he grinned.

Tom looked down at her glass. 'Are you on the white wine?'

'I seem to get a marginally less worse hangover,' Cassie admitted. 'But then I can drink twice as much of it. Swings and roundabouts. Now bugger off, you lot. I have some cooking to do.'

'God forbid,' Nat said, ushering them out into the

hall and into the sitting room where Cassie had laid a fire. The doorbell rang again.

'Little present,' Laure said, as Cassie opened the door, handing her a bunch of beautiful yellow roses. In her other hand she held a bottle of champagne. She looked at it and said, 'It's a celebration, darling. I have been given another commission.'

'That's brilliant,' Cassie said, kissing her on the cheek, breathing in her Chanel perfume. On Laure, it smelled gorgeous. On herself, she thought it smelled like air freshener. 'The others are in the sitting room, I'm just wrestling with the vegetables.'

'I'll come and help you,' Laure said. She shrugged off her velvet coat and hung it over the bottom of the stairs.

'Hello, Cassie.' Gerard brushed his cheek against hers.

'Go and get a drink, the others are in the living room,' she said. Laure followed her into the kitchen, and plonked her bag down on the table. On closer inspection, Cassie saw she didn't look so great. Her nose was slightly pink, and her eyes were red-rimmed. Almost as if she had been crying. And she was even thinner than usual. She was wearing a long chocolate brown suede skirt which Cassie had seen many times before, and it hung off her. The bones at the base of her neck looked oddly pronounced, like chicken wings. Her hand shook slightly as she took a glass of white wine from Cassie. Laure realized she was being studied, and wouldn't meet her eyes.

'Are you all right?'

Laure glanced at the open doorway. From beyond the hall came the sound of animated conversation and laughter. She grimaced. 'It's Nick,' she said.

'What?'

Laure lowered her voice. 'He and Gerard had a

terrible row on the phone last night. Gerard's been going on about the fact that he isn't working hard enough and yesterday morning we got a letter from school saying that we had to go in to see his tutor. Apparently his grades aren't very good. I told Gerard that boys of his age go through ups and downs,' Cassie nodded, 'and it wasn't anything too serious. But he just exploded. He told Nick', Laure hesitated, as if she might cry again, 'that he was going to take him away. Make him come home.'

'No!'

'I know. I tried to calm him down but he wouldn't see sense. Then Nick started shouting back – I couldn't hear what he was saying and Sophie ran out of the TV room because of all the noise and then she was in tears, and – oh, it was so stupid. One of those awful family arguments that go too far. Maybe it will blow over.' She didn't look very convinced.

'What happened then?'

Laure took a sip of wine and appeared to be considering something. She looked directly at Cassie, and swallowed. 'I was trying to persuade him to ring Nick back and say it was all a mistake but he must work harder, and I was blocking the door to the kitchen and he, well – he pushed me out of the way.'

'Pushed you?'

'Yes. I know it sounds so silly, it was only a push, but it really – it really shocked me that he could think he could treat me like that.' Laure glanced back at the doorway, and then reached out and firmly closed the kitchen door.

'Forcefully?'

Laure looked down into her wine.

'Quite. He hurt my shoulder. It's a little bruised. But it was my fault in a way,' she added quickly. 'I didn't support him. I stood up for Nick, and I was

167

deliberately blocking the door. I wanted to stop him, and make him see sense.' She looked up at Cassie, and her eyes were full of tears. Cassie stepped towards her and hugged her.

Laure started to sob. 'You won't say anything, will you?' Her voice was frightened. 'I feel like I don't know what he will do.' The words came out in a rush. 'One minute he's normal and the next minute he is almost out of his mind. He scares me,' she said, her voice muffled against Cassie's shoulder. 'It is as if he's out of control.'

'Why?' Cassie said, slowly. 'Why would he be like this? You've never told me he can be like this.' I knew, she thought. He's a bully.

'Oh, he can,' Laure said. 'He can be quite frightening sometimes. It's not something you talk about, though, is it? It's a private matter. But it's the first time he has ever gone so far.' She hesitated over the word. 'And been almost, well, violent. What can I do? I cannot talk to him.'

'I don't know what to say. I can't believe it. Did he say sorry? Has he apologized?'

'Oh yes,' Laure said, rubbing the back of her hand across her eyes and stepping back from Cassie. 'Sorry,' she said, with a weak laugh. 'I must look awful.'

'You look fine. What are you going to do?'

'I don't know,' Laure said. 'I really don't. What can I do?'

'He's got to do more than apologize,' Cassie said, angrily. 'He can't do this. Did Sophie see what happened?'

Laure's lip quivered again. 'Yes,' she said, quietly. 'He shoved me back against the door frame and he slammed the doors into the kitchen.' She gazed at Cassie with wide open eyes. 'I just stood there and Sophie was crying, and I hugged her. She was so shocked. We both were. What could I say to her?' Cassie shrugged, helplessly. 'I said that Daddy wasn't feeling well and we should leave him alone for a while, and I took her upstairs for a bath. Then I heard the front door slam and he went out.'

'When did he come back?'

'He was gone for ages. I gave up waiting – actually, I thought about locking the door, but I was worried that with the mood he was in he might break a window, and that would wake Sophie, especially if he'd been drinking, which would be so awful and frightening for her. I went to bed. Of course I couldn't sleep, and he came home about midnight. He stank of alcohol, God knows how he'd driven the car.' She smiled, weakly. 'Things like this don't happen to people like us, do they?'

'And what did he say?' Cassie's mouth was pressed into a thin line.

'I shouldn't be telling you this,' she said. 'It's so disloyal. He would be so angry if he knew. He held me, and he cried. He said he was so sorry, and that it would never happen again. He said – he said he loved me, and that he was terrified of losing me. He could not go on.'

'And did you forgive him?'

'I said I did. But – oh, God, how can I? You don't know, you really don't know—'

The door opened. In the doorway stood Tom. 'Is this a private conversation, or can anyone join in?' he said, his voice apparently cheerful, but, Cassie could see, underneath it he appeared nervous, ill at ease. Then he saw Laure's face. 'What on earth is the matter? What has happened?' he said. His face registered a mixture of concern and something else, something much more intense. Cassie felt as if she had been physically struck. Oh, God, no. Not this. Time stood still as she looked from one to the other. Tom made a move as if he was going to throw his arms around Laure, and she seemed to quiver, as if she was desperately trying to stop herself running to him. She brought a hand up protectively, in front of her, as if to ward him off. Cassie stood rooted to the spot. They could not be so stupid. She must be imagining it. But pieces of an intricate jigsaw were slowly beginning to slot into place.

'It's nothing. I'm just feeling a bit down, not very well. How are you? You look smart,' she added, nodding furiously and wiping her eyes. Tom looked at her as if she was talking rubbish, and seemed as if he was going to say something, and then thought better of it.

'I'm fine. Sod me. What's happened to you? For God's sake, tell me.' Laure shook her head. There was an awkward pause as he stared hungrily at Laure, who avoided his eyes.

Cassie looked rapidly between the two of them. 'Tom, could you give us a few minutes? Thanks.' He stared at her wildly, as if only just noticing she was there. Seeing the look on her face, he nodded. 'OK,' he said, slowly, and backed out of the kitchen. His eyes never left Laure's face. He looked as if he wanted to snatch her up and run away. Cassie's heart sank. Stupid, stupid boy. So that was it. How far had it gone? She wondered fleetingly if she should tell Nat. No. She knew exactly what he would say. It was none of their business. They were adults, and had the right to make their own decisions, cataclysmic as they might turn out to be.

'What don't I know?' Cassie said to Laure, once Tom had gone. 'Tell me. Please. What the hell is going on?' They both knew she was not talking about Gerard.

'I need another glass of wine,' Laure said. Cassie looked at her, surprised. She so rarely drank. 'They'll wonder why we aren't going through. Gerard must know I am talking to you. He'll be so . . .' Her eyes flicked nervously over to the door. Her eyes told Cassie not to ask her about Tom.

'Tom will stall them,' Cassie said.

Laure took a deep breath. 'He will. Gerard's business is in big trouble,' she said. 'That is what is behind this.' But that's not it, Cassie wanted to say. Is it? Do you think I am stupid? This is far, far more complicated than that.

'So that's why he said you might have to sell the house?' I will let her tell me in her own time, she thought. She has clearly been through enough. But she could not stop her mind racing. Was it reciprocated? Did Laure know that he was in love with her? Had they . . . God, it was unthinkable. And she was so vulnerable, no wonder Tom . . . and. And. Part of her could see that it was quite understandable. That Laure was everything that Tom needed.

'Yes. We could lose everything,' Laure said, simply.

'Oh, God. I thought you said the house was in your name, for tax purposes or something?'

'So did I,' Laure said. 'Apparently not. He's mortgaged us up to the hilt and now there is nothing left. Well, a little bit of equity but it isn't enough security. And with interest rates rising as fast as they are, it means that all the money we have saved over the years could be lost.'

'Aren't you furious with him? You've no savings left? No security?' Despite the fact that she was reeling from Tom's unspoken revelation, she could not believe that things had got so bad and Laure had not told her.

Laure laughed wryly. 'Whatever I or Gerard had invested has long gone into the business. Oh Cassie, I have been so stupid. I have believed all the excuses he has been fobbing me off with for over a year. The only things we have left are my mother's furniture and paintings. We might have to sell those, just to raise enough to buy a much smaller house to live in, or rent. But all that doesn't matter. If only he would let me help, or talk to me about it, none of this would be important. They're only material things, we don't need them. What does matter is the children, our marriage. But the thing is . . .'

'The thing is what?'

'I don't know if I want to stay with him. Oh God.' Her hand flew to her mouth. 'I can't believe I have said it. I just do not know, I am in such a mess. All I want to do is grab the children and run away, but I have nowhere to go.'

Cassie felt cold with shock. Tom. She was in love with him, even if she hadn't yet admitted it to herself. There was no mistaking the emotion that flashed between them. She could not interfere in their relationship, that would have to be Laure's decision, and hers alone. Although Cassie's advice would have been that it was suicidal.

Cassie took a deep breath. 'Is it permanent, though? Is there no hope of saving the house? Maybe Nat would be able to do something. You've got to let us do *something* to help. You can stay here, of course you can, if you really want to leave . . . just don't . . . he isn't in a position, neither of you are . . . I can't quite . . .' The words tumbled out, in confusion.

Laure looked at her in horror. 'I can't leave him!' she said, half to herself. 'What am I thinking? He would have no-one, I can't take the children away from him. And it isn't totally his fault, Cassie, I can see that he's been trying to protect me from it and the strain must have been awful. That's why he has been so foul. I have to try to understand and not judge him,' she said. 'I can't just make a knee-jerk reaction and leave. It would not solve anything. Just because I . . . it isn't possible, I don't how we thought it could ever . . .' Her words trailed away.

'You've only just found out?' Cassie suddenly thought that she could not bear to discuss Tom.

Laure nodded. 'In the last month or so. Of course I saw the bank statements but he kept telling me it was only temporary, that the American investment would come good, but now the house is threatened . . .' She left the sentence unfinished.

'And you can't afford the school fees.'

'No. But that's why I want to sell the furniture – it would buy us a little time, and I think it's the most important thing in the world, to keep the children stable and happy. They don't know anything about losing the house.'

And what about you? Cassie wanted to shout. What effect will it have on them if this relationship with Tom develops? That would make their lives anything but stable and happy. But then how could she stay with Gerard when he had treated her like this?

'So what are you going to do?'

The door flew open. Gerard stood swaying in the entrance to the kitchen, and Cassie could immediately tell that even in the relatively short time they had been talking, he must have drunk several glasses of wine. He'd put on weight, and his skin was sallow and unhealthy. He looked warily between Cassie and Laure, taking in the atmosphere. Anger crossed his face and – something else, Cassie thought. He looked both guilty and exhausted. Laure stepped towards him, putting out one hand. 'Hi, darling,' she said. 'I was just helping Cassie with the food. Do you want to take through another bottle of wine?'

'No thanks,' he said. 'I – er, I just wondered where you'd got to. You've been ages.'

'I'm just going to the toilet.' Laure, picking up her

173

bag, kept her face down as she brushed past him, and walked swiftly out of the room.

Gerard stood awkwardly in the doorway.

'Did you want something?' Cassie said. She was aware that her voice had a hard edge. Try as she might, she could not erase from her mind the image of him pushing Laure. How could he? How could he be so cowardly and cruel as to take it out on Laure? But oh, poor man, if her instincts were correct. Gerard was watching her closely, as she turned to lift the plates out of the warming oven. He didn't say anything. She wished he would go, as she didn't trust herself to speak to him, or know what to say.

'Is there anything I can do to help?' he said, eventually.

'No, thanks,' she said. 'I'm fine. I'll come through for a drink in a sec. Can you take this bottle with you?' She handed him another opened bottle of red wine. It was an unmistakable invitation to leave. Gerard looked beseechingly at her. He wants to talk to me, Cassie thought, but I do not want to hear his side of the story. I don't want to hear him justifying himself, I simply cannot cope with any more information. She couldn't meet his eyes. He clearly realized that Laure had told her what had happened. Despite her anger, there was a tinge of sadness for him. He looked on the edge of a breakdown. What a mess, she thought. What a bloody mess.

'Do you think Laure is OK?' he said.

Cassie thought hard. 'No,' she said, slowly. 'I think she is very confused.' That was true enough. He dropped his head.

'She told you, then.'

'Yes.'

'You've no idea what this year has been like for me. I know I can't make excuses but at least I can try to make you understand a little. I can't talk to anyone and there is so much pressure, day after bloody day. I was holding it together and I thought I had protected Laure pretty well from the full horror. Can't you see? I wanted to make it better and solve everything myself, but I can't and I feel I have failed. I would never, ever hurt her, you know that. She won't forgive me, Cassie, and I need her so much.'

Cassie looked at him, and thought, God, he's going to cry. What on earth am I going to say? Standing before her was the antithesis of the man Gerard had always been, so sure of himself, so confident. She could not believe he was opening up to her like this, although most of her wished he hadn't. What the hell should she do? Clumsily, she reached forward and took his hand. It was clammy, and shaking. 'I really appreciate the fact that you've talked to me so honestly,' she said. 'I still think you've been a bloody idiot, and I think you have to talk to each other. You need help, Gerard. You've got to talk to someone. Maybe a doctor?'

Gerard shook his head. 'I can't. I have to sort this out myself. I've reached the point of no return with the business but I have to save my marriage. Losing Laure is unthinkable. Do you think she will ever forgive me? Without her, I haven't got anything. I could not go on. I'm not joking.' His voice rattled with despair. 'That would be it.'

Cassie felt physically sick. The relationships of her closest friends seemed to be twisting and turning into powerful knots, and there was nothing she could do to prevent it happening, or protect any of them. It was too great a responsibility. How could she attempt to untangle any of this? It was all too, too much.

'Maybe you should go away,' she said, a thought striking her. It wasn't very coherent, but it was all she had to offer.

175

'What?'

'Sell up. Leave the house, and move right away. You can put the children into different schools, and start again. You could work for someone else. God, Gerard, you can't just give up, and I know Laure wouldn't want to lose you.' Not quite so sure about that one, she thought. But it was what he wanted to hear.

'But moving away is defeat,' he said. 'That's giving up.'

'That's common sense,' she said. She would miss Laure terribly, but she could see quite clearly, in that instant, that they had to go. They had to make a fresh start. Laure was far too vulnerable at the moment. Factor in Tom . . . and, well, it was a disaster waiting to explode, from which no-one would escape unhurt or damaged. Not least the children.

'I can see you're right,' Gerard said, the beginning of a smile on his face. 'I'll talk to Laure,' he said. 'You're pretty clever, you know.' Cassie pulled a face.

'Oh no, I'm not,' she said. If I'd been clever, she thought, I would have seen this coming. He stepped forward, and put his arms around her. He smelled strongly of aftershave, wine and sweat.

She let herself be hugged, but part of her recoiled. I don't want you to touch me, she thought. Despite everything you have said, I do not know if I trust you. God, she thought. I can see every side of this and I do not know who is right. Least of all me.

'Thanks,' he said. 'Please don't tell Nat or the others, will you?'

'Of course not.' She smiled what she hoped was a reassuring smile at him. Now go, she prayed. Give me a moment to think. 'Thanks,' he said. 'You may have saved my life.'

Unlikely, she thought. Unlikely. Once he had gone, she quickly laid the table in the kitchen. She could have used the big old dining room, but it was freezing and too far away from the kitchen. There was an open fireplace, but it didn't heat the room properly, whereas the kitchen was beautifully warm with the Aga and the log-burning stove at the far end. Hector, despairing of being given the attention he was due, had curled himself into an angry ball in his basket, and was regarding her with one beady black eye. She lifted a loaf of crusty bread out of the bottom oven, and put it on a chopping board. Minutes later, she put her head around the door of the snug.

'Tilly, darling, can you tell everyone to come?'

'Anything else?' Tilly said in a martyred way, unwrapping herself from the duvet which covered herself, Arthur and Beth. It was way past Beth's bedtime, but Cassie didn't have the energy to chase her upstairs. She felt completely exhausted, longing for the haven of Nat and bed. And she had dinner to come. God. Nat could put Beth to bed, later. She was much better with him. It was all too much information, she thought, wearily, as she trudged back into the kitchen. Too much responsibility for one small person to bear.

After the first course Tom leant back in his chair. Cassie had noticed that throughout the meal his eyes had hardly left Laure, who was sitting at the far end of the table next to Nat and Sarah. 'Not too bad,' Tom said, wiping a piece of bread around his plate. 'Reasonably edible.'

'I thought it was lovely,' Laure said. Cassie smiled at her. In the soft candlelight she looked quite lovely again; the colour had come back into her face. Cassie, feeling hypersensitive, noticed that she deliberately avoided looking at Tom.

'How's the book going?' Carole said to Tom.

'It isn't,' Sarah said, sharply. Cassie heard Tom sigh.

'It's been months and months and so far he's only written a sentence.' She waited for everyone to laugh, but no-one did. She looked discomfited. Cassie wished that Sarah wouldn't use public occasions to belittle him. You're driving him away, she thought. Why hadn't she seen it before?

'Have you got a title yet?' Nat asked, pouring more wine.

'*Conflict of Interest*,' Tom said. 'I know, crap, isn't it?'

'I think it's good,' Laure said.

Cassie realized she was clenching her fingernails into her palm under the table. To her, the atmosphere was palpable with the sexual tension radiating from Tom and Laure. Could no-one else sense it?

'What is it about?' Nat said.

'God knows,' Sarah said.

Tom ignored her, and smiled at Nat. 'It's about my daring escapades in Sierra Leone when I was shot at and nearly arrested for being a diamond smuggler.'

'Wow, sounds great,' Carole said.

'So it's autobiographical?' Nat said. 'Or are you making it into a thriller, a novel?'

Tom nodded. 'It's based on my experiences, but I have invented a main character who is of course much more brave and handsome than me. It is a work of genius, if I say it myself, only at the moment it is more at the thinking stage. On paper, it may well be complete balls.'

Sarah laughed. 'If only you would write something, then we might be able to find out.'

Tom inclined his head towards her. 'As my wife intimates, unless I get on with it, it will remain in the pensive rather than the actual. Only writing is awful, really it is. The only good thing I can say about it is that it makes everything else enjoyable. I sing when I am unloading the dishwasher. I look forward very much to going to the loo.'

Cassie smiled helplessly to herself. I love you, she thought. You hopeless, deluded, reckless boy. You never stopped to think, did you? As a teenager, Tom was always the one who could be relied upon to take the plunge, who'd jump into an ice-cold river, who'd steal alcohol from his parents, who'd race the train on his motorbike. You will quite possibly destroy yourself, she thought, but you will always be my friend. 'It can't be that bad,' she said.

'Oh, it can, believe me. It takes me hours just to switch the bloody computer on. I wander round the table, clean the keys, resist the temptation to check my email, go and look in the fridge, switch the tumble-dryer on – you have no idea how many fascinating things there are to do around the house.'

'It can't be that hard,' Gerard said. 'Try running a business.'

'It's the fear of failure,' Tom said. His hair had fallen over one eye and he pushed it back, in a frustrated, angry gesture. 'In business, you aren't faced with the reality of your own inadequacy every second, in quite such a brutal way.'

'Oh, believe me, you are,' Gerard said. 'And at least no-one else depends on your inadequacy, as a writer.'

'What about his family?' Sarah said, sharply. They all turned to look at her.

'We depend on him. We care if he's a success,' she said.

Perhaps she's going to be kind, Cassie thought.

'It would make a fantastic change if he'd achieve anything.'

Oh no she isn't, Cassie thought.

Sarah continued, 'Look, darling, I do appreciate how tough it is for you to actually start and finish something for once in your life, but this is a golden opportunity and I have a horrible feeling that you're going to blow it. Again.'

An uncomfortable silence settled on the table, and Laure and Cassie exchanged embarrassed glances. Tom sat with his head down, his lips pursed, nodding as if he agreed. Then he lifted his head and looked directly at Sarah. Cassie saw there was no emotion in his gaze, no love, as if he was looking at a complete stranger.

'Thank you for pointing out what a completely useless prick I am,' Tom said, calmly. Then he laughed.

'Did you see that article in the newspaper?' Cassie said, quickly. 'They're planning to open theatres on a Sunday.'

'What a good idea,' Sarah said. 'It's *so* annoying that you can't see a play on the one free day I have a week.'

'I think it's awful,' Cassie said, realizing she had probably had too much wine, in desperation. At least it looked as if the conversation was moving away from Tom. 'It's as if God's getting lost.'

'Well, God is lost, isn't he?' Gerard said. His lips seemed out of synch with his words, and Cassie realized he was very drunk. 'You're the only person I know who goes to church. And whose fault is that? Religion these days is so bland no-one takes any notice. Last time I went to church the sermon was so dull I fell asleep. The church isn't saying anything that anyone wants to hear. They are just preaching the same old stories.' His hand moved to lift his glass, and he knocked it forward. There was no wine left in it, and Laure reached over with a practised movement to stand it upright.

'That's why no-one has any morals any more,' Carole said. 'If there isn't any exterior direction to people's lives, any authority, then of course people

180

will make up their own rules and indulge their basest instincts.'

'No prizes for guessing who she means,' Tom muttered to Cassie, shooting her a glance of complicity. Their eyes met, and Tom thought, She knows. He had a cold feeling in the pit of his stomach. He had wanted to tell her in his own time, in his own words, to get her on his side. He wanted Cassie, his dearest friend, to understand how this was both right and possible. She was the one person who could influence Laure.

Sarah perked up, sensing a possible feature. 'It's true,' she said. 'That's why so many people are turning to New Age remedies and yoga and all these retreats where you eat one hard rind of cheese and hit yourself with twigs. It's a search for a cause, a belief, to fill the gap left by religion.'

'But Christians are so boring,' Tom said, flippantly.

'I'm a Christian,' Cassie pointed out. 'Am I boring?'

'Sometimes,' Tom said. 'I can't bear all that happy clappy business, as if they have no brain. Fundamental Christians aren't happy, they're lobotomized.'

'But if you take away all the rules,' Carole persisted, 'then how do you live life by a moral code? I mean, we all got married in church, didn't we?' They all nodded. 'And we all made the vow to remain together as long as we both shall live?' More nodding. 'But how many of us will?' She glared around the table. 'Mike buggered off without any thought about the vows he had made before God. It's just become a nice thing to do, like having your child christened. No-one takes any notice of the actual words you say, they're irrelevant. I mean, I'm a godparent and I haven't seen my godchild for ten years. All it means is remembering to send her a present at Christmas and birthdays, and that's my duty done.'

'I think that is a very shallow view of the world,' Cassie said. 'And rather cynical of you.'

'Well, I would be cynical, wouldn't I?' Carole said, reaching for a piece of celery. 'I placed my entire security and future in what turned out to have been a long and cruel hoax.'

'You can't get rid of the church service though, can you? Because that would be like giving up and admitting that marriage is a temporary state that can be joined and broken at will,' Cassie replied.

'But it can, can't it?' Carole said. 'Maybe it should be stressed that it isn't likely to last for life. As long as you both shall live – or until one of you gets bored and fancies someone else. You should be able to buy a marriage, and then sell it when it's broken. Then you go for an upgrade or a better model and nobody beats themselves up about it or thinks they have failed "in the sight of God".'

'I think you're wrong,' Nat said. They all turned to look at him. 'I think that people take marriage just as seriously as they ever did. No-one goes into it lightly, and no-one breaks up a marriage lightly. It's just that the pressure from society has lifted.'

'But surely lifting the stigma of divorce means that it is easier to do, because no-one is going to point at you in the street any more, are they?' Cassie said. 'You're no longer some kind of social outcast. You're rapidly becoming the norm. Marriage has become too much of a commodity.' Listen carefully, Tom, she thought. You have to think long and hard about this.

'Perhaps that's a good thing,' Nat said. 'My mother and father would have killed each other if they'd stayed together. I was glad they split. By the law of averages, it can't work for everyone.'

'But you're not close to either of them, now,' Cassie

said. 'They lost you, in a way, when they lost each other.'

'That's because I don't like them,' he said.

'My PA who's in her early thirties says that nobody is prepared to commit themselves to a long-term relationship any more,' Sarah said. 'And marriage, it has to be said, is a leap of faith.' Tom was looking at her closely.

'So you think that if you don't do it – make that leap of faith – in your twenties, then by the time you are in your thirties and established in a career you are simply too intelligent and choosy to make the decision to even attempt to commit yourself to one person for the rest of your life?' he said.

Sarah thought for a moment. 'I suppose so, yes. It's quite possible that the only way to stay married is to bury your head in the sand and ignore opportunities which might actually make you much happier and lead to a more fulfilling life. You don't *have* to stay married, and as Nat says, there's no longer the social pressure.'

'You just have to believe.' Laure, who had said nothing so far, spoke with quiet intensity.

'What?' Tom said, leaning forward. 'What do you have to believe?'

'You have to believe that you have made the right decision because the moment you start questioning it then there can be no way back. Maybe blind faith is the only way to keep a marriage intact. Having said that, my parents should have separated when I was a child, because they were never happy and it ruined my childhood.' Tom hung on every word. Laure shrugged. 'I don't know if life would have been better with them living apart, but it certainly would have saved me from all those nights listening to them shouting and saying hateful things to each other.'

'I wonder what hope there is for any of us,' Cassie said.

'You'll be all right,' Tom said, grinning, trying to lighten the atmosphere. 'I mean, who would ever want Nat? I think you're stuck with him.'

'Quite right,' Nat said. 'Cassie was the only one who would have me.'

'Gee, thanks,' she said.

'Whereas Cassie was fighting them off with a stick,' Tom added, smiling at her.

Cassie drew herself up to her full five foot three. 'I will have you know I could have had anyone in this village. Nat was very lucky indeed.'

'Well, Tom, you got lucky with me,' Sarah said. Tom shot her a look which made Cassie's stomach churn. Don't go there, Tom, she thought. Please, please don't go there. Not now. You are way too drunk. 'Just think where you could have ended up,' Sarah added.

'She's right,' Tom said, refilling his glass. 'I got *so* lucky.' He took a long drink of wine. You will regret this, Cassie thought. Please shut up. Instantly.

'It's true!' Sarah laughed, bitterly. 'You were drinking half a bottle of whisky a day and smoking cannabis every night. And you were about to be fired.'

'I was quite a fascinating character,' Tom said, confidingly, to Carole.

'No, you weren't. You were a basket case.'

'And I just go on being hopeless,' he said. 'Until I make a decision.'

'What do you mean?' Sarah looked at him, shocked. 'What decision?'

'I think he does a brilliant job with the children,' Laure said, quickly. She had drunk a lot less than everyone else and Cassie looked at her gratefully. Not tonight, she thought. Let's not blow it open tonight. Thank goodness someone still had their wits about them. 'Gerard would never have been able to stay at home with our children. It would have driven him mad, especially when they were little.'

'True,' Gerard said. 'Boring as hell.'

'But women find it boring too, sometimes,' Cassie said. 'We just get on with it because we think it is our responsibility and we feel guilty even if we are working. It's still our primary role.'

'So where does that leave me?' Sarah said. 'Am I a really bad mother for spending so much time at work? Can you be a good absent mother, or are the two a contradiction in terms?'

Cassie groaned inwardly – it had been the wrong subject to bring up. 'No,' she said quickly. 'Because you and Tom have found a way of making parenting work, haven't you?'

'Have we?' Sarah said. Her meaning was clear.

'Cheese?' Cassie said.

'So you don't think our arrangement works all that well?' Tom said, calmly. 'In what way?'

An awful hush had fallen on the table, and Cassie noticed that Carole's face had positively lightened up at the whiff of marital strife. 'What she means', Cassie said, aware that she was digging an even larger hole, 'is that equality, or . . .'

'Equal amounts of work would be good,' Sarah said, nodding. 'It's quite a lot of pressure to be solely financially responsible for a family of three children on my own, you know.'

'It must be,' Cassie said, shooting a glance at Tom, who looked furious. 'I'll make some coffee,' she said, getting up from the table. 'Does everyone want some?'

'I'll get the brandy,' Nat said. 'Gerard? Tom?'

'Yes, please,' Tom said.

'Sarah, do you want some Cointreau?'

'Thanks, darling. Thank God we can walk home.'

185

'So in what way, exactly,' Tom said, slowly, 'do you feel that our situation does not work to your advantage?'

'To my advantage?' Sarah laughed bitterly. 'Er – hello, Tom, I'm the one who has to get up at the crack of dawn and get the train into London and deal with all the office politics and worry about paying all the bills while you ride with Cassie and have coffee with your friends. And go to the pub,' she added.

'And I do not look after the children? You chose to do that job. If you ask me, you should have left years ago and done something else. You love it, that's why you do it. You couldn't bear to be at home with the kids because there would be no-one to pat you on the back and tell you how wonderful you are all the time.'

'What!' Sarah exploded. 'How can you say that when I'm doing this for my children? Not for me.'

'I think', Cassie said, handing round the cups and saucers, 'we have kind of exhausted this. Look, Tom does a great job with the kids and you have a job you love and are doing fantastically well.'

'I don't love it,' Sarah said. 'A lot of the time it is a pile of crap and I would love to have the freedom to do less and get away from the constant pressure. But I don't.'

'Generations of men have been in the same boat,' Gerard pointed out.

'Yes, but they don't have to be a mummy as well,' Sarah said.

'Not that you do that awfully well, do you?' Tom said. Cassie stared at him in horror. Did he have some kind of death wish?

'What the hell do you mean?'

'I mean that you could spend a lot more time with the children than you do. You make excuses not to be

186

with them,' Tom said calmly. Sarah slammed her glass down on the table. She leant forward and spat the words out.

'You are an absolute bastard. How dare you say that in front of our friends when I have to support you every day of your life? Your novel! It will never get written because you have not accomplished one single thing, one fucking thing, in your spoilt, lazy little life. Your problem is that you cannot take on any responsibility whatsoever and you belittle anyone else who does. You have never, ever grown up and I am sick to death of being married to a child.' Turning, she snatched up her tweed jacket from the back of her chair, and walked swiftly towards the door. The door slammed, and there was silence in the room. Nat reappeared, holding bottles of brandy and Cointreau.

'Liqueur, anyone?' He looked around the table owlishly and Cassie realized that, unusually, he was quite drunk too. 'Where's Sarah gone?'

'Bit of a row,' Cassie said.

'That was a remarkably stupid thing to say,' Laure said to Tom. 'And really hurtful.'

'So it's fine for her to call me a lazy bastard, but not fine for me to retaliate? Very equal, I must say. I thought you would support me, but obviously I am mistaken. I better go.'

'Yes, go after her,' Cassie agreed. God, did she want this to end. The thing was, Sarah did have a point. Tom was a child.

An hour later Cassie wearily gathered the glasses up off the table, and wiped a cloth over it. It was two before they had been able to persuade Gerard, who was on his fourth glass of brandy, to leave. Laure was sitting on the edge of her seat, sober, brittle and desperate to go home. Tom had disappeared just minutes after Sarah. Laure refused even to look up when he left the table. Cassie's head ached.

'Well, that went well, didn't it?' Nat said. Cassie laughed. 'Are all our friends completely mad?' he continued, as he lifted the bin bag full of bottles out of the back door. 'Ow. My head hurts already.'

'It appears so. Oh God, I'm sure it was all my fault. I started the conversation, and look where it ended up.'

Nat put the bag down and put his arms around her. 'It wasn't your fault. Stop thinking everything revolves around you. You cannot sort out other people's lives. If you ask me, that has been coming for a long time. Sarah does have a point, Tom does do bugger all and he does spend a lot of time in the pub.'

'That isn't fair. He looks after the children brilliantly.'

'I am not', Nat said, gently, 'going to argue with you now. I think we are all argued out, don't you? Bed. It will all seem quite ridiculous and unimportant in the morning.'

Chapter Thirteen

Sarah

Sarah woke with a horrible dry taste in her mouth. She ran her tongue around her teeth, which felt furry. Her eyes seemed to be glued together, and she realized that she had neither taken off her make-up nor removed her contact lenses. Oh joy. She stretched out one hand, and encountered a warm body. Tom. So he had come home, after all. She raised her head slightly, wincing at the sunlight streaming through the gap in the curtains. But it wasn't Tom. It was Daisy, her huge blue eyes regarding her with an unblinking stare.

'Where's Daddy?'

'He must be here somewhere,' Sarah said, lifting her head and groaning. Why had she drunk so much? And, oh God, the storming out and all that bloody rubbish Tom had spouted about her in front of everyone. He was such a sod. He was really going to pay for this.

'Cuddle,' Daisy said, snuggling up to her.

'In a minute, darling. I need a drink of water.' Groggily, she fumbled by the bed but there was no glass. Her eye caught the alarm clock. Oh Lord, it was ten o'clock. It was amazing Daisy had stayed in bed so long. Where the hell was Tom? She sat up in bed and clutched her hair. Her eyesight was fuzzy, it was like looking at things underwater. She blinked several times, but her vision did not clear. 'Where's Mickey and Lucy?' she said.

'Watching TV,' Daisy said. 'I wanted to watch my programme but they said it was too babyish.' A big tear trickled down her cheek. 'I came to tell you but you wouldn't wake up and I looked and I looked and I couldn't find Daddy. I want him.'

'Don't worry, darling,' Sarah said. 'He won't be far away.'

She slid out of bed, wrapping her dressing gown around her. In the bathroom, she peered into the mirror. She looked awful. She stuck out her tongue. It was yellow. She rinsed her mouth out with water and spat into the sink. Her mascara had run down her face, making her look like a panda, and her hair, which had been very expensively cut and coloured on Friday in a luxuriously long – unusually so – lunch break, was standing on end. She felt utterly jaded, and furious with Tom. Pushing her feet into fluffy mules, she headed down the stairs. In the kitchen there was cereal all over the table, and a patch of spilt milk on the floor. There was also – God! – a hen in the kitchen, crapping on the floor and pecking at the milk. 'Mickey!' she screamed. 'What is this doing in here?' Mickey wandered through in the tracksuit bottoms he always slept in.

'Dunno,' he said, grinning. 'Daisy must have brought it in. Where's Dad?'

'I do not know,' Sarah said, grimly, switching on the kettle. 'Has Daisy had any breakfast?'

'I guess she did this,' Mickey said, gesturing at the mess. 'I haven't given her anything.' Muttering, Sarah went back upstairs. Daisy was sitting at her dressing table, thoughtfully outlining her lips with Sarah's Chanel lipstick.

'No!' she shouted. 'How dare you! That's mine!' Daisy, shocked, dropped it on the floor.

'Everywhere is such a mess,' Sarah said. 'Go and get your clothes.' Daisy looked at her hesitantly. 'Daddy does it,' she said. 'He puts them out for me but there's nothing there.'

'Bugger and blast,' Sarah stormed, heading for Daisy's room. Daisy and Tom had begun a big mural on her bedroom wall, of flowers and trees. 'Look at the picture,' Daisy said. 'We did it this week.'

'Later,' Sarah said, rooting about in her drawers. Daisy didn't seem to have any clean knickers, and a couple of the T-shirts that had been put back in were distinctly grubby. She held them out. 'Look at this! It's filthy.' She would have to do a wash. She looked around Daisy's room. It was urgently in need of a spring clean – her toy box was overflowing and every- thing in her drawers needed to be refolded. If only she had the time.

Daisy put her arms around Sarah's legs. 'I love you,' she said.

'And I love you too,' Sarah replied, absently. Where could Tom have gone? He clearly wasn't in the house. He must have stayed at Cassie's. After dressing Daisy she headed downstairs, picking up the phone from the hall table as she went. Tucking it under one ear as she poured out a bowl of cereal and heated some milk, after five or six rings she heard Cassie's answerphone click in. Damn. She was starting to leave a message when Cassie picked up.

'Hello? Sorry, I am here, stop it, you stupid machine. Just ignore it. Carry on. Hello?'

'It's me, Sarah.'

'Oh.' Cassie's voice was guarded. 'How are you?'

'Fine. Well, not fine really, I'm still livid with Tom. Did he stay with you?'

Cassie's voice registered complete surprise. 'No. He left just five minutes after you. He was going home.'

'Oh, Christ. Hang on, let me see if his car's here.' She carried the phone to the window. 'No, it isn't. He must have gone off somewhere, the silly sod.'

'But he had far too much to drink! God, I wonder where he is. Does he have his mobile on him?'

Sarah seethed quietly. Cassie seemed far more worried about Tom than she was about her, and she was the injured party. 'I have no idea,' she said, coldly. 'And I hope he spent a very uncomfortable night in the car. Look, can I come round for a chat?'

Cassie groaned inwardly. She desperately wanted to get on Fred and go for a good gallop to clear her head, which felt like it was being slowly crushed by big metal pincers. And she had a million and one things to do in the house.

'No, it's fine,' she found herself saying. 'It's a tip here, but that's nothing new.'

'I'll see you in a bit,' Sarah said, putting down the phone.

She was shouting at Mickey and Lucy to do something about the appalling state of the kitchen when there was a sickening crash. 'Jesus, what now?' she said, and ran upstairs. Daisy had been practising jumping on her bed, and had missed the side, crashing down onto the floor. She was sitting holding her head and howling. There was already a bump the size of an egg appearing.

Peace, Sarah thought. All I want is peace.

'Daddy!' Daisy howled. 'I want Daddy!'

'Let's go and see Cassie,' Sarah said. 'Beth will be there. You can play with her.'

Daisy stopped sobbing for a moment. 'And Tilly?'

'Tilly too. You can go and look after Dougal.'

Daisy brightened immediately. 'Can I ride him?'

'Not today. Come on, let's get your coat.' She picked her up, and thought how much heavier she was getting. On the way out she put her head around the living-room door. 'Don't you two have homework?'

'Weekend, Mother,' Mickey said, without looking up. 'Chill.'

Cassie opened the front door of the manor looking as if she had been pulled through a hedge backwards. She was wearing a horrible old holey jumper and jodhpurs which were frankly far too tight for her and showed her knicker line. As she turned to walk down the corridor to the kitchen, Sarah thought that if she looked like that from the back, she would never, ever wear anything so revealing. Didn't she exercise? Hadn't she heard of the Atkins diet?

'Toast?' Cassie said. Apparently not.

'No, thank you. So has he turned up yet?'

Sarah sat down at the kitchen table and shifted Daisy uncomfortably from one knee to the other. 'Can you get down, darling, you're squashing me. Go and find Beth.'

'She's at the stables. Is she OK to go there on her own?' Cassie asked.

'Tilly's there, isn't she?'

'I think so,' Cassie said, looking out of the window.

'She'll be fine. Just don't stand in any mud,' Sarah said firmly to Daisy, who was already running to the door.

'Hang on, darling,' Cassie said. She bent down and gave her a piece of toast. 'Here's a carrot for Dougal too. Remember to keep your hand flat.' Daisy nodded solemnly, sucking on the toast. Cassie opened the back door for her and watched her trot down to the stables. 'Tilly!' she bellowed over the half-door. 'Daisy's here. Keep an eye out for her, will you?' Tilly appeared over Shadow's stable door, a body brush in her hand. She waved to show she'd heard. Beth wandered across the

193

yard, dragging a towel behind her. Cassie thought about asking her what she was doing but decided she didn't have the energy. Everything felt like far too much effort this morning. Getting dressed had taken her half an hour, because she kept putting things on the wrong way round, and she actually fell over putting on her socks.

'Where's Nat?'

'Still asleep,' Cassie said. 'It's not like him to drink that much. He went out like a light.'

'I felt like an alien this morning.'

'Me, too. Who babysat?'

'Jo from the village,' Sarah said. 'I have no clear recollection of paying her or her leaving the house, which is pretty bad.'

'I can't believe Tom didn't turn up. Hang on. Let's try his mobile.' Cassie lifted up the Roverphone and dialled his number. It rang and rang, until his answer service picked up. 'Nope,' she said. 'He's not there, wherever he might be. That's the trouble with mobiles, you could be anywhere. Am I wittering?'

'Yes. I could fucking boil him in oil for last night,' Sarah said. 'I cannot believe he had the gall to say that I am a bad mother.'

'You did say he was practically an alcoholic,' Cassie pointed out, taking the kettle off the hotplate and wincing when it banged shut.

'He's getting more and more useless.'

'But what about the children? He does look after them pretty well.'

'With this new promotion I can just about afford a nanny,' Sarah said. 'Daisy's too dependent on him, anyway.'

'He is her father.'

'It's as if she hardly needs me,' Sarah said. 'She cried for him this morning.'

Cassie said nothing, and changed tack.

'You haven't told me about this new job. What will it mean?'

Sarah brightened and ran her fingers through her hair. 'It means I have control of all of the features department as well as the women's pages. It's a hell of a lot more responsibility but they are giving me more money and they've said I can have a car.'

'Brilliant,' Cassie said, trying to be enthusiastic. 'Won't you have to work harder, though? And you already work such long hours.'

'We should move,' Sarah said. 'It's only Tom that wants to stay here. The commute is really getting me down, and there are much better schools in London, I'm sure the children would benefit.'

'But this is Tom's home,' Cassie said.

'He's got more to think about than that,' Sarah said, sharply. 'He can't have everything all his own way. He has to think about me for a change. I know all his friends live around here and he's carved out this lovely little life for himself, but he has to stop being selfish. We depend on my job, and all the travelling is really wearing me out. I hate the country,' she said, staring moodily out of the window. 'It's so dirty. I cannot understand what pleasure you all seem to get from trudging around in mud. You can't buy anything here, there's no social life to speak of and I think it's a really bad environment for Tom. If he was in a city he could network, make proper contacts and get his freelance career established.'

He would hate that, Cassie thought. Making Tom live in a city would be like harnessing a peacock. 'It has to be a compromise, though, doesn't it?' she said, putting a mug of hot coffee down in front of Sarah.

'Is that decaff?'

'Yes,' she lied.

'I think I have compromised enough. We've lived here for five years, and I spend between three to four hours a day commuting. You can see how awful that must be.'

'Yes,' Cassie said. 'But the children love it here too.'

'They'd adapt.' Sarah drummed a long red fingernail on the table, then thoughtfully scratched at a bit of encrusted cereal. 'Do you have a cleaner?'

'No,' Cassie said.

'Good job,' Sarah said, 'because I'd sack her. What was the matter with Laure last night? She was very quiet.'

'Nothing that I know of,' Cassie said, carefully. 'She didn't say anything to me.'

'She looked dreadful. Gerard was knocking back the wine like there was no tomorrow, wasn't he?'

'So were you,' Cassie said, without thinking.

'So you think I was drunk?' Sarah said, crossly. 'And you think I was too hard on Tom? You don't understand, Cassie. He has to have someone to put a rocket under him or nothing will happen. I do think he has talent, really I do, and I think it is such a waste that he won't get on with things.'

'I do think you could be more supportive,' Cassie said, bravely.

Sarah looked at her malevolently. 'Really?' she said, slowly, raising one plucked eyebrow.

Cassie swallowed hard. 'Yes. He doesn't have confidence, Tom, surely you know that? His mother always told him that he was second best to Henry so he grew up feeling that he was some kind of failure, which he isn't. You're so strong, Sarah. Sometimes I think that you overpower him.'

'He doesn't need support,' Sarah said. 'What he needs is a kick up the arse.' She sighed. 'I know that I do nag him sometimes. But can't you see that it is hard

196

for me, too? I feel like I'm the one carrying all the pressure, and there's a part of me that really, really resents it. We're brought up to be big strong girls and I have to be tough in my world. I have to be like a man, think like a man. Then when I come home Tom seems to expect me to change into this girly, feminine little thing that he can look after. He knows that isn't part of the deal. He has to let me be in charge, or the relationship doesn't work. You can't back off from the responsibility of being a man but then still expect your wife to be the little woman.'

'I don't think he does want that,' Cassie said. 'I think he just wants to feel that he's appreciated. Needed. I suppose we all do.'

Sarah took a sip of the hot coffee. 'But I would appreciate him so much more if he earned my respect. I know he looks after the house and the kids, but he doesn't do it as well or as efficiently as I would. And it isn't very sexy, is it, having a man who spends his time washing up and looking after small children?'

'I think it's admirable,' Cassie said. 'And the children are really happy.'

'They'd be as happy with a nanny.'

'No,' she said. 'I don't think they would. I think they would be miserable – Daisy would, anyway. She adores Tom.'

'Too much. It's a funny world, isn't it? I fought so hard to get where I am, but there are times when I wonder if the sacrifice I've made has been worth it.' She looked at Cassie to tell her that yes, of course it had been. Cassie said nothing.

'I went back to work when Daisy was five weeks old,' Sarah said. 'There are times when I feel I hardly know her. Men must have felt like that for generations, mustn't they? And yet now women are being crucified for taking on male roles, and are being vilified as bad

197

mothers. I don't want Tom to be like me, we couldn't both work like this, but I can't bear the fact that he doesn't do anything. When people ask me in the office, I always say that he is writing a novel, and he's sold it to a publisher. Complete rubbish, obviously, but I somehow feel that I need to lie to myself to respect him. Sexuality is about respect, don't you think?' Cassie nodded. She felt rather sick. She might actually throw up. She swallowed, and tried to concentrate on what Sarah was saying.

'If Tom was really successful and powerful, like Nat or Gerard, then I would find him much more sexy. Men in suits are very sexy, aren't they? Instead I come home to find him slopping around in a horrible old pair of trousers, like a tramp. Just looking at him makes me angry.'

At that moment the kitchen door opened, and Nat wandered in. He was wearing just a pair of pull-on sailing trousers. Sarah gasped involuntarily. God, he was in great shape, muscular and still tanned from last summer. He ran his hand through his mussed hair, and blinked at Cassie. 'Hello, gorgeous,' he said. 'Have you thrown up?' He bent over the table and nuzzled her neck. 'Come back to bed and let me shag you sense-less. It's the best thing for a hangover.' Cassie made a furious gesture to look behind him. 'What?' He stood up. 'Sarah. Ah. Hi. Bit of a late start this morning, might just need some water, I think.' Cassie had to turn away she was laughing so much, and Nat was bright red with embarrassment.

'Sorry,' Cassie said to Sarah, who was hastily examining her perfect nails. She saw Nat pause in the doorway, and make a hanging gesture from the door frame, pointing at Sarah's back. Cassie smiled brightly, ignoring him, and made a quick shooing movement with her hand.

'We have to track Tom down. He might be hurt,' she told Sarah.

'Let's hope so,' Sarah said. 'Do you think I am being unfair?'

'Do you love him?' Cassie said.

Sarah looked at her, shocked. 'Of course,' she said, automatically. 'I think so. God, I don't know. How do you know if you still love somebody when you've been married for thirteen years? They're just there, aren't they, like the washing machine? We did a feature recently about dynamic marriages, and really the answer seemed to be that if you still slept together, then your marriage was OK. Well, we do, and it's pretty good. OK, anyway. I think people set too much store by love. Marriage is a partnership, and you shouldn't expect too much from it.'

You are quite indifferent to him, Cassie thought, studying Sarah's face. It was more handsome than pretty, with her strong jaw and wide-set eyes. She wondered how much of Sarah's background had coloured her attitude to marriage. Sarah had confided in her that when she was growing up her mother had frequently told her that men were the enemy, they always let you down. In many ways, she was quite similar to Nat in that he too was the product of an embittered, overly adoring single mother. God, your parents did fuck you up, as the poem said. She was so lucky, Cassie thought, to have had two parents who loved each other. You could not buy that kind of security, and she knew it was one of the things Nat found so appealing about her. The circle of love of a complete family.

Both Nat and Sarah had put leagues between themselves and their upbringing, but the shadows never left. And Tom? Tom was always searching and had only, she realized, found real happiness in his relationship

199

with his children. So far. He clearly hadn't found it with Sarah. Cassie had thought, before last night, that they had achieved a balance in their relationship with which both were reasonably content. Nothing, it seemed, could have been further from the truth.

There was a loud bang on the window, and Cassie, who was standing by the dresser, saw Tom first. His hair was standing on end, and he looked dreadful. Sarah had her back to the window, and he saw her before she saw him. He grimaced comically, in horror, at Cassie. She snorted, and then turned it into a cough. He stopped just as Sarah turned to see him. 'He would come here,' she said resignedly. 'You ought to untie him from your apron strings, Cassie. He's a big boy now.'

'I better let him in,' Cassie said, sidling to the door. God, Sarah could be a cow. Cassie knew she did have a point about Tom, but did she have to be quite so cutting?

She threw open the front door and there he stood, his neatly pressed chinos crumpled, his lovely new shirt torn. There was a deep scratch across his cheek. 'What on earth happened to you?' she said, keeping her voice low.

'I was going to follow her, but then I thought, sod it. I wasn't going to apologize. And in that pissed way that you do I decided to go for a long walk. I had a lot to think about. I set off down the bridle path – I realize now it wasn't the brightest idea I have ever had – and I got a bit stuck in a hedge.' Cassie laughed, despite how cross she was feeling with him. 'Then I realized I didn't have my front-door keys and I could not face trying to wake Sarah up but I did have my spare car key so I went for a bit of a drive about. Then I fell asleep. Thank God no-one saw me, I would have been done for drinking and driving. I was totally out of it.'

'You certainly would. It was a criminally insane thing to do.'

'I feel rather criminally insane. What am I going to do, Cassie?' He ran his hands through his hair. 'I don't know – I don't know if I do love her any more. I can't find anything to love in her. And I'm so desperately . . .'

'Shush,' Cassie said, putting her finger to his lips. 'Do not tell me more. Right at this moment, I cannot cope with any more revelations. Come in and have a coffee, or a bath, or whatever. I'm being nice to you, but really I'm fucking furious with you.'

'I have to get home for the children,' he said. 'Daisy must be wondering where the hell I am.'

'She's here with Beth,' Cassie said. 'At the stables.'

At that moment Nat came down the stairs, more reasonably dressed in a big old gardening jumper. 'God, you too,' he said. 'It's like fucking Piccadilly Circus this morning. Did you all sleep here, or what?'

'Nice to see you too,' Tom said.

Cassie took hold of Nat's arm and drew him into the snug. 'Make Tom a coffee and talk to him,' she said, firmly. 'He's having a bit of a crisis and I think he wants to talk. We have to keep him separate from Sarah for a while.'

Nat looked about him wildly. 'I don't know what to say to him,' he hissed. 'What crisis? It's Sunday morning. This is my house, not the bloody Samaritans. What am I going to talk to him about? I'm not a woman. Blokes don't talk like that, and the pubs aren't even open. Can't you deal with it? Way too much drama. Look, just tell them to go, will you?'

'You are not being very supportive,' Cassie whispered furiously.

'Oh, fuck that. It's their problem, let them sort it out. I really am not going to get involved, and nor should you. You'll get sucked in and just make everything worse.'

'Thanks,' Cassie said.

'Do you fancy watching the Test Match?' Nat said to Tom, who was gazing out of the window in the long hallway overlooking the stables. Daisy, he saw, was sitting on Dougal's back while Beth groomed him.

'OK,' he said, and they wandered into the snug.

'What did he say?' Sarah asked her as she went back into the kitchen. 'Where is he?'

'Er – watching the cricket,' Cassie said.

'What!'

'With Nat,' Cassie added, apologetically.

'I am having an emotional breakdown and he is watching sport?'

'Yes,' Cassie said. 'But leave him – please. You still feel too strongly, you'll only have another row. Look, leave Daisy here. I'll talk to Tom. I'm sure this is only a temporary thing. You've got far too much going for you both to think about doing anything – permanent – haven't you?'

'It's damn close,' Sarah said, grimly. 'I don't think I can ever forgive him for what he said.'

'But what do you have to gain?' Cassie said. 'How would you cope and where would that leave Tom? What about the children? He might get custody,' she added, a trifle evilly.

'Rubbish. I'm the breadwinner. I could move us all and then he could do what he sodding well likes,' Sarah said. 'He could buy a mouldering country cottage and drink himself to death and write his crappy novel all on his own. Because no-one else would want him, that's for sure. He's hardly a catch, is he? If he lost me he would have nothing.'

'But he can be lovely,' Cassie said, helplessly. 'He has lots of good points.' Don't throw him away, she thought. You have no idea how close you are to losing him. Lord. She felt like she was trying to fight fires without any water, running from one outbreak to the other with only a damp tea towel.

'You don't have to live with him,' Sarah said. 'Trust me. He hasn't.'

Chapter Fourteen

Laure

'I don't care if you're busy, I have to see you.' Cassie made a face at the phone. She'd been trying to talk to Laure for two days now. After she'd finally managed to get rid of both Sarah and Tom, she'd walked round to the Rectory, her head still thumping. Both cars were there, but no-one would come to the door. She thought about peering in through the snug window, or going round to bang on the French doors into the kitchen, but she really did not want to face Gerard. By the gate, she sat down on the wall and buried her head in her hands. Maybe Nat was right. Maybe she should butt out, and leave them all to it. But then he didn't understand the depth of the chaos. Perhaps she should have told Nat the full extent of her fears, but she suspected he would still say it was none of their business. People inevitably did what they wanted to do, even if it was a crash course to hell.

Laure had hesitated before she picked up the phone. She thought it might be Cassie, and she owed her an explanation. But the thing was, she couldn't lie to Cassie. And she was still lying to herself.

On the kitchen table lay her mobile. Inside it was Tom's message. She would have to delete it from her inbox, Sophie played with her phone all the time and read her messages. It was very simple. It said, 'Leave him. I love you.'

The phone had bleeped that morning when she was driving home after taking Sophie to school. She had seen him across the car park, and knew he was staring at her, willing her to come over and talk to him. Even from that distance, she knew exactly what he was thinking. She had stopped the car, and stared at the message for a long time. Such simple words. Words that would tear up her life by the roots. There was such a gulf, such a huge gulf, she thought, between doing what you wanted to do and what you ought to do. Could feeling like this ever be wrong? Would denying these emotions, so powerful they filled every waking moment, twist up inside her like a noose and make her live the rest of her life in bitter regret?

She should have deleted the message immediately, but she didn't. She kept it as a present, a secret, to herself, just for a little while. She would not act upon it. Just knowing that he loved her was enough. It would have to be enough.

'What are you doing?' Cassie said, down the phone line.

'Nothing,' Laure replied, reaching forward for her mobile. She scrolled down until she came to his name, and then activated the message. She read it for one last time, and then she pressed Options. Using the arrow key, she went down, down, down until she found Erase. And it was gone.

'Come over now,' she said. 'I've got half an hour before I have to get Sophie.'

Cassie sat in Laure's immaculate kitchen, having taken off her wellingtons at the door. Victor, in honour of her arrival, had pulled himself stiffly out of his basket and his nose, grey-whiskered, rested on her knee. Her hand stroked his old head, and his eyes looked at her with love. They were old friends.

'So,' she said, as Laure moved about the kitchen making coffee in their expensive Gaggia machine. She had to raise her voice over the sound of the milk steamer. Laure carefully poured the hot frothing milk into two beautiful French coffee cups, and then moved to the sink to rinse out the jug. Taking a cloth, she wiped around the nozzle, and then rinsed the cloth under the mixer tap, squeezing it out and folding it into four before hanging it over the edge of the Belfast sink.

'Will you bleeding well sit down and talk to me,' Cassie said, impatiently. Laure turned to her. Her eyes were huge, and haunted. 'I don't know what to say,' she shrugged.

Cassie traced the colourful pattern on the cup with the tip of her finger. 'Start at the beginning,' she said.

'Please don't say that's a very good place to start,' Laure smiled.

'Why didn't I know?'

'Because I didn't either,' Laure said. 'It isn't just something that happens. It – grew – on both of us, I think. Neither of us sat down and thought, let's fall in love.'

'So it is love.'

'Goodness, Cassie, I don't know. I can't even decide what jumper to wear in the morning at the moment. How do I know if I am falling in love?'

'But this is Tom we're talking about. Tom, remember? Our friend? The hopeless one? The writer who never does any writing? The man who can frequently be seen propping up the bar in the Slug and Lettuce wearing a muddy old coat and discussing the merits of the combine harvester? This isn't some gorgeous Lothario who would sweep you off your feet or offer you a life of Beluga caviar, swathed in mink, is it?'

Laure laughed. 'But life's not like that, is it, Cassie? That isn't what's important. What is important is finding someone who actually loves you, not the thought of you, an ideal version of you that has absolutely nothing to do with the reality.'

'Is that how you feel about Gerard?'

Laure sat down at the table. 'Yes,' she said. 'There's something . . .' she paused, and picked her words very carefully. 'There's something not quite real about him. It's as if he is always playing a part, someone he feels he ought to be. And I'm part of that fantasy. I make the perfect home. I look good. I cook lovely meals, I can be trusted to perform well in public. I'm an asset, Cassie, just like his company used to be. Only I'm not an asset. Certainly not at the moment. I'm me, and not very perfect at all. And me has felt rather ignored in the past few years. Then there are the rows, the shouting, the fact that he feels he can be any way he likes with me – you have no idea what he is like behind closed doors, you really haven't. I have put up with far too much, but then it has always been so important to me to keep the family together.'

'I can see that,' Cassie said. 'But surely you can see this, you and Tom, has no future . . .'

'Why not?'

She thought for a moment. 'Because Gerard would probably kill you.'

'Don't be silly.'

Cassie looked at her sceptically. Laure put her hand down flat on the table. 'OK, he would be furious beyond belief. But it isn't going to come to that, Cassie. I'm not going to let it go that far. How stupid do you think I am? It was just that we were both miserable and there was a, I don't know, a tiny spark and that's all.

We're both grown-ups. We aren't going to jeopardize our lives. Tom knows that too.'

Cassie raised her eyebrows. 'Does he? The thing is, Sarah had a point about Tom being a bit of a child. He doesn't see the boundaries that other people live by, he never has. In a way, it's part of his charm, the little boy inside the man. He's quite impetuous, and very passionate underneath that lazy exterior. You're playing with fire, you know. He isn't going to give up and listen to reason.'

'Oh, I know,' Laure said. 'Believe me, I know.'

Chapter Fifteen

Laure

'Let me do the talking.' Gerard's mouth was set in a grim line as they drove up the long drive to Uplingham. Laure smoothed down the soft material of her skirt. She opened her mouth to disagree, but then thought better of it. Talking to Gerard about anything was impossible and she had no energy for an argument. It was the Thursday after the dinner party, and Gerard had had to take the morning off work.

After Saturday, they stepped warily around each other, and treated each other with careful politeness. Gerard didn't seem to know what to say to her, and she often caught him staring at her, intensely.

In the early hours after the dinner party, as soon as Gerard fell into a deep sleep, she had climbed out of bed, and, picking up her alarm clock, she tiptoed into the spare room. The neatly pressed sheets felt cold. She slid between them, and waited for sleep to claim her. Her shoulder ached slightly, and she pressed her hand to it. Had she been right to tell Cassie? She thought hard. No, she decided. She should not have done. It was not fair to Gerard. Once you said something like that about someone, it could not be unsaid, and, to Cassie, he would forever be the man who had hurt her. And it was an accident, she told herself, an accident which would not be repeated. The other issues were so much more important. She could see that his anger was not really directed at her, it was directed as much at himself, at his apparent failure to find a solution. How much had Cassie guessed? She was not stupid, and she knew them both so well. And if Laure talked to her openly about Tom, she made it real. As if it might be possible.

Laure lay between the cold sheets, and tried to look into the future. But the only thing she could see was Tom. She couldn't help but sketch the outline of a future with him. A future without rows, where they were two grown-ups in a relationship and no one person had to be dominant. A relationship of loving equals, without fear. And sex, she thought. God, yes, sex. I want to make love to him so much. To make love with someone who genuinely desires me, who is wild for me. The thought of Tom next to her, naked, muscular, strong, made her burn with longing, and shame. I am a mother, she thought. Not simply a woman. A mother. I have no right to these feelings.

In the darkness, she looked into the place where her love for Gerard had been. There was a jumble of emotions, none of them clearly defined. Pity, anger, resentment, understanding, and a sense of loss. Her feelings for him were so interwoven with the children. They loved him – well, Sophie loved him, she wasn't so sure about Nick. What was utterly unchangeable was the fact that he was their father. Look at Carole. She would never recover from her divorce, Laure could see that. It hadn't solved anything, it had made her life – well, pointless. It was if she was constantly regretting, mourning, what she had lost, or what had been taken from her. I suppose it is the feeling of failure, Laure thought. That you set off with such high hopes, and then you realize it is not going to be perfect and you go through the storms, and then you learn how to handle the storms and then you try to carry on, but sometimes it is simply not possible. And then you fail.

What did Cassie say? Travelling hopefully, that was how she described her and Nat's marriage, which was just about the best example Laure could conjure up. They made room for each other and they genuinely seemed to like each other. As friends. She saw the little looks they exchanged, the way they touched each other so often, not necessarily in a romantic or sexual way, but naturally, a way of drawing strength from each other. I want that, she thought, hugging the pillow to herself. I want that in my life. Why shouldn't I have it? All I want is to love and be loved. Is that really so very selfish?

The love she and Gerard had was, she realized, in danger of being corrupted, twisted into something which did not bring pleasure, but pain. They did not seem to make each other's lives better. They did not enhance each other, they detracted. And Sarah – she was so awful to Tom. When she had been putting him down it was all Laure could do not to shout, 'Stop! Can't you see what you are doing?' but of course she had said nothing, and watched Tom's face working with silent fury. No man could put up with that kind of onslaught and say nothing, but to tell Sarah she was a bad mother – that was going too far. It wasn't Sarah's fault she had to work so hard.

What a tangled web we weave, she said to herself. What was the rest of it? Oh yes – when first we practise to deceive. The trouble was that they were not free to choose. How could anyone justify that kind of selfishness? Yet, behind the rational thought was the intensity of the sexual longing. The sheer animal

211

passion she felt for Tom was like a tidal wave, sweeping everything that made sense in front of it like so much flotsam. But she could not act upon these feelings. It would bring such chaos. They were not animals. They had a choice. To do the right thing.

'Please don't cry,' Gerard said, as they climbed the stone steps to the entrance hall to Nick's school.

'Why would I?' Laure said.

'Just in case.'

A pleasant-looking secretary motioned them towards a sofa in the waiting room to the headmaster's study, and asked them if they would like some tea or coffee. Gerard sat on the edge of the sofa, cracking his knuckles and fidgeting. 'I wish I could smoke,' he said, staring out of the window at a rugby game taking place on the pitch beneath the window. It was a cold, windy afternoon, and the boys' shirts whipped around their bodies. Laure wondered if Nick was among them. He wasn't to be present at the meeting, but his form tutor had said they could see him afterwards.

Laure wondered why the school made Gerard so uncomfortable. He had always been like this, at prep school too – he hated school events, and made any excuse not to turn up at speech day, or concerts or plays. He always said he was too busy, but Laure thought it was more than that – the atmosphere made him nervous, insecure. Perhaps it was because it was such an alien environment to him, and yet he had been the driving force behind the decision to send them to private school in the first place.

'The head will see you now.' His secretary ushered them in, and the head, a tall, grey-haired man with the benevolent air of a bishop, smiled at them. He motioned for them to sit.

'Nick, I'm afraid,' he said, 'has been fighting. We have two problems at the moment. He is not trying as hard as he could in the classroom, and his grades have dropped quite alarmingly for a boy so close to GCSEs. And then, last week, quite unprovoked, he started a fight. The other boy was not badly hurt, but very shaken up.'

Laure saw Gerard clench his right fist with his left hand. Please do not embarrass me, she thought. Please. How long have I been making excuses for his boorish behaviour, Laure wondered.

'He isn't a violent boy, but something seems to have happened which has upset him.' He looked from Gerard to Laure. 'What we have to consider is whether he is happy here and should remain in the school.'

Laure's heart fell. They were going to expel him. What else could happen this week?

'He needs a firm hand,' Gerard said. 'His behaviour at home last holidays left a lot to be desired.'

'He isn't a bad boy,' the head said, quickly. 'All teenage boys seem to go through this phase – a kind of testing their strength, if you will. He is doing exceptionally well on the sports field, and he's very popular. What do you think we should do?'

'Aren't we paying you to come up with the answers?' Gerard said. His voice was barely civil.

'Not necessarily,' the head said. 'We feel it should be a joint decision, and we see the school acting in partnership with the parents. Is there anything that you feel we should know about?'

'No,' Gerard said, tersely. 'Nothing.'

'I see. Then perhaps we should approach this, how can I put it – creatively? I am not going to suspend Nick.' Laure realized she had been holding her breath, and it came out with a rush.

'No, in fact I am going to give him more responsibility. I think he should be put in charge of the mentoring of new boys in his house. Academically, he needs to realize that, at this stage in his career, he cannot coast. That needs to be a two-pronged attack.' He smiled at them. 'Nick can get a lot out of this school,' he said. 'I see him having a great future.'

'You see?' Laure said, walking out of the school, down the steps. 'They value him.'

'He wants our money,' Gerard said. 'He's not going to kick him out, is he? Not when we are spending so much.'

'What will we do?' Laure asked quietly. 'Couldn't we have told him that we might— that— apply for bursaries, or try to pay on a monthly basis?'

'No,' Gerard said, shortly. 'It's not so desperate. Yet.'

'Will he have to leave?' Laure asked.

'We'll see,' Gerard said.

They sat in Starbucks half an hour later with Nick, avoiding each other's eyes. Laure reached under the table to hold Nick's hand. He squeezed it briefly.

'Right,' Gerard said. 'Listen to me. This is your last chance. Unless you pull your finger out and start working, you will be out of that school faster than you can say knife. If I hear of any more fighting, or trouble of any kind, you will leave.'

'I should leave anyway,' Nick said, looking directly at his father. 'We can't afford it. I'm not stupid, you know.'

'That is not your decision!' Gerard shouted. Two women at the counter turned to stare at them. Gerard coughed. 'That is not your decision,' he said, lowering his voice. 'What goes on in my business is nothing to do with you. But we are pumping money into you and we want to see some return. All that means is that you get good grades. You keep your nose clean. You work hard and you try to do something to make us proud, for once.'

'For once?'

'Please, Nick,' Laure said, putting her hand on his arm.

'What about sport? Does that count for nothing? I'm in the first team in case you hadn't noticed.' His voice was full of suppressed fury. 'Not that you ever bother coming to see me play.'

'That means nothing,' Gerard said. 'What matters are academic results. You've been too cosseted and protected and you have had everything your own way. It's partly my fault, I have let it happen. You have this arrogant attitude that the world owes you a living, and when you are at home you don't even lift a finger to help.'

'That isn't true,' Laure said.

'Be quiet.'

'Don't tell Mum to be quiet.'

'I'll do what I damn well please,' Gerard said. 'Don't you dare answer me back.'

'Gerard,' Laure said, as soothingly as she could. 'This is not the place to have an argument.'

'You're letting him get away with it. Christ, listen to yourself. If you stopped defending him and treating him like a baby then maybe he would have more respect.'

'I do have respect,' Nick said, in a low voice. 'For Mum.'

Gerard stared at him. 'What is that supposed to mean?'

'Just what I said. I have respect for Mum.'

'And me?' Gerard ground out the words.

'Stop this!' Laure said, more loudly than she intended. 'This isn't getting us anywhere. We are not going to have a public row. Nick will promise to work harder and will never – never – repeat this awful fighting incident. You have to appreciate, Nick, that it isn't easy for us to keep you here. Why did you start the fight, anyway?'

Nick said nothing.

'Why?'

He looked at the floor, his cheeks flaming red. Then he looked up. 'Because one of the boys in the class above me said something about you, OK? Are you happy now?'

'What? What on earth did he say?' Gerard was staring at him, intently.

'Nothing,' Nick said. 'Forget it. He just said you were good-looking, and what he would like to . . .'

Laure was horrified. 'That's just teenage boys showing off,' she said, quickly. 'It doesn't mean anything.'

Nick looked at her as if he was going to say something else, and then thought better of it. He said mutinously, 'Then why not do it? Why not make me leave?'

'Because we want the best for you,' she said, simply.

Nick slumped back against the chair, and ran his hand through his hair. His nails, she saw, were bitten so short. What did he do, when he was away from her? She had a longing to take him home, to tuck him up in bed, to make him safe, to make him hers again. In sending him away, they had forced an independent life upon him. And when she saw him, she always thought, I want you back. Are we really doing the best for you?

'If you want to leave, that can be arranged,' Gerard said, taking out his mobile, which had bleeped with a message.

'I don't,' Nick said, shortly. 'Can I go back now?' He stared at his father insolently.

'Only when you have said you are sorry.'

'Sorry. Will that do?'

'Please, Nick, don't . . .'

'I wouldn't,' Gerard said, 'I really wouldn't. Come on. I have to go, that was an important call, I've got to get back to the office.'

On the way back to the car, Gerard strode ahead and Laure tucked her arm through Nick's. He looked down at her. 'Are you really OK, Mum?' he said.

'There are problems,' she said, slowly.

'Like what?'

'It's up to your father to tell you.'

'Him! He'd never give me a straight answer.'

'Don't.'

'Don't what?'

Laure realized she had been going to say, 'Don't hate him,' and stopped herself just in time. 'He's got a lot on his mind.'

'He's a bully.'

'Nick!'

'Well, he is. I hate the way he talks to you. You shouldn't take it. You should stand up for yourself. If you won't, I will. How dare he tell you to shut up? I nearly thumped him.'

'That wouldn't get us very far, would it? Stop it, he is your father.'

'That doesn't give him the right to jackboot around.'

'Please, Nick.' She stopped, and pulled him round to face her. 'I need your support. There is enough drama in our lives at the moment without you two going at it hammer and tongs. It is only two weeks until the Easter holidays, when we have a whole month together. I cannot bear the thought of you two being at each other's throats. You've got to find a way of getting along. Of surviving.'

'Tell him to stop being such a fucking Hitler then and get off my case,' Nick said.

'Don't swear.'

'Sorry. I'll try. It's just that he sets my teeth on edge. I can't do anything right. It's like he's always looking for excuses to jump on me.'

'Don't react,' Laure said.

'Yeah, right. Like that's easy.'

They walked for a moment in silence, and then Laure said, 'What else were you going to say? About why you started the fight? I need to understand,' she added gently. Nick stopped walking, and looked at her long and hard. 'They said,' and his words came out with a rush, 'they said you were shagging that bloke you came to watch the match with. Tom. That he was all over you.'

Laure felt the blood drain from her face. 'What? That is complete rubbish. Nick! You don't believe that, do you? What an appalling thought. You know Tom is just a friend.' Nick looked thoroughly miserable. He scuffed the pavement with the toe of his grubby training shoe.

'I know,' he said. 'It's just that when I'm away I don't know what to think, and with things so bad between you and Dad . . .'

'I would never put you in such an awful position,' Laure said, her heart a hard, cold stone within her. 'I promise. That's such a farcical idea.' She tried to laugh, but no sound came out.

'I know,' Nick said. 'You're not like that. That's why I told the guy to shut his mouth, why I hit him.'

Gerard was already sitting in the car when they reached it, and Laure climbed into the front, Nick in the back. As they drove to school, Laure reached out hesitantly to touch Gerard on the arm, but he shrugged her hand away. Nick saw what was happening, and gazed out of the window, despairingly. He had to prepare himself for whatever was coming. He could not afford to be vulnerable. He would never let himself love anyone as much as he had loved his parents, because when you love someone that much you could be hurt too deeply, and it was not worth the pain.

Chapter Sixteen

Cassie

'Why won't you let me come with you in the team, instead of Tom? Please, please, please? It isn't too late.'

Arthur wrapped his arms around Cassie's neck as she stood in front of the sink and she felt his beanpole, bony fame through the thin cotton of his moth-eaten dressing gown. On his feet were huge monster slippers, a present from Beth at Christmas. He ate constantly, but never seemed to put on any weight. He'd inherited Nat's frame, not her own, and, at eleven, he was already two inches taller than she was.

'Because I say so?'

'Not a good enough reason,' he said, letting go and moving over to the table, where he began eating cereal out of the packet. 'I am the best rider in this house.'

'No you're not,' Tilly said firmly. She was copying cartoons at the kitchen table on a drawing pad, her pink tongue slightly protruding from her mouth, her hair still twisted into the dreadlocks of sleep. 'Who wins the most at shows? Me.'

'Stop squabbling. My mind is made up. You'll get other chances.'

There was the sound of the back door being pushed

open and the scrape of the riding boots which were stacked up against it. Tom climbed over them.

'God, you look clean,' Cassie said.

'Don't sound so surprised. I can scrub up quite well,' he said, turning this way and that so they got a better view. He was wearing a white shirt and navy-coloured stock, with his hacking jacket over one arm. His jodhpurs were, for once, clean, and he'd even polished his black riding boots. Studying him objectively, she thought he probably looked better now than he had in his twenties, when he had been a bit of a hippy with long hair, and her brothers and their friends had treated him like a sad joke.

Lucy peeped out shyly from behind him, and Daisy ran into the kitchen, to climb up onto Tilly's knee. Tilly, who mostly ignored Beth, adored Daisy and liked to make her up and do her hair. Hector, who loathed unsolicited children in his kitchen, growled ominously, his black nose poking out from under a chair like a small crocodile.

'Shut up!' Cassie, Arthur, Tilly and Beth shouted at him simultaneously.

'You are a grumpy little sod, aren't you?' Tom said, walking in and reaching down to rub Hector's head. He growled again in a low, menacing way, and Beth bent down to smack him.

'Too many people in his kitchen,' Arthur explained. 'If Hector was a person he'd be an SS officer.'

'Thanks for coming early,' Cassie said, beginning to clear the piles of breakfast dishes from the table, ringed with hardening cereal, and wiping the surface of the table littered with toast crumbs. 'We are a trifle behind.'

'You can say that again,' Tilly said.

'I don't care,' Arthur said, loudly. 'Because I'm not allowed to go. Someone' – and he shot a furious glance at Tom, who smiled back at him apologetically – 'is stealing my horse. So although this may well be my one and only chance of winning the team chase I am not being allowed to take part because I am considered too young.'

'Ohmigod,' Cassie said. 'We have to go in –' she glanced at the kitchen clock, permanently set ten minutes fast to give her a modicum of a chance of not being late – 'in under an hour. Fuck.'

'Swearing,' Tilly said. 'That's a quid in the box.'

'Please get dressed. And you too, Arthur,' Cassie said. Tilly reluctantly put away her pad and got up from the table.

'Arthur, can you come and help us once you've got dressed?'

'Er – snowball's chance, and hell?' he said, and walked out of the kitchen, slamming the door. Cassie sighed. She knew it was hard for him not to be able to go. God, she really ought to get organized, she should have done much more organizing last night, but after half a bottle of wine she couldn't be bothered. Actually, possibly a whole bottle of wine. With Nat staying over in London, she had meant not to drink anything at all but once she'd got all the children off to bed there was the siren call from the fridge – I am a cold bottle of Sauvignon Blanc, I am delicious, and I will help you relax. Just the one, she thought, pulling the cork out, and she'd sat down thankfully at the kitchen table to read the day's newspapers. All was calm and peaceful. It was utter bliss.

She was so heartily sick of worrying about Tom and Laure. She had definite compassion fatigue, and had, for the first time in years, not rung Tom all week until she had to, to make the arrangements for today. Laure had promised her faithfully that she was not about to do anything rash, and that Gerard was being much more reasonable. She said that everything was fine. Yeah, right, Cassie thought. But she had to let Laure do things her way, and, of everyone involved, she trusted Laure to be the grown-up. She would not mediate or fret about a situation over which she had so little control.

She had read through the features and opinion columns, making a mental note to try to see one of the films recommended with Laure. Two glasses had slipped down very pleasantly. Then she moved on to a celebrity magazine, which she'd forgotten she'd picked up in the village shop. Almost without realizing it her arm had snaked out and poured herself another glass, as she sniggered about the clothes chosen by the soap actress to welcome the magazine into her mock-Tudor mansion. How did you get to be bright orange like that, she wondered. Then she scanned the society pages and thought gloomily how women of exactly her age seemed to be so much slimmer and had no bags under their eyes. She looked down at her spreading thighs and the roll of flesh over the waistband of her jeans. Tomorrow the diet began. No bread. No alcohol. It was so depressing. The only thing that kept her going at the moment seemed to be alcohol.

It was the weekend before Easter, and the start of the team-chasing season. Cassie had been doing it for years, and adored it. Teams of three or four riders hurtled over a cross-country course of big hedges, post and rails and through water. The winner was decided on the closest to what was called a 'bogey' time, or there was a timed section in the middle of the course. Tom had joined her team several times when they had a gap, and this weekend one of their usual riders had dropped out because they had a lame horse and Tom had offered to step into the breach. Arthur had immediately piped up that he was definitely old enough now, but Cassie said it was too fast and furious.

It took them several minutes to load the overexcited horses, who spun around in the yard, knowing they were going to the horse equivalent of a party. Fred stood on Cassie's foot, and she hopped about the yard, swearing. There would be something vital she had forgotten, there always was. There was just so much to remember, taking a horse to an event. It was like trying to pack for a toddler on holiday.

The team chase was being held on the land of the Lockett family, who were friends of both Tom's parents and her mother. The two-mile course followed undulating parkland in front of a beautiful Georgian mansion, and the going was good – they'd walked the course the day before, and it was spongy but not too wet. They had a good draw, near the beginning, so the ground would not be too churned up in front of the fences, which could make it hard for the horses to take off.

All the children piled into the car with them, and Arthur and Tilly were under strict instructions to look after the little ones for the ten minutes or so they would be on the course. There would be a burger van, so they'd probably sit in the car stuffing themselves with food laden with E-numbers. Sarah, as Cassie had suspected, had said she was too busy to come. She had a lot of work to do at home, and would welcome the peace with all the children out of the house. Tom had told Cassie he and Sarah were simply existing together. They had to sleep in the same bed, because there wasn't any other room, but he said that she leapt a mile if he as much as brushed up against her.

Tom reached down to tighten his girth. Mulberry, normally so steady, was prancing about with his ears pricked, pawing the ground and desperate to get off. He loved team chases and was an old hand, a very useful third or fourth horse who didn't mind going at the back and popped his fences without doing anything spectacular. He could be guaranteed to take you round safely, and Tom had no fears. Cassie, on the other hand, was full of butterflies. No matter how often she did this, she still got the same sense of excitement and anticipation, the feeling that anything could happen. Fred had to go at the front because he pulled like a train, but then he was so fearless he could be relied upon to jump anything and not stop, which was very important in a lead horse.

Their two other team mates were old friends of both Cassie and Tom, and very competent riders. Cassie knew they stood a chance in their class, the big open. And it was big — some of the hedges were almost two metres high. On tiptoe, she couldn't see over them. A couple had ditches in front, which meant she'd have to let Fred stand back off them and give them an enormous leap.

They circled in the collecting ring, chatting and gradually warming up the horses. There were a couple of practice fences, and they jumped them in turn, each of the horses making nothing of them. It should be a breeze.

Out of the corner of her eye, Cassie caught sight of a familiar dark coat and blue and pink scarf. It looked very like Laure. She rode nearer. It was, with Sophie clinging excitedly to her hand.

'I didn't know you were coming,' she called.

Laure smiled up at her. She looked pale, and fragile. 'I wanted to get out of the house. I thought I would come and support you, even though you know this scares me stiff. Those fences are huge.'

'How are you?'

Laure gazed at her with dark-shadowed eyes. 'Not so good,' she said. 'Surviving.'

'Hi.' Tom brought Mulberry up to stand beside her. Laure turned away, to bend down and button up Sophie's coat against the biting wind, brushing away the hair that was blowing in front of her face.

'Good luck,' she said, looking at Cassie. 'I won't say break a leg.'

'Please don't,' Cassie said. 'That's the last thing we need. Are you staying to the end?'

Laure shrugged. 'I think so. I don't have anything else to do today.'

'I'm glad you came,' Tom said. 'It was nice of you.'

'That's OK,' Laure said, looking up at him.

'Come on, Tom,' Cassie said. 'It's us in five minutes.'

'See you later,' he said.

'Maybe,' she said.

Brilliant, Cassie thought. Bloody brilliant. She forced herself to put it to the back of her mind. You could not do a competition like this and think about anything else.

The four horses lined up by the starting tape, Fred backing up, desperate to be off. The man with the stop-watch counted down. Five, four, three, two, one – he waved his handkerchief and the clock started. Fred sat back on his haunches, and then launched himself forward, taking Cassie by surprise with his power. It was like sitting on an Exocet missile. Desperately, she tried to rein him in as they approached the first fence, a sturdy post and rails. Going too fast, he jumped in like a stag, but fortunately it wasn't too high and he didn't catch the top. She was at least ten yards in front, and behind her she could hear the drumming hooves of the three other horses. She flicked a quick look back over her shoulder, as she crouched low over Fred's extended neck, feeling the rhythmic pace of his gallop. All still there, with Tom at the back, going steadily.

She turned sharp left, through a gate, to start the long line of cut-out hedges. These were great to jump, because it didn't matter if you hit them, the horses just brushed through. The ground in front had churned up a bit, but Fred had no trouble leaving the ground – he just gathered himself up, and soared into the air. She stole a quick look at her watch. Two minutes. They were moving fast, but not too fast. No-one ever had an idea what the bogey time was, you just had to guess. She began to relax and enjoy herself. The wind hit her face, making her eyes stream, and her heart raced with the adrenalin of galloping at speed across country, with no possible thought but the fences ahead.

Through the lowest part of the course, she now swung Fred to the right, to begin the climb up the hill and into the wood. They flew a big log, with a rail on top, and behind her she could hear a crunch as one of the horses hit it. Please, not Mulberry. He was getting too old to bear an injury like that. She turned her head. No, they were all still there. 'Steady,' one of the riders shouted at her, as they skidded through a gate and into the wood. She would have to take it slower here, because the fences were more technical, with twists and turns in boggy ground before they hit the open country once more and the big hedge section on the last part of the course.

She pulled Fred almost back to a trot to jump a hunt rail under an overhanging branch, and then they were all through the water and galloping towards the first of the hedges. And it was big. Walking the course, she'd thought, that is a whopper, but now galloping towards it on Fred, she realized she would have to give this everything. She shortened her reins, squeezed her legs against Fred's sides and kicked. The horse responded immediately, like a beautiful, powerful machine. He saw the ditch and hit his stride just right, bunching his muscles to leap effortlessly into the air. Cassie was aware of the sensation of flying, of the wide hedge beneath her, and then the reins whipped through her fingers as Fred plunged back to earth. In that moment, she was as close to God as it was possible to be. She had to lean right back to stop herself being pitched forward and as she landed she shouted, involuntarily, 'Yes!' It had been a fantastic leap, they'd cleared it by at least a foot. He was the most amazing horse. There hadn't been a thought of stopping, not an inch of hesitation.

Still high on adrenalin, and looking towards the next hedge, she was suddenly aware of shouting behind her, and she turned. She could see, above the hedge she had just jumped, the figure of a rider, sideways on. One of the horses had stopped, overwhelmed by the sheer size. Then, sickeningly, she saw Mulberry rise into the air behind him. The fool, the old fool. He was doing his best. He wasn't going to stop, he knew it was important, a competition, he had to do his best. In slow motion, she saw him stretch desperately to make the width of the hedge, Tom letting the reins slip through his fingers to the buckle end, the blood-red of the horse's nostrils and the terrified whites of his eyes as he tried not to hit the top. But there was nothing he could do. There was no way any horse could make that kind of jump. His front legs buckled as they caught the top of the hedge and she was aware of herself screaming, 'No!' as his body began to turn, somersaulting over the top. Twisting, turning in mid-air, before his dark body hit the ground with a hideous crash and Tom, thrown forward, landed directly underneath the horse as he fell, crumpling like a rag doll.

Cassie slammed Fred to a standstill, and turned to gallop back. Already the course officials were running to Tom, lifeless on the ground. Mulberry, covered in white lather, had managed to get up, but in flailing about had kicked Tom. By the time she reached them Mulberry was standing, holding one leg up, by the side of the hedge. The other two riders, their faces as white as sheets, had found a gate further along and were trotting towards them, their horses blowing and pulling.

Cassie threw herself off Fred, and gave the reins to a bystander. Tom lay in a ball, his legs tucked underneath him. The official held out a hand.

'Don't touch him,' he said. 'The ambulance is coming.' Cassie pulled off her hat, and ran her hand through her sweat-drenched hair. Tom began to moan, and the man bent down and gently pressed his hand against his shoulder. 'Don't move,' he said. 'Help's on its way.'

'My fucking shoulder,' Tom said. Cassie walked over and looked down at him. If he could talk, he could not be too bad.

'Who gave you permission to dismount?' she said, trying to make him smile, to relieve the awful tension.

He looked up as far as he could, his face covered in mud, white underneath with shock.

'Can you feel your legs?'

'Hang on,' he muttered, trying to turn over. The official warned him again to keep still.

'Yes,' he muttered. 'I think so. How's Mulberry?'

'He'll be OK,' Cassie said. 'It was a spectacular crash, I'll give you that.'

'I'm glad I'm entertaining,' he said. 'I've got a mouthful of mud.' He spat it out. The ambulance jerked to a stop next to them. The paramedics started to bring out a stretcher, and one of them eased off Tom's hat. 'Does your neck hurt?' he said.

'Er – yes,' Tom said. 'Everything bloody hurts.'

'You're not being awfully brave,' Cassie said.

'Let's hope I'm not paralysed or you are going to feel really, really bad,' Tom said, smiling and wincing at the same time. But Cassie could see from the way he was moving that he hadn't done any permanent damage. With a paramedic's help, he brought himself up to a sitting position. The paramedic felt along his shoulder, under the body protector, while Tom twitched away from him. 'Broken collarbone, ribs and probably shoulder,' he said.

'I'm sorry I haven't got any more exotic injuries,' Tom said. 'Remind me next time to break my neck.'

The official coughed. 'We'll need to clear the course,' he said.

Cassie walked back to Fred, and the woman holding him gave her a leg-up. 'We may as well finish,' she said. 'Could someone bring Mulberry back to the trailer?'

Gathering up her reins, she kicked on. Poor, poor Tom. But thank God. It could have been much worse. The image of the somersaulting horse and rider replayed itself over and over in her mind as the three of them finished the course.

Back at the collecting ring, Laure came running towards her. 'What happened? Where's Tom?'

'He fell,' Cassie said. 'He's not . . .'

'Oh, my God.' Laure's hand flew to her mouth. 'Where is he? Can he talk? Is he badly hurt?' She looked as if she was going to faint.

You love him, Cassie thought. You do love him. And he deserves that kind of love. Sarah's first thought would have been how it would affect her life.

'He's OK,' she said. 'A bit smashed up, but otherwise fine.'

'Where is he?'

'In the ambulance. Can you go and tell Lucy and

Daisy – gently? God knows how Sarah is going to cope.'

'Sarah!' Laure said. 'Can I go with him?'

'No,' Cassie said. 'The children . . .'

'Of course.' Laure looked ashamed. 'I'll take them home with me. Is there anything else I can do to help?'

'You could ring Sarah,' Cassie said, without thinking.

'No,' Laure said, looking up at her calmly. 'I don't think I could do that.'

Chapter Seventeen

Tom

'I think I am bearing my pain with great stoicism,' Tom said, reaching forward stiffly to try to pick one of the grapes Cassie had brought him.

'Knowing you, that's not very likely,' she said.

'But I can't do anything,' he said, shifting his weight on the hospital bed. 'I am bedridden, and it is driving me fucking crazy. I've broken a bone in my knee, too,' he added, quite proudly.

'Which you walked on,' Cassie pointed out.

'Don't remind me. I hurt all over. How's Mulberry?'

'He'll survive, thank God, but he's got a big lump on his leg. He has become something of a hero at home, though, the horse that thinks he can jump over the moon. Like the cow.'

Tom laughed, and winced. 'Ouch. Oh, bugger this. I can't bear being so still.'

'How long do you have to stay in?'

'Just today and tomorrow. They want to X-ray me again and make sure I haven't done anything to my spine. Which I'm sure I haven't.'

'Thank God.'

'Have you seen Laure?'

'No, Tom, I haven't. I've been up to my ears getting

231

the horses home, and then I wanted to see you and make sure you hadn't died. She's been brilliant – she took all the children back to her house and cooked them an enormous lunch. She's still got them. They are all very excited about your injuries, you know how they love drama. Lucy said she was quite hoping you might be in a wheelchair for a bit.'

'Charming. My lovely children.' He looked guarded. 'Have you spoken to Sarah?'

'Er, yes,' Cassie said. 'Why on earth didn't you call her? She's not best pleased.'

'I couldn't, could I? They don't let you have phones in here. I thought you'd call her. I bet she's hopping mad. She didn't want me to do it in the first place.'

'Well, it does present her with some rather challenging logistical problems, doesn't it?' Cassie pointed out. 'Such as how to get the children to school, and how she's going to work. She says she's either going to have to take some time off or employ a temporary nanny.'

'And guess which she's doing?' Tom said.

Cassie nodded. 'She's already fixed it with an agency. The nanny starts on Monday. Just think, it could be great. She'll do all your washing and ironing while you sit in a chair and order her about. Anyway, this is a good chance to crack on with the novel.'

Tom raised his eyebrows sardonically at her. 'It hurts when I move,' he said. 'I'm not sure I can type.'

'You haven't had brain surgery,' Cassie said, briskly. 'Anyway, she may be a gorgeous young thing. That would perk you up.'

'I don't want a gorgeous young thing.'

'Nat's coming in later,' Cassie said, quickly. 'That is an honour, he hates hospitals. I was lucky he turned up for the birth of the kids. He said he was trying to think of an appropriate gift. I talked him out of the electronic stairlift. You were lucky, you know,' she added, more seriously. 'You could have been paralysed.'

'That's the risk we take,' Tom said. 'Otherwise you'd never do anything exciting. Not that Sarah will see it like that.'

'No,' said Cassie. 'She won't.'

Tom sat in the armchair in his living room, his mobile phone at his side. Two weeks since the accident, and he was bored stiff. The agency nanny had taken the morning off, after dropping Daisy at nursery. He couldn't even walk very far with the crutches and his knee in plaster, and his collarbone, shoulders and ribs hurt like hell. He was bored of reading, bored of not being able to drive and bored of sitting in a chair. He'd read a year's worth of books, and he ought to be writing, but he felt exhausted, demotivated and depressed. Sarah was furious with him, and they were barely speaking. He hadn't expected any sympathy, and had got none. The new nanny was a model of efficiency and for once the children's drawers and bedrooms were neat and tidy – even Mickey's, who followed the twenty-year-old girl about with slavish eyes when he was home from school.

Tom picked up the phone, and his fingers dialled the number as if automatically. His heart was beating so loudly he could hear it.

'I'm bored,' he said. 'Don't hang up.'

'How are you? Still in pain?'

'Fucking agony.' There was a long pause. 'Come and see me,' he said. 'I'm incapacitated. You're quite safe.' Laure laughed. 'Please. Please, please, please. I have to see you. Just for a moment.'

'OK. I'll bring you some books.'

'Not books,' he said. But she had gone.

Ten minutes later, Laure let herself in through the open front door.

'You could be burgled,' she said.

'Who'd want to burgle me?' Tom said, rearranging his sling. Getting dressed was a complete nightmare – he had to wear his baggiest trousers over the cast on his knee and every slight movement of the shattered bones in his collarbone and shoulder made him want to cry with pain. It took him over half an hour to get his shirt on. His face was also a mass of scratches and bruises, and he appeared to have chipped a tooth.

'That's true,' Laure said, looking at him. 'You'd scare anyone away.'

'I had hoped my beauty was undimmed, but thanks.' She sat down opposite him, and carefully arranged the folds of her long skirt, which she was wearing with a white T-shirt. She had no make-up on and was much thinner than usual. She looked quite, quite beautiful. They sat and stared at each other. She leant forward, and very gently took his hand. He stared down at it. 'We're not very good at this, are we?' he said.

'What?'

'Not seeing each other. I've been fucking miserable. I can't bear not seeing you. If I don't see you it's like the world has gone dark.'

'Surely you can think of a better analogy than that,' she said.

'Don't tease me,' he said. 'I'm the sick person here.' She smiled, and tightened her grip on his hand. Without quite knowing what he was doing, he began to pull her towards him. At first she resisted, and then she began to flow towards him, until she was kneeling in front of him, his leg in the cast propped up on a chair beside her. Their faces were almost touching, and she could feel his breath on her cheek. 'I don't care,' he said. 'I don't care at all any more. I just have to do this . . .' He leant towards her, and his lips touched hers, as softly as a baby might kiss. She gently put her hands either side of his face, trying desperately not to hurt him. He felt the butterfly whisper of her breath against his skin, the unbelievable pleasure of her mouth under his. His good arm slid round her and pulled her much closer to him. She was half lying, half kneeling against him. 'Ouch, ouch,' he said. 'Oh, sod it.'

Laure drew a little away from him and laughed. 'You are in no fit state . . .'

'Oh, fuck that,' he said. 'I'm not letting you go. Follow me. You can hold my crutches.'

I just want to lie next to him, and hold him, Laure thought. Nothing else. I need to know what his skin tastes like, what it feels like to have his body against mine, just once. That's all. Then I'll make it all stop.

Gingerly, he hopped upstairs, with Laure following behind, supporting him. In the bedroom he turned, and leant against the door to close it. He put his hand into her hair, drawing her face to his. 'I don't care if this kills me,' he said. He tilted her head back, feeling the long hair flow over his fingers. His mouth found hers, and he pulled her hard up against him. Then he drew away from her.

'Mine?' he said, barely breathing. 'All mine?'

She looked at him with half-closed eyes. 'Yes,' she murmured. 'I give in.'

Half an hour later they lay entwined, their eyes centimetres apart. She'd tried to be so careful when she touched him, but he had moaned when he tried to put weight on his knee, and they had to lie facing each other, his good leg draped over her. But there was no embarrassment, no hesitation. At the moment of orgasm his lips were against her ear. 'You can never leave me now,' he whispered. 'I love you utterly, utterly, utterly.'

Chapter Eighteen

Nat

Nat stretched out his long legs in club class. Next to him, a Japanese businessman fiddled with the earpiece connecting him to the in-flight movie, being shown on a DVD player which flipped up from the armrest.

'Blanket, sir?' The blonde stewardess offered him a thick, soft-looking blanket. He smiled and took it off her, as her eyes never left his face.

This was the last trip before Easter, he thought. Thank God. He spread the blanket over himself, and eased off his shoes. He should have booked the seat next to him, as well, because he could hear the bloody film through the man's tinny earpiece. He turned over, away from him, and closed his eyes, resting his head on a pathetic little blow-up pillow. He was so very tired. He had been working sixteen hours a day on the proposals for the New York office and from the moment he landed at JFK there would be meeting after meeting with his PR staff, the hotels who wanted promotional DVDs, the technical staff and the American website designer. Plus the fact that a show they had had commissioned in the UK was likely to be picked up as an option by CNN. He also had a meeting fixed with the light-entertainment controller at NBC.

It was all looking good. Too good. If it took off, it meant that he would have to spend at least half the year in the States. Almost half the business was likely to be over there, and he couldn't just leave it to his staff to deal with, the heads of the networks wanted to deal with him direct, which was understandable. Five, ten years ago, he would have been thrilled. I am losing the appetite for the chase, he thought. He and Cassie hadn't talked any more about Scotland, but that didn't mean he had given up the idea. The thought of the vast open spaces, the simplicity, the absence of stuff, and people, was violently attractive. Life was getting far too complicated at home, and Cassie, he could see, out of the kindness of her heart, was getting sucked in. All that nonsense with Tom and Sarah.

Nat sighed. He had no patience with it. If two intelligent adults could not find a way of living in reasonable harmony, then they ought to have their heads knocked together. They had married in the first place, they must have loved each other. So what happened? How could you let a marriage slide into going so badly wrong without recognizing the signs and doing something to tackle it. Maybe he was just lucky being married to Cassie, who thought that family was as important as he did. It wasn't just that. Marriage shouldn't just be a duty, but a joy, a haven.

He had friends who also put great store on family – but then slept with other women. How could you be that dishonest? Sarah was intelligent, she must be, to hold down her job. He would not have liked Cassie to work at that kind of level. You can't have two stars in a marriage, he thought, and argue as you might, men still wanted to be the main breadwinner. Tom must have that urge – he was just lazy. He liked Tom, but he could not see why he was prepared to be effectively a househusband. Having said that, part of Nat's desire to move to Scotland was being able to spend far more time with the children. He smiled at the thought of them.

The stewardess saw him smile with his eyes closed, and wondered what he was thinking about. It was at that moment that the plane lurched violently forward. 'What the hell?' Nat said. He sat up, throwing off his blanket. All around him people were pulling off eye masks, removing their earpieces. The stewardess reached out to pull herself back to her feet, having been knocked to the floor, spilling gin from a half-open bottle all over the carpet.

'What's going on?' A dark-suited man called to her. 'There was no announcement about turbulence.'

The overhead seat belts signs flicked on. That must be it, Nat thought. Odd. Then the plane seemed to stop, and dropped what felt like almost a hundred metres. Nat's stomach rose into his throat, his head jerked painfully forward, and he grabbed onto the arms of his seat, then fastened his seat belt as hurriedly as he could. He flew twenty or thirty times a year, and this was the worst turbulence he'd ever encountered. The man next to him was as white as a ghost, his lips moving as if in prayer. At that moment, the entire left-hand side of the plane seemed to tip on its side. Nat felt his face bang against the window, and all around him cases, coats and files were falling out of the overhead lockers, glasses were flying, newspapers and magazines filled the air. There was a muffled sound of shouting, and a woman screamed, a high-pitched, awful, unearthly sound. The plane seemed to be going into a free fall, and no-one was doing anything to stop it.

Nat's brain raced. This wasn't turbulence. No air current, no matter how strong, could make a plane lurch like that. It couldn't be a bomb, obviously. There was no extra wind noise within the cabin, nothing seemed to have been punctured. With all his might he hauled himself out of his seat, and climbed over the Japanese man, who had thrown his head forward between his knees into the crash-landing position. The blonde stewardess was lying on the floor, blood trickling from one corner of her mouth. Hanging onto the arm of a seat, he felt her pulse. She was still alive, she must have knocked herself out. 'Help me get her up!' he shouted, but no-one was listening.

The plane was flying at a crazy right angle, bumping and lurching, as if thrown around by a vast, invisible hand in the sky. The cabin staff, he could see, had fastened themselves into their seats at the front, and two were crying as they desperately tried to keep their balance. The cockpit. There must be something happening in the cockpit. On his hands and knees, he inched himself forward. It was almost impossible, because he had to hang onto the right-hand seats, and with each move his knees banged painfully against the seats on the left. A woman in front of him was frantically counting her rosary beads, and from behind he heard the sound of children screaming. His ears were roaring with white-hot noise, as the sudden dips had changed the pressure within the cabin. For a moment, the plane seemed to right itself, and then, horrifyingly, the nose went down.

Nat was pitched forward, and he was flying through the air, to land with a crash against the door to the cockpit. This is it, he thought, and was amazed at how calm he was. I am going to die in a metal tube hundreds of miles up in the sky. We cannot take this kind of pressure, the plane must start to disintegrate. I love you, Cassie, he thought. I have loved you so much, and I am a lucky, lucky man to have had my life. The plane levelled out. What the hell was going on? One of the stewards banged into him. 'Get back, sir,' he said. 'Please.' He motioned at the other first-class passengers, all of whom were now bent double into the crash position. 'Please, sir, get back.'

'No!' Nat shouted, above the noise of people screaming. 'Something's going on – come with me,' and he reached up and forced open the door to the cockpit. The sight inside made him gasp. At the controls of the plane was a dark-haired man, and wrestling with him was the captain, his face contorted. Behind him the co-pilot was slumped in his seat, blood running down his face.

The captain saw him just as Nat launched himself forward and hastily stepped back. Taken by surprise, the man did not react at first when Nat pinned his arms to his side. Then he went wild. Bellowing with rage, he wrenched open his arms with extraordinary force for such a slight man, knocking Nat in the mouth, and he felt his front teeth smash. He was overcome with what felt like a superhuman anger. No way was this lunatic going to kill everyone on board. No way was he going to kill him. He wasn't going to die at the hands of some possibly religious fanatic or outright lunatic who thought that slaughtering hundreds of innocent people was going to guarantee him a place in heaven. He lunged forward, and wrapped his arm around the man's neck. He realized he actively wanted to kill him. With all the might of his six foot three frame he dragged him back, over the top of the seat. The pilot immediately threw himself back into his seat and began to ease the controls level. The steward, who had been completely paralysed by what was happening, seemed to come to his senses and grabbed the man's flailing arms. He was getting weaker, as Nat was cutting off his air supply.

'Get a fucking rope,' Nat shouted. Two stewardesses ran into the cabin. 'Rope!' Nat yelled. 'Anything.' The man was trying to chant, Nat could hear, his lips moving in a language he could not understand. You poor bastard, he thought. And this will bring you salvation? He was clearly insane. The man's body was beginning to slump in his arms. He had to release the pressure, or he would kill him. The man's eyes had shut, and he was going pale. Nat let go slightly, and he fell forward, unconscious, against the pilot's back. Nat flipped him over, and half carried him to the co-pilot's seat. God, he was little more than a boy. Maybe eighteen, nineteen years of age. He looked like any Middle Eastern young man, in jeans, a sweatshirt, trainers. He had a peculiar symbol tattooed on his arm and he was unshaven, dishevelled. Swallowing blood, Nat helped the stewardesses tie him up.

The pilot, sweat running down his face, was flicking dials and checking his instruments. 'The bastard knew how to take it off autopilot,' he said. 'It's amazing what they know, isn't it?' He grinned at Nat. 'I'm Greg,' he said, holding out his hand. Nat smiled. Only the British. He shook it. 'Nat.'

'I suppose we ought to tell people what has happened,' Greg said, flipping on the tannoy. He coughed. 'Ladies and gentlemen,' he said. 'A lunatic just tried to kill us all. But he is now safely overpowered and we owe a big thanks to a guy named Nat. We should be landing, safely, thank God, in about two hours.' There was a stunned silence, and then applause rippled through the plane, followed by wild cheering. A baby continued to scream.

'What shall we do with him?' Nat said, checking the man's pulse. 'He's out cold.'

'Lock him in one of the lavatories,' the steward suggested.

'Can you do that from the outside?'

'We can.'

'Your mouth,' one of the stewardesses said. Nat put his hand to his mouth. There was blood pouring down his chin, and he gently ran his tongue over his teeth. One had gone completely, another had been pushed back. It hurt like hell. She passed over a wad of cotton wool, and Nat held it to his mouth. 'I could do with a drink,' he said, through the cotton wool.

The pilot laughed. 'You lucky sod. I'll have to wait hours until I can have one.' They turned to look at the co-pilot, who was just coming round, shaking his head.

'What the fuck happened?' he said. He rubbed his head. 'Something hit me.'

The stewardess held up a bottle of vodka. 'This.'

'Ow,' he said. 'Some security.'

When they arrived at JFK airport, there was a fleet of ambulances and police cars, sirens blaring, waiting to greet them. Nat had spent the rest of the flight being patted, hugged and cried over. He felt terrible. He hadn't done anything anyone with half a brain wouldn't have tried, and the last thing he wanted was any publicity. Bit late for that, he thought, as he pushed his way through the terminal, flashlights popping, TV microphones being thrust under his nose and reporters shouting questions at him. The airline had arranged to transfer him straight to hospital to have his mouth dealt with, and it was only in the ambulance that he could use his mobile.

'Hi,' he said.

Cassie's voice was sleepy. 'Oh, hi. What time is it?'

'About ten a.m. our time.'

'Well, it's the middle of the night here. How was your flight?'

Nat smiled. 'Eventful.'

'You sound odd. What's the matter?'

'Someone decided to rearrange my teeth.' Cassie sat bolt upright in bed, and switched on the bedside light. 'How? Why?'

'It's a long story,' he said. 'It might even be in the papers.'

'You had a fight on the plane?' Cassie sounded horrified. 'That isn't like you. What on earth happened?'

'A lunatic tried to kill us by grabbing the controls of the plane,' he said.

'You're having me on.'

'No, honestly.'

'And you stopped him?'

'Er – yes. With some help.'

'Am I dreaming this?'

'No, really. It happened, trust me, it happened. I've lost one of my front teeth, which is pretty inconvenient. Look, I have to go. I'll ring you as soon as I can. Tell the kids I love them, will you?'

'We love you.' Nat could hear the smile in her voice. 'You mad hero. Just don't ever do anything like that again.'

Chapter Nineteen

Gerard

Gerard stared at the front page of the newspaper disbelievingly. Splashed across four columns was a huge picture of Nat, a white pad held to his mouth, his head down and a look of weary irritation on his face. The headline said it all. 'HERO!'

He could not believe it when Cassie called to tell them about it. This kind of thing didn't happen to people you knew, it happened to strangers, people who did not touch your lives. You could read avidly the dramatic eye-witness accounts, enjoy the vicarious thrill of trying to imagine what you would have done in their shoes, and then close the paper and forget them. But this was real. It was also, for him, disastrous.

The young man had been a member of a Middle Eastern terrorist group. When they landed at JFK, FBI agents had ordered everyone off the plane before throwing open the door to the toilet. Instead of an unconscious boy, they found a dead man. Somehow, he had managed to slip the ropes off his hands and had slashed his wrists with a knife he had smuggled onto the plane. The ramifications were enormous, and quite understandably the public were up in arms. How had a member of the group which was the major terrorist threat in the world today been able to smuggle a knife on board a plane, despite all the supposed security checks? Surely he had alerted suspicion?

He had paid for a seat in first class, which should have rung alarm bells at the desk in the terminal, because with his dishevelled air and appearance, he hardly looked like a standard business-class passenger. The knife could have been a gun, and if that had gone off, they would all have been dead in minutes. How had he gained access to the cockpit? Since the last major terrorist threat, all planes had been fitted with security locks, the number known only to the in-flight staff. How had he been able to get hold of a whole bottle of vodka, which he'd used to knock out the co-pilot?

The litany of blunders reflected incredibly badly not only on the Government but also the airline itself. What it also did, extremely effectively, was re-ignite the intensity of fear of terrorism and emphaize the vulnerability of the West to Islamic extremism. Which meant that people were reluctant to fly. Which meant that an American company thinking of commissioning a big order from Britain was far more likely to turn to its own suppliers within the States than risk a series of transatlantic flights they did not have to make. Rationally, people knew that it was very unlikely to happen again. But when a disaster of this magnitude nearly happened, everyone's instinct was to pull up the drawbridge and stay at home.

It was exactly the same in the aftermath of the last attack – many of the population, brainwashed by the alleged threat of nerve-gas attacks on the underground and bombs at strategic targets, simply closed their front doors and stayed at home. Transatlantic flights were cancelled and shares in the airlines nosedived.

Gerard could see it was a natural reaction – when under threat, you wanted to dig in and feel safe.

The effect on international trade was disastrous, and the value of the pound plummeted against international currencies. It was very cunning. This young man had not mattered. He was a pawn in the much wider, clever game masterminded by a man who knew just how to hit the West. British Muslims had been quick to condemn and distance themselves from the extremists and the terrorism attempt, but already bone-headed thugs were arranging marches. Membership of extreme right-wing groups doubled overnight. Idiots.

Gerard put down the newspaper, leant back in his chair, and sighed. He looked around the office. Once, there had been ten people working in this office. Now it was like a ghost town. Just Margaret, his personal assistant, remained, and she was only working two days a week. He had had to let them go. Paying their wages for work that was not there was idiotic, although he had been doing it for over six months. Several had offered to work on without pay, but he said that was ridiculous, that they must leave and find other jobs to support themselves. He stretched, and put his hands behind his head. The lighting in the office was dim, as it was lit in two sections and there was no point switching on the lights at the far side, as there was no-one who needed to see.

He looked at his phone. Once, it had been red-hot, with red lights flashing of calls waiting, the buzz and fun of being busy, busy, busy. He had run on that. And now, like a train being shunted into the sidings, it was all grinding to a halt. Without the American order, there was nothing. He could not tender for new work because he not afford to wait to be paid.

A manufacturing business, like his, depended on a

rolling programme of work to finance itself, because contractors were notoriously slow payers, especially the small firms. Their cash flow depended on a policy of delaying sending out cheques to the last minute, which meant it was a constant juggling act to keep his suppliers sweet by actually paying them. For years and years he had been part of the delaying process, balancing the books with a policy of crisis management. But staff had to be paid – you could not delay that.

The warehouse was now being operated by a skeleton staff of just two. He had had to lay everybody else off. They were more used to it, because the work did tend to come and go, and there were periods of months when they had no work. But Gerard had always made up for that by paying them over the odds when they were busy, often double time. He had two senior craftsmen, and he kept them on permanently. One of them had been with him right from the beginning, twenty-one years ago, and had moved his whole family down to the Midlands. His wife was ill with breast cancer and they had three grandchildren. He was only two years from retirement, sixty-three. His pension – Gerard could not bring himself to think about it. He cracked his knuckles. Whatever happened, he must get his pension when they sold the house. When.

He picked up the glossy brochure the estate agents had sent him last week, which was lying on his desk. The perfect small country house, as it was described. He looked at the cover. It was perfect, all right. Perfect for them. He flipped open the pages. Laure's beautiful rooms, so lovingly created, were laid out in all their stylishness. Open fires flickered in every hearth, and if he was a buyer, he would have put in an offer on the spot, house unseen. It looked so welcoming, a house in which you could not fail to be happy. Already, it felt as if he no longer lived there. The home, their castle, had been made of straw, after all. And now it had been turned into the styled shoot of an interiors magazine – there was no sign of their family. Just in the kitchen, Victor had been used as a prop. Gerard smiled. Only because they couldn't persuade him to get out of his basket. Poor old boy. He could hardly lift himself up at all now, and Gerard said that the moment he became incontinent that would have to be it, they couldn't let him suffer. In his youth he had been a fine hunter, lolloping after pheasants and rabbits – he never caught anything, but he loved the thrill of the chase. He was also a real 'water dog' – he adored launching himself into the river on one of their favourite walks, to swim with strong strides in pursuit of sticks. He must have that memory, Gerard thought, having watched the old dog asleep, his nose twitching, his paws paddling. Dreams. They both had dreams, but Gerard's dreams woke him, sweating, his heart racing.

Last night he had dreamt he was being arrested. He was being dragged down a corridor, away from Laure and Sophie. He kept trying to hang onto the steel bars of cells as he was manhandled along, but they were too strong for him. And then he had been lying on his back on a hard, narrow bed, and there was a tiny window up above him, high, far too high for him to reach and escape. When he woke, he found he had been crying in his sleep.

He spread his hand out on the newspaper. Laure had moved permanently out of their bedroom. She had done it very quietly and without drama. One night he had come home from another day uselessly firefighting problems to find she had taken her clothes and her books into the spare room. Nothing was said. He wondered what she had told Sophie. Maybe that he snored.

In every respect, Laure was being perfectly controlled. He could not reach her. Gradually, she was withdrawing from him. She had stopped offering to help. Only with other people and Sophie was she anything approaching her old self. With him, she was a careful, polite stranger. She cooked his meals, and they ate them in silence. She gave him all the post to deal with, and there were no more discussions about their future, what they would do once the house was sold. He wondered if she was making plans – she must be. But there would be no money. She had her furniture and paintings, of course – that would give her enough for the deposit on a house, if she intended to leave him. He did not know. She was working every day now, either up at the manor or on the phone to suppliers and shops in her neat study.

He crunched his hand up into a ball. The only thing he had was Sophie. She was the only ace he had to play to keep Laure. He knew she would not willingly split up the family. Nick's fees were paid up to the end of the spring term, and then, if the house was sold, Gerard planned to use the small amount of equity to pay the school until Nick's exams, after which he would have to leave and go to a local college. Sophie would have to leave and start at a state school in the summer term. Wherever they might be. Wherever he might be. Wherever Laure might be.

She had to talk to him. He could not go on like this, not knowing. There were times when he wanted to grab her by the shoulders and shake her, to force a reaction out of her, but he could not do that – he could not touch her in anger again. He was filled with shame at the thought of the incident which had set, in his eyes, this whole thing off – losing his temper with Nick, taking it out on her. He could still see her horrified face as he pushed her, hard, against the door frame. In that split second he had wanted to hurt her. He wanted to make her pay for taking sides with Nick against him, for refusing to support him because he was her husband and she should love him the most. All the insecurity he had tried to submerge had rushed to the surface, and he had lost control. He was an idiot. And now, understandably, he had lost her trust. His head slumped forward onto his chest. He had violated that trust, and in front of Sophie too.

Last year he had felt great swings of emotion – energetic and optimistic one moment, plunged into the depths of depression and hopelessness the next. And he had taken that out on Laure, he could see that. Even last week, at Nick's school, he had been thoughtless and cruel. When would he learn? Without physically hurting her, he had brutalized her with his temper and his mood swings. And now he had frightened Sophie too. What kind of a monster had he become? Sophie would not let him hold her. A sigh escaped him. Last night he had bent down to give her a goodnight kiss and she had shrunk away from him. He had to bend lower, and physically reach out for her, whereas before she would have wrapped her arms around his neck and clung to him. Naturally, as he was her father. Now she let herself be hugged, but did not return the embrace.

How much he had taken for granted. How he had sailed through his days, breezing in and out of the perfect house, cosseted by the luxury of the life Laure provided for him. Did she have any idea how much he loved her? Had he shown, in any way, that without her he was nothing? He thought hard. No. Because he had never thought that it would end.

His hand reached for the phone on his desk. He would call her, suggest they go out for a meal that night, to talk. His heart lurched. She couldn't, wouldn't, want to leave him. Where would she go? She wouldn't go to her father, God, he was getting married in three weeks' time, he'd forgotten about that. Cassie had asked them to go skiing with them at Easter, but there was no way they could – it wasn't just the cost of the chalet, Cassie said that was all paid for, but the cost of ski hire, lift passes, tuition for the children. Lunches, meals out – there was no way they could do it. What would he do? Pass the bill to Nat? Laure did not understand how much male pride was wrapped up in money. You provided. Take that away, and what were you? Sure, you could be a great father and spend lots of time with your kids, and be a loving husband, but your raison d'être was to support, protect and care for your family.

He could not understand Tom at all. At the dinner party, Gerard had been on Sarah's side. Why should she support Tom? What kind of pride did he have to take money from a woman without contributing at all? He could pay lip service to men and women having interchangeable roles, but it was rubbish. Women wanted men to look after them, and women were the most natural primary carers for children. Of course men could do it, but they didn't have the instinctive feel. Sarah, he thought, for all her high-flying career and independence, wanted a man who would support her, and treat her, and make her safe. Tom didn't do that. He did not give that marriage long.

His hand hesitated on the phone. Would she speak to him? Laure was too polite just to put the phone down, but she had developed a way of talking to him that was not a conversation in itself – she failed to engage. She just said 'yes,' or 'no,' or 'if you think it is a good idea,' and afterwards he realized that she had not really been there at all. Whatever he said made no impact. She seemed to have made herself immune to him. The only faintly positive thing he could see was the fact that they were not arguing, there were no rows. Instead of a tense atmosphere at home, the mood was subdued. They tiptoed around each other and no-one raised their voice. It was almost, he thought, as if someone had died. They had not told Sophie or Nick about selling the house yet. There was no point, they agreed, until people started coming to look round, and even that could be done when Sophie was at school.

He was on the knife-edge of bankruptcy. Some mornings he woke and thought, Sod it. It is the easiest option. But bankruptcy meant that he would not be able to be the director of a company for three years at least, so he wouldn't be able to set up on his own again for a while. If he ever dared. No, he would have to go and work for someone else, and bite his lip when the managing director told him what to do, and engage in office politics and be a good boy so he might get a rise. Indignation seethed inside him. He had been the boss of a multinational company, and now he would have to kowtow to some ignorant git who would give him orders. He could do it. He would have to do it. The offer from the consortium had been withdrawn. That lifeline had gone.

There was a big textiles-manufacturing company which was looking for a marketing director. He could do that standing on his head. The salary was half the amount of money he had been earning ten years ago. And would they want someone like him? Would they want a big personality to rock the boat in their stream-lined operation? The answer was quite probably, no. They would think he would just be waiting for the right time to go off and set up on his own again, and pinch their ideas and their customers.

He could retrain, start a new career. He thought hard. He had always wanted to be a lawyer, but there was no way he could go to law school now, nor could he afford it.

He dialled the number of the Rectory. It rang so long he thought that she was not there.

'Hello?'

'Laure? It's me.'

'Oh, hi.'

'Are you busy? In the middle of something?'

'No, just working.'

'Oh. I won't be long.'

'What did you want?' Her voice was distant, polite.

His hand gripped the phone. I want you to say that you love me. I want you to say that everything is going to be like it was before. I want you to say that you understand that I am sorry. But he could say nothing of this. He knew that the moment he tried to talk to her openly she would back off, and close up, and they would take another step backwards away from each other.

'I'm just closing up the office.'

'Oh.' There was pity in her voice.

'Did you see Nat on the front pages?'

'I did. It must have been awful for Cassie.'

How would you have felt if it had been me? he thought.

'Have you spoken to her?'

'Oh yes, I saw her yesterday. She's fine. Very shaken up, but fine. Nat's coming home at the end of the week. It was very brave of him to decide to stay.'

'Typical Nat.'

'Yes, he's apparently trying to pretend it was no big deal. Arthur is basking in his reflected glory.'

Gerard laughed mirthlessly. 'Laure—'

'What?' Her voice, which had relaxed, became tense, guarded, again.

'I need to talk to you.'

'Oh.'

'Can't you say anything else but "oh"?'

'I'm a bit busy now. My other phone is ringing, I have to go—'

'Laure!' He tried to stop himself shouting, and the knuckles on his hand were white where he gripped the phone.

'Please don't shout,' she said.

He forced himself to breathe calmly and deeply, to keep his voice normal. If he lost it, that would be it, she might put the phone down.

'I'm not shouting. It's just a really, really bad day for me. Margaret is coming in later and I have to tell her we are officially closing down next week. I will pay her until the end of the month.'

'Can you?'

'No. Look, we have to make plans.'

There was silence.

'Laure?'

'I heard you.'

'Well?'

'There is no point making any plans until we know we have a buyer. Then we will see.'

'See what?'

'See what we can do.'

She said 'we'. It was a glimmer of hope.

'We *can* start again.'

Another silence.

'Laure, I'm not going to beg.'

'I wouldn't expect you to.'

'I can't sleep without you.'

Silence.

'I am literally cold without you.'

'Don't.'

'Don't what?'

'Don't make me make a decision.'

254

He paused and stared at the phone.

'What kind of decision?' His heart was beating uncomfortably.

'About where I will go.'

'Where will you go?'

'Gerard, this is pointless. I do not know. I do not know anything, at the moment. I am living from day to day, putting one foot in front of the other.'

'Is that all?'

'It's all that I can do. Nick will be home next week, and we need to keep everything calm. I mean that.'

That was quite an order, coming from Laure.

'I'm not going to argue with him, if that's what you mean.'

'Good. I better go.'

'Don't!' The words came out far more sharply than he intended. 'I mean, just let me talk. Even if you don't want to say anything. Please, please. I love you. I cannot live without you. I feel like I am going mad not being able to hold you and make love to you. I cannot bear the fact that you have shut yourself off from me. The only way we can make this any less awful than it really is, is by being together. Is by going through it together. Houses don't matter. Schools don't matter. Fuck that. What matters is us, and the children. We can start again. I have plans, I really, really do. You don't have to work if you don't want to, it can be just like it was before. Please, Laure, I'm—'

'I don't want it to be like it was before,' Laure said, quietly. 'I don't know if it can be. It is too late.'

'Then it will be different! I didn't mean that! I meant that you can do whatever you want to do and I will support you, and yes, we'll have lost a lot of ground, but it's only temporary . . .'

'You don't see, do you?'

'See what?'

'See that I don't want anything to be like it was before.'

'But you were happy!'

There was a long pause.

'Laure? You were happy, I know you were. Our life was not some kind of charade. The birth of the children . . .'

'You weren't there.'

'I know! I was wrong, I can see that now, my priorities were wrong. But I was doing it for you, for us . . .'

'Really?'

'I thought I was. You have to let me try.'

'I don't know. I just don't know.'

'Now this is some kind of barking-mad mind game!' he exploded.

'I will put the phone down,' she said, firmly.

'OK, OK. I thought we were happy. You certainly seemed happy. Nick, Sophie – we have children, Laure. Together. Nothing can change that. I know I haven't told you, but you are a fantastic mother, a fantastic wife, the best—'

'I know.'

'Just give me some hope,' he said. 'Please.'

'I don't know what there is to give.' Her voice was weary. 'I don't seem to know anything any more.'

'That's shock. It will pass. What matters is the fundamental truth that we love each other and we love our children. If we have that, then we have everything we need.'

'It might be too late for that.'

'What in God's name do you mean?'

There was a long pause and then Laure said, in a rush, 'You took advantage of it, Gerard. You took our life for granted and you abused us and shouted at us and treated me as if I was some kind of servant and you wanted everything to look perfect but you didn't give me anything or make me feel that I was of value to you, or even as if you liked me and found me interesting or funny or any of the things that people need to feel that they are worth something. You didn't give anything of yourself. I cannot tell you how lonely I have felt at times, shut out from you. And then when you were at home you were like this kind of – tyrant – whom everyone had to obey. You cannot turn around now and say that you need us when you are down. We have learnt, Gerard, that we do not need you. We do not have to take it. We can live without you.'

'What about Sophie? What about Nick?'

'Sophie is very young. She will adapt. You have treated Nick appallingly and I am not sure if he wants to have anything to do with you.'

'Are you saying that you are leaving me?' He spoke the words very slowly and carefully, and then held his breath.

There was a long pause. 'I cannot say,' she said.

'Please, God, now I am begging you, please. Don't. I don't know what I would do – I couldn't . . .' Tears were pouring down his face. 'You can't. Not now. I don't have anything . . .'

'Don't do this. Not over the phone. Nothing is decided, Gerard. The children do love you, yes, even Nick, and there is nothing in the world I would do to separate you from them.'

'And you? Do you love me?'

But she had gone.

Chapter Twenty

Sarah

'I don't care if it costs five thousand pounds, we have to get it done by Thursday. Do you hear? Thursday. And don't tell me you have lined up five women who look like moose. I want them slim, and young, and attractive. Or you won't get paid.'

Sarah banged the phone down. This job was impossible. Impossible. She had thought that Charles would appoint someone into her old job behind her and leave her free to oversee both departments. Oh, no. Clever old Charles had meant that he would simply sack Venetia, who had promptly been offered the same job on a rival newspaper for more money, and let Sarah fill both roles. Venetia then subtly hinted to Sarah, via the grapevine, that the position she had now was a poisoned chalice and that, unless she succeeded, Charles was thinking of incorporating the magazine into a colour section within the newspaper itself, thereby saving hundreds of thousands of pounds in printing costs. It was not, in fact, true, but it was an extremely useful rumour to spread and one which would have the maximum impact of making Sarah feel both under pressure and insecure.

Charles was wondering if maybe he had

underestimated Venetia and shouldn't have sacked her in the first place. He heard very good things about the regime she was imposing at his rival's paper. Maybe he should take her out for lunch in the near future and smooth things down, pave the way for a possible return. In the short term, he did not want to find a replacement for Sarah's old position. Which meant that Sarah, great worker as she was, would just have to soldier and cope. It was a good test for her. She'd taken her PA Cosima with her, and the poor woman was running around like a headless chicken.

So Sarah had double the work. Double the amount of shoots, double the amount of commissions, double the amount of both staff and freelance journalists to deal with, double the amount of office politics and warring staff, jockeying for position. One of her favourite commissioning editors, Claire, was off on maternity leave, which meant she did not have anyone close to her to whom she could let off steam. She could not confide in anyone in the department, or show any sign of weakness. It was battering her down. She had taken to spending more nights in the hotel near to the office, because she simply could not face getting on a train at ten o'clock at night, to get up at five to be back on a train at six. Besides, she and Tom were not speaking to each other, which meant that the atmosphere in the house was awful. The nanny was running the house very efficiently, but she was showing signs of unease at the unspoken tension.

Mickey had stayed out all night the previous Saturday, claiming to be with a friend, but when they had rung the friend had denied all knowledge. God knows where he had been. Lucy was being downright rude to her, and Daisy looked at her as if she had two heads and was clinging to the new nanny. Tom's accident had upset her a great deal, and she could not understand why Daddy could not drive or pick her up. Tom, meanwhile, seemed to be using his leisure time to read books and stare out of the window, instead of getting down to some writing while he had the child-care back-up.

'Can I come in?' Cosima stuck her head around the door.

'Sure.' Sarah spread three layouts out in front of her. 'You can help me choose which of these are the least unattractive.'

Cosima looked over her shoulder. 'Oh, dear,' she said. 'Were they very expensive?'

'Five grand each.'

'Oh. Charles is not going to be a happy bunny, is he?'

'I think we can safely say that. Why in God's name aren't people jpegging the case-study pictures in the first place to the picture desk? Can't we select these women before it is too late? Does no-one out there have a brain?'

'It is a bit tough with Claire away,' Cosima nodded. 'And I think people feel . . .'

'What?' Sarah said, sharply. Cosima was about the only person in the office who ever dared to speak honestly to her.

'There's a bit of a feeling of lack of direction,' she said. 'You're in here, on the phone all the time, and no-one's making any decisions. We doubled up this week on that commission on the diet women, you know, because no-one checked who had rung whom, so two journalists did exactly the same feature and we only found out when the pictures came in.'

Sarah put her head in her hands and groaned. 'Everyone has to check everything with me. I want to see all case studies before they are commissioned, I want to see every picture before we book the shoot.'

'You don't have time,' Cosima said, gently.

'I know I don't have fucking time. Sorry. I know I don't have time but otherwise we are going to hit our annual budget in about, oh, three months, and then I will be fired. It's all these bloody meetings I have to go to. Most of them are just a chance for the editorial team to show off and score points off each other, and put each other down in front of Charles. And they go on for hours. Policy this, policy that. None of it gets pages made up.'

'You need a break.'

'Which is precisely what I cannot have.'

'Easter's coming up. You ought to go away, with the family.'

Sarah looked at her. The very last thing she could do which would be relaxing was parcel herself and Tom up with the children in some remote cottage, where they could explode the myth of the nuclear family once and for all.

'I don't think so,' she said. 'I don't have time.' The only possibility they did have was a suggestion Cassie had thrown out weeks ago, before the dinner party, which was for them to join them in France because the other family they had been planning to travel with had cancelled, and now they had four spare bedrooms. Cassie had implied, which was very good of her, that they needn't pay for the chalet, which was already booked, but just for the flights and the normal skiing costs like lift passes and so on. It was a catered chalet, which meant there wouldn't be many meals to pay for, just lunches and one meal at night when it was the chalet staff's night off.

God, it was tempting, because she wouldn't have to be alone with Tom, which would have been impossible, and it would mean she could spend some time skiing, which she loved and was good at, and the children would be out of her hair because they would have ready-made friends to play with. Nat and Tom were so good with the kids that she would get some vital 'me' time. Plus the fact that Courchevel was a very chichi resort and it would be good to say that was where she was going. Far better than some grotty cottage, which would simply remove their bickering to a seaside location.

'Actually,' she said, thinking aloud. 'We might need a bit of cover over Easter. I might be going away. Could you call Claire and see if she's actually popped yet? If not, could you offer her double freelance time to come in and cover, maybe just for four days? Or she could work from home, if she likes.'

'OK.'

Sarah didn't ask Cosima if she was going away, but then she was used to not being the centre of attention. It was part of being a good PA. You had no life outside the office.

'I'll go and make those calls, then. Is there anything else?'

'Yes. I want to pick your brains. Sit down.'

Cosima pulled up a chair.

'What do you think about doing a series on modern relationships? The relationship revolution? Battle of the sexes?' Cosima nodded. She was used to Sarah bouncing ideas off her.

'Sounds good. It's the thing that everyone talks about all the time.'

'Do they?' Sarah said, sucking the end of her biro. 'What about your friends? What do you talk about over your vodka martinis?'

Cosima laughed. 'Men, obviously,' she said.

'Men and . . .'

'Their reluctance to commit. I'm thirty-two, and no nearer marriage than I was when I was twenty-two. Well, actually, probably further away, because a couple of the men I could have married have got married to other people.'

'So why didn't you marry them?'

'They weren't perfect,' Cosima said. Sarah nodded. 'They had to tick absolutely every box because I want a man who is handsome, kind, successful, loving . . .' She smiled at Sarah's disbelieving face. 'OK, too perfect, I guess. But it's no longer any good to go out with a man who is right for now. They have to be right for ever, and that's a massive order for anyone.'

'I see,' Sarah said.

'Only I am learning', Cosima went on, 'that it's very hard to be a successful independent woman and then be expected to look after a man as well. The older you get, the fussier you get, and it gradually begins to dawn on you that men haven't changed all that much after all, they still want their mummy. They want someone who is going to make their life comfortable and perfect, and yet they also want someone who earns their own money, but is sexy and feminine.'

'So why is that so hard?' Sarah leant forward.

'Because I am not going to run around after some man when I'm exhausted too. I'm not going to play the little woman and pander to their ego,' Cosima said. 'I lived with Alistair for three years and that made me realize that even though we worked exactly the same hours, he expected me to clean the toilet and do all the washing!' She laughed, in a horrified fashion. 'Can you believe it! I thought we would be absolutely equal but he treated me as if I was some kind of servant. Imagine what it would have been like if we had had children. He would have thought they were just my responsibility.'

'So you don't think that permanent relationships can work?'

'Not until I find the perfect man,' Cosima said. 'But

once you're in your thirties, if you're like my friends, you end up in this big group of people, most of whom have slept with one another at some point because you all know each other so well, and you go around in a big gang which is great fun and we have fantastic parties, but it does mean that people don't pair off. It's almost as if we're scared to. We're too scared of getting it wrong. Even just living with someone is such a huge decision, I think we're terrified of making the wrong one so we're just kind of paralysed and we end up taking no decisions at all, just crashing from party to party.'

'But you have great friends,' Sarah said, thoughtfully.

'Oh yes, masses of friends. It's like this huge, supportive network of people.'

'A kind of urban group hug,' Sarah smiled.

Cosima laughed. 'I guess so. And we turn to each other for support, and people are kind of interchangeable, men and women. Actually, two of my closest friends are gay. They're brilliant. I just – I just don't want to sit there with a fag in one hand and a bottle of wine in the other, and think I will still be doing the same thing when I am fifty. I want responsibilities. I want children.'

'So will you get married?'

'Married?' Cosima laughed. 'It seems like a long way off at the moment.'

'But you're thirty-two?'

'I know. My dad keeps teasing me that unless I get a move on I'll be like that woman in Romania, you know, the one who'd had a baby by IVF at the age of sixty-five or whatever she is. I know I need to get a move on but I don't want to have a child with just anyone. Although,' she said, leaning forward, 'I do have a friend who's just had a baby using a sperm donor. She was absolutely fed up with waiting for Mr Right to come along, so she bought a designer baby.'

'Good story,' Sarah said.

'I know, I've asked her but she won't talk. Don't worry, I'll keep on at her.'

'Offer her money.'

'I've tried that. She says she doesn't want to be made a public laughing stock or an object of curiosity.'

'She's a woman of our times,' Sarah said. 'We wouldn't send her up.'

'I know. She still won't do it. But now she's got this gorgeous little baby, Charlie, and she's happier than I've ever seen her. I always thought that babies were pretty revolting but he is just adorable. She isn't even going back to work.' Cosima shook her head, disbelievingly.

'And does the father support her?'

'That's the point – she's no idea who he is. She paid for the sperm, and Charlie is entirely her responsibility. I think it's brilliant. I might do it, if I get to thirty-five and I haven't met anyone special.'

'Are you looking?'

'God, all the time. But everyone is scared of making the first move. I suppose what I want', she laughed, 'is a knight in shining armour to come and carry me away. But then if he did I'd think he was a sexist oaf. You're so lucky,' she said.

'What?'

'You have the perfect solution. You have fabulous Tom who looks after the children and you've got this amazing job. Maybe that's the way we ought to go – all women work and men stay at home.'

'But would you want a man who stays at home?'

Cosima looked at her consideringly. 'Yes,' she said, tactfully.

'Liar,' Sarah said. 'Anyway, it isn't all perfect. I work

every hour God sends and I am never at home with my children and I think they all hate me.'

Cosima looked shocked. 'I'm sure they don't.'

'It just feels like that sometimes. No, tragically, there does not seem to be a perfect solution out there.'

'Don't you have friends who both work full-time and share all the responsibilities?'

'And are still together?' Sarah thought for a moment. 'No.'

Once Cosima had gone she sat and stared into space. She was supposed to be reading copy and making marks but the words blurred in front of her eyes. She rubbed her fingertips over her forehead, and rolled her head around on her neck. She really needed a massage, her neck was clicking. Cosima thought she was lucky. That was rich. At the moment she felt like the most put-upon woman on earth. Everything would be fine if Tom sold his novel. His accident was so irresponsible, and now she had to find the money to pay for a nanny, too.

They hadn't had a proper conversation for weeks. She thought hard for a moment. Did she want a divorce? To leave Tom? She thought of herself, a single mother, trying to juggle work and childcare without his help. She had no doubt that she would get custody, because she was the breadwinner. Even though she didn't think Tom worked particularly hard around the house, it did occur to her that she would miss him and all the things he did. She was, in practical terms, much better off with him, and the children adored him. But did she? She leant her elbow on the table and put her hand to her face, staring unseeingly at the computer screen.

When they met she'd thought Tom was so clever, so funny, so unlike anyone she had ever known. A bit crazy and prone to do rather dangerous things, certainly, but that was a big part of his sexual attraction. He never put her down, he always encouraged her and they had a great time in bed. But over the years it had just trickled away – quite possibly, she could see, because they had not taken care of what they had. He wasn't gorgeous, like Nat, or dynamic like Gerard, but he was charming. That was the one thing everyone always said when they met Tom – he had charm. I don't really want anyone else, she thought. I have been guilty of taking him for granted.

She would have to make more of an effort. They'd go skiing, with Cassie, and have a great time, and there was a chance everything could be just like it was before.

It was up to him to say that he was sorry, and she was prepared to be magnanimous.

Chapter Twenty-One

Cassie

She felt her hips beginning to sway. She hadn't heard this record in years. She shook her hair back and let rip, dancing around the kitchen. If there was one thing Cassie could do, it was dance. Though she didn't have a model-girl figure, even as a teenager, she had always been a great dancer. Her shoulders moved backwards and forwards in time to the music, her body fluid. She was the embodiment of soul.

'What the heck are you doing, aged Mother?'

'What does it look like?' she said, trying to grab hold of Tilly's hands. 'Bopping.'

'I don't think so,' Tilly said, standing still, her hands on her hips, as Cassie shimmied around the table. 'Are you barking mad?'

'No, I love this one. Come on.'

Reluctantly at first, Tilly started to shuffle her feet. This was way too embarrassing. But it did look kind of fun, too. Cassie took one hand and soon they were dancing around, Tilly doing her own thing while Cassie imagined she was twenty years old. Attracted by the noise, Beth and Arthur appeared. Arthur contented himself with banging a spoon against the table, while Beth climbed on the table and did a very passable imitation of a pop star, using the tomato-ketchup bottle as a microphone.

Nat opened the back door, his feet, in wellingtons, caked in mud. He had been walking around the garden, trying to decide if it was dry enough for the first mow of the season. He loved mowing, and he especially loved his sit-on tractor. The ground was a bit spongy in places, but he'd probably get away with it without making too many deep grooves in the lawn. He looked around the disco kitchen and raised his eyebrows. Tilly had Hector in her arms, and, as his front paws imitated John Travolta in *Saturday Night Fever*, his face registered extreme disapproval of such liberties. Hamish thumped his tail against the floor, in time to the beat.

'Come on, Dad!' Tilly yelled. 'Get on down!' All too soon, the record finished.

'That was fun,' Cassie said, and danced towards him. 'Take your wellingtons off.'

'Why? Do you have evil designs on me?'

'No, I don't want mud all over the floor.'

'Shame about the cat, then,' he said, and they both looked at the perfect row of cat paw marks heading towards the plastic laundry basket where she slept during the day. Cassie had to poke about before she piled clothes into the machine, because it would have been all too easy to add grey fur to the coloureds wash. Spin, and cat, were not a good combination and Cassie was fairly sure Sooty had 'hand wash only' on the label.

'It's the have-a-go hero,' Arthur said, grinning. This was Nat's new nickname, funny at first but now the joke was wearing a little thin. Nat reached out and ruffled Arthur's brushed-forward hair. 'Shut up,' he said. 'Tufty.'

Cassie was glad that he was in a good mood, because

she had something to tell him that would possibly not please him.

'Can you mow?' Best to adopt the sideways approach.

'I guess so. It's a bit early, but what the heck. What's this?' He picked up a letter confirming the details of the chalet, and including everyone's air tickets. 'There seem to be a lot of these,' he said, riffling through them.

'Ah,' Cassie said. 'That's what I was going to tell you. Um . . .'

'Mum invited Tom and Sarah and Laure and they're all coming,' Tilly announced, happily. 'And all the children. Everybody.'

'What!' Nat exploded. 'Are we paying for all this lot?'

'Not exactly,' Cassie said, quickly. 'Well, not at all, really. Just the chalet. They've all paid me back for the air fares.' Well, Tom and Sarah had but she had yet to get a cheque from Laure.

'Why', Nat said patiently, 'are we going on holiday with a small travelling circus?'

'That isn't fair,' Cassie said. 'It will be fun.'

Nat raised his eyebrows at her.

'I couldn't say no,' she said, shrugging. 'You know me. I'd completely forgotten that I'd invited them, it was so long ago and then Sarah rang and said they'd been considering it and they'd love to come, and then I had a long chat with Laure and—' she glanced at the children – 'at the moment, you know, it seemed a great opportunity for her to have a break with Nick and Sophie.'

'What?' said Nat, completely lost. Cassie made a 'don't go there' face at him. Laure had made her promise not to tell her children that the house was on the market because Sophie and Nick didn't know yet and she didn't want village gossip. There was no For Sale sign and it was all being done very discreetly.

Cassie had run out of trying 'what if' scenarios, as in 'what if the business picks up' because Laure had told her, and again made her swear to secrecy, that Gerard was quite likely to be made bankrupt and that would be it. No going back. She seemed, to Cassie, far too calm and she kept saying everything was 'fine' in the manner of a person tranquillized. She also deflected any of her questions about Tom, and he wasn't giving anything away, either. When pushed, Laure said they both knew it was impossible, and then stalled further questions, saying she had to decide her own future first. Cassie suspected that they had reached some kind of pact and were not telling her, which on the one hand made her feel left out, and on the other hand was something of a relief, because she could see no way out without chaos and mayhem.

Everything was so up in the air at the moment, she felt as if she was living in the middle of a surreal film. Laure and Gerard were barely speaking to each other, and Gerard seemed to be spending hardly any time at home as he wrapped up the business and they waited for a buyer for the house. Tom and Sarah were not speaking at all. Tom had locked himself away and was now trying to write his book, and hadn't been out for a ride for ages. Sarah seemed to be living in the city for most of the week, while the new nanny cared for the children. Laure was also busy working, saying that she had to start building up her career because she had to have some financial security.

Nat had pronounced one opinion on the subject, that he and Cassie should leave them all alone to get on with destroying their lives, and that he wanted no part of it. Subject closed. Which was why this joint holiday was going to be very tricky indeed to sell to him. He rarely lost his temper with her, but this might just push him over the edge. He had told Cassie quite firmly that they had to put their own family first, and that she would do no good in dabbling in other people's affairs, which were none of her business. Cassie replied that you had a duty to close friends, but Nat said life had to be about survival, and his family would always come first. Nor, he said, did he want any of their children to know anything about this. Let them grow up in some kind of innocence. And she hadn't even told him the full extent of the Tom and Laure affair.

'You never know what?' Cassie had said, as they sat having coffee in Laure's kitchen earlier that week.

'You never know what might happen. I have to establish some kind of independence.'

'I can see that,' Cassie said. 'Are you sure?'

'What?'

'That you're going to leave him when the house is sold?'

Laure wrapped her arms around her too-thin body. With no make-up on, she looked about sixteen, and her hair hung loosely about her face. The kitchen, always so immaculate, had, for Laure, something of a neglected air. There were toast crumbs on the chopping board, and a pint of milk stood in its bottle on the kitchen table. Normally Laure only ever used jugs. She caught Cassie's gaze around the kitchen.

'I can't bring myself to care,' she said. 'It's starting to feel not like my home any more.' She bent her head, and Cassie realized she was crying. She motioned towards a big pile of letters on the work surface. 'All bills,' she said. 'We can't pay any of them.'

'Have you tried any debt agencies? Or a consolidating loan?'

'We have no credit rating,' Laure said. 'Ridiculous, isn't it? We live in a million-pound house but we can't borrow a hundred pounds. I couldn't afford to buy food this week.'

Cassie gasped. Laure nodded. 'I tried to pay with my one remaining credit card in the supermarket and it refused to swipe. Then the boy on the checkout said, very discreetly, "I'm sorry, it won't accept this," and there was a big queue of people behind me, and they were all looking at me. I was only buying the bare essentials, bread, milk, cheese. I used to spend hundreds of pounds in one go,' she laughed. 'And now I couldn't pay for fifteen pounds' worth of food. I said something stupid like, "It must be past its expiry date, how silly of me," but he looked at it and said no, it was fine. Then he tried to swipe it again and it made that awful pinging noise. So I looked in my purse, although I knew I only had a couple of pounds, and I took out the milk and paid for that and then I ran out and left everything else by the till. There was a woman in the queue from Sophie's school and, oh God, I was sitting in the car crying and she knocked on the window and offered to pay for me. I have never been so humiliated in my life. She was so kind, which made it even worse, and I pretended that I'd left my other cards at home. Then I switched on the engine and the car wouldn't start because I didn't have any petrol.'

Cassie rubbed her hand up and down Laure's arm. 'Why didn't you call me?' she said, gently.

'I would have done, but I can't use my mobile now. The bank has frozen all our standing orders and the network has cut me off.'

'Christ!'

'I got the bus home, because I had just enough money for that. You know, it's the first time I've been on a bus for years. I quite enjoyed it. I felt –

273

anonymous. I left the car there and asked Tom to pick up Sophie for me, and then Gerard filled a petrol can and picked it up later. He's borrowed some money from one of his friends. He will pay it back,' she added.

'You can't live like this.'

'What choice do we have?'

'How long will it be until you get paid from the manor house?'

Laure sighed. 'I've asked for an interim cheque, and they looked at me really oddly too – you never get paid on a commission until you've finished it. But they said they would see what they could do next week. I felt like I was asking for charity. It was awful.'

'But that's silly – they do owe you the money.'

'I know. But I still felt like I was begging. You cannot understand what it's like, Cassie. I daren't answer the phone. I daren't open the post, I freeze when there's a knock on the door. I am terrified that one of the credit-card agencies will send the bailiffs round and Sophie will be here.'

'How much do you owe?'

'I have no idea, that's the problem. Gerard won't tell me. I know I only owed a thousand or so on my credit card, but then he took out at least four more when we started to get into trouble, and you know how high the interest rates are on cards when you don't pay it back in full . . . it's affecting everything. The phone may be cut off soon, as well as my mobile. The only money I can use to buy food is child benefit – thank God I had some saved up.'

'Can't you borrow against the house?'

'There's not enough left. And if he does go bankrupt, then all of that will be swallowed up by the debts he owes his creditors and suppliers, which means that Nick will have to leave at the end of this term.'

'It isn't the end of the world.' As soon as Cassie said it, she realized the words were totally inadequate.

Laure laughed, bitterly. 'It may not be. But it feels like it.'

'How is Gerard?'

'Desperate. We're not sleeping in the same room. I can't bear him to touch me.'

'It isn't entirely his fault.'

'You know it's not that. It isn't just the – the incident, it's the lying to me. He's lied to me for years, you know. We could have prevented all this, if he'd told me how things were going.'

'But the business is his concern, you know that. He wouldn't have taken your advice.'

Laure nodded. 'I know. And it isn't just the money, Cassie. It's the way he has behaved to us. I feel like I have been living on a knife-edge for years, and all the time I thought it was fine because soon it would be all right again and things would go well and he would go back to being the man I married. Only I think that the man I married has gone. He's never going to be like that again.'

'Are you sure?'

Laure nodded, chewing on her dry lower lip. 'He says he can be – he said so on the phone yesterday – but I can't trust him. That's it, really. I feel that I can't trust him again. I'm terrified of what he might do. I feel like I'm stalling all the time, trying not to make decisions which I ought to make. I need to make plans, but I feel paralysed.'

'You have to think what is best for Nick and Sophie.'

'I know,' Laure said, rubbing a tired hand through her long hair. 'They will be appalled at the thought of moving, but Nick is old enough to understand. Sophie won't. Even now, she expects her father to make everything all right, but she's changed towards him, too. It's as if she is wary of what he might do, ever since . . . it can't be undone.'

'Can you forgive him?'

'I can understand him, which isn't quite the same thing. I can understand why he is so angry and hurt that he is flailing around and not really aware of what he is doing. But that doesn't make it right. He says he can change, but God, Cassie, I don't honestly know if I want him any more. I feel totally, totally burnt out by all this. He tried to plead with me on the phone yesterday, but I couldn't bear to listen to him. He said he loved me but . . .'

'And what about Tom?' Cassie asked, quietly.

Laure looked wary. 'What do you mean?'

'I mean, are you seeing him? Are you thinking . . .' she swallowed. 'Might you leave Gerard to be with him? Is he going to leave Sarah?'

Laure looked horrified. 'God, no. I see him, of course I do. We see each other at school, around. But no, Cassie, I could not push him to do anything like that. To leave Sarah.' Cassie thought that she might not have to push Tom very hard. 'I could not face seeing another family destroyed.'

'Have you told him that?'

'Yes,' she said. 'Trust me, Cassie, I have. I need to sort myself out before I can even think about the future, and the children have to come first. I have to make a home for them.'

Cassie let out her breath with a small sigh of relief. But a shadow of doubt remained. Both Tom and Laure seemed far too calm. Laure might be putting the children first, but she suspected they had made some kind of plan and were not telling her. Maybe being together was years hence, but some kind of decision had been reached.

'Let me give you some money,' Cassie said.

'No, Cassie, how on earth can I take money from you?'

'You bloody well can, because if this was me you would force me to take it.'

'Gerard would kill me.'

'He borrowed from a friend.'

'A business acquaintance. Not a real friend. Not someone like you and Nat.'

'Don't tell him. What matters is that you and Sophie have enough money to eat – God! – and you can pay your phone bill.'

'You really don't have to do this, it is so embarrassing . . .'

'No, it isn't. I could have done much more. You will take this.'

'Don't write me a cheque,' Laure said. She grimaced. 'It has to be cash. A cheque would just get swallowed up.'

Cassie sighed. 'Right. You need to open up your own savings account that Gerard does not know about. You will put the money I give you into the account, and draw it out whenever you want. And you ought to be sending some of your furniture to an auction house, and you have to make sure that you are paid in your name.'

'This sounds very clinical and organized,' Laure said, with the ghost of a smile.

'This is survival, Laure. You need to protect the children's future, and it sounds to me like once the house is gone there isn't going to be anything left.' Laure shook her head. 'What does Gerard say he's going to do?'

'Find a job. Work for someone else, or set up on his own again if he is allowed to.'

Cassie looked searchingly at her. 'Will you stay with him?'

'I've told you I do not know. I feel like I don't know anything. I'm like a dead woman walking at the moment.'

'We have to make plans. You have to make plans, and the first step is setting up this account. Right. What time is it?' She looked at the clock. It was two. 'We've just got time to go into Claydon and get to the building society before I have to pick up the kids.'

Filling out the forms seemed to take forever, and Cassie was worried sick she was going to be late. Laure was almost sleepwalking – she had to help her into the car. How on earth she was managing to work at the moment, God only knew, Cassie thought. Once Laure had her paying-in book, she turned to Cassie. 'I can put my child benefit money in here,' she said. 'And it will be safe.' Cassie nodded, and brought out her cheque book. She swiftly filled a cheque in, and handed it to Laure, her eyes daring her to refuse it.

'I can't take all this.'

'Yes, you bloody well can.' Cassie had written a cheque for thousands.

Laure started to cry, then she wrapped her arms around Cassie's neck. 'You will never understand how much this means to me,' she said. They both began to laugh.

'We must look like lesbians,' Cassie giggled. 'Shut up, and do not refer to this ever again.'

'I am not, repeat not,' Nat said, holding onto the bulging envelope full of airline tickets, 'going on holiday with mad people.'

'Who are the mad people?' Arthur said, with interest.

'I told you,' Tilly said, delighted to know something that her brother did not. 'Tom and Sarah and Mickey and Lucy and Daisy and then Laure and Nick and

278

Sophie. Honestly,' she said, rolling her eyes. 'Don't you ever listen?'

'No Gerard?' Nat asked.

Cassie shook her head.

'Isn't the chalet going to be a bit – crowded?' Arthur said, raising his eyebrows. 'But all the girls can share a room, can't they?'

'No way!' Tilly said. 'For a start Lucy is friends with Sophie and I'm not – I am a whole year older, unless you had forgotten, Mother, and there is no way I am sharing a room with them and her.' She looked accusingly at Beth.

Nat and Cassie looked at Beth, who was cramming chocolate cake into her mouth, sitting cross-legged in the middle of the kitchen table.

'It's not a person,' Tilly said. 'It's a troll.'

'Am not!' Beth shrieked, jumping from the table onto her, pulling her hair.

Nat expertly caught Beth and tucked her under his arm so she could not reach Tilly.

'Apologize,' he said sternly to Tilly. 'Your sister is not a troll.'

'Yes she is. She's a horrible troll who steals my clothes and all my felt tips.'

'Do not!'

'Do.'

'Shut up,' Nat said, putting his hand over Beth's mouth.

'Women,' Arthur said. 'Pathetic.'

'Shut up,' Tilly and Beth said together.

'Nobody is going to be going anywhere unless you lot start behaving. Dad and I will go on our own and leave you all in a cupboard.'

'You can't do that. It's against the law.'

'Not against troll law,' Tilly said. Beth shrieked against Nat's hand and bit it.

'Ow! Now that's enough,' he said, sternly and loudly. Beth looked up at him uncertainly. She was more than happy to disregard her mum but her dad was another kettle of fish entirely. If he said something was going to happen, it tended to happen, such as not being able to ride Dougal for a week or missing out on a swimming trip. She had pushed him before, and it wasn't worth it.

'I love you, Daddy,' she said, winding her arms around his neck and gazing up at him.

'Little creepy troll,' Tilly said. She opened the chalet brochure. 'It's got a plasma-screen television,' she said. 'Dreamy. We'll be able to sit up and watch films while Beth is in bed.'

'You will not!' shouted Beth. 'I will not be in bed!'

'Enough,' Nat said. 'Arthur's got a point, though. It is going to be a bit crowded, Cassie.'

She looked crestfallen. 'It is my fault. But I've done it now. I can't un-invite them and the tickets have been issued. Everyone is really looking forward to it.'

There was nothing she could do. Gerard would not come, and she hadn't had the courage to turn Sarah down. She had winced when Sarah said, 'It will do Tom and me a lot of good to have time together, and Laure has been through so much.'

Chapter Twenty-Two

Tom

'I do not want to go. How much more plain can I make this?' Tom said. 'The last thing in the world I want to do is go away with our friends and try to pretend that we are one big happy family.'

'What are we going to do at Easter? Sit and stare at each other for a week in this house?'

'You can work,' Tom said. 'And I will entertain the kids.'

'Which means you'll tap away on your computer and the kids will run riot, as usual.'

'I thought you wanted me to tap away on my computer,' he said, reasonably. 'I am doing what you want. I am writing my novel.'

It was, in fact, the only escape for him and he had found, once he'd written the first chapter which was like pulling teeth, he was quite enjoying it. When he was writing, he entered a kind of weird parallel universe where time stopped, and he was often amazed to find he had been sitting at his computer for three hours at a time. Then he would be late for Daisy, driving like a bat out of hell towards her nursery while his head fought drug-crazed terrorists.

At first he had sat down and tried to plan all the

chapters. It was like doing a school essay, and after half an hour he was bored stiff and ripped it up. Then a phrase, a comment he liked floated into his brain and he typed it, and then, suddenly on the screen in front of him there was a conversation between two people he had never met but whom he knew. One was a gung-ho, naïve young man who was escaping from a drugs charge in Britain – that would make Laure smile – and the other was a world-weary, Edward Farrell-type figure wearing a smartly pressed linen suit and smoking an expensive cigar. He was an ex-pat who'd settled in Africa, living alone in a vast and quite empty villa on the beach, with only a manservant for company. He had millions from diamond smuggling stashed away in a Swiss bank account and he gave wild parties for the other expats, attended by beautiful hookers. He'd bumped into the young main character Ted (Ned? Michael? Reuben? Hector? Names were awfully difficult) at the airport, when he was in danger of being arrested for not bribing the customs officer to let him through. Miles, the patrician diamond smuggler, had seen what was happening and shoved a fistful of dollars into the hands of the fat, sweating man with a gun at his belt. Spotting a prospective runner, he invited the young man back to his amazing house and plied him with brandy. They had a fascinating conversation about philosophy – Ted, no, Ted wouldn't do. Not romantic enough. Henry? Gah, no, his brother would think it was him – Chris, yes, likeable, friendly. Chris and Miles had talked late into the night and Miles had offered some opium, whereupon things had gone a bit weird and veered off from Edward Farrell into Joseph Conrad territory. Which was fine, because they were both dead so he could nick their ideas.

Tom quickly realized that what he was doing was

living out his fantasies – as a troubled teenager he had longed to drink his way around the world and have adventures under swirling tropical fans while wearing a linen suit, smoking Havana cigars. When he was writing he left reality, and when he looked up and saw the familiar wall of his office he had to shake himself, because it seemed far less real than the world in his head. It was a kind of madness, a form of schizophrenia with voices talking to him, unbidden, in his mind. No wonder so many writers drank themselves to death, he thought, or went potty.

The only person he wanted to show his work to was Laure. He thought about her all the time. From the moment he woke, to the moment sleep finally claimed him, she lived inside his head, smiling, talking to him, making love to him. How often he replayed that morning, the morning that Laure would not repeat until things were sorted, the house was sold, and she had left Gerard. When he was driving, he invented all kinds of situations about how they were going to tell Sarah and Gerard, how they were going to break the news to the children and how they going to set up a home together and everything would be perfect. Only even Tom had to admit that it was unlikely to be perfect. Parts would undoubtedly be chaos and hell. That was the trouble. No matter how idyllic his imaginings of the future, there was no way of avoiding the hurt and implosion of two families. Quite a few people would never speak to them again, quite possibly Nat included. They would be pariahs. Which was fine by him, but he could not bear the thought of Laure being ostracized or regarded as something she quite patently was not.

There was no going back with Sarah. He did not love her any more – his feelings for Laure made that obvious. He wasn't even sure if he liked her. All she could ever see was what she wanted. He laughed bitterly to himself – what had he once read in one of her women's magazines? That the thing that attracts you to a person most strongly in the first place is the thing that will eventually turn you against them. In Sarah's case, it was her strength, her single-mindedness and her determination to push him, to make him the man she wanted him to be. Well, he wasn't the man she wanted him to be. He never would be. He was a romantic idealist who would prefer to be in a derelict cottage with love, than in a big house surrounded by the trappings of wealth, living the kind of life that other people deemed successful. He didn't care about money, and he was not going to climb any kind of ladder, corporate or otherwise. He found Sarah's goals empty and shallow, and he longed for an existence where he did not have to pretend, where he could be honest to himself.

The children's school was not doing them any favours. Mickey was getting out of control, rude and aggressive, mainly because he could not keep up in class and felt he was stupid. His teachers were talking about putting him into a dyslexic unit, and Tom was furious that it was only now, at the age of thirteen with his common entrance exams looming, that they had picked up on his problem. Lucy was becoming stroppy and Daisy – Daisy was adorable, but she'd be fine in a state school. And just as well, if not better, with two parents who were far happier apart. He and Laure could create a proper loving home. It would be much better for them to grow up around two adults who loved each other, than two adults who barely co-existed.

'Why don't you want to go skiing?' Sarah had cornered him in the kitchen, when he was making Daisy a cheese sandwich for lunch.

'What are you talking about?' He parked Daisy on the work surface by the sink, and wiped her nose with a piece of kitchen roll. 'Not cheese,' she said, firmly. 'Ham.'

'Not ham,' he said. 'Lovely cheese.'

'Yuk.'

Mickey was in town, and Lucy was playing at Sophie's, which gave him an excuse to see Laure later on. He lived for those snatched five minutes when they could exchange pleasantries and social arrangements for the children, and he could at least be physically close to her. Nothing was said, but nothing needed to be said. He'd hoped to try and get another hour or so on his book while Daisy had a nap. At three, she still needed a sleep in the afternoon or she was awful by teatime. Sarah had said she needed to work today even though it was Saturday, so he thought he was safe, but then he'd seen her car pull into the drive half an hour ago. She was now driving a maroon BMW, very sleek and sporty. It drank petrol, and looked outrageously new and shiny next to Tom's grubby old estate. The nanny had departed the day before, now that Tom was off crutches and he could drive again, although the doctor said he shouldn't. He was fine, apart from not being able to turn his head without wincing.

'I desperately need a break,' she said, reaching past him to flick on the kettle. She was wearing a smart black trouser suit and shiny black stilettos. She had lost weight and it suited her. 'I don't know if you have noticed, but I am working flat out.'

'Of course I've noticed,' Tom said, neutrally. The last thing he wanted was an argument. They still slept in the same bed, because there was nowhere else for him to go, apart from sleeping on the sofa, and Sarah had said he was absolutely not going to do that because then the children would realize how bad things had become. So they slept side by side, carefully making sure they did not touch each other, while he dreamed of Laure and she dreamed of – what? He could no longer see inside her head, if he had ever been able to.

'So don't you think I ought to be allowed to have a break? The children would love it. I thought Cassie was one of your greatest friends.'

'I love Cassie and Nat,' he said. 'But a) we cannot afford it and b) it hardly makes sense to go away together when . . .'

'When what?'

'When we don't know what is happening . . .'

Sarah swung round, and for the first time in what felt like years, he saw real emotion in her eyes. 'What's happening to us, you mean?'

'Yes,' he said, awkwardly. He didn't want to get into this, right now. He hadn't planned what to say. He had toyed with so many ideas, so many scenarios, such as moving out himself, but then who would look after the children? And he couldn't leave them. It made far more sense for Sarah to leave and live in London, but then he knew she would never agree to give the house and its equity to him, and the children would miss her . . . It was complicated, he admitted. But something had to be done. He and Laure had to be allowed to be together. That was the beacon of truth he held onto, repeating it to himself like a mantra. It had to happen, because it was right. Being so in love made them blameless.

'There you go.' He handed Daisy the sandwich and lifted her down. She put her hand in his. 'Video,' she said.

'Oh, all right then.' He took her into the front room, and slotted in her favourite video. She reversed onto the sofa, and began to eat her sandwich around the thumb that was almost permanently parked in her mouth. Tom debated how he could avoid this discussion, and, if possible, leave the house. But his car keys were in the kitchen. He sighed, and walked back in. Sarah was wiping up the crumbs from Daisy's sandwich, an irritated expression on her face. That lifted as she turned towards him.

'Tom,' she said, softly, 'I don't want this.'

'What?' He stalled, backing up against the dishwasher, picking up the knife to clear it up. Sarah trying to be nice was almost worse than Sarah being horrible, or ignoring him.

'I don't want us to be like this.' She reached up and ran her finger down his chest. To his horror, he felt himself becoming aroused. She moved smoothly up against him, and he could feel her breasts through her jacket. 'Daisy's watching TV. She'll be fine. Put the knife down.' He put it down, obediently, as if hypnotized. Laure wouldn't make love to him again, and he was so desperate for her, all the time . . . He thought about being in bed with her, constantly. Sarah lifted her face to his and kissed him.

Twenty minutes later, he lay on his side, his mind churning. At the moment of orgasm, he had only just stopped himself calling out Laure's name. He put his hands to his face. What a bloody mess. And now Sarah would think that everything was fine, all was resolved. How could he be so weak? If Laure ever found out . . . They had promised each other they were not sleeping with Gerard or Sarah, nor would they.

'Why are you in bed in the middle of the day?' Daisy's face peered at him enquiringly. He opened his eyes and looked at her, his mind desperately searching for a reason. 'Mummy and Daddy were feeling tired,' he said. Daisy put down the pink rabbit she was holding and started to climb into the bed.

'Why have you got no clothes on?'

'We were feeling a bit warm,' he said.

'Snuggle,' she said, tucking herself into his arms. He let his chin rest on her head, breathing in her familiar smell. He felt Sarah move beside him. She stretched languorously, her leg brushing against his. She rubbed the sole of her foot up and down the back of his calf. 'I'm going to have a shower,' she whispered into his ear.

'Fine,' he said. 'I'll get up in a second.'

'Hello, Daisy,' she said, leaning over and kissing her on the cheek. 'Was the video good?'

'I've seen it before. It's boring. I didn't know where you had gone.'

Tom heard Sarah slide out of bed, and then the door to the en suite bathroom banged shut. The whir of the power shower began, and he could hear Sarah singing softly to herself. He rolled over onto his back, and Daisy put her hand on his chest, lifting herself up.

'Can we go and see Dougal?' she said. 'And you promised you'd take me to the park to ride my bike.'

'I did,' he said. 'And we will.' Seeing Dougal would give him a chance to talk to Cassie and try and sort this out. Surely the last thing Cassie would want would be him and Sarah on holiday with them. He had almost nodded off to sleep with Daisy in his arms when Sarah padded back into the room, swathed in a towel. 'I'll ring Cassie now,' she said. 'You know, I'm really looking forward to this.' He groaned. There was no escape.

Chapter Twenty-Three

Laure

Laure paused at the top of the mountain, her breath visible in the air before her, her nose pink with the cold. She tucked a stray tendril of hair into her chocolate-brown faux-fur hat, and pulled on her black ski gloves, wriggling her toes in the rigid ski boots to keep them warm.

'I think my testicles have frozen,' Tom said, behind her. 'I thought it was supposed to be warmer at Easter. It's bloody freezing up here. Where are the others?'

'Already gone,' Laure said, watching the line of figures zigzagging down the gentle Bellecôte piste, the tall figure of Nat in front. 'You've got to take it steady, remember. You shouldn't really be on skis.'

'Stupid doctors. What do they know?'

'They know that if you fall again the bones will not knit together properly.'

'Have you said where we'll meet them?'

'At Le Jump for a coffee in about an hour,' she said, moving the sleeve of her chocolate-brown all-in-one ski suit back to look at her watch.

'Fantastic,' he said. 'I have you all to myself. For a whole hour.'

She turned to smile up at him.

'I hate to say this,' she said. 'But I love you.'

He bent his head, and kissed her.

'This is so cool,' Lucy had said, standing in the living room, looking around her with wide eyes. The main living area of the chalet was open-plan, with a huge fireplace in the centre. All the bedrooms opened off a circular balcony on the first floor. Running the entire length of the vast room were windows giving a panoramic view of the snow-covered mountains. The light was blinding. All the floors were wooden, with Indian-style rugs dotted around and snow-scene paintings hung on the walls. It was like living inside an exceptionally luxurious cuckoo clock.

'This is amazing,' Sophie said, running down the stairs into the basement. 'Come and look!' she called over her shoulder. All the children followed her, their feet pounding on the wooden staircase.

Mickey shouted up the stairs, 'There's a sauna! And a jacuzzi! This is so freaky.'

Lucy rushed up to the first floor. 'I'm having this bedroom!' they could hear her cry. 'It's got its own bathroom with a shower and everything!'

Cassie pulled off her hat and shook out her hair.

'It is nice, isn't it?' she said. 'We've never been able to book it at this time of year.'

'Haven't you stayed here before?' Sarah asked. She was looking about her with a thoroughly pleased air. It was so luxurious. There was even a TV room just off the main living area with a vast plasma screen, and the table in the far corner of the living area was already laid as if for a formal dinner party. Their host, Thomas, an Austrian chef, had been at the door to greet them, and his girlfriend, Anna, who looked after the chalet, immediately asked them if they would like a drink. On the sideboard was an array of delicious-looking cakes.

290

'Where do you want us, Cassie?' Sarah called, climbing the stairs. In the hallway stood mountains of luggage, which Thomas was starting to carry up behind her.

'I thought you and Tom could have this room,' Cassie said a few minutes later, putting her head around the door of the smaller of the double bedrooms. She saw a shadow cross Sarah's face. 'It has an adjoining door to the children's room,' she explained, motioning to it with her hand, 'so you can be close to Daisy. It was either that or putting up a camp bed in your room. Otherwise of course you could have had the big bedroom with the en suite. You can, if you want.' She could see Nat pulling a face behind Sarah's shoulder.

Tom jumped in immediately. 'Of course we're happy with this. Thanks, it looks perfect. Doesn't it, Sarah?'

'I suppose so,' she said.

Living in close proximity with Sarah for a week, Cassie ruminated, was not going to be entirely easy. At the airport, she arrived dressed up to the nines in a floor-length fur coat and pale blue Mukluk boots, whereupon Tilly promptly informed her that anything up to four rabbits had died just so she could have those fluffy pompoms. She had three suitcases just for herself, far more than you needed for a week's skiing trip. Cassie had explained that the evenings weren't usually dressy – she and Nat tended just to wear jeans and comfortable sweaters. She hoped Sarah would not want the high life: there were some great clubs in the resort but she was always so tired at the end of a day's skiing that after dinner all she wanted to do was have a bath and go to bed. Cassie also noticed how Tom did everything – he carried Daisy, he lifted the suitcases off the carousel, he fetched the trolleys at Geneva airport, while Sarah snapped orders. At one point she caught Nat's eye, and had to stifle a giggle.

Sarah turned to her. 'Will the chalet staff babysit?' she said.

'I'm sure Anna would if you asked her, but you'd have to pay extra, I think. Anyway, I'll be here because the younger ones will need an early bed.'

'Great,' Sarah said.

Cassie and Laure exchanged glances.

'Tom and I might go out for a meal on our own tonight,' Sarah announced. 'A friend in the office says there's a fabulous Michelin-starred restaurant here.'

'What?' Cassie said. 'Sorry, I mean, this is the first night and the chalet staff will have made a meal. It isn't really worth spending money on going out, is it?'

'We hardly ever get a chance to go out on our own though, Tom, do we?' Sarah said, smiling up at him, tucking her arm through his. Tom disengaged his arm.

'I would not dream of going out on our own tonight,' he said. 'Why would we? Come on, Sarah, let's unpack.' He closed the door to their bedroom firmly, and Laure raised her eyebrows at Cassie.

'I am going to have to kill her,' Cassie muttered. 'She has to be the most selfish woman in the universe.'

'She doesn't get a break very often,' Laure said, soothingly. 'Although I do rather agree with you.'

'But did you see what she was like at the airport? When we were walking towards the plane Daisy reached up to take her hand and she just snatched it away.' Then Cassie stopped. The last thing she wanted to do was portray Sarah as a monstrous mother, because it would give more weight to the argument that the children could survive without her. Oh, God. This was all too complicated, there were far too many undercurrents. But Laure, as ever, seemed quite calm and unperturbed. She seemed to have detached herself from the entire situation.

Laure looked thoughtful. 'She's just used to Tom doing everything for the children.'

At that moment, Tilly raced past in her swimming costume.

'Where are you going?' Cassie said. 'You haven't unpacked yet.'

'Details,' she said. 'Too, too dull. Come on, Lucy, Sophie, last one in is really sad!'

'Jacuzzi,' Laure explained. 'They'll never be out of it. This is lovely, Cassie. I can't get over how beautiful it is. You are so kind . . .'

'If you start thanking me I will have to never speak to you again,' Cassie said. 'It's great having you here. You deserve a holiday. Only . . .'

'Are you sure I'm not in the way?' Laure said, quickly. Cassie realized the last thing she wanted to do was talk about Tom, and she made a mental note that she would push it to the back of her mind this holiday and not obsess. There was nothing she could do.

'You are beginning to sound like Carole. If you start collecting plates and tidying up you are on the next plane home.'

'God forbid. I will not moan, and I will not be grateful. OK?'

'Fab. Now I am going to have a shower and then I am going to have a very large glass of champagne and lots of canapés.' She twirled the word around her lips, and Laure smiled. She felt as if a great weight was lifting from her shoulders. It was wonderful to be able to spend a whole week so close to Tom. She had no fears that they would reveal themselves, because they had become so adept at acting. They no longer had to look at each other, they just knew how the other one was feeling. She felt she could bear anything, because in the future they would be together. The only really hard part was the fact that he was sharing a bed with Sarah.

But he had promised her that they never slept together now.

It was unlike Laure to take any pleasure in a situation which would cause hurt, but there was something very seductive about having such a huge secret that no-one else knew. She hugged it to herself, at night. He loves me. Utterly. In her bag was a purse containing the money she had drawn out of her new account. That would mean she could pay her way and the whole nightmare was put on hold this week, thank goodness. It had blown a big hole in the money Cassie had given her – lent, she said firmly to herself – but it would be worth it. She would pay her back, every penny, once her design cheque came through.

Sophie had ripped open her bag to get to her swimming costume, and there were clothes, shoes and knickers all over the floor. Sighing, Laure began to tidy up, and unpacked all her clothes and Sophie's, hanging them neatly in the wardrobe and putting them in symmetrical piles in the chest of drawers. There was a sink in their bedroom, thoughtfully provided with soap in a wrapper, and a selection of shampoos, shower gels and conditioners in monogrammed bottles. She had a fleeting sensation of guilt. Gerard would love this, it was just his kind of environment. He would love the resort, too. Driving up through the winding streets on the coach from the airport, she thought what a smart place it was – all the houses, shops and hotels were built in traditional wood and already, as the sun went down, the town twinkled with fairy lights. Browsing around the shops were chic-looking women swathed in furs, children in the latest skiing outfits.

Her mother had always wanted them to buy a skiing lodge, but her father said it was too much of an expense and they would never go. She hadn't been here before – I must get to know more of my own country, she thought. It would be lovely to be able to speak her native language this week. Having lived away for so long, she now even thought in English. Nick was pretty fluent in French but Sophie, who had been bilingual as a young child, was losing a lot of her vocabulary.

Laure sat on the bed, and stretched out her arms behind her. Why didn't she and Tom come and live here? Why not come home? They could parcel up all the children, there were great schools over here. Sarah wouldn't mind – she was so busy working anyway, and they could put them on cheap flights to come back. She did not think of Gerard.

Maybe somewhere in the south, where her grand-parents were from, in the lush, rolling countryside, she could buy a small *mas* and – what? What would she do for money? Her business was only at the fledgling stage, and she knew nothing of how to set up in France and the tax laws. Besides, French style was quite different. They might not like her ideas. And Sophie and Nick did not think of themselves as French. Would it be fair to uproot them and take them to live in what was effectively a foreign country? Tom could write anywhere, that wasn't a problem. They could make it work.

Her heart had lifted with relief when Gerard had told her he didn't want to come on the holiday. He had insisted that he had to stay at home to show people around the house and tidy up the loose ends of the business. Really, Laure knew he would not come because he couldn't bear not to pick up the tab in restaurants. He would have hated to have not felt equal to Nat. That would be far too humiliating.

Laure sighed. This was probably the last holiday she would be able to take the children on for years and years, and it was unlikely that she would be able to afford anything as luxurious as this ever again. But did it matter? If Gerard had not wanted so much, they might not be in this predicament. Life is not about what you have, she thought. It corrupts the things that do matter. She lay down on the bed, suddenly exhausted, and closed her eyes.

The next thing she knew, Cassie was knocking on the door. Not getting an answer, she tentatively opened it. Seeing Laure on the bed she said, 'I'm so sorry, I should have let you sleep. Only it's seven and they're about to serve the canapés. I knew you wouldn't want to miss that.'

'Where's Tom?'

'God knows, I haven't seen them for an hour.'

Laure felt a wave of jealousy. What was he doing?

'Where's Daisy?'

'With me,' Cassie said. 'We've been doing puzzles. They have a great selection of games here.'

Laure lifted herself onto one elbow and shook her head. 'I was out like a light. What are the children doing?'

'Watching a film wrapped in towels,' Cassie said. 'They all seem to be getting on like a house on fire. Nick is a sweetheart, isn't he? He's been lovely with Daisy and Beth. Come on. The man's due to come to take our sizes for the boots and skis in half an hour or so.'

'Wow, he comes to us?'

'No expense spared,' Cassie said, then saw Laure's face. 'The martyr look. Take it off. Now. Can you—' She gestured awkwardly. 'The skis and stuff, lift passes . . .'

'Yes,' Laure said, firmly. 'And don't you dare offer another thing. I am fine. I'll be down in a minute.'

'Don't get too dressed up, will you? I don't want you

to show me up because I can't be bothered to get changed.'

'I promise I will make no effort whatsoever,' Laure laughed.

'Good.'

It was odd that Tom and Sarah had disappeared into their room and left the children alone, Laure thought.

Half an hour later, Cassie, Nat and Laure were sitting on the sofa in front of the fire sipping champagne. 'This is hell, isn't it?' Cassie said, stretching her toes out towards the flames. Nat was reading a newspaper he'd bought at the airport, lounging back against the cushions. Laure stared into the fire. 'Are all the children eating with us?' she said, lazily.

'I think so,' Cassie said. 'Other nights Anna says she can make them some tea at about five or six if we want – something simpler, like chicken and chips.'

'They'll want to stay up,' Laure said. Cassie nodded. She heard the door to Tom and Sarah's room open.

Tom wandered downstairs wearing a pair of jeans, no socks and shoes and a loose-fitting white collarless shirt. Behind him came Sarah. She was wearing a skin-tight turquoise knee-length satin dress and black stilettos. Laure heard Cassie choke back a laugh, and she had to bite the inside of her cheek. Sarah sashayed across the room, slowly taking in the fact that Cassie was in jeans as was Nat, and Laure was wearing baggy combat trousers and a T-shirt.

'Lovely outfit,' Cassie said.

'You might have told me you weren't going to dress for dinner,' Sarah said, crossly. She was wearing full make-up, and her hair was blow-dried into shining waves.

'I thought I did,' Cassie said, apologetically. 'I'm afraid we aren't very smart here.'

'So I see,' Sarah said.

'What are the kids doing?' Tom asked.

'Watching a film.'

He turned and walked away, and minutes later he reappeared with Daisy in his arms. Her thumb was plugged into her mouth and her little head was drooping. 'I don't think she's going to last,' he said.

'Am,' Daisy said, sleepily.

'Well, come and sit with me for a bit.'

Tom sat down in one of the big armchairs, and Daisy snuggled into his chest. Cassie handed him a glass of champagne.

'Thanks,' he said. 'So what's the plan for tomorrow?'

'Dividing up into groups for skiing, I guess,' Cassie said. 'Does anyone have any preferences?'

'I'm going to introduce Daisy to the joys of the slopes,' Tom said, looking down at her. She had fallen fast asleep, her rosebud mouth pursed, one hand grasping Tom's shirt. He smoothed a lock of hair on her forehead, and bent to kiss her.

'Why don't you put her down to sleep?' Cassie said. 'I don't think she's going to wake.'

'I will in a mo,' he said.

'What about Beth?' Laure asked. 'Will she stay on the nursery slopes with Daisy?'

'Are you kidding?' Nat said, lifting his eyes from the newspaper. 'You haven't seen her on skis. She's an absolute demon. She's faster than I am.'

'She is pretty amazing,' Cassie nodded. 'She kind of sits back into the snowplough position and – whoosh.'

'Like a small but very dangerous arrow,' Nat said.

'More champagne?' Anna asked. She was a pretty girl, with long brunette hair tied back in a ponytail. Like Thomas, she wore a chef's white apron.

Sarah held out her glass without acknowledging Anna. 'I'd like to hire a ski guide,' she said.

'That's quite expensive,' Tom said, 'and I don't

think all the children would be able to ski at that level.'

'I meant for me.'

'Ah. And are you going to be so selfish all holiday?'

There was a long silence. Sarah reached forward and put her glass, very deliberately, on the table in front of her. She stood up, and walked with great elegance and poise to the stairs. Without looking back, she climbed them and then they heard the sound of the bedroom door closing.

'Tom! Did you have to?'

He looked down at Daisy. 'I'm just going to put her to bed,' he said. 'Back in a minute.'

Once he had gone, Laure and Cassie gazed at each other in horror.

'This is your fault,' Nat said. 'I warned you.' He stood up, and walked off towards the television room. 'Lunatics,' he said, over his shoulder.

'I ought to go to Sarah,' Cassie said. 'She'll be upset.'

Laure, to her amazement, started to laugh. Then Cassie started to laugh too. They laughed until the tears rolled down their cheeks. 'The dress!' Cassie spluttered.

'And the shoes!' Laure yelped.

'We're not being very kind,' Laure said, wiping her eyes. 'Tom shouldn't have said that.'

'He was right, though. Does she ever think of anyone but herself? Poor, poor Tom. I don't know how he has lasted, all these years.'

At that moment, they heard Tom's tread on the stairs. They both hastily stopped laughing.

'Has she gone to sleep?' Cassie asked him as he joined them.

'Daisy, or my darling wife?'

'Daisy, you fool,' Cassie said. She noticed he didn't look at Laure, who was sitting with her legs tucked up under her on the sofa, gazing into the fire. There was an aura of peace around the two of them, as if they didn't need to communicate.

'Yes. Where's my drink?'

'Here.' Cassie handed it to him.

He looked at them both. 'What?' he said. 'What do you expect me to say?'

'I don't know,' Cassie admitted. 'Sorry?'

'I'm not sorry. She is a selfish cow.'

'But you can't take sides against her in front of all of us.'

'Why not?'

'Because you are married to her,' Cassie explained, patiently.

Tom glanced at Laure, who looked away.

'I don't know,' he said.

Cassie looked at him sternly. 'What don't you know? Shush.'

'She can't hear. She's on the phone. Probably calling the truth police to come and take me away.'

Cassie snorted. 'This is going to make things quite hard for the rest of us,' she said.

'Well, you can't expect me to sit here and listen to all that shite, can you?'

'Couldn't you have had a quiet word, you know, in your room? Away from your very embarrassed friends? Don't bring it here, Tom, please. Let's just have a truce for a week.'

'It was rude of me,' Tom admitted. 'I just can't seem to bite my lip any more in the way I used to.'

'Try,' Cassie suggested.

Tom stared moodily out of the window at the dark navy blue night. Below them twinkled the lights of the town. It looked enchantingly pretty. 'I feel like getting exceedingly drunk,' he said.

'I'm not sure that is the answer,' Cassie said.

Laure had leant back into the sofa. She was still

looking into the fire, apparently not listening, in a world of her own.

'What are you thinking?' Tom asked, softly. Cassie looked from one to the other.

Laure raised her head. 'I think I will go to bed early,' she said. 'I need to sleep.' In one fluid movement, she stood up and walked towards the stairs. At the bottom she turned. 'Tell Nick and Sophie where I am, will you? Sophie must be in bed by nine, no later. You don't mind, do you, if I skip the meal?' She looked utterly exhausted, on another planet.

'No,' Cassie said, understanding perfectly. 'I'll sort the kids out. You sleep.'

When Laure had disappeared, Cassie looked at Tom firmly.

'What is going on?' she said, in a low voice.

'What do you mean?'

'You know perfectly well what I mean. Is this totally over or have you hatched a plan, the two of you? Please tell me, because I feel that I am going mad. I'm so worried about all of you it's keeping me awake at night. I know it's not up to me to interfere in any way, you're both adults, but I love you both so much I can't bear to see you make a decision that might ruin everyone's lives. You can see that, can't you? I feel in a way responsible.'

Tom put his head down, and stared at his hands. 'I love her,' he said.

'I know.' She reached forward and held one of his hands. 'But I'm not sure that gives you the right to make a decision which is, to be fair, totally selfish.'

'I know that in the tiny logical bit of my brain, but try telling the rest of me.' He laughed, quietly.

'You are both my dearest friends,' Cassie said. 'And that is why I don't think I can let you do this. It isn't just about your lives, you know . . .'

'Yo, Mum!' Arthur wandered into the room. 'Cool film. When's dinner? I'm starving.'

'Soon.' She smiled up at him.

Arthur looked about. 'Where is everybody?'

'I thought Dad was with you, and Laure's gone to bed. She's really tired. Sarah's just – coming down in a minute.'

Arthur picked up a tangerine from the large fruit bowl in the centre of the coffee table, and tossed it in the air. 'Nick said he'd take me to a club.'

'Nick is not going to a club, he's too young, and so are you. By miles.'

'Thanks for reminding me. Can I have a beer?'

'Ask your father.'

'Ask me what?' Nat said, appearing in the doorway with Beth in his arms. She was looking sleepy.

Cassie looked past him. 'Do tell the girls to get dressed,' she said. 'They're going to freeze.'

'Get dressed, you are going to freeze,' Nat said, over his shoulder.

'Dinner in half an hour,' Cassie called, as they raced up the stairs, towels still wrapped around them.

'Can Arthur have a beer?'

'I should think so. One.'

'Have they got any alcopops?' Arthur asked, hopefully.

'Don't push it,' Nat said. 'Where's Laure gone?'

'Sleep.'

Nat rolled his eyes. 'Is everyone going to be this weird all week?'

Tom laughed. 'I could murder a pint.'

'Have we got time?' Nat raised his eyebrows at Cassie.

'Yeah, why not. The girls will be a while getting changed. Don't be ages.'

Great, she thought. That leaves me with Sarah, if she

302

hasn't gone to bed too. She picked up one of the magazines on the table, and was enjoyably reading about fashion faux pas at the Oscars when she heard the tip, tap, of Sarah's shoes. She arranged a bright smile on her face before looking up.

'Where is he?' Sarah said.

Cassie resisted the temptation to say, 'Who? George W. Bush? Elvis Presley? Goofy?' Instead she said, 'Gone for a drink with Nat.'

'Figures.' She sat down next to Cassie, and smoothed her hands over the turquoise satin. 'Does this look silly?'

'A bit,' Cassie said. 'But it's lovely.'

'Lacroix,' Sarah said. 'I've never stayed in a chalet before.'

'Really? But you said you'd been skiing a lot.'

'Yeah,' Sarah nodded. 'In my twenties. We usually stayed in hostels. We couldn't afford anything like this. I didn't know', she smiled at Cassie, 'what to wear.'

Cassie's heart melted. 'We didn't support you,' she said. 'I'm sorry.'

'I suppose I did sound awful,' Sarah said. 'You must think I am selfish.'

'No,' Cassie said. 'Well, a bit.'

'I seem to get everything wrong,' Sarah said, leaning forward with her hands on her silk-stockinged knees.

'It must be really hard,' Cassie said, 'trying to be everything.'

'That's it,' Sarah said. 'I feel that I'm trying to be three people at once, mother, wife, career woman, and not being any of them very well. Did Tom say anything?'

'No,' Cassie lied. 'Nothing at all.'

'Laure seems rather sad. Do you think she and Gerard will stay together?'

Not fair, Cassie thought. I can't give those secrets away. 'I don't know. It isn't really anything to do with me.'

'You're her best friend,' Sarah said. 'She's beautiful, isn't she?'

'Yes,' Cassie said, looking at her warily. Where was this going?

'She's got a fabulous natural style. I try too hard.'

'No, you don't.'

'Yes, I do. But at least I try,' she said, turning to look at Cassie.

'Ouch,' Cassie said.

'Sorry, uncalled for.' She stretched out her slim legs. 'My job calls on me to be a bitch and sometimes it's hard to draw the line.'

'Do you like it?'

'Yes. It's what I am,' Sarah said, simply. 'I moan and moan about Tom not being the breadwinner but I couldn't give up my job. I have spent so long getting where I am that chucking it all in would be pointless. I'd hate it at home. I'm not a natural mother,' she said, turning to look at Cassie.

'I'm not sure I am either,' Cassie admitted.

'No,' Sarah said. 'And at least I have my career. Is there any more champagne?'

'I'll get some.' Cassie stood up and headed in the direction of the kitchen. Grr. Grr. She'd been lulled into a false sense of security and then pow! She'd got her again. It was like swimming too near a jellyfish.

Nat and Tom stuck their heads into what was described as an English bar, and then swiftly retreated. Too noisy. Too pubby. Too many loud young people.

'Let's try this,' Nat said. He was standing outside a chic-looking bar and restaurant called La Cloche.

'Fine,' Tom nodded.

It was perfect. An old wooden bar, an old French guy sitting in the corner, a low beamed ceiling and beautifully laid tables, unoccupied as yet. And a very pretty barmaid. She smiled flirtatiously up at them.

'*Deux bières*,' Tom said. '*Merci*.'

'No problem,' she replied, in perfect English.

'Why do they do that?' Tom said, as they hitched themselves onto high bar stools. 'How does she know? I only said two words.'

'You look English,' Nat said. 'You are the quintessential Englishman.'

Tom perked up. 'I like the idea of looking like that,' he said.

Nat sipped his beer. They drank in silence for a while, savouring the peace.

'This is a great bar,' Tom said, looking around. 'We should have a beer here every night. If we're allowed.'

Nat laughed. 'What do you mean?'

'Sarah does not like me sneaking off on my own. She says I am a slave to pub culture.'

'Cassie doesn't mind,' Nat said, as if the thought was ridiculous.

'That is because Cassie is a saint,' Tom said. 'You cannot judge other women against Cassie. She is an honorary bloke.'

'But if I pull my weight during the day with the kids, which is only fair, then surely I should be able to have a pint before dinner, which I enjoy?'

'That is a perfectly reasonable argument,' Tom said. 'But Sarah sees it as a personal affront. That I do not want to spend the time with her. That I am somehow abdicating my husbandly and paternal duties.'

'I think you do more than your fair share of duties,' Nat said. 'I don't know how you stand it.'

'I enjoy it,' Tom said. 'I love being with the kids.'

'But every day? All day?'

'What's the alternative? Putting on a suit and spending hours on a train? Come on. Which would you rather do? They're at school a lot of the time, anyway.'

'I don't know,' Nat said, turning and putting his elbows on the bar. 'I don't know. Maybe you have a point.'

'The plane . . . it must have been fucking scary.'

'It was. But only afterwards. At the time I just – well, you just react. Instinct takes over. You would have done the same.'

'I like to think I would,' Tom said. 'But I don't know if I would have had the guts. I may well have run to the back of the plane flapping my arms and hidden under a stewardess.' There was a pause. 'How's work?' he asked.

'I hate that question,' Nat said. 'Work is work. Busy. Shit. You know.'

'Poor Gerard.'

'Poor Gerard indeed. I don't quite know where he will go from here. Having said that, he has been a complete idiot.'

'Really?'

'Oh, yes. Total tosser. You could have seen the collapse coming a mile off but he kept throwing more and more money at the problem. And not his own.'

'Oh.'

'Yeah. He'll have to go bankrupt. There's no other way. Two more beers, please.'

'Have we time?'

'Stop being such an old woman.'

'Cassie said . . .'

'Cassie will be fine. Trust me.'

'You are lucky.'

'I know.'

'Have you ever . . .'

Nat's glance was amused. 'What?'

'You know.'

'Played away?' Nat smiled. 'No.'

'That's bloody amazing.'

'Why? Have you?'

Tom blushed to the roots of his hair. Nat noticed and thought, I have hit a nerve, and I am not sure I want to know the answer. Tom seemed to be thinking hard, and then he said, 'What would you say if you had a friend who had fallen very deeply in love with another friend's wife? Really deeply, you know, not just sex. Do you think there is any circumstance in which he could be justified in leaving his wife and moving in with her?'

Alarm bells rang loudly in Nat's head. What had Cassie said? Maybe she had not been so far off the mark, after all. He decided to play Tom's game. 'So if this – friend – thought he was so much in love, would he break up his marriage for her?'

'He might,' Tom said hesitantly, not meeting Nat's eye.

'And leave his children?'

'No,' Tom said, quickly. 'He'd take his children with him. They'd set up together.'

'As one big family?'

'Yeah.'

'Wouldn't work,' Nat said. 'Not a chance in hell. The kids wouldn't leave their mother and the other bloke would kill him. Do you fancy another?'

'I'm fine. Surely if you really love somebody then you have the right to leave? If you're very unhappy?'

'Life isn't that simple,' Nat said, draining his glass. 'You don't always have the right to choose, do you? Not when you have children. You have to give things up or your life would end up one bloody big mess, wouldn't it? I mean, most blokes have shagged around, haven't they, I think I am quite unusual. But to actually leave your wife and children ... that really opens up a can of worms. I know blokes who are on their third, fourth marriages now, with abandoned kids all over the place. Costs a fortune, too. You can't justify that kind of hurt. Not just for your own pleasure.'

'Oh.' Tom looked down into his beer. 'What if he can't live without her?'

'You've been watching too many films,' Nat said.

'But you couldn't live without Cassie, could you?'

'This is getting a bit personal, isn't it? I only came for a pint and a chat. No, I couldn't live without her, I suppose. I just got lucky in that she's a great friend as well as the mother of my children. That counts for a lot, you know. The mother bit.'

'I know it does.' Tom looked morose. 'Do you really think it would never work?'

'Nope,' Nat said. 'Never. Too much chaos and recriminations. Tell your mate to keep it in perspective. Just enjoy an illicit shag and then go home.'

Chapter Twenty-Four

Laure

'We'll be fine, won't we, *chéri*?' Laure said to Arthur, who was putting out the chess pieces on the board. He had decided not to ski that morning, because he had fallen over on his knee, which was beginning to swell.

'I hope you're not very good,' she said, 'because I'm rubbish.'

'I'm only in the second school chess team,' he said.

'Great,' she said, ironically.

'So we'll see you at the mountain bar?' Cassie had said. 'The one by the second lift? About one?'

'Yes, go,' Laure said, without looking up. She felt a hundred times better for having slept so well for the last two nights. The moment her head hit the pillow she fell asleep, and slept solidly for twelve hours. She had fared much better than the other adults, who had arrived at the breakfast table groaning and clutching their heads after the second night of drinking heavily.

'Very bad idea, champagne,' Cassie said. 'And then lots of wine.'

'Beer,' Tom moaned.

'And brandy,' Nat reminded him.

'No! This is supposed to be a healthy holiday.'

'I don't feel too bad,' Sarah said, tweaking her pink

fluffy collar. 'I managed not to go over the top. You just have to say, I'll stick to three glasses, and then move on to water.'

Cassie shot her a poisonous look. 'I'll bear it in mind,' she said. 'Only for me there's a tipping point when I think one more won't make any difference because I am still aware of my surroundings and if I stop I will become a miserable cow and want to go to bed, but then the one more becomes another one and then I lose the ability to count. And climb the stairs, and clean my teeth. At least the mountain air will sort us out,' she added. 'It's impossible to keep a hangover on the mountains. Right. Assemble, you lot.'

The children stood in a colourful row in front of them. Cassie grinned. 'On the count of one, all hold up your skiing gloves.' They did so. 'Good. On the count of two, all hold out your ski passes.' They all did so, barring Tilly. 'Where?' Cassie raised her eyebrows. Tilly turned and ran up the stairs.

'This week you are all responsible for your own stuff. Which means that if you arrive at the lifts without your ski pass or your gloves or your goggles or your hat then it is your responsibility, which means you have to go back to the chalet. This is a holiday for the grown-ups too, and we don't want to spend all week rushing round after you.'

They all nodded. From upstairs came a series of muffled thumps and then Tilly's voice yelled, 'Found it!'

'Good,' Cassie called. 'Right, goggles.'

'I wear shades,' Nick said, looking affronted.

'You would,' Cassie said. 'Very dashing.' She noticed that Tilly, who had arrived panting back in the line, was looking up at him with blatant adoration. She smiled to herself. Both Tilly and Lucy clearly thought he was gorgeous.

'Teams like yesterday,' Cassie said. 'Nat, you don't mind taking the girls, do you? Tom's taking Daisy on the nursery slopes and the boys can ski with me.'

Nat appeared from the stairs, pulling on his ski gloves. 'No, that's fine. What about Sarah?'

Cassie looked around. She'd disappeared again. She kept doing this, leaving Tom to be responsible for Daisy, or Cassie. Last night she'd spent over an hour in the bath. When any of her children were Daisy's age, Cassie remembered, she'd never spent more than five minutes in the bath, or they'd been in with her.

Tom had gone to the loo, and was taking absolutely ages. Nat hated having to wait for anyone, and Cassie knew he was desperate to get out on the slopes. It was very good of him to ski with the little ones – tomorrow she'd take the girls and he could ski black runs with the boys.

'Do you mind skiing with Sarah?' she said to Nat. He pulled a face, making Tilly and Arthur laugh. Tom reappeared.

'I wouldn't go in there for a while,' he said, gesturing at the downstairs loo.

'You are disgusting,' Sarah said, from the bottom of the stairs. 'I can't take you anywhere.'

Ask what you can do to help, Cassie thought. She paused. Nothing happened. Sarah was carefully applying lip balm. Cassie took a deep breath.

'Who do you want to ski with, Sarah?' she asked, pleasantly.

'I'll go with Nat,' she said.

'Right. Let's go. It's nearly half past nine and the lifts are getting busy.' Cassie looked at her watch. 'Let's meet at one then, all of us, at Le Jump. Has everyone got a watch?' They nodded. She turned to Laure. 'Are you sure you'll be OK?'

'Goodbye,' Laure said. 'Have fun. And do not, I repeat, break anything. Any of you.'

'Please do,' Arthur said, a touch mournfully. 'I'm a bit sick of being the only incapacitated person here.'

'You get to stay with Laure,' Tom said. Sarah flashed him an irritated look. 'Which is pretty special, mate.' And then they were gone.

Laure found Arthur a stimulating and funny companion. After he thrashed her at chess, twice, they moved on to Cluedo. It took ages with just two people, because you had to throw the dice to get into practically every room and Arthur kept nicking her as Miss Scarlett to suspect her in the ballroom with the lead piping. Eventually he beat her at that, too.

'Monopoly?' he said, holding up the red and white box.

Laure shook her head. 'I think I would lose the will to live,' she said. 'What's the time?'

Arthur looked at his enormous diver's watch. 'Twelve. Bit early to set off, yet.'

Laure had an idea. 'Let's go and see if we can see Tom on the nursery slopes. They're right by the village. Will you be able to manage in the snow?'

'I think so.' Gingerly, he levered himself up. Laure fetched his ski jacket, and bent down to fasten the velcro on the training shoe of his injured leg. 'You'll fall over,' she said.

Arthur looked down at her shining curtain of hair, as it hung above his leg and foot. There was something to be said for having to stay behind. He was in serious danger of developing a huge crush on her. She was so nice. And she didn't talk down to him at all. She was just like his mum, only, well – beautiful. She was so slim, and she wore lovely clothes. He could see that Sarah was attractive – he had recently started giving girls marks out of ten for their looks – but she was too impatient and bossy. He couldn't quite see what she and Tom had in common. He was so laid back, and she was always fussing over things that didn't matter.

Thomas and Anna had tidied up all of the breakfast things. They had laid on a wonderful spread, including bacon and eggs, delicious fresh croissants – chocolate ones, too, which had been devoured – and freshly squeezed orange juice. Anna was now hoovering the bedrooms. Cassie had told them all sternly they needed to keep their rooms tidy because otherwise it wasn't fair to Anna, but Laure knew the girls' room, in particular, looked like a bomb had hit it.

'Anna!' Laure called. 'Do you know the number for a taxi?'

'Of course,' she said, in her strongly accented English. 'I will ring.'

Laure pulled on her jacket and her hat, looking into the mirror above the coat rack. All the boots, skis and poles were kept in a heated room at the bottom of the chalet, accessible only from the outside. She'd put on a little make-up first thing this morning, and she had a sudden urge to make herself look better. She ran up the stairs, and rooted about in her cosmetics bag. She brushed her hair, and came back downstairs, her hair glossy and her lips a subtle shade of pink. Arthur thought, Wow, and had a brief fantasy that they would somehow bump into some of his friends from school and he could say, casually, 'Hi, guys, this is my friend, Laure.'

The taxi arrived promptly, and Laure held his arm as he lowered himself into the back. She'd pulled on a pair of fluffy yeti boots she'd had for ages, tucking her jeans into the top. Packing for the holiday, she had unearthed a coat she hadn't worn for years – it was in denim, with a high collar and lined with faux rabbit fur. It had belonged to her mother, and had apparently been the height of chic at the time – looking at the label, she saw it was by Dior. Good old Mother. She never did anything by halves. Trying it on in front of her bedroom mirror, she thought it hadn't dated at all. She had wanted to get it dry-cleaned, but that would have been too expensive, so instead she simply shook it out, sponged off a couple of marks and then hung it up on the outside of the wardrobe to air.

The taxi dropped them off at La Croisette, the main lift area, where many of the bars and restaurants within the town were sited. Up to their left was the longest of the nursery slopes, a gentle run served with a button tow, divided by a small island of trees.

'Are you OK on the snow?' she asked, as one of Arthur's feet briefly skated and he had to hang onto her to stop himself falling.

'Oops, sorry,' he said. 'I'll get my balance in a minute.'

She ruffled his hair. 'You're being really brave,' she said. 'Nick would be moaning like mad.'

'It's OK,' he said, grinning and hanging his head. She saw his cheeks had gone pink.

'Look – there they are!' she said, pointing up as the blue ski-suited figure of Tom appeared around the island of trees. He was holding Daisy in front of him, between his knees. She was wearing a bright orange all-in-one ski suit that was a bit too big for her, with a red crash hat and orange goggles. She looked like a skiing tangerine. Even from this distance, Laure could see that she was laughing. Tom guided her down the slope towards them, bending low over her shoulder as he gave her instructions. He had almost skied past them when Laure called out to him, and he stopped dead, lifting Daisy up off the snow. He flicked his skis into a neat parallel stop, sending a spray of cold snow over Laure and Arthur.

'Show-off!' she said. His face had caught the sun already, and his hair flopped over a brightly coloured bandanna he had tied around his head. He looked, for Tom, quite glamorous. He lifted his sunglasses, and perched them on his head.

Daisy was beaming and shrieking. 'Again! Again!' she cried. 'Daddy ski again!'

'I'm knackered,' he said. 'I think I'm doing my back in. I feel like a skiing paper clip.'

'Daisy seems to be loving it,' Laure said, smiling at him.

'God, yeah, she's taken to it like a duck to water, haven't you, honey?' he said, lifting her goggles away from her eyes and wedging them on the top of her helmet. She stamped her feet on her tiny skis. 'Let's do it again!' she ordered.

'Give me a break,' he said. 'Let Daddy get his breath back.' He looked at his watch. 'We're a bit early for lunch. Do you fancy a coffee?'

'Oh, yes, please,' Laure said, looking at Arthur, who nodded, obligingly.

Tom, with Daisy in his arms, skied over to a rack where skis and poles were hung in front of the terrace of a restaurant. Putting her down, he clicked off the bindings of his skis, and leant them against the wooden frame, before bending down to lever off Daisy's. She protested vehemently, trying to push him away. He lifted off her helmet, and knelt down in front of her. 'If you are a good girl – a very good girl – I will let you ski again before lunch. If not, you're going back to the chalet.' Daisy eyed him thoughtfully. It seemed a reasonable deal. She nodded. 'You can also have some chocolate.' She nodded, much more enthusiastically.

Laure had found a table for them, next to a roaring log fire, and he pushed open the swing door and clomped in, Daisy in front of him. He swung her into a chair, and turned to Arthur. 'Hot chocolate?'

'Yes, please.'

'With whipped cream and a Flake?'

Arthur tried to look nonchalant. 'I suppose so.'

'Me too!' Daisy said.

'It might be too hot,' Laure said.

'I'll get them to put more milk in,' Tom said, and walked over to lean against the bar.

Once he had carried the drinks back to the table, Laure stirred the froth on the top of her cappuccino. She knew his eyes never left her face. They couldn't talk here, not with Arthur around. He moved one of his feet to rest against the fur of her yeti boot.

'Is Sarah OK now?' she said, eventually.

Tom grimaced. 'As fine as she's going to be. We had a long talk last night.'

Laure's head lifted. 'Really?'

'Yeah,' he said, 'I'll – I'll talk to you about it later.'

'I need to go to the loo,' Daisy said, loudly.

'I'll take her,' Laure said.

'No,' Tom said, 'I'll do it. She's shy of other people.'

When they came back, Arthur said he needed the toilet too. He grinned at them as he stood up. 'I can go on my own,' he said.

Tom watched him negotiate his way around the tables.

'He's a lovely boy, isn't he?'

'Fantastic. Cassie should be so proud,' Laure replied. Daisy got up, and wandered over to a window seat covered in cushions. She started to lever herself up. Tom looked fondly at her orange back in the puffy ski suit, as she stared out at the skiers on the slopes and the people walking past. She was fascinated by the cable cars, and her little head lifted as she watched one slide up the metal ropes fifty or so feet above the ground.

'I need to talk to you,' Tom said, quietly. He reached over the table and took her hand. Laure looked at the toilet door. 'He'll be ages,' he said.

She stared down at their hands, transfixed, but did not make a move to pull her hand away.

'I do not think I can wait. I know that we said we would leave everything until next year but being here with you now, not able to touch you, to hold you – do you see what I mean? It feels like living a lie, Laure. I want to be able to hold your hand and put my arm around you without the constant dread of being seen. It's ridiculous that we feel we have to hide our love. I want to walk down the street with you. We're not like this, are we, Laure? We're not two idiots having a sordid affair. I love you, and I want to tell the world. I want to make plans. I want to know that there is a definite time frame so we can stop this bloody lie. It will be kinder to everyone in the long run.'

'Gerard . . .' she said.

'Look. He will be furious, of course he will, but you have to tell him. Stop putting it off. If you don't, I will. I can't tell Sarah now, not on holiday, but I will as soon as we get home. I promise you. We have to start working out what we're going to do and once we have told them, that's it. No going back. You're mine, remember. You told me. You promised me.' He held her hand up against his cheek.

'I do remember,' she said. 'I think about it all the time.' She reached up, and touched his face. He turned his cheek towards her palm, and she caressed him.

He closed his eyes. 'All I can see is you,' he said. 'I have to stop myself saying your name over and over again. Everything I do, from waking up, to writing, to looking after the children, to emptying the bloody bin bags, is filled with you. I am so committed to you, you know. This is for ever. Fuck knows where we will live, I don't care. I would live anywhere, with you.'

The toilet door banged, and Arthur appeared. Laure snaked her hand back under the table. She looked at Tom, nervous once more. 'Don't,' she said quietly. 'You have to give me time,' she added. 'Trust me. I know when it will be right.'

'I am very sick', he said, urgently, 'of waiting.'

'Right,' he said loudly, leaning back on his chair, as Arthur came to sit down. 'I'll pay for these and then I have promised Daisy another half an hour. We're meeting back here for lunch, aren't we?' He looked at his watch, before getting up and walking over to scoop Daisy up from the window seat.

Laure's heart lifted. He was right, they had to make definite plans. The situation might be impossible, but she could not prevent the feeling that she was happier and more alive than she had been for years. Truly, truly, happy. Euphoric. She was full of energy. He was right. It would affect everyone around them, but they would do everything they could to minimize the hurt. They were all rational adults.

At the door he turned to smile at her. His hair was sticking up over the bandanna, and he looked in his twenties. 'Ciao!' he said, and smiled at her, his face full of love. Daisy waggled her fingers at them, and they were gone. I love Daisy too, she thought. His children would be a big part of her life. My stepchildren. She must make more of an effort to get to know Mickey. He was the only one of Tom's children who was something of a closed book. She felt that he was an unhappy boy, which was why he could be aggressive and quite rude sometimes. She would get to the bottom of it, and Nick could help. It would be great for Nick to have a brother, and thank goodness Sophie and Lucy were such pals. It would be bumpy at first, but they would love being all together, eventually.

'He's great, Tom, isn't he?' Arthur said. 'I really hope his book's going to be a success.'

'I think it will,' Laure said. She shook herself. 'Come on. What would you like to do? It sounds a bit tacky but in the arcade on the bottom street I am sure your mother said there are some pretty cool clothes and music shops. I'll treat you to a T-shirt or something.'

'Will you be my mother?' he said, taking her hand and batting his eyelashes at her.

She laughed loudly, joyously. 'Idiot!'

Nat walked into the restaurant with a face like thunder. Cassie was already there, sitting at the big table by the window she had commandeered for all of them, telling the man behind the counter there were lots of people still to come. There was no sign of Laure and Arthur. She'd had a pleasant enough morning on the slopes with the boys. After lunch she planned to take them up Verdun, which had a little black run at the top and then went into a long red.

Nat all but threw his goggles down onto the table. Sarah had gone to the toilet and Nick and Tilly were standing at the bar ordering drinks. Cassie noticed that Tilly had a new gesture, flicking her hair away from her face while gazing up at him. Lord.

'That woman,' Nat hissed.

'Who?' Cassie said, her face the picture of innocence.

'You know. Me, me, me,' he said. 'Every bleeding time we got going she shouted at us to stop because she had to adjust her goggles or her bindings were too tight or she thought her skis were a touch too long and could we go back down the mountain so she could change them? And Lucy took not a blind bit of notice of me and was skiing off piste where it is actually quite dangerous – showing off – and then Tilly tried to follow her and slipped and bruised her back. And then when we did get everybody together and set off she—' he glanced angrily at the toilet door – 'fell over and said that she thought she had sprained her wrist.' He held out his hand like a helpless paw. 'She wasn't sure if she could go on, and could I call the ski ambulance? I said it was hardly worth calling them out at a cost of hundreds of pounds with a stretcher when she had a slightly sore hand. Then she went in a huff and wouldn't speak to me, so I just left her.'

'No!'

'Well, the kids had gone shooting on ahead and they're much more important than she is. I didn't think she was really hurt, or I wouldn't have left her. Anyway, she managed to ski down all right despite her serious injury, ha, ha, and then she said she wanted to stop for a coffee. We'd only done an hour,' Cassie nodded in sympathy – Nat hated stopping once he had got going – 'and I said she could but I was going back up. So I left her again. She was not', he said, 'a great help. She can bloody well ski on her own this afternoon.'

'Shush,' Cassie said. 'She's coming.' It occurred to her it was rather like being back at school, with people falling out and taking sides. She felt as if she was caught in the middle, and it dawned on her that she had been in this situation at school too, pulled this way and that by warring friends. Maybe it meant she was a nice person. Or maybe, she thought, it meant she was a mug. She must practise being less of a pushover.

'Nat skis so fast,' Sarah said, sitting down next to her, as Nat wandered off to the bar. 'He hardly waited for me at all. He wasn't very chivalrous.'

'He does like to get on,' Cassie said. 'I did warn you.

Why don't I ski with him this afternoon and you can go off on your own?' she said, sweetly. 'Or maybe you could take Daisy and give Tom a break. He must be dying to ski properly. He's really good, isn't he? Although he shouldn't do too much.'

'So he says,' Sarah said, picking up the menu on the table. 'Are we having the à la carte or just the snacks?'

'The snacks, I thought,' Cassie said. 'We'll have a big meal tonight,' she added.

'I didn't think the food was awfully good last night,' Sarah said. 'The sauce was a bit too creamy and that ice cream was not home-made.'

'You seemed to eat it OK,' Cassie said, pleasantly.

'Oh, I can eat anything,' Sarah said. 'I'm not fussy.'

After lunch they lingered over espressos, while the gang of children played the slot machine at the far corner of the bar. Tom, leaning back in his chair smoking, seemed quite at peace with himself, Cassie thought. Like the cat with the cream. Nat put his cup down. Cassie knew he was eager to be off again.

'What are you going to do, Tom?' she asked.

'Daisy and me are going to have a bit more of a play about, and then she's going to have a kip,' he said.

'Am not,' Daisy said.

'Am so,' said Tom, 'if you want to come swimming with me at teatime and then stay up really late with all the big ones.'

Daisy eyed him consideringly. 'OK,' she said.

'I'll take the rest of the hordes,' he added. 'They'll want to swim, won't they? Laure, will you come?'

'Yes,' said Laure. 'I will. That would be nice.'

'I'm glad my plans please some people,' he said, shaking Daisy backwards and forwards on his knee, growling.

Sarah reached over to wipe Daisy's mouth. 'Do you mind if Mummy goes off and skis?' she said.

'No,' Daisy said, as if the thought wouldn't occur to her. 'Stay with Daddy.'

'What about you two?' Cassie said, turning to Laure and Arthur.

'Laure bought me this really cool T-shirt,' Arthur said, holding up a bag.

'You shouldn't have.' Cassie shook her head.

Laure smiled. 'It was nothing. You really think that buying clothes is a hardship for me? We had a fun time, didn't we?' Arthur nodded. 'It's great, that arcade, they have really loud music and there's a rope ladder in the centre for the kids.'

'And an amusement arcade,' Arthur said.

'Oh joy,' Cassie said. 'I remember it well. My favourite place. Not. So what will you do this afternoon?'

'I think I'll watch a film,' Arthur said, looking at Laure, 'so Laure can ski if she wants.'

'Nope,' she said. 'I'll watch it with you.'

'As will I,' Tom said. 'All sorted.'

Sarah looked from Laure to Tom. 'Very cosy,' she said.

'We can't all get what we want, can we?' Tom said, smiling blandly at her. 'Go ski. You can do your bit with Daisy tomorrow. I'm going to ski with Nat on La Face.'

'Can I come with you?' Nick said.

'Only as long as you promise not to be better than us,' Tom said. 'Old men's egos are very fragile, you know.'

Arthur chose a DVD, and he and Laure settled themselves down on the sofa in front of the screen. Arthur was just about to press the 'play' button when Laure called to Tom, who was upstairs putting Daisy to bed. 'Are you ready yet?'

'Coming,' he said.

Minutes later he sat down next to Laure. She could feel the warmth from his body through his T-shirt and the jeans he'd pulled on after taking off his ski suit. She tried to concentrate on the film, but she could feel his breath on her shoulder. After half an hour she said, 'Does anyone want a drink or some cake?'

'Cake, please,' Arthur said, his eyes never leaving the screen.

'Tom?'

'I'll help you,' he said. She made a face at him, which he ignored. Thomas and Anna were due back in an hour, having said they were going to spend the afternoon snowboarding. In the kitchen Laure held the kettle under the cold tap, and then switched it on.

Tom's arms enfolded her from behind, and for a blissful minute she leant back against him. 'Turn round,' he murmured, into her neck.

Unable to stop herself, she swivelled around so her face was only inches from his. She looked up at him. His eyes were opaque with lust, and she closed her eyes as his mouth brushed against hers. Gently, he parted her lips and then he was kissing her deeply, and her arms moved up around his neck. She could feel every inch of him as he pushed her back up hard against the sink, and his hand slid up over her stomach to touch her breast. She felt as if a fire had been ignited, and they were a single flame. He paused, and she opened her eyes to look at him. 'Oh, dear,' she said.

'Not awfully good restraint,' he said, 'admittedly.'

'I love you,' she said.

'I know,' he whispered. 'I'm clever like that.'

There was a crash, and they jumped apart. 'Sorry!' Arthur yelled. 'Dropped a cup. Are you coming back? I've got it on pause.'

'Just coming,' Laure called, turning back to the sink. Tom put his arms around her waist, and pressed up against her from behind. 'You're never going to get rid of me now,' he said.

'Get off,' she said, but she was laughing. 'Show some decorum. I cannot believe I am doing this.'

'This is only the beginning,' he said.

Chapter Twenty-Five

Laure

'Why won't Dad come?' Laure was sitting on Nick's bed as he tightened his tie in front of his bedroom mirror, grimacing. 'I look like a pillock.'

'Too busy,' Laure replied. 'Tom', she went on, casually, 'said he'd come along for moral support.'

'Good of him.'

'He likes my father. I rang Papa and he said I was more than welcome to bring him.'

'They're a bit similar,' Nick said, peering at what looked horribly like a new spot.

Laure looked horrified. 'No, they are not! Not in the slightest.'

'Neither of them are very good at facing real life, are they? Anyway,' Nick said, turning to her, 'at least it gets us away from Dad and his foul moods.'

'You know how hard this is for him,' Laure said, quickly.

'Oh boy, do I. As if he ever lets us forget it for one minute. I'm a bit worried about him, Mum.'

Laure felt a twinge of alarm. 'In what way?'

'He's drinking a lot on his own. Look, I know you two haven't been getting on so well and you're sleeping in separate rooms and all that,' he looked awkwardly away from her, 'and I just wondered . . . no. It's OK. Nothing.'

'Wondered what?'

'Wondered if you're going to split up.' The words came out in a rush and Nick stood stock still, staring warily at her. 'Where we're going to live. After the house is sold.'

'Where on earth did you get that from?'

'I'm not stupid,' he said. 'I can see what's happening.'

Laure's heart was beating so fast she thought that she might faint. 'What . . . is happening?' she repeated. He could not have noticed on the holiday. They had behaved entirely normally around everyone else, and Tom had calmed down a lot once she had promised she would tell Gerard in a week or so, after they had returned. Only she hadn't been able to find the courage. Next week, she said. Once the house was settled.

A buyer had been found for the Rectory. He worked in the City, she was a lawyer and they had two young children. They said the house was perfect and they didn't want to change a thing. They offered over the asking price. Gerard had managed to narrowly avoid bankruptcy which meant they had just enough to keep Nick at school until his final exams, and Sophie until the end of her prep school. Last night Gerard had left out on the kitchen table the details of a house for rent in the next village. Laure knew she had to tell him. She could not leave him to make plans that were never going to happen. It was too cruel. But something inside her delayed. She was, she knew, terrified of taking the final step.

She stood up and put her arms around Nick. 'I'm not exactly sure where we're going to live yet. I'm working that out. I think we'll have to rent for a while, but it will be fine. We'll find somewhere.'

Tom had said on the phone that morning they had to choose a definite date and tell Sarah and Gerard simultaneously. Tom too had found a cottage he said they should rent until both houses were sold and they could see if there was enough to buy a house between them. It was rather run down with four small bedrooms and would be a squeeze, with seven of them, but they would manage. They wouldn't have much money, but that did not matter. There would be no suggestion of not letting Sarah or Gerard see the children as often as they wanted, wherever they were going to choose to live. When Tom talked, he managed to make the situation sound as if it was all quite possible, logical, even. Then Laure thought about telling Gerard, and the house of cards came crashing down.

Laure had to admit that her father looked good for a man in his mid-sixties. He took them all to an extremely smart restaurant for lunch after the register-office wedding, and made an emotional speech about how Rachel had made him such a happy man, and how delighted he was that his family were there to share his joy.

They were sitting drinking coffee, after the meal, when Laure bent down to pick up her handbag. 'It's time we went,' she said to Tom. 'We don't want to get stuck in the traffic, and I've got to drive Nick back first thing in the morning.'

'Sure,' Tom said, easily. He put his hand under her elbow as she stood, and as she turned she was aware of her father watching them. Laure went to fetch Sophie's coat and Nick's jacket left hanging on the back of the chair. Then she turned to hug her father.

'Bye, Papa. Thank you. It was lovely, and I do wish you all the best, really I do. She's very—'

she cast around for an appropriate word – 'special.'

'And you take care,' her father said. As he released her, he looked at Tom, and then he winked. Laure stared at him in horror. It was a wink of complicity. He knew. The sleaziness made her gasp. He was implying that they were like him. She was on his side. She wasn't the white-as-snow martyr her mother had tried so hard to be. She was like him. Living a life of lies to get what she wanted.

Suddenly cold, she wrapped her coat tight around her, and snapped at Sophie, 'Come on! Stop messing about!'

Tom looked at her in surprise. 'What's the matter?' he said.

'Nothing,' she said. 'Not now.'

On the way home she stared out of the window and would not look at him. Tom was driving her people carrier, because he said it was her party and she ought to be allowed to have one or two drinks if she wanted to. She had thought how sweet and caring that was – she always drove Gerard, who could not bear not to have a drink. Tom kept glancing at her, and longed to say something, but there were too many witnesses for honesty. They could only talk in code.

Sarah was away working that weekend, and Gerard had said he was going to stay over with one of his new business contacts. He had an important meeting on Monday with an investment company which was sure to get the business started. Laure listened, and nodded, and did not care. Soon you will not be my responsibility any more, beyond the tie of being the father of my children. Looking at the situation like that, it was a huge relief. Cassie was looking after Daisy and Lucy, Mickey was staying with a friend.

Dusk was falling as they drove across the green, and

at first Laure did not register the fact that Gerard's car was parked in the drive.

'Dad's home,' Sophie said.

'Oh,' Laure said, her heart beating uncomfortably. Tom had left his old car on her side of the garage. She told herself to calm down. Gerard would not think there was anything unusual in that, Tom often popped round bringing the children to and fro. Gerard wouldn't immediately think Tom had been to the wedding with them.

Tom glanced at her. 'You've been very quiet,' he said.

'I know,' she tried to laugh. 'Too much to drink, I expect. You know me. Two glasses of wine and I'm completely *ivre*.'

'It isn't that,' he said. 'Something's wrong.'

She flicked a glance at Sophie and Nick in the back of the car. Nick was listening to his iPod, and Sophie was plugged into her portable CD player, humming. 'Call me later,' she said. 'Or I'll call you.'

'Do you want me to come in?' he said.

'No. Thanks.'

'I don't want to leave you like this.'

'Tom, please, just go, I'm fine. Come on, kids,' she said, loudly. 'Out.'

Tom waited for the children to climb out, then he pressed the automatic lock and handed the keys to Laure. 'You're being weird,' he said. 'Don't do this. We don't pretend to each other.' Nick and Sophie had walked on ahead to the house.

'Trust me, Tom, I'm not being weird. I'm just tired and right at the moment I can't think straight.'

'Is it because he's back?' He gestured at Gerard's car.

'Yes. No,' she said, pressing her fingers against her temples. 'I don't know. I suppose it's Papa's wedding and everything . . .'

'We will be happy,' Tom said, every word insistent, a tiny hammer blow in her ear. 'No-one can stop us.'

'I know.' She wanted him gone. She smiled at him wanly. 'I need to sleep.'

'Sleep,' he said, 'and think of me.'

It isn't going to work, she thought, looking up at him. It isn't simple, and it won't go smoothly, and it isn't going to work. We are hiding like children.

I am afraid, she thought, closing the big front door behind her, the door that used to make her feel safe. Something is very wrong. Nick had gone upstairs, and Sophie had switched on the TV in the snug. Laure walked slowly towards the kitchen. She gently pushed open the oak doors. The room was shrouded in darkness. She reached out with her right hand to find the switch. She flicked the lights on. Gerard was sitting at the table, his head in his hands.

'Why were you sitting in the dark?' she asked. Her voice was light, tremulous with fear. He raised tearstained, weary eyes to her.

'Victor is dead,' he said.

'No!' Tears started in her eyes. 'When?'

'He must have died when you were at the wedding.'

Laure's hand flew to her mouth. 'He was alone. He died alone. Where was he, when you found him?'

'By the front door. He must have been scratching to get out. His heart must have just given up.' He drew back from the table and Laure saw he had the old dog spread across his lap, his hand compulsively stroking the black head, the grey muzzle pressed into his other hand. She bent down by Victor's head, and looked into his lifeless eyes. She touched him, and her hand met Gerard's. She drew a long, shuddering breath.

'I can't bear the thought that he died in an empty house. After so long with us.'

330

'He was the best of dogs,' Gerard said.

Laure sank back on her heels, rocking herself backwards and forwards. Victor seemed always to have been a part of her life, his eyes following her as she moved around the kitchen, his tail thumping against her leg as she drank coffee and read the paper, his big fat paw on her knee when he wanted a walk. He was part of the geography of her existence, and now he had gone, leaving an irreplaceable void. It was too much to take in, too great a loss.

'He would have hated moving,' Laure said, quietly.

Gerard nodded. 'He was a bit too old for change,' he said.

'Will you tell Sophie and Nick?' Laure said, wiping her eyes. 'I don't think I can.'

'OK.' Gerard stood up stiffly, and carried the dog's heavy body over to his basket. He gently rested him in it, and then covered him with a blanket.

'We'll have to take him to the vet,' she said. 'For cremation.'

'We can bury him here,' Gerard said, looking out of the window. 'Beneath that apple tree he bloody well dug up when I first planted it.'

Laure laughed softly. 'I guess that's appropriate.' He turned to her and, without warning, took her in his arms. He buried his face in her hair.

'Come back to me,' he said. 'Please. I can't do anything without you. I'm trying to get going again but there feels no point. You have to tell me. You have to tell me what you are going to do. I am in hell, Laure, without you. We have both been completely insane to let things go this far. It's crazy. We are married, Laure, married.'

She drew away from him. She did not think, in shock, and the words came out unbidden, in a rush, incoherently. 'I can't. It's . . . I am in love . . . Tom . . .

I'm so sorry . . .' she said. She took a deep breath. 'I am leaving you. Tom is leaving Sarah.'

He dropped his arms as if he had been shot.

She hadn't meant to say it. Even as she said the words, she thought, is this what I want? What I really want? Victor's death would mean nothing to Tom. He does not know my life. We haven't lived in the same house together for sixteen years. We haven't had two children together. All we have is sex, not love. Not love. Not history and experience love. It isn't real. How can I give this up?

Gerard stepped towards her, his arms thrown out as if he wanted to hold her, and as she turned, his hand accidentally hit her hard above her cheek. She reeled back, banging into the kitchen table. As if from a distance, she felt her hand reaching up to her face, and automatically she ducked, as the door to the kitchen was flung open. She heard Nick's voice, as she tasted blood in her mouth, and she heard herself shout, 'No!' as he threw himself at his father. Her head swam, as if she might faint, and she forced herself to stay conscious as Nick wrestled Gerard to the floor, shouting over and over again, 'You bastard! You bastard!' She staggered forward, and tried to hold Nick's arm, but he wrenched it away from her, and, distracted, let go of his father.

Gerard immediately jumped up, pinning Nick's arms to his sides. His face was contorted with grief and he could barely speak. 'Don't – do – that,' he said. 'Don't – come – near – me. I can't – I don't know . . . I'm so sorry . . . It was an . . .' He pushed Nick away from him, against Laure, and they fell, Laure hitting her head hard against the chair. Then she heard Sophie scream, and the front door slammed.

'Mum?' Nick was bending over her. 'Mum, for God's sake! Are you all right?'

'I'm fine,' she said, the awful salty taste of blood still in her mouth.

'He's gone fucking mental,' Nick said. 'What the hell is going on?'

Just then they heard the sound of a car engine. Laure ran to the window. Gerard's car screeched backwards out of the garage, and then roared away down the drive, leaving deep gashes in the gravel. Her hand flew to her mouth. 'Sophie!' she cried. Nick ran into the hall and then into the snug. She heard doors being flung open. He ran back into the kitchen.

'She's gone,' he said. 'Dad's taken her.'

Laure slumped over the sink, fighting hard to stay conscious, fighting hard not to collapse. 'Ring the police,' she said.

'What?'

'Just do it!' she screamed. 'Ring the police! He's not in his right mind! He could do anything!'

'Jesus,' Nick muttered as he dialled the emergency number with a shaking hand. What the hell was he going to say? He tried to breathe slowly and calmly. The voice on the other end was urgent. 'Police, fire, ambulance?'

'Police.'

'Wait one minute.'

Laure heard him give their address, then say, 'It's my father. He's taken my sister. He's – he's hit my mother. He's not thinking straight. We – no, he hasn't done this before. Ever. No. I know he has no history of violence. It's just . . . Please. Can you find him?' She heard him giving Gerard's registration number and the make and model of his car. Then he said, 'Thank you. We will. Thanks.' He put the phone down.

'They're sending someone over now and they're try-ing to trace Dad. Are you OK? Christ, look at you.'

Laure ran her tongue over her teeth. She felt her

face. Her hand came away sticky with blood, her head was banging and her vision blurred. 'I'm fine,' she heard herself saying. 'Where would he go? I'll call him . . .'

'No,' Nick said. 'I will.' He dialled Gerard's mobile number. After a minute he said, 'He's not answering.'

'Leave a message. No. Don't.' Her mind raced. What should she do? There was no point driving after them, because she had no idea where he had gone. Think, she told herself. Where would he go with Sophie? He wouldn't go to his parents. Too far. He would never turn to them, anyway. She could not put the thought of Sophie's terrified face out of her mind. She had screamed. What had he done? Had he hit her, too? She must be wondering what on earth he was doing, the father she loved and trusted, snatching her up, throwing her into the car, with his eyes wild, driving at that speed . . .

'Ring Cassie,' she said to Nick. 'Nat will know what to do.'

Cassie held her in her arms, gently, as if she was a baby. She had bathed the side of her face, which was red raw, and given her painkillers and a glass of brandy. The policewoman had asked Laure all sorts of awful questions – had he hit her before? Did he have a history of mental illness? Did she have any idea where he might take the child? The child. Sophie. Frightened, lost Sophie. Abducted Sophie. Could you abduct your own child? She tried to tell the policewoman she thought it had been an accident, but she couldn't get the words out. Besides, she did not know. Had he meant to hit her? It did not matter. Not any more. Thoughts that made no sense ran through her mind, and she jumped each time the phone rang.

The police said it was best not to try to call him on

his mobile again, because if he was driving in such a heightened state of emotion he might crash. Laure let out a wail as the policewoman said that. Crash. He might mean to crash. He might mean to crash or drive over a cliff with Sophie in the car. And it was all her fault. All her selfish fault, for thinking that she could tell him that she loved someone else and that she planned to leave him and he would say – what? OK? Fine? Nothing could justify – this – but she understood. She understood. Because the one thing, the one thing she had overlooked was the fact that he loved her. He loved her passionately and now she did not love him there was no need to live. But Sophie. She could not imagine he could take the life of the child he loved so much.

The policewoman bent down next to her. 'Can you think,' she said. 'Think. There must be somewhere he might go. Parents. Friends. A holiday home.' Laure shook her head. Gerard didn't have many friends. He was always too busy with work, and he let her arrange their social life. Really, she thought, Nat was about his closest friend.

She heard Nat's voice above her head. Everything was happening in slow motion, as if she was in a dream. 'Can you get a helicopter up? Bugger the cost. Look, if it comes to that I'll pay.'

'It's my fault,' Laure whispered to Cassie. 'I told him.'

'What?'

She screwed the handkerchief she was holding into a ball. 'I told him about Tom and me. I told him I was leaving. I told him I loved Tom.'

'It's all right,' Cassie said, holding her. 'It isn't your fault.'

'But it is.' Laure nodded, her tears dripping onto Cassie's hand. 'You can't do that to a person. I deserve this. I had no right to think it would be possible.'

At that moment, the door flew open. Tom pushed Cassie out of the way, and threw his arms around Laure. 'My love!' he said. 'What the hell has he done? The bastard! Why?'

Cassie looked at him. 'Go,' she said.

'What?' He looked wildly at Laure. She nodded. 'Go,' she whispered.

'This isn't my fault!' he shouted. Everyone in the kitchen stopped talking and stared at him. 'I love you!' he shouted.

Nick dropped his head. 'Fuck,' he said. 'Oh, fuck.'

Nat took Tom's arm. 'Come outside,' he said. 'Laure can't deal with this right now.'

'Let her tell me!' he yelled. Cassie stared at him. She had never seen Tom out of control like this. He was sobbing. 'It has to be now!' he shouted.

'Make him go,' Laure said, quietly. Cassie nodded and looked beseechingly at Nat. He put his arm around Tom, and led him out of the kitchen.

It was two a.m. Laure lay in bed staring at the ceiling. Cassie lay next to her, breathing heavily in her sleep. Downstairs, the policewoman and two more policemen sat in her kitchen drinking tea and trying to stay awake. Nick sat with them. She had wanted to stay up, but Cassie said that she must try to sleep. Nat had gone home to look after the children, taking Tom. Once the children were in bed they sat drinking whisky until Tom could drink no more and fell asleep in his chair. Nat covered him with a blanket, and wearily climbed the stairs to bed. Lord, he thought. What fools we mortals be.

'He must be a lunatic,' Tom had said as they sat drinking. 'And we never knew. How could he hit her? How could he do it?'

Nat said nothing for a moment. 'He was having everything taken away from him,' he said. 'What would you do?'

'Not this,' Tom said. 'Not this. He can't stop us.'

There were many, and incorrect, sightings of Gerard's car through the night. A similar car was seen speeding up the motorway. A similar car was involved in a head-on collision. Nick's nerves were on a knife-edge. Every call, every bleep of the police's phones and he thought that his father and his sister were dead. The police were talking in low voices about possibly giving a press conference to appeal for information. And all the time, Sophie might be lying dead. Dead in the mangled wreckage of a car. Dead in her father's arms. Why? He wrapped his arms around himself. Why had his father been driven to do something so crazy? How could normal people like them be tipped into this bizarre nightmare? He did not know if he could ever forgive his father. If he ever saw him again. And Tom. Tom was in love with his mother. He wasn't surprised, not really. Now, it was quite, quite obvious. He looked into the future, and it was like stepping off a cliff.

At four, Laure managed to sleep. Her dreams were filled with images of a car chase, tyres screeching, Sophie being just out of her reach, falling, falling – and then she woke with a jerk. She lay quite still. It was a dream. Sophie was asleep in her bed down the passage, her arm around her teddy bear. She gently threw back the covers, and slipped out of bed. She tiptoed down to Sophie's room, and pushed open the door. The bed was flat and empty. Neatly made. The bear lay on the cover, his sightless eyes staring at the ceiling. 'No!' she screamed. Cassie ran down the corridor, and put her arms around her. Laure turned, shaking. 'Is there any news?'

'I don't know. Go back to bed. I'll go and ask.'

In the kitchen their faces were grey with exhaustion. There had been no more sightings. Gerard and Sophie seemed to have disappeared off the face of the earth. Cassie made a cup of tea, and carried it up to Laure. She was sitting up in bed, rocking backwards and forwards.

'She's dead,' she said, over and over again. 'I know it.'

'No you don't. Gerard would not kill her. He wouldn't.'

'He was mad,' Laure said, grasping Cassie's hand. 'You didn't see him. He could have done anything. He was driving so fast. He wants to hurt me as much as he can.'

'He loves Sophie,' Cassie said, gently. 'He could not do that.'

'You don't see!' Laure said. 'He doesn't have anything to live for! He said that – he's said it before. If he doesn't have me he doesn't have anything. His life isn't worth anything. You don't understand how far I have pushed him because I thought – I thought – I had the right to leave.'

'You do,' Cassie said. 'You have that right.'

'But I expected him to just accept it! I have been so, so stupid. Where's Tom?'

'Nat took him home.'

'I can't see him again,' Laure shouted. 'We've killed them.'

'You're hysterical. Hush, hush.'

Then the phone rang. Laure stared at Cassie, a wild elation in her eyes. 'It must be news!' she said. She ripped back the duvet and pulled on her dressing gown, running down the stairs. She got to the phone before the policewoman. She snatched it up. It was Gerard's voice, and yet not. It was quite, quite dead, as if there was no life in him.

'Speak to me!' she shouted. 'Sophie!'

'I don't know where I am,' he said, quietly.

The policewoman mouthed at her, 'Keep him talking.' Then she gestured to one of the policemen to pick up the phone in the kitchen. There was a faint click on the line, but Gerard didn't seem to hear it.

'Please,' Laure said, gripping the phone until her knuckles turned white. 'Please put Sophie on,' she whispered.

'Mummy?'

'Oh, thank God.' Laure fell back against the wall. 'Thank God. Darling, where are you? Where's Daddy?'

'We're in a phone box. It's cold, Mummy. We had a crash in the car, and Daddy hit his head.'

Laure's heart was pounding. She forced herself to breathe. 'Can you see any signs? Did you drive a long way?'

'Yes.' Sophie's voice was tiny. 'On the motorway. I was scared. Daddy wouldn't talk to me. I'm hungry, Mummy, and I'm really, really cold. I can hear the sea.'

'Hang on, darling, we'll find you. We'll be with you as soon as we can. Put Daddy back on, will you?

'Bring her home,' Laure whispered. 'Please. Whatever you want, I will do. Just come home. Or tell me where you are.'

'Mr Chadwick?' It was the policeman's voice. Hard. Impersonal. 'Are you there? Just tell us . . .'

And then the line went dead.

Laure ran into the kitchen as the policeman was putting the phone down. 'Why?' she screamed. 'Why did you do that? He was going to tell me . . . you idiot.'

'Calm down,' he said, sharply. 'I think we have a

trace on the call.' His mobile phone rang. He turned away from them, and walked outside.

Nick stepped forward and put his arms around Laure. 'It's OK,' he said. 'They'll find them.'

'She was cold,' Laure said, into Nick's shoulder. 'She was cold and hungry and frightened and I haven't protected her. It's my job to keep her warm and feed her and make sure she is safe and I have not done it. I let her go.'

'They're by the coast,' the policeman said, stepping back into the kitchen. 'In Cornwall. A phone box. We've got cars heading there now.'

Laure slumped down on one of the kitchen chairs. 'We've been on holiday there,' she said. 'With our friends. We walked the coastal paths, and Gerard sailed. Do you remember, Nick?' He nodded. 'Why?' she said to herself. 'Why would he go there?' She looked into the distance. 'Because the cliffs are high,' she said, slowly, in realization. 'Because the cliffs are high.'

She turned to look beseechingly at the policemen. 'How long will it take to get to them? They've had a crash. I don't know where they can shelter. It's cold.' She looked out at the black night. The branches of the old tree by the church were bent low with the wind, and the window was spattered with silvery raindrops.

Cassie put her arm around her. 'They will find them,' she said, certainly. 'They will.' She wanted to ring Nat and tell him that Gerard had rung, but she didn't want to leave Laure. She was very worried she might break down completely.

Sophie saw the lights first. Daddy seemed to have gone to sleep, and he was lying heavily on her arm. They were huddled in the car, the bonnet bent backwards into a snarl. They'd hit the wall head on, Gerard losing

340

control of the car on the wet road, the blackness engulfing him as he spun the wheel. And then they'd slid for what seemed like an eternity in a spiral that was beautiful in its way until it had ended with the sickening crunch and Daddy had hit his head on the steering wheel. She had to shake him to wake him up, it had taken ages, and he had blood coming from his forehead. She tried to mop it with her sleeve, but there was too much. 'We have to ring Mummy,' she had whispered. 'She'll come and get us.' Daddy had nodded, and she'd held his arm as he tried to lift himself out of the car. There was a phone box all lit up just yards away. Daddy's mobile had no charge left. There was one house she could see, but it was quite a long way away and she couldn't see any lights. She had to heave open the phone-box door and help Daddy in, and then she took the coins from his pocket and dialled their number.

Daddy was not like Daddy. While they had been driving she'd tried to put the radio on, and he'd said no, and she kept asking where they were going and he said nothing. It was as if he was a stranger, and she felt as frightened of him as if he really was a person she did not know. The lights got nearer, and Sophie decided to get out and see who it was. It was a police car. She waved, and the lights stopped just in front of her.

Laure held her as if she would never let her go. 'You are the bravest girl in the world,' she said. 'Did you hurt yourself?'

'No,' Sophie said slowly. 'But I am starving. And very cold. Why are you crying?'

'Because I'm so happy to see you again.'

'Where's Victor?' Sophie looked around the kitchen.

'I'm so sorry, darling, but he died. Nick's dug a big

341

hole for him and we're going to put up a cross so you know where he is.'

'But we're leaving here. He won't come with us.'

'He'll be with us,' Laure said, hugging her more tightly. 'You never lose someone that you love. They are always with you, in your mind.'

'Will Daddy be in hospital long? I want to see him.'

Whatever he did, Laure thought, whatever he did, he would always be her father and she would love him. And that was right. 'We'll go and see him tomorrow,' she said.

'What happened to your face?'

'I fell. It's nothing.' Sophie touched it gently. 'There,' Laure said. 'You've made it all better.'

Chapter Twenty-Six

Laure

He held her hand very tightly, as if he would never let it go. Sophie sat on the edge of the bed next to her, and Nick hovered, uncertainly, at the foot.

'Could you give us a moment?' she said, gently, to them. 'Take Sophie for a drink, would you, Nick? There's a canteen in the next wing.'

'Sure,' Nick said. 'Come on, Sophes.'

'Please don't cry again,' Laure said.

Gerard turned his head away. 'I can't help it. You have no idea, Laure, how close I came to . . .'

'Shush. Don't tell me. You both survived. That is all we need to know.'

'And you?'

'And I, what?' She turned her head to him, and he reached up, with his bandaged hand, to touch her hair.

'What will you do?'

'I will stay.'

He pressed his lips together. 'Not because you think I will do something like that again? Not out of pity? Or fear? I could not bear that.'

'No.'

'But do you love me?'

She looked at him consideringly. 'I am not sure if I trust love, any more. Could we settle for trust, and friendship?'

His lips curved into the shadow of a smile, his fingers entwined in her hair. 'I don't care,' he said, quietly. 'I don't really care what you say as long as I know that you will not leave.'

'I won't leave you,' she said. 'I promise.'

'And Tom?'

She bit her lip. Tom. Cassie said that when she had finally got home he was asleep, but then he woke an hour later, crying, determined to see Laure immediately. She said it was terrible, he'd woken the children. For what remained of the night she sat with him, while he sobbed. She said she had never seen him like that, as if something inside him had broken.

'Tom will survive,' she said. 'He has the children.'

'We have to leave.'

'I know. I know that.'

'Where will we go?'

'You know,' she said, looking at his fingers as they played with her hair, 'I really do not care.'

'Do you want to go to France? I'm happy to do that, I'm sure I could find work.'

'I can work too,' Laure said.

'You will. It is going to be quite, quite different,' he said. 'I promise.'

'Hi.'

'Hi, darling. Did you get something to eat?'

'Just a biscuit. Nick's coming. How long will you have that plaster on your arm, Daddy?'

'Not so long. A few weeks, maybe. Come here.'

Sophie sat on the bed, and leant towards him. He put his arm around her shoulder, and she gently pressed her face against his. Laure saw him close his eyes, blissfully. Nick's hand squeezed her shoulder. 'Are you OK?'

She reached up and took his hand. 'Yes,' she said. 'I'm fine.'

Chapter Twenty-Seven

Tom

Sarah sat with Cassie at her untidy kitchen table. On it lay several glossy brochures for houses in Scotland. 'Will you go?' Sarah asked.

'I don't know,' Cassie said. 'We're going to go and have a look at a couple. The children are very excited.'

'And what about you?'

'I will be happy as long as they are happy.' Cassie smiled. 'You know me. I could be happy anywhere. Anyway, I think a new start might benefit us all. With Laure leaving, it doesn't feel quite the same. Time for a new chapter,' she said, decisively. 'Mum says it's a good thing. She's even threatening to come with us.'

'I wonder if anything will ever be the same.'

'I don't know,' Cassie said. 'It was a savage lesson, wasn't it?'

'You can say that again. Did you know?' Sarah said, brusquely.

Cassie looked at her uncertainly.

'I – suspected,' she said. 'But it wasn't my business, was it? I did not know all the details.'

'I'm glad,' Sarah said. 'Because if you were my friend you would have told me.'

'That's a big responsibility,' Cassie said. 'I'm not sure you are right.'

Sarah sighed. 'I've decided to leave work,' she said. 'At last, Tom has taken my advice. He was offered a job this week, and he's putting the novel on ice. I'm going to work from home and give myself at least a chance to try to be a mother. God knows if I'll be any good, but we'll see. I'm so glad that he's finally facing up to his responsibilities. But then he has a hell of a lot to repay.'

'I hope you will be happy,' Cassie said. She knew that Tom would not.

'How's Gerard? I haven't seen him since he came out of hospital.'

'He seems fine. They're leaving tomorrow, you know.'

'Good,' Sarah said. She caught Cassie's eye. 'I know you think I should be charitable, what with everything Gerard's been through, but I'm not that kind. Laure behaved appallingly. When I think that all the time we were on holiday . . .'

'I know,' Cassie said. 'But I think they just . . . they couldn't help themselves. It was a kind of madness.'

'They did not have that right,' Sarah said. 'I don't know if I can ever trust Tom again.'

Don't make his life hell, Cassie thought. But Sarah would not listen to her. She needed to extract revenge for the way that Tom had publicly humiliated her.

His hand shook as she handed him a cup of coffee, and his face was ashen.

'Gerard won,' he said.

'It's not that simple,' Cassie said. 'Don't think of it like that.'

'You have no idea,' he said. 'No idea.'

'You have to go forward,' she said.

'What a fucking cliché.'

'I know. I'm sorry. Count up all the positives in your life. Keep busy. You're going be working, I hear.'

'Yeah, fucking great, isn't it? The local newspaper. The career I gave up over twenty years ago. Don't go. I couldn't bear it if you left as well.'

'I don't think we will. I'll just go and look, to keep Nat happy. He's been really affected by all this, you know. He thinks there was a lot more he could have done.'

'There wasn't.'

'It would have been disastrous,' Cassie said, gently. 'Honestly, it is better this way.'

Tom laughed, mirthlessly. 'I'm the only real casualty, aren't I? And I don't matter.'

'I'm sure that Laure feels just as strongly as you do.'

'Then why did she go back to him? Why won't she talk to me? Why?' He could hardly get the last word out, he was crying now, and Cassie wrapped her arms around him. 'I can't even look at the children without thinking . . . everything makes me think of her. We would have had such a great life, and now it's all fucked up. For the first time in my life I thought I could be happy.'

'You don't know,' Cassie said, hugging him. 'You don't know that. You've got to let it go, Tom, or you will go mad.'

'And we don't want that, do we?' he said, bitterly, drawing away from her. 'Because everything is tidily sorted out, isn't it?'

'Hardly.'

'That's how it feels. Whereas inside I have this huge, gaping hole and I am so fucking angry. There is nowhere for these feelings to go. I'm sorry.' He smiled, and shook his head. 'Stupid Tom. Idiot Tom. I always got things wrong, didn't I? I always screwed up.'

'No.'

'And for once, I'd thought I got things right. No—' He stood up, and walked towards the back door and then paused, thumping his hand against the frame. 'I know I got things right. Only nobody would believe me.' Opening the door, he paused. 'Can I borrow Hector?'

'Sure. Why?'

'I'll go and sort out those rats.'

'Fine.' She looked puzzled. Why now? She shrugged. It would keep him occupied today, the day that Laure was leaving. He whistled for Hector, and he jumped up out of his basket, and followed Tom out of the back door.

Laure turned the big old key for the last time. She put her hand on the heavy oak of the front door. 'Goodbye,' she said. She smiled, sadly. No turning back. They all had to look forward, not back. She reached down and put the key under the terracotta pot, where she had said she would leave it for the new owners who were arriving later today.

She climbed into the front of the car, as Gerard drummed his fingers on the steering wheel. He turned to smile at her and she smiled back, reassuringly. Sophie reached forward and put her arms around her neck.

In the distance, there was the faint sound of a single gunshot from the lower barns.

'I love you,' Sophie whispered.

'I love you more,' Laure said.

THE END

HOMING INSTINCT
Diana Appleyard

When having it all just isn't enough . . .

It's time to start thinking the unthinkable . . .

Carrie Adams, successful television producer, mother and wife, is about to return to work. Baby Tom has fallen in love with the new nanny; six-year-old Rebecca isn't too keen, but hopes the nanny will at least be better organised than Mummy. Carrie meanwhile is desperate to reinvent herself from housewife to svelte career woman.

Because this is what today's women do, don't they? They're smart, successful, glamorous wives and perfect part-time mothers. They can be brilliant at work and brilliant in bed. Carrie lives by the maxim that working full-time is no problem as long as she has the right child-care, and has never doubted for a moment that this is her path in life – until reality begins to hit home. She isn't happy, the children aren't happy, and husband Mike – until recently trying desperately to be a New Man – is now becoming more and more detached from family life. She begins to think the unthinkable. Perhaps, just perhaps, she doesn't *have* to do all this . . .

'A FABULOUS, FUNNY NOVEL . . . THIS WONDERFUL BOOK IS ESSENTIAL READING FOR MOTHERS TRYING TO DO IT ALL'
Daily Mail

'RUTHLESSLY AND HILARIOUSLY FRANK'
New Woman

'A BRILLIANTLY FUNNY READ'
Woman's Realm

0 552 99821 4

BLACK SWAN

OUT OF LOVE
Diana Appleyard

'VERY, VERY TRUE AND TOUCHING . . . PACKS A
HUGE EMOTIONAL PUNCH'
Sarah Harrison

It has been an idyllic summer, Tess reflects, as she packs
up the Cornish holiday home in preparation for plunging
back into the cold reality of normal life. An idyllic
summer, and there will be more – so why does she feel
awash with a nameless fear about returning home?

Alone at the holiday cottage for one last night with
her young daughter – Mark and the boys have already
returned home to London – she has the time, and the
silence, to take stock of her life. A life, which, on the
surface, has everything a woman could want. So why,
now the children are growing up, does she want more?
The dramatic decision she takes that night sets her off
on a quite new journey – but one for which she may
need the courage to travel alone . . .

'WARM, WITTY AND ULTRA-ASTUTE'
Mail on Sunday

'HER NARRATIVE WRAPS YOU ROUND ITS
LITTLE FINGER . . . A STORY ABOUT LOVE,
WRITTEN WITH LOTS OF IT'
Daily Mail

'A SENSITIVE AND ALL TOO CREDIBLE PORTRAIT
OF A MODERN MARRIAGE'
Woman and Home

'A PERCEPTIVE LOOK AT THE CRACKS THAT CAN
APPEAR IN MODERN MARRIAGES'
Woman's Own

0 552 99933 4

BLACK SWAN

EVERY GOOD WOMAN
DESERVES A LOVER
Diana Appleyard

A warm and compelling novel about a woman
who has to break free.

Sasha feels that she is captive in a life which no longer
satisfies her. Her children are critical, her husband
unsupportive, and she is bored and unfulfilled. So, with
two good women friends, she escapes to darkest Peru,
to take on the challenge of a lifetime – to walk the Inca
Trail. Amongst the grandeur of the mountains, and the
glorious ancient civilisation of the Incas, she discovers
that she can grab hold of her life and wrench it back before
it's too late. She embarks upon a love affair which takes
her completely by surprise; she also finds disaster and
the sound of her own laughter once more.

0 552 99934 2

BLACK SWAN